Four Brothers In Love

JEL JONES

PublishAmerica
Baltimore

Softcover 9781630842062
PUBLISHED BY PUBLISHAMERICA, LLLP
www.publishamerica.com
Baltimore

Printed in the United States of America

Chapter One

The warm June breeze blew softly against Veronica Franklin's face as she smiled toward Janice and Ralph Sterling that Saturday afternoon as they sat on the old couple's patio sipping tea.

"Have you two decided yet whether you'll sell and move to Florida?" Veronica asked with her focus on Janice. "I have given this a profusion amount of thought and I'm convinced that you and Ralph would be much happier there." She paused. "Plus, you two mentioned awhile back that many of your friends have moved down to the sunshine state."

Janice nodded. "That is correct, many of them have; and seem well adjusted to their new surroundings," she said, sipping from her teacup with both hands. "Never-the-less, dear, you don't understand our special bond to this place. Ralph and I were both born just miles from here and wouldn't quite feel at home anywhere else. When we were younger and first married fresh out of college, we tried settling in Michigan, but ended up back in Illinois just eight months later. We purchased this piece of land and we both watched the builders build our home from the ground up. We designed and specified every detail, right down to the designs on the staircase. It's our home," Janice stressed passionately.

"That was sixty years ago." Ralph nodded. "I was just twenty-four and Janice was twenty-four; but it seems like just yesterday," Ralph uttered with a sparkle in his eyes. "And at that time it was just a few homes in this section of Barrington. Sterling House is one of the first homes built in this subdivision. Your house was standing but it was a much smaller version than what it is now; and a couple years after the completion of our home, Ellen and Samuel Franklin added a new wing to the house and made it grandeur. However, most of the houses you see in this section today had not been built yet." He nodded, glancing about the grounds with a gleam in his eyes.

"Now look at this community." Janice stretched out both arms. "It's a live with beautiful landscape and grand homes galore! Ralph and I wouldn't know how to feel at home anywhere else."

Veronica sipped her tea in silence as they talked. She was anxious and could sense from their love of the area and the grand house that it wasn't going to be easy to persuade them to move out. Yet her determination knew no limitations toward the task and hoped it would be tied up in a neat knot before she took her last sip of tea.

"Janice, Ralph, you are just wasting your life away now; and I think too much of the two of you to just sit around and not speak out."

"Speak out about what?" Ralph asked.

"Speak out about what I think is best for the two of you." She smiled at Ralph and then reached across the table and touched the top of Janice's hand. "Especially, since the two of you remind me of my parents. They would be around your ages if they were still alive."

"That's mighty nice of you, dear," Janice nodded as she nervously lifted her teacup to her lips. "You and your boys are quite dear to us as well. We watched your sons grow into fine young men. They are the split image of their father." Janice smiled. "Just can't believe it's been twenty years since you lost your sweet husband."

Veronica face stiffened with sadness as she thought of her late husband. "It's hard to believe that Ryan has been gone from me and the boys for twenty years," she said sadly. "I still miss him and mention him to the boys every chance I get."

"It seems like yesterday when that tall, good looking husband of yours, the famous Ryan Franklin, brought you to his home to live at Franklin House right before his folks passed away," Janice smiled. "And we never told you, but Ralph and I were friends with your late in-laws, Ellen and Samuel Franklin. We were friends with Robert and Patricia Coleman as well. I'm not sure if you knew the Colemans that lived to the right of you. They moved away years ago right after your husband passed away."

"Yes, I knew the Colemans," Veronica nodded. "I went to school with Jack Coleman. He was my husband's best friend, who also managed his career."

"I figured you probably knew the Colemans. Yes, we were friends, but not as close as we were with Ellen and Samuel," Janice said, smiling.

Ralph lifted one hand and grumbled as if it irritated him for his wife to mention that bit of information. "Yes, we were friends with Ellen and Samuel, but they were a rather sickly couple and stayed to themselves a lot." His hand slightly shook as he lifted his teacup. "Although, I'm now reminded that they were not always sickly and to themselves," he stressed and stared hard at his wife.

Veronica noticed the expression on Ralph's face and wondered what had taken place between the late Franklins and the Sterlings. Her mind entertained the thought that there could have been rough waters between Ralph and her late-in-laws.

After a moment of silence, Janice smiled. "Ralph is right; we were never as close to them as we are connected to you and the boys. From the day you moved into Franklin House, watching you and your young family grow has been a treasure to Ralph and me. Watching your family and being close neighbors has meant a lot to us," Janice explained in a heartfelt manner. "We have the births of all your sons written in our bible: 1987, 1988, 1989 and 1990; each time you brought home a new baby from the hospital, Ralph and I would have our own private celebration as if the infant was a new addition to our family."

"This is true," Ralph agreed. "Being connected to your family has been quite uplifting for us; and moving away we would miss you all." He held up one finger. "Also, we don't want to forget Catherine, that sweet sister-in-law of yours; she has been a dear to us as well. She drops by to see us quite often just like her dear brother used to do before his death." He looked toward Janice. "That reminds me; you have a piece of jewelry for her."

Veronica exchanged looks with the old couple and smiled. "You have a piece of jewelry for me?" She touched her chest.

"Yes, I have it right here." Janice pulled a small black velvet pouch from her dress pocket and placed it on the table in front of her. "I originally thought Catherine would like the piece, but maybe you'll like and enjoy them." She handed the pouch to Veronica.

Veronica pulled both strings on either side to open the small black pouch, pouring the long string of white cultured pearls on the table. Her eyes lit up at the striking elegance of the necklace. The word expensive radiated from the sight of them. "Oh, my goodness, this necklace is precious." Veronica held the string of pearls in her hands as they felt like silk. "And you are giving this beautiful necklace to me? This is an incredible gift. Thank you. They look like they cost a fortune."

Ralph nodded. "They almost did; and I should know. I bought those pearls forty-seven years ago for a special event we were invited to," he said, smiling as he glanced at his wife. "I can still see them hanging down the front of that long flowing pink dress you were wearing. You looked so beautiful that evening," he said and stared into space.

"It's quite obvious that's a very special memory that the two of you share; are you sure you want to part with this exquisite necklace?" Veronica asked.

"Yes, dear, I'm sure," Janice assured her. "I never wear much jewelry anymore and I have donated a great number of fine pieces, but Ralph and I felt these pearls should go to someone special," she said sincerely and stared at the necklace as it sparkled in Veronica's hands from the reflection of the sun. "Something as elegant as that necklace is something you would give to a daughter if you had one. So, Ralph and I decided not to put it in the donation pile."

"A daughter, I feel honored." Veronica smiled. "But you thought of Catherine first?" Veronica said under her breath.

"What was that, dear," Janice asked.

"I said I can't wait to show these to Catherine," Veronica said, forcing a smile.

"Please, do," the old lady smiled. "I'm sure the two of you get invited to lots of parties that you can wear them to," Janice said sadly as she sipped her tea. "I have nowhere to wear my fine pieces to anymore so it's best if someone else enjoy them."

"That doesn't sound true. I'm sure there are lots of places you can wear these beautiful cultured pearls to."

"Yes, dear, that may be true, but the invites are not that plentiful anymore for Ralph and me. When you stop giving parties you end up off many guest lists. Therefore, we know you and Catherine will enjoy those set of pearls."

"Thank you again for these beautiful pearls and I know exactly what I'm going to do with them." She paused. "But first of all, I need you two to do me a favor?" Veronica exchanged looks with the old couple.

"What favor is that, dear?" Janice asked.

"I need the two of you to keep a secret and not reveal to Catherine that you gave me this exceptional string of pearls; because I would like to hold on to them and give them to her as a birthday gift from the two of you."

The old couple smiled and nodded. "That's a lovable idea. I'm sure Catherine is just like a sister to you," Ralph said. "The two of you have stuck together since her brother's death," he paused and coughed a couple times, but he cleared his throat and continued. "But I should just tell you that the necklace you are holding is not the typical birthday gift," he said with pride, exchanged looks with his wife and she nodded toward him. "If I recall correctly, I think I paid in the neighborhood of $20,000 for that string in the summer of 1966."

The old lady smiled and looked toward the old man. "The summer of 1966 was a very good year for us," Janice mumbled with warmth in her voice.

Veronica smiled and thought to herself. "I'm sorry Catherine, but you'll never see these pearls until you see them on the person who buys them from Keith's Re-sell Corner. Keith will give me at least $15,000 for these and I can use the money to pay the household salaries for an entire month." She stared pleasingly across the grounds toward her big white house.

Janice touched Veronica's hand to get her attention. "Is everything okay, dear? You seem a bit quiet suddenly."

Veronica looked around and smiled. "I'm just fine. I was just thinking about the two of you. And based on your warm memories, how much the two of you miss the past." She touched the old lady's shoulder.

"This is true; Ralph and I miss the good old days of the past, and especially the summer of 1966. Getting old isn't easy."

"I'm sure it isn't, but 2013 can be a very good year for the two of you as well; all you need to do is just rid yourself of this big beautiful grand place you have here." Veronica held out both arms. "And all this responsibility and just take off to Florida and live carefree for the rest of your lives. Now is the time. Just pack up and do it right away," Veronica stressed.

"Pack up and move to Florida right away?" Janice asked.

"Yes, just do it. You have nothing stopping you. You have lived your life and had your parties here in this big house, now it's time to let all of this go and live carefree without attachments," Veronica suggested strongly.

Janice took a napkin and patted her forehead as the hot June sun beamed down on their shoulders making her uncomfortably warm and uneasy. She wasn't just edgy from the warm weather; she was anxious from the discussion of giving up her home. "It sounds tempting and I know you are thinking of our wellbeing, but it's not easy to just pack up and move," Janice mumbled sadly. "We have lived here in this same house for the past sixty years."

"I don't know, Janice. I have been thinking and maybe we should consider selling this place." Ralph lifted his teacup to his mouth and took a sip. "It is a bit too much for us now. And besides, Veronica only has our best interest in mind. She is saying to us what our own children would say if we had any. It's time for us to think of our future and settle into a more simple way of living. Living in this twenty-five room house has lost its appeal since I have only seen six rooms of this huge place in the past three years."

"Ralph, would you really consider relocating to Florida?" Janice glanced at her husband of sixty-two years with a surprised look on her 84-year-old face.

"Yes, Janice, I would consider it because I read it's a good place to retire to. Plus, once we settle there, we'll be able to socialize more."

"How do you figure that?" Janice asked. "We are not socializing now, what will make us socialize more in Florida?"

"Because that's where most of our socializing friends have moved off to. They are all living in some town called Jupiter," the old man reminded his wife.

Veronica quickly added. "I have read about Jupiter. It's one of the wealthiest towns in the whole state of Florida."

"That might be, but Ralph are you serious?" Janice stared at her husband.

"Yes, I'm serious, Janice; I think we should move to Jupiter, Florida."

"Ralph, if we move to Florida what about the staff. They will be out of a job after twenty years of steady work."

"Why not take Mr. and Mrs. Westwood with you?" Veronica suggested.

"Janice, she's right. Sam and Carrie just might welcome the change. They are welcome to relocate with us. Besides, we will need staff wherever we end up, might as well take the ones we have; that is, if they are willing to relocate," Ralph said.

Janice frowned at her husband. "You have really surprised me, old man. I didn't think you would be so eager to leave Barrington. It's almost as if you are eager to give up Sterling House. I thought we would think about this a little longer."

"What is there to think about, Janice? We have been thinking about this since Veronica first suggested it to us a couple weeks ago. Besides, if we are going to sell Sterling House and relocate to Florida, I think we should get on the ball and do it before summer is over. I don't want to do all of this during a cold Illinois winter."

Janice shook her head. "No, I don't think I want to leave Barrington. I'm not ready to give up Sterling House," she protested.

Veronica frowned and placed her tea cup on the little round table that she was seated at. "I realize it's not easy to move from a home that you have lived in for sixty years. But you are in the prime of your live and need to have less responsibility to deal with. You both should be traveling and enjoying the rest of your life. How many good years do you have left? You shouldn't be tied to some gigantic house, right? I lost my parents right after my college graduation, but if they were still alive I would give them the same advice I'm giving to you two. Go now, and enjoy the rest of your life while you still can!" Veronica said with conviction.

Ralph looked at Janice and nodded; and then they both looked at Veronica and smiled. "We will miss you and Catherine and your nice sons," Janice said with a smile. "But you have convinced us that giving up this big house and moving to Florida is in our best interest."

"That's wonderful," Veronica said as she subdued her excitement. "You two are making the right decision." She quickly hopped out of her seat and hugged the old couple.

"We think so too," Ralph said, and Janice nodded in agreement.

Veronica stood there smiling with the black pouch in her left hand swinging at her side. She reached down and lifted her teacup from the table and took the last sip of tea. She placed the cup back on the table and smiled. "I'm going to take off now, but I'm sure you two will be very happy in Jupiter, Florida." She paused. "But I would like to say, I think you should put your house up for sell and move as soon as possible," she suggested. "I heard the property value in this area is dropping. And since you are planning to sell, it's best to do it as soon as possible. But I would advise you not to mention your move to anyone, not even Catherine."

"Why shouldn't we?" Janice asked.

"I know you two are close with Catherine and I love my sister-in-law, but Catherine has a tendency to spread information; and if word got out that you two are moving it could have a negative affect on property values in this area."

The old couple exchanged confused looks and then Ralph lifted one hand and said. "I doubt that would happen. But be assured that we will keep our moving plans to ourselves just in case what you said made some kind of sense that we didn't pick up on." He grinned. "Thank you so much for looking out for us and encouraging us to make this move for ourselves."

"It was my pleasure and I hope you two will have a wonderful life in Florida," Veronica said, smiling triumphed as she waved and headed across the grounds toward Franklin House.

Chapter Two

Ralph and Janice Sterling moved out of Sterling House on Saturday, June 22, exactly twenty-one days after Veronica much persuaded conversation with them; and their property went on the market the next day. Veronica made it a priority to handpick the precise prestigious family that she felt suitable to move in next door. When the tall, thin, selling agent, Julian Bartlett, pulled into the driveway of the old Sterling estate, Veronica rushed across the grounds to greet the middle-aged, dark haired gentlemen.

"Good afternoon," she said, smiling as she headed across the patio toward him. "My name is Veronica Franklin. I live next door." She pointed toward her property. "I just wanted to come over and meet you."

Julian Bartlett was dressed professionally in gray slacks, a white shirt and a gray tie. He held a clipboard against his chest with his left arm as he reached out his right hand to shook hers. His eyes and mouth were smiling but his brain was curious about why she wanted to meet him. "My name is Julian Bartlett, the real-estate agent for this property. Do we know each other?" he asked, staring almost too long into her dark brown eyes.

"No, we do not know each other, but I'm curious to get to know more about what agents like you do," Veronica looked at him sincerely.

"You're kidding right?" Julian grinned. "Don't get me wrong, I'm very flattered, but this must be my lucky day to greet an attractive woman like you in the middle of the day, tearing yourself away from all of that." He pointed toward Franklin House, just to inquire about what I do?"

Veronica felt awkward after he put it that way. She was hoping he hadn't figured her out, but also felt there was no way he could. "What can I say, I'm just curious about what real-estate agents do," she said nervously.

"That's easy," he said. "We sell properties." He glanced at his watch and back at her. "You wouldn't happen to be in the market, are you; and looking to sell that spread." He pointed to Franklin House. "It's just as grand as this one."

Veronica glanced at his clipboard, trying to get a glimpse of his notes or paperwork. "No, Mr. Bartlett, I'm not in the market to sell my home, but you would be the guy I would call if I were," she said hoping to soften him up.

"That's a good answer." He reached into his shirt pocket and pulled out a business card and passed it to her.

"Thanks, I'll keep your card and pass it along to one of my friends that may be in the market." Veronica slipped his card into the pocket of her long rose colored sundress.

"Thank you, I would appreciate that. Word of mouth really helps in this tough market now." He lifted his reading glasses and glanced at her stunning face as she pulled his business card out of her pocket and examined it closely. He was in awe of her striking features and her long wavy black hair that hung gracefully to her shoulders, parted to one side and pulled behind her left ear.

"Yes, I'm sure." She glanced at the agent and stuck the card back inside her pocket. "And speaking of a tough market, I know the Sterling property has only been on the market for one day but do you have any prospects?"

"A matter of facts, yes. That's why I'm here this afternoon. I have a couple, the Reeds, that's interested in this property," Julian said excitedly.

"Do they have any children?" Veronica asked.

He stared at her curiously for a moment as if her question caught him off guard. She smiled and quickly replied before he could. "I'm just curious since we don't have many youngsters in this section."

He quickly flipped through his notes. "As a matter of a fact, this couple does have a couple of youngsters."

"How young are they?"

Julian felt a bit anxious in Veronica's company. "The couple or the kids?" he asked and then answered himself. "You mean the kids, of course. They have a set of five-year-old twins," he said and glanced at his watch again. "They should be here at any moment now." He stared toward the end of the driveway for a moment and then glanced at Veronica. "It was nice meeting you, Veronica, but I need to get focused here and get ready to show this property." He headed toward the patio glass door, slid it open and stepped inside.

No more than two minutes after he stepped inside, the couple he was waiting for pulled into the driveway, but before they could turn off the engine and step out of their shiny red Lexus, Veronica met them at the car.

"Good afternoon, are you Mr. and Mrs. Reed to see the property?" Veronica smiled as she stood there with her arms folded.

"Yes, we are, I'm sorry we are a little behind schedule," Mr. Reed glanced at his watch. "But we are only ten minutes behind schedule. Traffic on a Sunday afternoon is murder around here."

"I'm so sorry, but this property is no longer for sell. We just sold this estate," Veronica informed the young thirty-something couple.

"You got to be kidding us. We just spoke to a gentleman by the name of Julian Bartlett about an hour ago when we made our appointment and the property was still available an hour ago," Mr. Reed protest.

"I'm so sorry, but we just sold Sterling Home and took it off the market a few minutes ago," Veronica explained.

The young couple was so upset and disappointed until they didn't say another word. They backed out of the driveway and drove away in a rush. By the time Julian stepped back outside five minutes later, he was surprised to discover that Veronica was still on the premises.

"Hello again," he said. "Are you still here?"

"Yes, I'm still here. I was waiting to get a glimpse at my possible new neighbors." She smiled.

He glanced at his watch. "I actually expected them to be here ten minutes ago. I'm not sure what happened. Maybe they couldn't find the place. I think I should give them a call."

Veronica heart raced at the thought of him calling the couple and finding out how she had sabotaged his sale. It wouldn't take much for him to figure out that she was the woman in the driveway who had announced to the couple that the property was no longer on the market because it had sold.

"Julian, why waste your time calling that couple. Maybe they changed their minds. Besides, with GPS nobody gets lost anymore," Veronica reminded him.

He nodded and wiped the back of his hand across his forehead. "Yes, I do believe you're right. I'm sure if they are interested they will show up or call me," he said anxiously as he rubbed his hand down his short black hair that he wore closely cut to his head. "But if they don't call or show up in the next fifteen minutes I will have to leave for another appointment elsewhere."

As he stood there restlessly looking out toward the end of the driveway, Veronica took a seat on the patio furniture. He glanced over his shoulder and smiled at her. "Well, it's starting to look more and more like this couple stood me up. I pegged them to be serious, interested buyers. They mentioned how they had driven by the property and loved what they saw and just wanted a glimpse inside. I was positive they would show up and bid on the place," he explained. "So, there you have it, Veronica. You wanted to know more about what I do; well as you can see, sometime I wait for possible buyers who never show up," he said disappointedly.

"I'm sure this doesn't happen often that you get stood up," she said, smiling to herself.

"You are right, it doesn't happen often, but it shouldn't happen at all." He glanced at his watch again. "And now I'm out of here if I want to reach my next appointment on time," he said, heading toward his car.

Veronica hopped out of the patio chair and rushed toward him. "Wait up Mr. Bartlett." She reached him just as he grabbed the handle of his car door. "It was nice meeting you; and thanks again for allowing

me to hang around and watch you work to get an idea what agents do."
She reached out and shook his hand goodbye.

"The pleasure was all mines, but all you saw was me standing and
waiting," he said, smiling. "It's usually more involved than getting stood
up," he joked.

"I'm sure it is; take care," she said, turned on her heels and headed
across the grounds toward Franklin House.

Veronica had spent nearly an hour at Sterling House with the selling
agent, but she headed across the grounds toward her home feeling
triumphed. She had accomplished what she set out to do, but her work
wasn't finished with Julian Bartlett until Sterling House was sold.

Chapter Three

Three days later, that Wednesday afternoon around one o'clock, Veronica was standing in the window looking out when Julian pulled his new white Chevy Malibu into the driveway of the old Sterling estate. She rushed outside and hurried across the grounds to greet him before he could get out of his car.

He was seated looking through his notes for awhile, and then slowly opened his car door and stepped out of his vehicle. He was looking professional and well groomed as he was the other day. With his clipboard under his arm and his cell phone in one hand, he had a surprise look on his face when he shut his car door and noticed Veronica standing near the patio furniture.

He smiled, walking toward her. "What do I owe the honor of your lovely presence again?" he said in a friendlier manner than when they first met. "If you keep showing up like this, you could give a guy the wrong impression," he joked.

"And what impression would that be?" Veronica asked, caught off guard by his carefree manners with her.

"I didn't mean to sound fresh and I hope I didn't offend you," he apologized. "That was just my lousy attempt at friendly humor."

"No offense taken," she said, glancing toward the clipboard under his arm.

"That's good, but really what do I owe the honor of your presence here at the Sterling estate today?" he asked seriously.

"It's a hot day and I thought you could use a cold drink." She handed him a bottle of ice cold water.

He smiled and reached for the bottle of water. "Thank you. You are right. This is the hottest June I can remember."

"So, did you ever hear from that young couple you were waiting for when you were here on Sunday?" Veronica asked.

"No, nothing." He placed his clipboard and phone on the patio table. "And I don't expect to," he twisted the cap off the bottle of water and turned the bottle up to his mouth and gulped down a quick swallow. "I'm waiting for another couple." He glanced at his watch. "They should be here shortly. It's one o'clock and they said to expect them by five after. I just hope they don't stand me up the way that young couple blew me off on Sunday."

"Is this couple young as well?" Veronica inquired.

"No, this is a more settled couple, Jett and Roberta Sanders. They are both retired and are looking to buy in this area from southern Illinois."

"A retired couple is looking to buy a house this size?" Veronica asked curiously.

"Yes, they are retired and if they got the money and want to buy we don't care how old they are," Julian stressed.

"Oh, sure," Veronica mumbled anxiously. "I know a sale is a sale."

Before she could continue questioning him about the Sanders, they pulled into the driveway sporting a shiny burgundy Cadillac Deville. They were a well-dressed, upbeat seventy-something couple. Julian greeted the couple with a smile as Veronica followed Mr. and Mrs. Sanders and Julian inside of the property. She also followed as he showed the property. And after Julian had showed the entire property, the Sanders were very pleased and quite excited with what they had seen. They were hundred percent sure that they wanted to put a bid on the property. And just as they were expressing their enthusiasm, Julian phone rang. He glanced at the incoming call and couldn't ignore it.

"I'm glad you both love the property and think it's a good fit for you," he said. "This is fantastic news, but I need to take this call." He held up one hand. "Please excuse me for a moment. I really need to take this call." He pointed toward the living room sofa. "Just be seated anywhere. This call will only take a few minutes, no more than five," he said and rushed out of the room toward the patio door to take his call.

When Julian rushed outside, Veronica took a deep breath. She felt anxious knowing her window of opportunity to question the Sanders was limited. She had not been afforded the privilege of learning about their background ahead of time as with the first couple. She didn't want to discourage the older couple without all the facts. She felt time wasn't on her side to find out their background, and if it didn't fit, discourage them not to buy within a window of five minutes. However, she was determined and would find away. And just as they took a seat on the long black sofa, Veronica took a seat on the twin sofa facing them.

"This is a beautiful place. Do you plan to live here alone? Do you have any children?" She quickly asked with nerves.

The old couple stared at her peculiarly as if they found her annoying. Then the old lady answered. "Yes, we have seven children, but they won't be moving in here with us. They are all grown and married. It will just be the two of us, our workers and two caregivers," Mrs. Sanders uttered arrogantly.

Veronica shifted in her seat and swallowed hard after Mrs. Sanders spoke. Their seven married children made them an unsuitable fit to occupy the estate. She didn't want her efforts to be for nothing. She had rid the estate of one elderly couple and knew she had to pull out all the stops to keep the Sanders from buying the mansion.

"Don't mention this to the agent, but he's keeping a secret from the two of you. It's a big secret that could make the difference in whether you buy this property or not," Veronica stressed, but keeping her voice low.

The older couple appeared preoccupied and not looking in her direction until she made that statement. They quickly stared at Veronica with their undivided attention. Her statement had aroused their curiosity. "If we don't mention it, how are we going to find out the secret?" Mr. Sanders asked.

"I will tell you, but when he walks back inside, you have to promise not to mention to him that I told you the secret."

Mr. and Mrs. Sanders exchanged looks with each other and appeared suddenly shaken. "You have our word. What is the secret?" Mr. Sanders asked.

"The secret is bed bugs. I heard that the owners abruptly moved out of this elegant place because of a bed bug problem. You two seem like nice people and that's why I'm telling you," she whispered.

"Thank you, young lady. We will decline on this property, that's for sure," Mrs. Sanders said with her head in the air. "We have enough problems without buying another." Mrs. Sanders grabbed her husband's hand. "Jett, we need to leave. This dump gives me the creeps," she said arrogantly.

"This is hardly a dump with a price tag like this," Mr. Sanders disagreed, pointing to the price of the house on the listing in his hand.

"I know it's on a grand scale." Mrs. Sanders glanced about the refined house. "But I don't care what the price tag says, being infested with those revolting creatures makes it a dump in my eyes," she said condescendingly.

"I understand how that information would turn you off, but please do not relay this information to the agent. I don't want him to know that I informed you of the bed bug problem and knocked him out of a sale," Veronica whispered, smiling inside.

"Don't worry, he'll never hear it from us," Mr. Sanders assured her. "But we are out of here."

They both stood up from the sofa and headed out of the big house, passing swiftly by Julian who was still on the phone. Julian managed to end his call and approached them as they had just gotten seated into their car.

"I'm sorry my phone call took longer than I expected." He stuck his phone in his shirt pocket. "Are you leaving?" Julian asked, bewildered at their decision not to bid on the property after they had given it unlimited praise. "Did I miss something?" he asked politely. "I was under the impression that you wanted to bid on the property."

The Sanders sat in their luxury car with the engine running. They realized that they needed to give some kind of explanation for not bidding on the property after they had made it certain that they would, but they were in an awkward spot of what to say.

"We are sorry, Mr. Bartlett, we seriously considered purchasing the property but after some further thought decided it's not for us. It wasn't your phone call that discouraged us. We just changed our minds," Mr. Sanders assured him.

After they had driven completely out of view, Julian shook his head, pulled his phone out of his pocket and powered it off. "I don't need any more calls to interrupt my sales; therefore, at least my phone won't ring during my next appointment."

"But they just told you it wasn't the phone call that changed their minds," Veronica reminded him.

"So they said, but I'm sure they didn't like waiting after pulling a complete 180 on me. They were set to sign on the dotted line and then pulled a complete about face on the sale. Maybe you were right in your assumption?"

"I beg you pardon," Veronica inquired. "May I ask what assumption are you referring to?"

"You seemed surprised that an elderly couple in their age category would be interested in purchasing such a huge estate to maintain. Maybe they were inclined to agree with your assumption," he said casually and smiled at her. "You didn't happen to enlighten them on your theory, did you?"

Veronica heart raced with nerves for a moment, although she had not mentioned their ages in particular, she had still sabotaged the sale with a complete fabrication to the buyers. She looked at the agent and then glanced down at the driveway so he wouldn't see the obvious guilt on her face. She was lost for words until he remarked. "Of course, I'm just kidding. I didn't think that about you, just my peculiar humor at work again," he assured her.

The lump left Veronica's throat and she could smile again. She looked at him and said, smiling. "I knew you were just kidding, but it's hardly anything to joke about. I'm sure you wanted to wrap up the sale."

"It's true." He nodded. "But it's all in a day's work. I'm not concerned. This place won't be on the market long; but in the meantime, you wanted to see what agents do and at the moment I'm giving all agents a bad rap." He held up both arms. "I have single-handedly managed to somehow botch two appointments that should have gone off without a hitch." He glanced at his Timex watch. "Hopefully, I'll have better luck with the Taylors. They are due here in the next thirty minutes." He strolled over to the patio.

Veronica strolled over to the patio as well and took a seat in a patio chair as she curiously watched Julian flip through his clipboard. The name Taylor appealed to her, but she was hoping it wasn't another older couple with married kids or a younger couple with small children or babies.

Julian glanced over his glasses and saw her sitting there and suddenly her presence slightly irritated him. His mood was somewhat subdued and her beauty was rather distracting. He felt he desperately needed to concentrate on his work. He didn't want to miss out on another sale.

"I'm sorry your other buyers didn't come through for you. Maybe the Taylors will take Sterling House off the market," she said, hoping he would perk up and volunteer some information about the couple.

He threw her a quick glance. "If anybody can, they can," he said, and then buried his face back in his paperwork, carefully looking through his clipboard.

"What do you mean by that?" Veronica casually asked, as if she wasn't sitting on the edge of her seat to hear his answer.

He didn't readily answer her question as he seemed engrossed in his notes. Veronica shifted in her seat impatiently as she kept her eyes glued to him. He had aroused her interest and now she was waiting on his confirmation that maybe the Taylors would be the suitable couple, according to her expectations, to buy and move into the old Sterling estate.

Julian pulled off his glasses and placed them on the patio table, and then wiped his forehead with the back of his hand. "I mean this guy is a CEO of some huge corporation in Chicago." He put his glasses back on. "My other buyers were financially set well, but this Taylor clan is filthy rich," he finally relayed.

"When you say filthy rich, do you mean multi-millionaire?" Veronica inquired.

He stared at her, lifted his reading glasses and placed them on top of his head. "No, I mean multi-billionaire."

Veronica was so excited until she almost couldn't contain her emotions of anxiousness to press him for more information. "Why do you call them a clan?"

"Because it's a houseful, believe me. Besides the Taylors, five others will occupy this huge house if they buy it." He glanced down at his notes. "There will also be Mr. Taylor's mother and father and the Taylor's three young daughters."

"So, these buyers have three young daughters?" Veronica discreetly asked as her heart was racing with anticipation. "How young are they?" Veronica anxiously asked.

"They are all quite young, in their early twenties," he uttered as he continued to look through his notes.

Veronica grabbed her cheeks with both hands but kept her composure not to give away how excited she was. The Taylor family sounded perfect.

"Julian, do the Taylors appear to be very interested as your other two buyers appeared? You mentioned that you can usually sense if a buyer is going to bid."

"Yes, I usually can, but I was completely off the mark with my other two. I would have bet the farm that they would have made a bid, but either did."

"That being so, how would you label these buyers? Do you have a strong sense that the Taylors will bid on the property?"

"My gut tells me that this is a done deal. After they drove past the house and toured it online they were ready to bid. However, they decided to take a walk through. They informed me in no uncertain terms that they loved the property," he assured her.

Veronica glanced at her stylish Rolex watch. "I can see it's almost time for the Taylors to show up and I think I should head home and get out of your way and let you do your job."

"It's fine by me if you want to continue hanging around to watch me work."

"Thank you, Julian, but I think I have seen enough." She glanced over her shoulder and waved good-bye. "But thank you for selling Sterling House to a fine couple like the Taylors."

"I don't want to count my chickens before they hatch, but in this case I think I can." He waved back at her as she headed across the grounds to Franklin House.

Chapter Four

Veronica stood staring out of the living room window at her new neighbors' front door. She was standing in the side window of one of the six windows that graced the enormous room. Franklin House elegant living room was like a stylish showcase all decorated in four shades of white, from old lace white carpeting and walls, to snow white long sheer curtains hanging from all six windows, to off white twin sofas and four off white matching chairs, to the eggshell white fireplace mantle, coffee table, two end tables and frames of the paintings on the wall. The room had a refined touch of three shades of delicate blues scattered throughout it, from the exquisite center piece on the coffee table to the graceful array of throw pillows, exclusive vases and display items in the room.

It was a cool Sunday morning right before nine o'clock. She stood there smiling as she sipped from a mug of coffee. She thought to herself how everything seemed to be on track as she hoped. She had persuaded Ralph and Janice to move to Florida and sell their home. The old couple agreeably moved out of Sterling House on June 22nd, the estate went on sale on June 23rd and sold on June 26th, the new family moved into the enormous white house on August 3rd.

"Did you see the new Taylor family that just moved in yesterday into the old Sterling estate next door?" She asked her sister-in-law, Catherine Franklin.

Catherine had just walked into the spacious living room and was now seated on the long off white sofa with her head buried in the Sunday paper.

Veronica glanced over her shoulder toward Catherine. "What are you reading? Did you hear what I just said?"

"Yes, I heard you," Catherine glared toward Veronica. "I haven't seen a soul yet. But they just moved into the place a day ago. I think it's a bit too soon to expect them to make their way across those grounds to pay us a social visit."

"You're right, of course. We need to give them time to get settled." Veronica continued to stare out of the window as if she was frozen in that spot. "I just wondered if you had caught a glimpse of any of them yet."

Getting up from the sofa, Catherine smiled and slowly made her way over across the room as she waved the Sunday paper above her head. "I haven't seen any of them, but I just read about the whole Taylor clan in the paper."

Veronica looked around and smiled. "You what, you just read about them?" Veronica was surprised and delighted. "They made the Sunday paper? Are you sure it's the Taylors who just moved next door?"

"Yes, I'm quite sure since 606 Academy Place is mentioned as their address."

"Okay, it's them alright," Veronica said. "So let's have it. What did you read?"

"One thing for sure, they are a far cry from the very sweet old couple who up and sold the place so quickly. Roger and Janice were the best neighbors anyone could hope for. Now with this new Taylor clan we don't know what we'll get."

"I know what we'll get," Veronica mumbled, staring out of the window again.

"Did you just say you know what you'll get?" Catherine asked.

Veronica shook her head. "No, I meant to say that we knew what we had with Roger and Janice and I miss them as well."

"I'm really surprised they up and moved so quickly," Catherine uttered sadly.

"At their ages they should be able to do whatever they want. Besides, I wouldn't call sixty years quick," Veronica stressed. "They just needed a change."

"They waited sort of late in life to start over in a new home, wouldn't you agree?"

"It doesn't bother me one way or another. They were good people, but they wanted to relocate to Jupiter, Florida," Veronica announced.

"Oh, is that where they moved to? I had no idea. I was pretty close with the old couple, but they never mentioned a word about moving to Florida."

"I found out when I was over for tea one afternoon right before they moved out," Veronica mumbled.

"I see," Catherine nodded. "You seem to know more about their business than I thought. But don't get me wrong, I'm happy for them. It's just odd that they never mentioned Florida to me when I was much closer to them than you were. But yet, they mentioned it to you."

"Get over it, Catherine. I'm sure they didn't mean to exclude you and you'll hear all about their moving adventure in a long letter that will be coming your way."

"I surely hope so. It's just that, when I visited them a couple weeks before they moved out, they seemed content to stay next door for the rest of their lives."

"Catherine, just drop it," Veronica snapped.

"Drop what?"

"All this talk about how Ralph and Janice Sterling moved so quickly."

"Sure, I'll drop it. But why are you so uptight all of a sudden. It's not like you had anything to do with their travel plans."

"That's right I didn't; besides, I'm waiting to hear what you read in the paper about our new neighbors. So go on and tell me. What did you read about them?"

"Well, apparently the head of the household, Charles Taylor, decided to relocate his family from their Chicago penthouse after his newly appointed position as CEO of some huge corporation in Chicago that he partly owns."

Veronica dropped the curtains and stepped away from the window to give Catherine her full attention. "What a lucky clan our next door neighbors seem to be. They don't have to just look the part. Big house, nice cars and a bank account to go along with it," she mumbled and nodded as her mind seemed deep in thought.

"Please, Veronica, is money the only thing on your mind? Before you throw too much praise toward Charles Taylor, I read his wife is crippled due to some accident and bound to a wheelchair for life."

Veronica grabbed her face and paused for a second. "I didn't know that."

"Of course, you didn't know. How could you have?"

"That is just awful. I had no idea. I figured if they could afford the old Sterling estate, they had more money than anyone; and I didn't stop to think about the possibility that they could have any misfortunes," Veronica said with empathy as she took a seat on the sofa.

"Veronica, what's with you this morning?"

"What do you mean what's with me?"

"You are carrying on a bit odd. You seemed annoyed to discuss why Roger and Janice moved so quickly; and now you seem quite emotional about our new neighbors that you haven't even met yet. Do you mind letting me in on what's going on with you?" Catherine took a seat on the sofa beside her. "Is something troubling you?"

"Yes, something is always troubling me!" Veronica snapped. "It's the same thing that should be troubling you, since you live under my roof."

"Can you think of anything else to concern yourself with other than this constant worry about your funds drying up?" Catherine stressed.

Veronica shook her head. "Are you kidding me? How can I think of anything else? Look around this place if you will. This big house will not run itself and our monthly overhead is going to always be the same no matter how hard I try to cut corners with the budget."

"I know that, Veronica. But you should count your blessings. My brother left you set for life; and I know you and I foolishly spent like crazy when he first passed away. But we know better about budgeting now."

"Yes, you are right," Veronica nodded. "We are better at budgeting now. But look how long it took us. Think about it, Catherine, for twenty years you and I spent my husband's fortune like it would always be there."

"Yes, I admit we had no sense about the value of a dollar." Catherine nodded. "But nobody else had that much money sense back in 1993. Everybody spent money and used credit cards like it was going out of style. We just did what everyone else was doing, just on a greater scale. We wanted what we wanted," Catherine said regrettably and narrowed her eyes at Veronica. "Although, come to think of it, I did try on many occasions to talk you into not shopping and traveling abroad as much, but you wouldn't heard of it."

"I know I wouldn't listen to you, Catherine. But in all fairness, I have to admit, you were more leveled headed than I was when Ryan died. We were both rather young. You were just thirty-seven and I was just thirty-eight and I had just lost my thirty-eight-year-old husband who had left me with four young sons to raise. I was grief stricken and overwhelmed at the thought of being without Ryan. You were like a life saver. You showed up and took care of the funeral and never left me and the boys."

"Being there for you and the boys helped me get through my own heartbreak at the time," Catherine sadly admitted.

Veronica stared at her and patted her shoulder. "That's right; you had just suffered a disappointing miscarry just a couple months before your only sibling died. And on top of that, you were just getting over your bitter divorce to Antonio Armani. That guy had caused you a lot of heartache to the point that you had sworn off love. But I have to admit, I was pleased beyond words when you sold your condo and accepted my offer to move into Franklin House to help me with the boys."

"Your offer was what I needed at the time. It was devastating to lose my brother on top of the void of losing my parents all those years before, but knowing I was moving back home after all those years of feeling like an outsider made me feel whole again and it healed something in me," Catherine sadly shared. "And yes, I was glad to help you and be close to my brother's kids, but as you know I wasn't completely selfless since I wanted to fade out any reminder of my former life being married to Antonio."

"Yeah, Antonio was not good for you. But you were young and in love and completely misguided in your devotion and love for that man." Veronica shook her head. "He cost you a lot. Going against your parents' wishes to marry him caused you to be disinherited and your new husband barred from Franklin House," Veronica reminded her. "And since he was barred from the house you barely came around."

"I know, but when Ma and Pa said they would cut me out of the will if I went ahead with my marriage to Antonio, I didn't believe them. I didn't believe it until after their death and the reading of the will when the attorney announced that they had indeed left their entire fortune to Ryan: the gas station, the house and all the cash. On top of that, Ryan was already filthy rich, but I was penniless with nothing but a broken heart and my folks stuck to their word and didn't leave me a dime," Catherine sadly reflected back.

Veronica shook her head. "I loved your folks and they were good to me, but in my opinion I strongly feel they were wrong to cut you out of their will. I would rather cut out my own heart before I would ever do something like that to one of my sons," Veronica said with conviction.

Catherine gave Veronica a humble glance. "You and I may not see eye to eye on many things, but one thing I know to be for sure; and I would state my life on it! You love your sons with everything in you, just like a tree planted by the water that can not be moved. That is your single most redeeming quality and one that I admire," Catherine said sincerely.

"Thank you for that acknowledgment, and as I stated before, your folks were wrong and that's one of the reasons I was so pleased that you moved in with us after Ryan's death. I wanted you to be able to enjoy some of your rightful birthright," Veronica explained.

"Thank you for that acknowledgement, and I'm sure you know that before Ryan died, he was giving me a monthly allowance," Catherine shared.

Veronica nodded. "Yes, I knew about it and approved. "But look, enough of the sad memories; get back to telling me what you read about our new neighbors. I'm fascinated by them, but it's sad how his wife is bound to a wheelchair."

"From what I read, Mrs. Candace Taylor has been bound to a wheelchair for nearly four years from injuries she suffered from a skating accident."

"That part is sad. I want to hear the more exciting news. What else did you read about them, something less depressing, of course?" Veronica asked. "I like that name."

"What name, Candace?"

"No, silly, I like the Taylor name. It's a traditional well-known name that's attached to famous people like one of the world's leading living **philosophers** who's name is Charles Taylor. Did the article mention any other family members other than Charles and Candace Taylor?"

"Yes, it did. Charles Taylor's parents, Claire and Archie Taylor, reside with them along with three daughters, Sabrina, Samantha and Starlet, and one small dog named Queenie."

Veronica lit up at the mention of the three daughters. "That's just wonderful to hear. Finally neighbors with filthy rich daughters." She smiled. "Did it mention their ages? They are probably too old to have real small children."

Catherine shook her head. "Yes, the article did happen to mention their ages: 24, 23 and 22." She paused and stared at Veronica. "You know you're kidding yourself? I know what you're thinking, but the Taylors are out of our league."

"What do you mean by that?" Veronica snapped.

"You know what I mean by that. Those young ladies wouldn't be allowed to date any of my nephews."

"And why would you say something as stupid as that? My sons can hold a candle to anybody's daughters. They are smart, good looking, well-mannered young men. Any girl would be lucky to have anyone of them."

"I know that, and you know that," Catherine explained. "They are my nephews and perfect in my eyes. But really Veronica, Rome, Britain, Paris and Sydney do not have the stuff that they would need to impress one of the Taylor girls," Catherine argued.

"And how would you know that Catherine?" Veronica snapped, irritated with Catherine's pessimistic comments. "What stuff are they missing?"

"They are missing the green stuff, remember? The millions you went through like it was growing on trees after my famous brother died from depression leaving you a boatload of cash," Catherine pointed out.

"Shut up, Catherine. You are such a downer. You had your own credit card and didn't miss out on much yourself."

"I know I didn't, but I'm trying to live in the real world now. Because I realize how blessed we still are to have Franklin House, all the original furniture and paintings that my grandparents, parents and Ryan purchased. We are still able to keep our butler, cook, housekeeper and the grounds person, even if they only work five days out of seven instead of six as they did before Ryan's death. Therefore, I think we should count our blessings and try not to live above our means."

"Catherine, I am counting my blessings. But we are not broke yet."

"Not yet, but close enough if you don't watch your bankbook. Trying to live up to the standards of the Taylors just to impress their daughters so they'll take an interest in one of the boys is a sure way to lose sight of your cash."

"Catherine, please, why do you always have to be such a downer all the time? Instead of reminding me of what we once had, why not try to do something about having it again? That's my aim. I will not sit and wait on a sinking ship without trying to save the whole boat. We will be back on top again. Mark my word."

"Okay, Veronica. How do you see that happening? Are you going to marry another famous actor? At 58, it won't be as easy as it was to snag my brother."

"Who said anything about marriage and snagging anyone? That ship sailed for me with Ryan. We were married for only fifteen years before I lost him, but those were happy years. We traveled a lot before I started having my kids and being pregnant every year for four years in a row." She paused and smiled. "But my sons will one day have the life Ryan and I had that Ryan intended for his sons to have as well. I spent a lot of their inheritance but I will see to them gaining the same advantages and success as their father. They are fine looking young men and there's no reason why they can not follow in their father's footsteps." Veronica smiled. "Just think how gorgeous they would look on the big screen."

"I agree that they would look damn good on any big screen. They are all drop dead gorgeous young men, but your oldest, Rome, is sinfully good looking."

"Yes, he is, isn't he; but all of my boys are sinfully good looking. They are the split image of how Ryan looked when he and I first met and fell in love," Veronica said, smiling. "So, you agree that my sons are all that, but you have the nerve to say they don't have what it takes to cozy up to our neighbors' daughters?"

"I just mean, they could get their foot in the door with the Taylors. That part would be easy since they live in the same community in a house just as grand. But once the Taylors became aware that no overflowing bank account was attached with the big house, then that would be the end of any relationship between the boys and their daughters before it started," Catherine explained strongly. "And as far as the four of them looking good on a big screen, is a moot point."

"It might be moot to you but it's not moot to me," Veronica snapped.

"It might as well be moot to you. You seem to be forgetting how Rome, Britain, Paris and Sydney has made it quite clear that they wants nothing to do with the kind of lifestyle that they feel destroyed their father. They are completely content and happy working at the family business."

"I know they are completely content and happy working at the family business, but I'm not happy. Working at Franklin Gas is beneath them all. Ryan never meant for his sons to work at a gas station. When he inherited the business from your parents, he never worked one single day at the place."

"Of course, he didn't, but it wasn't because he felt it was beneath him," Catherine quickly replied. "It's just that he never had too. He was filthy rich and too busy making movies."

"But even if he wasn't filthy rich and making movies, he wouldn't have settled to work at a gas station. He wanted so much more for himself and his children," Veronica stressed.

"That's probably true, because he was a born achiever. But your boys think their father would still be alive if he had chosen the simple life over the fame and riches he sought. They are convinced that making it all the way up to the top of the movie chart just to be tossed aside after the car accident that damaged his face was the sole reason for Ryan's depression. They feel that's what ended up taking my beautiful brother's life," Catherine explained.

Veronica shook her head. "Catherine, you are so right about that. They do think that way right now, but you need to realize that they are still young with their whole life ahead of them. I'm hoping they will follow in their father's footsteps and strive for more than just making a living," Veronica said with conviction.

"I know you want the best for them, but that's a thin line to walk if you try to control their destiny to fit with what you want for their future instead of what they actually want for their own future," Catherine stressed. "Because you may refuse to accept it, but your sons are happy just making a living."

Veronica flew off the sofa and grabbed her face. "I know they are happy working there, but you have to help me encourage them toward the movie business. They all took drama in college and won awards with their acting abilities, but now they are content pumping gas. I can't fail Ryan and them by allowing them to settle for less than their birthright. They need to use their talents."

"They are just not that interested in the movie business. They only took drama lessons because they wanted to please you. You couldn't have forgotten how they protested until you started crying and then they all agreed to do it just to make you happy. But they told you they would never seek a professional acting job and end up dying from depression as their father," Catherine said firmly.

"Catherine, you are right. They are determined to throw their lives away because of that kind of thinking. They were so young when Ryan died, six, five, four and three, but just old enough to experience such a painful experience of missing their father. And as time went by and they grew older they never forgot the many lies and rumors that floated around surrounding his death. Plus, they ended up reading all those damn articles that you saved in that silly scrapbook. I don't know why you saved all those articles when some of them were just plain garbage stating that Ryan died from a broken heart because no one would hire him after the car accident. That was a lie. He got calls for work after the accident; he just wouldn't take any. He lost his passion for work because he didn't like his looks anymore. It was Ryan who gave up on his career not the other way around," Veronica pointed out. "I need you to help me encourage my sons to make something of their lives besides slaving at that gas station! That place is beneath my sons!"

"Veronica, I know you want the best for Rome and his brothers, but how can you say what you just said?"

"How can I say what?"

"How can you call Franklin Gas that place? After all, that place, so you call it, is responsible for putting all your boys through college and allowing you to stay afloat. It pays the taxes on this big house, puts food on the table, pays all the bills; and at the end of the day, your four sons end up with a decent weekly paycheck," Catherine pointed out strongly.

"So what, it's still a gas station," Veronica snapped. "I know it's our bread and butter, but I don't have to like it. Besides, you are missing the point. I don't mind owning the place and reaping the rewards, I just don't want my sons working there. When Rome graduated from college and insisted on working there, I didn't put up a fuss because I thought it would be temporary until he got bored. But I looked around five years later and all my sons were working there. They insisted. But the clock is ticking and they are not going to be young forever. I need to find away to encourage them toward the movie business while they are still young enough to make an impact as their father did. All it takes is one great movie, and you're a star. That's what happened with Ryan. He was an instant star and the public couldn't get enough of him."

"Veronica, you can't relive the past. That was Ryan's time and your life with him. You can't live your sons' lives for them. You can't shape and control their lives to make them what you want them to be. You should count your blessings. Since the boys took control of the management of Franklin Gas the profits are up. You have to admit business is doing great since they took over the management. People drive from miles around just to buy gas from your sons in hope of getting a glimpse of their good looks."

Veronica smiled. "That is true. Just like a local article stated six months ago."

The Franklin boys have grown into the image of their famous father. They have the looks and the charm, but will they end up on the big screen? It appears they are content dazzling the public with their good looks and smiles as cars drive up for gas?

"But I'm determined to make that article into a lie. I will see to them not staying content at Franklin Gas."

Chapter Five

It was lightly raining that Monday afternoon on the twelfth of August when Veronica parked her shiny black Bentley in front of Franklin Gas for the first time. Rome had called and asked her to drop over. He and his brothers wanted to show her the finished results of the remodeling.

"Rome, Sweetheart, why did you summon me here this morning?" Veronica asked, standing in front of her son's large Mahoney desk.

"Hey, Mother, I'm glad you could pencil me in." He smiled, holding out both arms. "Have a seat." He pointed to one of the two comfortable chairs that sat at either side of his desk. "Look around while you're in here. Tell me, does my office look like something you couldn't get used to?"

Veronica took a seat across from her oldest son. She was surprise to see how upscale his office was. After all, she had never sat foot in the business before and had no idea how it looked in side. "Sweetheart, I can see how you and your brothers have managed to make this business rather attractive." She glanced at the paintings on the wall in his spacious office that housed the finest office furniture and first rate carpeting on the floor.

"Mother, you need to realize that although this is a gas station, we actually enjoy working here. Besides, what's not to like? We are building up our family business. Our quarterly report showed profits way up." He pointed toward the hallway that was slightly visible through the small opening in his office door. "Before you leave make sure you step down the hallway to the first door on your right."

"What's the first door on the right?" She curiously asked.

"That would be the office of your CFO," Rome answered, looking through a stack of file folders.

"Is Mr. Fenton still in that office? That man must be near 90 by now. He was the finance head back when Ryan's parents owned the company," Veronica recalled.

"Mother, focus for a moment," Rome glanced at his mother from his files. "Mr. Fenton retired awhile ago long before Britain took over the office."

Veronica nodded. "That's right, that's Britain's office," she remembered.

"Yes, its Britain's office and you should stop by there before you leave and pick up a copy of the quarterly report."

"Stop and pick up a copy of the quarterly report?" Veronica glanced at her diamond Rolex watch. "I don't' have much time, dear; it's almost noon and I have another appointment I must get to."

Rome shook his head as he stared at his mother sitting there in her navy blue two piece suit and finest jewelry draped around her neck and dangling from her ears. "Mother, please. This is your first visit here and you have been here all of ten minutes. Where are your priorities? This is our company and you treat it like something to frown on."

"I'm sorry, my darling son, of course I can reschedule the other appointment. You are right. It's my first visit and I should see the entire facility and all of your offices here and what you each do." She glanced about. "Based on your office I'm sure the rest of the entire facility and the other offices look just as nice. The four of you have spared no expense at remodeling and beautifying this place." She nodded. "I must admit I taught you all well. This facility is first class all the way."

"Well, Mother, you told us not to spare expense when we discussed the remodeling last year. Everything was upgraded as well as that huge section of property that's behind the office building which was originally the old repair shop. We converted it into a four car parking garage for our cars. We don't use it right now, but just in case we want or need to, its there."

Veronica nodded. "That was a brilliant idea."

Rome smiled. "I think so as well since it was my idea."

"So, you had all seven floors remodeled?"

"Yes, Mother; even though, Basic Storage is still leasing the top three floors from us, we also had those three floored remodeled with new windows, woodwork and carpeting. It only made sense to remodel the entire building since it hadn't been upgraded since Father died."

"No argument from me. I just can't wait to see what you have done with the place. It definitely doesn't look anything in here the way I thought it would." She kept looking about his office. "So, I take it, all the business offices are on this floor?"

Rome nodded, tapping his pen on his desk. "That is correct. All the managerial and administrative offices are here on the fourth floor," Rome eagerly said, pleased to tell his mother about the business. "And as you know, the service counter, the mini-mart and auto supply store is all on the first floor. The cafeteria and exercise room is on the second floor; and the conference room, storage room and supply room is all on the third floor."

"I thought the cafeteria was offsite in that fancy building across the street? I recall eating there last year and it was quite nice."

"It was nice, but we had the space and decided to remodel a portion of the second floor into the cafeteria for the employees to have lunch onsite," Rome explained. "I know the lunch room across the street was more spacious and to your liking, but we just figured, and it was originally an idea that Paris came up with, why not have the entire company under one roof. Therefore, we decided to stop leasing that space, and now the workers don't have to leave the building for their lunches."

"I'm not complaining, sweetheart. I think it's a great idea to have the cafeteria in the same building as the managerial and administrative offices. You boys have done well with this place," Veronica complimented.

"We have done well, Mother. That's all you have to say?" Rome asked.

"What more do you want me to say? You have done an excellent job." She smiled. "Before I walked inside I was worried about a place to sit without snagging or spoiling my outfit. But this is upscale all the way," she said sincerely, smiling and then frowned. "But only if it wasn't a gas station."

Rome shook his head. "Mother, I don't know why you have this thing against gas stations, especially the one we own. Besides, its good business and good money; don't you know that, Mother?" He leaned back in his chair and placed both hands behind his head.

Veronica slowly nodded with serious eyes. "I guess I know that, but."

"You don't have to say it. We have heard it a hundred times. You feel as if we are doing work beneath us by working here. But Mother, that's not true. We are not the ones out there helping at the pumps or waiting on the customers. We have forty other employees who do that, but even if we were the ones doing it, it's honest decent work and nothing to be ashamed of. This is a blue collar operation but Britain, Paris and Sydney and I are all white collar workers. We are the executives behind the desk pushing the paper and pencils just like that crew we used to pay all that money. Britain, Paris and Sydney and I are doing what those people used to do for us. By doing so, we are saving a boatload of money. Its not going into their pockets, it's going into ours," Rome explained.

Veronica nodded. "Sweetheart, I understand what you are saying and everything is just beautiful here, right down to the landscaping outside, but no matter how you try to sell me on you, Britain, Paris and Sydney working here, I just can't see it in my mind's eye. A gas station no matter how fancy is still a gas station where people come for gas and snacks and a quick car wash," she argued. "And I want more for you and your brothers. You should be doing what you went to college for."

"Mother, what are you talking about? We are doing what we went to college for. I'm the CEO, Britain is the CFO, Paris is the CIO and Sydney is the COO. We wouldn't be qualified or skilled to hold these positions if we hadn't obtain the knowledge from college. The four employees that held these positions before us were qualified and paid good salaries. But we are also qualified and paid good salaries but we are not giving ourselves as much as we paid the employees who held these positions before us. Therefore, that helps save the company money by the four of us working here," Rome pointed out.

"Yes, it does. What is a COO?" Veronica smiled. "My baby is holding a title that I have no idea what it stands for."

"Mother, will you answer me one thing?" Rome asked.

"What's that, dear?"

"Why do you keep calling Sydney your baby?" Rome teased.

"Because he is my baby no matter how old he gets."

"That might be true, but Mother, he doesn't care to be called that in public."

"He hasn't complained to me about it."

"And he probably won't, but just so you know, he doesn't like being called your baby. He's a grown man."

"Alright, I'll try to keep that in mind. But you didn't answer me. What in the world does COO stand for?"

"Sydney title stands for chief operating officer. He pretty much oversees the employees and operations of the business. And if for some reason I step down as CEO, he'll be next in line for the position."

"I see; what a mess." She shook her head.

"Mother, what do you mean?"

"Rome, I mean, when I said you and your brothers should be doing what you went to college for, I meant acting. Your father is dead and gone but that's what he wanted for you boys. No fancy office anywhere is going to sway me from your birth right."

"Mother, we all took those drama classes in college just to please you. We never had any intentions of perusing an acting career and you know why," Rome said with an irritated edge.

"Yes, I do know why and it's a waste for the four of you to throw your talents away sitting behind some desk when the world is waiting to see you on the big screen," she said passionately.

Rome shook his head and just then there was a knock on his office door.

"Yes, may I help you? He asked.

"Rome, it's me, Sydney."

"Come in, of course," Rome replied.

Sydney walked in smiling. He looked very professional dressed in a white shirt with a pale yellow tie and matching pale yellow dress slacks. He had his shoulder length black hair pulled back in a pony tail. "Wow, I don't believe what I'm seeing. Mother, you stopped by. Is it going to storm?" He grinned. "What do we owe the pleasure?" he teased his mother.

"I'm only here for a short while, but figured it was about time I took a look at the place where the four of you stick to like glue," she said.

"It's almost lunchtime, join us for lunch," Sydney suggested.

"Where would we eat?" She asked.

"What do you mean where would we eat?" Sydney smiled. "We can eat here in the cafeteria, or we can all go to some restaurant up the street."

Veronica interrupted him. "I was referring to here. Where would we eat if we stayed onsite for lunch? I know you told me that you moved the cafeteria onsite to the second floor but I'm not sure I'm ready to try their menu."

"You should try it. The food is quite good," Sydney assured her.

Veronica shook her head. "Some other time, dear," she glanced at her watch.

Rome stared at his mother. "Mother, why are you checking the time? I thought you were going to cancel your other appointment, so why not have lunch with us?"

"Yes, Mother, why not? We don't have to eat in the lunchroom, which I think you would like if we did, but since you don't want to we won't. We can all eat in Paris office. His office is almost twice the size of ours. There's a large round table with six chairs in his office," Sydney said.

"I thought all your offices were the same size. Why would Paris have a larger office than the rest of you?"

"Mother, does that really matter?" Rome snapped. "Is everything about appearances to you?"

"Rome, lighten up; Mother didn't mean it like that," Sydney quickly jumped to his mother defense. "She just thought all the offices were the same size."

"I just think it's a non issue to discuss," Rome mumbled.

"Of course, it's a non issue," Sydney glanced at his diamond Omega watch. "It's time for lunch. I'm starved actually." He smiled at his mother. "Mother, what is it going to be, lunch with the best looking brothers in town or not?" He held out both arms.

She smiled. "When you put it that way, how can I refuse? Sure, I will join you boys for lunch. What's on the menu, and I don't mean the menu here."

"Pizza is on the menu," Sydney answered. "It should be arriving at any moment now. I'll check with Courtney and have her bring the boxes up to Paris's office after they are delivered. And I need to give her some cash for the tip."

"Who is Courtney?" Veronica asked.

"She's that very pretty young lady at the counter down there," Sydney opened the door and stepped out of the office.

Veronica glanced at Rome. "Which one is Courtney? When I walked in, there were four young ladies at the counter. They all seemed okay with average looks." Veronica stared at Rome with a curious look in her eyes.

"That's Shanell Davis, Vickie Simpson, Trina Ross, who is Courtney's younger sister, and Courtney Ross."

"Does Courtney work at the left end of the counter closest to the front entrance?" Veronica asked.

"No, she works in the middle, and just so you know." He paused. "Courtney is anything but average in looks. You probably didn't get a good look at her mother. She's the one with black tight curls sweeping just below her shoulders. She has deep brown eyes and she's exceedingly friendly and easy to talk to," Rome said with a certain look on his face.

Veronica didn't care for that look on his face. "Keep in mind, my son, these young ladies that you have working here are not girlfriend material for any of you," Veronica stressed strongly.

"Sure, Mother, I'm starting to think that according to you, no girl is."

Rome picked up his office phone and dialed Paris office. "Hey, Mother is here for lunch. Guess what, we're having lunch in your office. Give Britain a buzz and let him know."

Fifteen minutes later, as they awaited the arrival of the pizza, Veronica seemed bored sitting at the opposite end of Britain's desk glancing through the quarterly report file. Numbers and charts were not her strong area. However, she read it with interest.

When the pizza arrived, they were all gathered in Paris office sitting around the table when Courtney softly knocked on the office door and brought the four large boxes of steaming hot pizza in.

"Come in Courtney," Paris said, smiling. "Thank you. Sit the boxes over there." He pointed to the file cabinet next to his desk.

Courtney glanced toward Britain who was checking his phone, and then she glanced toward Rome and smiled as she placed the boxes on top of the file cabinet. Rome smiled toward her and Veronica noticed the line of warmth between the two. As Courtney turned to head out of the office Veronica frowned at the young lady's shoes and outfit. Then Britain lifted a finger.

"Courtney, wait up." He smiled. "Our manners seem to be lacking today. We are all sitting here and not one of us thought to introduce you to Mother. I would like for you to meet our mother, Veronica Franklin." Britain waved his hand toward his mother. "Mother, this is Courtney Ross, one of our dependable counter assistances."

"It's nice to meet you, Mrs. Franklin. I have heard a lot about you and your late husband, Ryan Franklin. He was my folk's favorite actor." She smiled.

"Thank you, dear. Do you work for us full-time?" Veronica asked.

Courtney nodded. "Yes, ma'am, I do."

"Do you live nearby?" Veronica asked.

"Yes, ma'am, just a few blocks away. I go to St. Mark's Church. You may know my parents, Raymond and Mildred Ross."

Veronica shook her head. "I'm sorry, dear, but I have never heard of your folks. We probably don't go to the same places."

"I'm sorry, but Britain mentioned he goes to St. Mark and I just assumed it was your church," Courtney explained.

Veronica nodded. "St. Mark is our church," she said quickly and changed the subject. "So, I take it, you are out of college?"

"Yes, ma'am, since the first of the year," Courtney answered.

"And you have settled in here for us as a counter assistance? What did you major in?"

"Education and I hope to get a teaching job next year," she said with excitement.

"A teaching job, you're not that ambitious are you?" Veronica waved her hand and mumbled in a slow voice.

"I beg you pardon," Courtney said. "I couldn't hear what you just said."

"It was not important," Veronica smiled. "It was nice meeting you, Courtney. Thanks for the good job you're doing for us."

"You are welcomed," Courtney said and left the office.

When Courtney shut the door closed behind her, the four brothers exchanged looks, knowing their mother had a hundred questions about Courtney. They all hopped up from the table at once and rushed toward the pizza. They left their mother sitting there tapping her fingernails on the table.

"Which one of you hired Courtney Ross?" she asked in a firm voice.

They all kept busying themselves with the pizza and said nothing.

"I know you heard me when I asked which one of you hired that girl. As you just heard, she doesn't plan to stick around that long. Next year she plans to teach school."

"Mother, we all know, but she's a nice girl and a good worker," Britain stated.

"And according to her, the two of you have exchanged personal conversations."

Britain slightly smiled as he exchanged looks with his brothers. They all knew that Britain shared his lunches with her and conversed with her during the lunch hour. He and Courtney had not socialized off the premises. They were solely lunch partners. However, they all knew Veronica would blow a gasket if she knew even that bit of information; therefore they were all mute on the subject.

"Mother, please," Britain smiled. "Telling someone the name of your church is hardly that personal. What's the big deal? Can we just enjoy our lunch without you giving us the third degree about one of our workers?"

"That's just it, Britain; I don't believe this Courtney is just another worker. I think she's crushing on one of you. Whether you, or the rest of you are encouraging her feelings. It's quite obvious to me that she likes one of you." Veronica held up one finger. "My point is, just don't encourage her. She could have an agenda to snag one of you. Maybe she orchestrated getting herself hired here just for that purpose."

"Mother, I'm not sure that makes sense," Britain smiled. "I'm wondering how she could orchestrate such an elaborate scheme. I guess by walking in and completing an application and being hired because she's over qualified?" Britain joked.

"You can make a joke about it if you like, but I just want the four of you to keep in mind the bottomline, which is, Courtney Ross is not girlfriend material for any of you. Do I make myself clear?"

They were all busy putting slices of pizza on paper plate, not acknowledging their mother and the statement she had just made.

Taking a seat at the table, Paris smiled. "Mother, Britain is right, and we all would agree that Courtney is a very nice young lady and as you can see, polite and exceptionally easy on the eyes."

"I agree, she is a pretty girl, but I want more than just beauty for you boys."

"What about what we want?" Rome said under his breath.

She glanced toward Rome. "What did you say, dear?"

Rome just stared at her and held out both hands as if he had said nothing. Then suddenly they all were trying to keep their composure and not laugh out as she stared at him wondering had he said what she thought he had said. But she quickly focused back on the subject of who had hired Courtney.

"So, will one of you please tell me who hired her? I will find out," she stressed.

"Mother, what difference does it makes who hired her?" Rome asked.

"I just want to know because that might tell me who she has her eye on. Some women have been known to fall for the man who gives her a job."

They all looked toward Paris and smiled, and she noticed. But before she could say a word Paris said.

"Yes, Mother, I hired Courtney Ross."

"Paris, dear," she said firmly. "Why would you hire someone who tells you she's only going to stick around for a short time? Besides, I thought Sydney did the hiring."

"Oh, Mother, that's the problem with you," Rome snapped. "You don't know what goes on here because you don't try to know and you don't want to know. Sydney does most of the hiring, but any of us can hire and fire employees," Rome stressed seriously. "You would know how the business worked and what we do around here if you took the time to find out."

Britain, Paris and Sydney gave Rome a solid look that meant they were not pleased with his rudeness toward their mother. "I think we're getting a bit loud," Britain touched Rome on the shoulder. "Remember, these walls are rather thin." He smiled and winked toward Rome. "Pretty soon I'm going to think you like for Mother to rag on you," Britain joked to lighten things up.

Rome was still a bit irritated that his mother was not pleased with Courtney for no apparent reason that he could think of. "What are you talking about?" Rome asked.

"I'm talking about how you know exactly how to keep Mother going," Britain turned a bottle of cola up to his mouth and finished a fourth of the cold drink before he lowered the beverage.

Rome nodded toward Britain and stood up from his seat. "I definitely do not want to keep Mother going." Rome grinned as he adjusted his chic silver belt around his model built waist. He was wearing a pair of black slacks, black shirt, silver tie and a pair of black Christian Louboutin shoes that shined from the reflection of the overhead office light. He was the picture of a magazine model with his ear length black waves combed back off his face. He stepped across the office for another slice of pizza.

"Mother, I apologize for my rudeness. I don't mean to be rude, but it's just irritating how you don't seem to show any interest in our business or what we do here," Rome explained.

"No apology is needed, sweetheart. I was not offended. You are right, but I'm trying to show some interest now. It's clear you all need help in hiring staff. Forget the beauty and hire someone who might actually want to work here and stick around," Veronica suggested, looking down at the plate Sydney placed in front of her. The three slices of pineapple pizza was more than she wanted but she didn't comment.

"Mother, did I give you too much, not enough?" Sydney asked. "There's plenty of pizza here. Probably more than we'll be able to finished off."

"It will keep in the lunchroom fridge," Paris winked at Sydney.

"It will keep for you, I guess. I don't eat leftover pizza," Sydney laughed.

"Well, I don't eat leftover pizza either," Paris laughed.

Veronica exchanged looks with Rome and Britain and they shook their heads. Then they all laughed at the same time. "But we know who do eat leftover pizza," Britain said to his mother.

"Okay, you have my attention. Who eats leftover pizza?" Veronica asked.

"Aunt Catherine does," Britain said. "We can take the leftover pizza to her."

"Sure, if you think she'll eat it," Veronica said, not sure.

"Yes, Mother, she will eat it," Sydney nodded. "Whenever we order pizza at home on the weekends, there's usually a lot left. We stick it in the fridge and Aunt Catherine eats it." He laughed. "We all saw her eating leftover cold pizza one night."

Veronica was quiet for a moment and Sydney asked. "Mother, why are you quiet all of a sudden? Is anything the matter? We are just teasing about Aunt Catherine. It's cool if she likes cold pizza. We just thought it was kind of funny when we all caught her eating it straight from the box."

"Nothing is the matter. I was just thinking about your father."

"Why are you thinking about Father right now, during the middle of our lunch? Is it his birthday or something?" Paris asked, exchanging looks with his brothers.

"No it's not your father birthday or anything like that. I was just thinking about how blessed I am to have all of you. You are just like your father. He didn't eat leftover pizza either." She smiled. "He loved pizza, but would never eat any leftover pizza."

"Maybe we took that after you instead of Father," Paris smiled. "You don't eat leftover pizza either."

"That's true, but I used to before I married your father. I stop eating leftover pizza after we married and he absolutely was against it. He would tell me how leftover pizza never measured up to fresh baked pizza. So, I stop eating leftover pizza."

"Now that we all know who does eat leftover pizza," Paris said jokingly and paused. "We can move on to another topic, which is a serious matter that I would like to clear up. We don't want you to leave here thinking we don't know how to hire the right employees," Paris said seriously. "Mother, when I hired Courtney and her sister Trina and the other two young ladies that work at the counter, we were all aware that they would only be with us temporary," Paris explained. "If you didn't know it, working as a counter assistant at a gas station is not a career job for most people."

Veronica slapped her hands and smiled, exchanging looks with all her sons. "I hope you all heard what your brother just said. I have been trying to concrete that bit of information into your heads, but nobody is listening to me."

"Mother, wake up," Paris grinned. "It's not a career place for the average worker. But we are not average workers. We own the place. I think there's a difference, since the average worker can only earn an average salary at a gas station, but the owners can make millions as we do," Paris pointed out.

"I know it's a money maker and that's great. I just want so much more for you boys. I want you to follow in your father's footsteps."

"Mother, please drop your pitch about the movie industry. We are not going to make a movie." Britain picked a chunk of pineapple from his slice of pizza and placed in his mouth. "Besides, you make it sound as if it's ours for the taking. We are not interested in the business that killed our father, and even if we were, who would hire us and put us in a movie?"

"That's right, Mother, who would give us a part in a movie?" Paris asked. "You just want us in the movies because father was famous and you think we can be too." Paris turned a bottle of water up to his mouth and took a swallow. "But seriously, Mother, nobody is going to take a chance on four unknowns like us. Besides, we are not actors anyway."

"You are all born actors. Just as your father who was one of the best," Veronica stressed passionately.

"Yes, Mother, we have heard," Rome mumbled. "But we are not our father. You need to accept the fact that we are not destined to be big stars as Father once was. We want to follow in his footsteps in terms of all the great things he did to help others with his wealth, but that's where the trail stops."

"That's right, Mother, we do want to follow in our father's footsteps and be the best human being that we can by supporting and standing up for the causes he believed in and fought for," Sydney added. "Like his quest to put a dent in world hunger and homelessness; and how he stood up for women's rights and civic rights and the list continues! Those are the ways we want to follow in our father's footsteps and not by making movies."

"Mother, that's my point. Just as Sydney just explained we feel we are following in Father's footsteps by supporting the many causes he believed in and supported when he was alive like the ones Sydney mentioned, civil rights and equal rights for women and helping others with food and shelter where needed," Rome said heartfelt. "But also as Paris just mentioned." He exchanged looks with Paris and then looked back toward his mother. "We are just not actors."

Veronica was silent for a moment as Sydney reached over and placed his hand on top of her hand and rubbed it lightly to soften her distress.

"Well, I respectfully disagree and feel you all are actors," Veronica stated. "Have you all forgotten that I saw all of you perform on stage during your college days? You were all wonderful and a big hit on campus."

Her sons exchanged looks and Britain nodded. "Mother, that's true. We were great in our performance of My Three Sons; and it was fun for all of us. But our hearts are not into it," Britain said seriously. "Besides, Mother, as we mentioned before, who would hire us and put us in a movie?"

"If you boys wanted to get in the movie business, I have all the connections you need. Just say the word and your father's old agent, Jack Coleman, would have you signed up for a movie within twenty-four hours. He has been waiting and contacting me for years for the four of you. He knows the industry will bank off of your father's name. The four of you would be instant stars over night," Veronica said with great confident. "I know you have beautified this place and you love this work and you feel the movie business destroyed your father, but your father was a go-getter. He didn't settle; he went all the way to the top and I'm sure he doesn't want any less for his sons. The four of you are still young and this opportunity will not always be knocking at your door," she stressed strongly and exchanged looks with them all. "Just say the word and I'll make the call to Jack Coleman."

"Mother, No," Rome spoke first. "For the last time, it's not what we want."

"Maybe, it's not what you want, but I need to hear all of you say just that," Veronica stated as the other three raised their hands in agreement with Rome. "Okay, but I'm not giving up," she said firmly as she got from her seat to head out of the office.

Sydney followed his mother out of the office, onto the elevator and out of the building to her car where it was parked on the street in front of the building. He felt bad that she was disappointed. He gave her a hug after he opened the car door for her.

"Mother, why did you park here on the streets? We have a parking lot in the back of the building."

"I didn't know," she mumbled with no perkiness to her voice.

"Okay, Mother, but next time park there. This is a no parking zone and you're lucky you didn't catch a ticket."

"Some luck is better than no luck. I didn't have any luck convincing the four of you to do what I feel you were born to do." She slowly took a seat in the car.

"I know you didn't convince us, but it was great having you pay a visit. We know how you feel about the business. Therefore, it meant a lot to us that you dropped by to have lunch with us." Sydney touched his mother's shoulder. "I know you are disappointed that we don't want to make movies, but we just hate what making movies eventually did to our father."

"Sydney, I think you are curious and would like to give acting a chance. Do you deny that?" Veronica looked in his eyes.

"I don't deny it, Mother, but I'm also happy where I am. Besides, we are a team. It's all or nothing. We made a decision that if we somehow got into the movie business, it would be all of us or none of us."

Veronica smiled. "So you have talked about the possibility among yourselves?"

"Of course, Mother, how could we have not, the way you are constant on us about it. But so far, we have all agreed to stay clear of the movie business."

"Sydney, you need to be the one to help me convince your brothers that this is a good idea. You are the youngest, the one they have always looked out for and wanted to please. I feel if you explained that it's something you want to give a chance, they will all jump onboard for you. Then the four of you would be on your way. You should think about talking to them," Veronica suggested. "Do you promise to do so?"

Sydney nodded. "Sure, Mother. I can't promise the outcome, but I will talk to Rome, Britain and Paris and see if I can encourage them to at least give it a shot."

Chapter Six

Leo's Fine Eatery was decorated in three shades of light green with expensive lighting and mirrors that made it breathe elegance and class. The song playing in the background, Unforgettable by Nat King Cole, was so soft it could hardly be heard as Veronica made her way toward the corner table.

"This is a very pleasant surprise, lunch with my wonderful sons two days in a row. I could get use to this." Veronica smiled. "But I must ask, what's the occasion? Why have you summoned me to this fine establishment for lunch?" she asked, smiling with a curious look on her face. "I would like to think it's just because I'm the most wonderful mother in the world, but something tells me that's not quite your reason." She smiled at her sons standing at the round table waiting for her to be seated, and just then it dawned on her that Sydney wasn't standing there with them. "She took her seat and then glanced about the place. "This is my first time here. It's quite nice, the new Italian restaurant that Catherine read about."

"Yes, Mother, it is. Welcome to Leo's Fine Eatery." Paris smiled as they all took their seats. "We asked you to lunch because we wanted to talk to you in privacy away from Sydney," Paris said passing his mother a menu.

"Why is that, are you boys planning some kind of party for him?" She connected eyes with all three of them. "He already celebrated his birthday back in May."

"Mother, it's not about his birthday. It's about the talk he had with us yesterday." Britain smiled. "After the talk you had with him shortly before," he said as he took the white napkin out of the glass it was sticking in and placed it on his lap.

Veronica went to sip her iced water, but lowered the glass back to the table when Britain relayed that bit of information. "Oh, I see; your brother talked to the three of you about considering the idea of giving your acting a shot?"

"Yes, Mother, did he ever." Rome raised one hand to get the waiter attention.

The tall, thin, dark-haired waiter, wearing all white attire, hurried over to their table with a pad in hand. "Are you ready to order?" he asked.

Rome nodded and pointed to his mother. "Yes, thanks, we are," he said to the waiter and then looked at his mother. "Mother, what would you like?"

"I'll take the soup and salad, and a tall glass of iced tea," Veronica said.

The waiter looked at Rome. "And you, Sir?"

"We will all take what she's having," Rome said with a smile.

The waiter nodded. "Okay, I got it. Four orders of soup, salad, tall glasses of iced tea and all the breadsticks you can eat," the waiter said and hurried away.

"Yes, Mother." Rome nodded. "Sydney is now quite convinced that we should all jump on board and give acting a shot to make you happy."

"Well, it would make me happy, but I think it will also make all of you happy as well." She nodded and tapped her finger on the table.

"That's debatable, Mother," Rome added. "The four of us have maintained our persistence about not wanting to get into the movies. You just won't let it go."

Just then the waiter rolled a serving cart over to their table. He placed their soup and salad in front of them along with a basket of eight bread sticks; and a tall glass of iced tea for each of them. "Can I get you anything else," the waiter said and when they all shook their heads, he then rolled the cart away.

After the waiter was out of earshot, Paris reached for a breadstick and dumped it into his soup and then into his mouth and took a bite. He gracefully chewed the piece of bread and then lifted his glass and took a swallow of iced tea. "Yes, Mother, we feel it's going to dishonor father's memory in some way," he explained. "We realize that you probably don't see it that way, but it's the way we see it. We have always tried to do what we felt best in terms of trying to honor father's name."

"And you boys have done a great job at that. Look what you have done with the gas station. I never would have thought that you would have managed to remodel and make that place look like a modern office building and not just some old building with unused office space and an old aging gas station out front," Veronica said with conviction. "It's not what I would have recommended since I felt putting your energy into such common work were beneath you," Veronica arrogantly admitted. "But believe it or not, I do know why you chose too."

"Do you really, Mother?" Paris took another bite from his breadstick.

"Yes, really, your mother knows. It's probably because you recall your Aunt Catherine and me telling all of you how your father regretted not fixing up the place and spending at least a little of his time there." She paused. "Yes, he regretted that in the end," Veronica shared. "But believe me, your father wasn't absence from Franklin Gas because he looked down on the business or felt it was beneath him. Ryan didn't have an arrogant bone in his body. I on the other hand, was pleased that he never spent any time at the family business. But he didn't stay away on my wishes. I had my thoughts and your father had his, and mostly his thoughts never mirrored mine."

Rome, Britain and Paris exchanged looks and smiled. "Mother, one day you'll have to tell us, what you and Father had in common?" Paris smiled.

"In a nutshell, your father and I had mutual respect for each other; and we loved each other and all of you with our whole heart and soul," she eagerly shared.

"Mother, in a nutshell, that was awesome what you just shared about you and father," Britain said. "But tell us why was father full of regret at the end about Franklin Gas? If he was too busy to spend time there, he was just too busy. Why did he have those regrets like that?" Britain curiously asked as he took a sip of his iced tea.

"He regretted that he never sat foot in the place," Veronica said, eating her salad. "It wasn't intentional as I pointed out before. Your father was just so busy with his acting schedule until it just happened that way. And during the end of his life he reflected on that. He had regrets and wished he had fixed up the place for the workers and also in honor of his parents for leaving him the family business."

"So, Mother, that's why you think we chose to work at the family business because we wanted to fulfill father's dream of getting the place in shape?" Paris asked.

"That's right," Veronica uttered seriously, lifted her glass and took a sip from her iced tea. "You boys had a vision and a goal to upgrade and beautify that old office building and gas station to honor your father's business. I heard you discuss it back when you were all still in high school. I hoped it would slip your mind by the time you finished college but it never did. Now look at you all." She held out both arms. "You have made the place unrecognizable in a pleasing way."

Britain nodded with a glow in his eyes. "Wow, Mother, I guess you do know what the family business means to us and why," Britain said as he dipped his spoon into his veggie soup and took a spoonful. "We just want to do all we can to honor father's name and getting into the movies isn't on our list."

Veronica looked from Rome, Britain and Paris and then lifted her glass and took a sip of iced tea. "So, I guess the three of you asked me to lunch to give me your final no, which is probably coming next. But as strong as you boys are against the movie business, I'm for it just as strongly. We just have different opinions. You boys think it's dishonoring your father and I happen to think it will be honoring Ryan," she explained, and then looked down at her half eaten salad and pushed it aside.

Britain looked toward his mother's salad. "Mother, you don't like the salad?"

"The lettuce isn't crisp," she complained. "Maybe this new restaurant isn't all it's talked up to be." She glanced about.

Rome looked at his mother and smiled. "Mother, we know what you are doing. You are pouting because we don't share your opinion about the movie business," Rome grinned. "But, Mother, Sydney isn't here to give in to your pouting and say what you want to hear." He exchanged serious looks with Britain and Paris. "However, we have decided to take Sydney suggestion and give acting a shot," Rome announced to her.

Veronica shifted in her seat and almost lost her composure at Rome's announcement. She pointed to each of them one at a time. "Did I hear you correctly? You, you, and you have decided along with Sydney to try acting and make a movie?"

"You heard right, Mother," Paris nodded. "However, we decided that we are keeping our positions at the business as well."

"But how will you boys be able to manage that?" she asked. "You are already busy as a bee, when would you find the time?"

"We have decided to only give acting a shot for your sake. Just to make you happy, Mother. Plus, our baby brother asked us to give it a shot and we didn't want to turn him down. But we are keeping our positions as Paris just said," Britain reminded her. "And we only plan to make one movie."

"That's right, Mother," Paris placed the last of his salad in his mouth. "We are only agreeing to one movie deal if anyone will sign us on."

"That's a done deal." Veronica nodded. "But just one movie, I'm not sure how Jack will feel about signing you on for just one movie, but it's a start." Veronica smiled.

Rome shook his head. "No, Mother, it's not a start. It's the start and the finish. We need you to understand that we are just doing this one movie for you. We want to make you happy, but this is not our happiness." He paused. "Do you get us, Mother?"

"Yes, I get you." She nodded. "You are only agreeing to the one movie. I will contact your father's old agent and manager, Jack Coleman, and set an appointment to take you boys into his office. He will be over the moon thrilled to get the four of you into a movie. It's what he has waited for all these years since your father passed away."

"Do you keep in touch with Mr. Coleman after all this time?" Britain asked.

"We are not close friends, but I do receive calls from him about once a month inquiring about the four of you."

"Inquiring about what?" Britain asked. "Why does he inquire about us?"

"You know why? He wants the four of you to follow into your father's footsteps just as I do," Veronica explained.

"Mother, I know why you want us in the movies, but why is it so important to Mr. Coleman?" Britain wondered.

"It's obvious he feels your father's name will boost your career and therefore make it easy to sign a movie deal for the four of you." Veronica nodded.

"Is he looking to bank off of us?" Britain narrowed his eyes at his mother.

Veronica nodded. "Of course, he feels one of your films will do well at the box-office with a Franklin name; and I'm inclined to agree with him. I feel as Jack does that the four of you will be an instant success due to your father's great movie record."

Paris grinned and exchanged looks with Rome and Britain. "Mr. Coleman most likely thinks he's going to make the kind of money with us that he made with Father, but if he thinks that, he needs to be enlightened on our acting skills."

"There's no need for concern about your acting abilities," Veronica quickly stated. "These people in the business know how to make it work. If they sign you for a movie deal, they will use every means possible to get the product they are after. They have acting coaches, voice coaches, hair stylists, makeup artists, costume designers, personal trainers and a host of others on hand to mold the individual into the character they are supposed to portray."

Britain nodded and looked toward his mother. "That's good to know, but Mother, money has to be Mr. Coleman's big interest in us."

Veronica nodded. "Well, of course, he's looking to make lots of money. That goes without saying. But what's important is that he feels the four of you will pull it in."

Britain smiled. "It's flattering that he has great confidence in us, but it's all based on Father's track record."

"That may be so, but I have great confidence that the four of you will do an amazing performance in any movie you star in," Veronica stressed.

"Thanks, Mother, but Mr. Coleman needs to be informed on our lack of enthusiasm for the entertainment business." Britain exchanged looks with Paris and Rome and they both nodded. "So, please don't forget to relay to him that this is just a one time movie deal, and it's sort of a gift to you." Britain nodded at his mother, then lifted his glass and took a sip from his iced tea. "Make it crystal clear to him that after the movie, we won't be shooting another one," Britain stressed strongly.

"Of course, I will relay your terms," Veronica said excitedly. "I'll call his office tomorrow and he'll probably want to see the four of you as soon as possible."

"How soon is that?" Rome asked.

"My best guess is that he'll probably want to see all of you a couple days after that, in his office by Friday at the latest."

Chapter Seven

During dinner, while they were all gathered around the dinner table, after the cook, Natalie Madden, placed the dish of sliced beef and gravy on the table and stepped out of the dinning room, Veronica raised both hands.

"Before we start dinner I have good news to share," she said.

Her sons were already reaching for the food, passing it to each other and filling their plates. But Catherine was curious. "Go on, what's the good news?" she asked.

"Look what I'm holding in my hand." She lifted a small envelope and waved it in the air.

"What's that, Mother?" Paris asked, passing the serving bowl of breadsticks to Britain, who was seated to his right.

"We have been personally invited to attend the Taylor's house warming and get acquainted party for tomorrow night," she said with great enthusiasm.

"They didn't give a lot of notice, did they?" Catherine remarked, passing the breadsticks to Rome.

"That part is my fault. The invitation arrived a few days ago, but I just noticed it today. Therefore, if any of you have plans for tomorrow, you need to cancel them. This is a very important party," Veronica stated. "They have lived next door for nearly a month, and this is our opportunity to meet and get acquainted with our new neighbors.

"Mother, I do have other plans," Britain announced as he took his fork and removed the cucumbers from his salad.

"So, do I," Paris nodded. "Why do we need to cancel our plans for the Taylor's party anyway? What's so important about this party? You get party invitations all the time and don't usually press us quite as strongly to attend."

"Mother, that's true, you're always getting these invitations," Sydney sprinkled black pepper on his salad. "People you know in this area are always having parties. Sometime you don't even attend. So why is this one so special?" Sydney narrowed his eyes and smiled toward his mother.

"Can the four of you just do as I ask? I would just like all of us to attend this party as a family," Veronica stressed humbly.

"Mother, we hear you," Rome paused from his meal and looked at his mother. "But we would like to know why you are insisting that we drop everything just to attend this party."

"I thought it would be obvious." She paused. "Apparently, it's extremely important to me. They have lived next door to us for a month now and we have never formally met any of them. I would think you all would be interested in meeting your next door neighbors."

"That's cool, I don't mind meeting them and welcoming them to the neighborhood, but spending a Saturday night at one of those parties will most likely be boring for all of us," Rome grinned.

"I second that," Sydney lifted his hand and smiled. "But I'm in. I'm willing to show up with you Mother and make an appearance if it means that much to you."

"Thank you, sweetheart, mother can always count on her sweet baby to come through," she caught herself. "I'm sorry I called you baby. I'm aware that you would prefer that I wouldn't refer to you as a baby; even though technically you are my baby. Anyway, I'm trying to break the habit of referring to you as such," she said, and then lifted her cup and sipped her hot tea.

"Hey, sweet baby," Paris teased and elbowed Sydney.

Then Rome and Britain teased him and the four of them laughed just joking around about their mother calling Sydney, sweet baby.

Veronica wanted their attention. "What's so funny about being called baby?"

"It could have something to do with the fact that your twenty-three-year-old son stopped wearing diapers years ago," Catherine mumbled in a low voice.

"Okay, enough about that already," Veronica raised her voice over everyone's chatter. "I'm still waiting my sons for the rest of you to get onboard." She stared toward Rome, Britain and Paris. "Can I count on the rest of you to attend this party with me as well?"

"You have your sweet baby, why do you need the rest of us?" Paris teased and then held up one finger. "I was just teasing, Mother. You can count me in. I'll be there," Paris smiled and exchanged looks with his brothers. "I'm sure we'll all end up there at your side. But I hope the Taylor's party doesn't turnout as boring as most of the parties we attend with you. And if you're wondering why we are not excited, why should we be excited to flock to a gathering of people twice or more our ages. We are usually the youngest guests at those parties," Paris finished his glass of iced tea and nodded toward his mother. "Mother, I'm just letting you know that's the major reason why we are not the least excited about the parties you want to take us to."

Veronica picked up a bottle of salad dressing, read the label and placed it back on the table. "Britain, please pass me the French dressing that's sitting near you."

Britain passed her the bottle of French salad dressing and she poured just a small amount on her salad. She smiled and looked out across the dinner table. "Thank you all for agreeing to attend the Taylor party; and I understand that my usual party crowd bore you, but this party will be different from all the others."

"And why is that?" Catherine asked. "I'm sure it won't be much different. It's just another high hat party with elevator music and too many waiters."

All the Franklin boys laughed. "Mother, Aunt Catherine is right," Rome stressed. "That's why we are not eager about this affair."

"Your Aunt Catherine is not right this time. The Taylor's will probably have lively music and their entire guest list will not consist of individuals twice or more your ages," Veronica assured them. "If nothing else, their three beautiful daughters will assure that."

The four Franklin brothers exchanged looks with each other and smiled, and for a moment the entire dinning room was quiet enough to hear the smooth tick tock of Britain's white gold Movado watch. Then suddenly the four of them stared at their mother speechless.

"Now, I guess I have your attention. Yes, the Taylor's are not some very old couple as our last next door neighbors. They have three very good looking daughters."

"Have you seen any of the daughters?" Paris curiously asked. "How do you know they are beautiful?"

"We haven't seen the girls," Catherine answered. "But after they moved next door, the local paper printed two articles on the family. The last article listed their pictures, and I must agree with your mother that the Taylor daughters are quite attractive young women, all in your age group, 24, 23 and 22," Catherine explained.

"Wow, Aunt Catherine," Paris smiled. "That's news to us. We had no idea we were living next door to three beautiful females."

"Yes, you are; and you have my blessings to date anyone of them," Veronica announced.

"What wrong with this picture?" Rome smiled. "Mother, you are giving your approval of these young women when you haven't even met them yet? You have never given your approval of any female that we have brought home to meet you."

"Come to think of it," Britain added, "That's true, Mother. Therefore, the Taylor's must have really impressed you," he said getting up from the dinner table, as they all left the dinning room laughing and chatting among themselves.

Veronica and Catherine were left seated at the table finishing up their meals. Catherine glanced across the table at Veronica with a curious look. "What's that look for?" Veronica asked.

"Why didn't you tell my nephews what all your fuss over the Taylors is really about?"

"And what is that remark supposed to mean?" Veronica snapped.

"It means you are still trying to control their lives. You want them at that party not to welcome the Taylors to the neighborhood as a family, but to meet the Taylor girls."

"So, what if I do? What's wrong with looking out for my sons? I'm trying to give them every advantage that they would have had if they hadn't lost their father at such a young age. And I wouldn't call it control. I call it setting the stage and what happens after that happens," Veronica explained. "You are their only Aunt and I wish you would take an interest in their wellbeing."

"I dare you say that to me. Why do you think I'm still here and have devoted twenty years of my life here at Franklin House with you and the boys if I'm not looking out for their wellbeing," Catherine said firmly and raised both hands. "I know you love your sons and mean well, but I just don't agree with your methods."

"You don't have to agree, but you can keep your negative opinions to yourself; and by doing so the water will stay calmer between us. Besides, the Taylor's daughters seem to be nice young ladies with a great future ahead of them. Why wouldn't you want them with nice young ladies as the Taylors?"

"I'm fine with them dating or even marrying a Taylor girl, but frankly I have met other nice girls they have introduced to us but you didn't approve. And it was for the sole purpose of them not having what you called a suitable background or the right bottomline in their bank account. So, I'm going out on a limb here to put two and two together that you approve of the three Taylor girls, not because they are pretty and nice, but because they are filthy rich. Am I getting warm?" Catherine smiled.

"Shut up Catherine, I certainly do not want my sons to get stuck with some female with a fading bank account."

"Like yours," Catherine snapped.

"Look, let's drop it. They have agreed to attend the party and that's all I wanted was for them to have an opportunity to meet Sabrina, Samantha and Starlet." Veronica smiled. "Who knows those young ladies may end up being my daughter-in-laws."

Catherine got out of her seat and headed out of the dinning room. "If you have the last word, I'm sure they will."

Chapter Eight

Veronica and her sons arrived at the Taylor's housewarming party around eight-thirty that cool Saturday evening on the last day of August, thirty minutes into the gathering. Veronica purposely never arrived at a party on time. She felt it wasn't in good taste and she always wanted the entire guest list on hand upon her arrival. When they reached the Taylor's front door, Paris elbowed Britain in approval of the decent party music that echoed from inside. The front door was closed but unlocked with a sign taped on the door and one taped near the doorbell that read: "Please come in." They twisted the gold plated doorknob and stepped inside to find a rather large gathering. People were mingling and standing around with glasses of champagne in their hands. The music was not too loud and the crowd was well-dressed in expensive evening gowns and suits and ties with sparkling expensive jewelry hanging from their necks and wrists. The entire crowd consisted of mostly middle-aged men and women. Then suddenly as Veronica and her sons headed from the front entrance, all eyes looked in their direction and at that moment all the chatter stopped and someone screamed in a loud, exciting, complimentary voice. "Oh, my goodness, who are they?"

Veronica and her sons stopped in the middle of the room as the entire crowd was instantaneously motionless staring at them and then everyone started glancing about the room to see who had screamed out. Then all the chatter started back as a waiter dashed to their sides with a shiny silver tray loaded with glasses of sparkling champagne. They all reached out and took a delicate crystal glass filled to the brim with champagne from his serving tray. By the time they were all holding a glass of champagne in their hands, a tall elegant looking gray-haired gentleman, dressed in a lavish three piece dark gray suit, walked up and tapped Veronica on the left shoulder to get her attention.

"Welcome to our home," he said and reached out his hand to her. "I'm Charles Taylor." He smiled. "And if I'm right, you are my next door neighbor."

Veronica shook his hand with both hands. "You are right. I am your next door neighbor. I guess you have spotted me at some point going in or coming out; but I don't think I ever got a glimpse of you before now," she explained laughingly. "Anyway, it's our pleasure to welcome you and your family to the neighborhood," she said and pointed to her sons. "I'm Veronica Franklin and these four handsome young men: Rome, Britain, Paris and Sydney are my sons who also reside next door at Franklin House."

Charles shook all of their hands and then he was off to mingle with other guests. Veronica scanned the room for Charles; she wasn't pleased that his hello had been so abrupt. She wanted to get more acquainted. She was looking forward to her sons meeting his daughters but she hadn't spotted any of them so far. And as she headed in search of Charles, Sydney took the last gulp of champagne from his glass and placed it on the tray of a passing waiter. He glanced about the spacious room.

"This house looks like a different place from when the Sterlings owned it." He nodded toward his brothers.

"That's because they replaced the Sterlings' expensive antique furniture and paintings with expensive traditional stuff," Paris remarked. "See that small plant stand over there. It's no antique but it probably cost more than your shoes." Paris pointed toward Sydney's black Gucci loafers.

"There isn't a plant stand built that could ever cost more than my shoes," Sydney assured him.

"So much for the new décor and how much you pay for your shoes, where are those young ladies we were supposed to run into at this party?" Britain asked Sydney.

"I wish I knew. We are all hanging around wondering the same thing; that's for sure," Sydney grinned.

"Aunt Catherine and Mother said the Taylor girls would be here," Britain smiled, glancing about the room. "But I haven't spotted one yet."

They were all restless standing around bumping shoulders with mostly people their mother's age. However, they were dressed to the nines in identical two piece suits of different colors. Rome was dressed in dark gray, Britain was dressed in light gray, Paris was dressed light blue, and Sydney was dressed in black. Their suits were tailor-made and fitted them like a glove. They all looked like they belonged on the cover of a fashion magazine. They were tall, about 6'1, slender built with radiant tanned skin and coal black hair that grew in loose waves. Rome wore his ear length loose waves parted to one side; Britain wore his hair exceptionally long, parted down the middle. Paris wore his neck length loose waves parted to the left side. Sydney wore his neck length hair combed back.

"I was wondering the same thing," Rome smiled. "This party is turning out to be just what we all expected. But the music isn't completely dreadful." He glanced at his watch. "But maybe we'll be out of here soon." He winked at Paris.

"If Mother ever turns back up," Paris grinned. "She would have a fit if we all left without her knowing."

They all laughed. "A fit is putting it mildly," Britain laughed. "It's more like she would have two fits."

They continued laughing until Sydney elbowed Paris to his right and Britain to his left. "Look toward the left of the room, near the entrance of the dinning room. Those must be the Taylor girls," he replied with much interest.

"Yes, it must be, it's three of them and they are young and super fine looking from where I'm standing," Britain nodded with a small intriguing smile at the corner of his mouth. "Mother and Aunt Catherine didn't exaggerate on their fine looks."

"All three are looking straight at us and headed this way," Paris said in a discreet mumbled, not to appear obvious that they were discussing them.

By the time the Taylor girls made their way over, Veronica stepped up at the same time as if she had been waiting for them to appear. She reached out her hands before the Taylor girls or her sons could say a word to each other.

"How are you young ladies this evening? I'm Veronica Franklin, your neighbor from next door and these are my sons, Rome, Britain, Paris and Sydney. I introduced them in order of age, of course."

"We are pleased to meet you Mrs. Franklin and your sons," Sabrina smiled. "I'm Sabrina Taylor and these are my sisters, Samantha and Starlet," she smiled. "And I just introduced us in age order. I'm the oldest."

The three of them were dressed in expensive, fashionable evening gowns. Sabrina wore a stylish white sleeveless dress that respectfully showed off her slender shape and neckline. Samantha wore an elegant lavender sleeveless dress that hung gracefully off her slender frame. Starlet wore a chic blue dress that charmingly fitted her slender stature as if it was tailor-made for her.

"First of all I want to apologize," Starlet quickly said. "I'm sorry I screamed out like that when you all first walked in." She grabbed her mouth. "It's just that we didn't expect anyone to show up in our age group, especially as handsome as all of you," she explained and paused. She was too embarrassed to continue. She stood there in the middle of her two sisters smiling.

"Thank you for the compliment and its nice meeting you, Starlet." Sydney smiled and winked at her, and then nodded toward Sabrina and Samantha.

After a moment of silence, the Taylor girls walked away. Veronica gave her sons a sharp look. "Well, don't just stand there, run after them or something. Do whatever it is you all do," she urged. "Don't' be rude and give the young ladies the impression that you're not interested. Go ask them to dance."

"Mother, please," Rome snapped. "Don't stand here in the middle of this room at this high hat party and tell us how to hit on girls. We have all had lots of practice in that area. Besides, who can dance off this music? Its okay, but it's not dancing music."

"I think the music is pretty good," Veronica replied.

"It is pretty good, Mother, compared to some of the music played at other parties we have attended with you; but it's not something to dance off of," Britain agreed.

"Forget how the music isn't perfect for dancing. Just dance to what's playing." She glanced at her watch. "It's still early and we are in for a long night here."

"Say it isn't so," Paris teased.

"But it is so; so I want you boys to help liven up this party with some dancing. By dancing you can become more acquainted with Sabrina, Samantha and Starlet on the dance floor," she encouraged.

"Mother how much of that champagne did you have?" Paris asked, smiling. "It's not like you to show interest in our social life that includes a female. I'm not particularly complaining, but what's with pushing us toward the Taylor girls?"

"I'm not pushing you toward them. I just figured the four of you might enjoy yourself more in the company of someone your age. That's what you said at dinner yesterday. You don't care for attending the parties I attend since there's usually nobody around your own age," Veronica explained. "Maybe if you get an opportunity to dance with those girls, you won't complaint later about how bored you were at this one."

"Mother, I'm all for dancing with one of them," Paris smiled. "I wouldn't mind spending some time on the floor with Samantha. That girl has some pretty eyes."

Sydney elbowed Paris and grinned. "I think you were looking at more than just her eyes."

Paris winked at Sydney. "You could have a point."

"Samantha is quite stunning without a doubt, but so is Sabrina and Starlet," Britain agreed. "Right now it's a toss up between the three. I'm not sure who has the edge?" He fixed his focus toward Sabrina. "But I definitely wouldn't mind spending a little time on the dance floor with the one in those shiny red shoes."

They all threw a quick discreet glance toward Sabrina's nice red Louis Vuitton shoes, including their mother and then placed their attention on Britain as he continued. "I'm positive that long haired Sabrina would be my type," Britain said, smiling. "Her hair is super cool. It's pretty long, don't you think?" He glanced at Rome.

"Yes, it is," Rome nodded. "It's almost as long as yours."

"No, Sabrina's hair is much longer than mine. Mine's is just middle-ways my back but that girl's hair is almost to her waist," Britain pointed out.

"Who cares about how long Sabrina hair is, you should care if she's going to dance with you," Veronica said firmly.

"Mother, drop the dancing stuff, nobody is listening," Rome said. "Besides, we have already mentioned that we can not dance to this slow music. How are we supposed to dance to all this slow music? Whoever is in charge of the music needs to play something with more of a beat."

"Maybe, but I'm sure you can dance to this too." She waved her hand. "Just try; will you? Ask one of the girls," Veronica urged and then left their presence in search of Charles. She desperately wanted to find him and become better acquainted before the party ended. As she searched the room for him, Rome, Britain, Paris and Sydney busied themselves enjoying more champagne. They knew they were stuck at the party at the mercy of their mother until she was ready to head home. However, they started to feel less stuck as they couldn't seem to tear their thoughts away from the Taylor girls; and the Taylor girls couldn't seem to tear their thoughts from them.

Samantha was especially moonstruck by Paris extraordinary good looks and she couldn't take her eyes off of him. She was captivated by his perfect jaw structure and enticing light brown eyes. Just his smile touched a special place inside of her and drew her to him. She had never felt so enchantingly overwhelmed by the presence of a man. She sneaked looks at him discreetly as Sabrina and Starlet couldn't take their eyes off of Britain and Sydney. Rome was otherwise preoccupied in search of their mother as Britain, Paris and Sydney smiled and conversed between the three of them. Sydney said something to Paris and Britain and then they all looked toward the refreshment table where Sabrina, Samantha and Starlet were gathered. When Sydney eyes connected with Starlet, she became breathless at the thought of him looking in her direction; and for a split second the crowd in the room seemed invisible except for the two of them. She grabbed her stomach discreetly and kept her composure. Just the thought that he was possibly interested in her made her heart race faster than it ever had. Suddenly she felt like a princess living in a castle and her prince had just arrived to claim her. Her mind was focused on a fantasy until suddenly he was standing there in front of her smiling.

"May I have this dance?" he asked.

She stared at him speechless as he took her hand and led her to the center of the room. He held her close as they slow danced to a Neil Diamond song. When the song ended he looked at her and smiled.

"Thanks for the dance, Starlet, but what was that we just danced to?"

She grabbed her mouth and slightly laughed. "That's some song my father likes. The entire collection of music that is being played tonight is from my father's music collection. This is sort of an old folk's party."

Sydney nodded. "Yeah, I know the type," he assured her.

"This party was thrown to basically get to know our neighbors, but most of the people here are people that my father know or work with," Starlet glanced about the large room as the two of them headed back toward the refreshment table. Starlet held out both arms toward the food and refreshments on the table. The round table had eight chairs around it with a white tablecloth draped on it. A twelve inch crystal vase with a lit candle sat in the center of the table. It displayed a delectable looking spread of appetizers, an array of desserts and bowls of chopped fruit.

Sydney stood near the table against the wall with his arms folded. He was looking attentive at Starlet as if her every word was important to him.

She looked at him and smiled. "Sounds like you have been to your share of stuffy parties."

"Yes, I have attended one too many. But this is one I'm glad Mother insisted on us attending. Otherwise, I would have missed a most special opportunity." He smiled.

"And what special opportunity is that?" Starlet asked and lowered her eyes.

Sydney very gently lifted her chin to see her eyes. "That would be the very special opportunity to meet a most ravishing beauty as you," he whispered.

Starlet stared longingly in his light brown eyes. She was awestruck by his good looks and charm; and she was enthralled by his every word and alluring voice. His entire presence overwhelmed her.

"I'm glad you came too. I'm standing here talking to you and looking at you, but I still feel like I'm dreaming," she said as her eyes never left his.

"Why does it feel like a dream?" he asked curiously.

"It feels like a dream because you are the kind of guy that I have always dreamed about. You have no way of knowing this but our parents have been fairly strict with the three of us. Our lives have been more sheltered than the average young lady our ages."

He rubbed his chin and listened with an interested ear. "Yes, I read a little about you and your sisters."

"That article that was written about us, I'm sure. It was pretty accurate. My parents, both my mother and father have always told us to be selective in dating and to hold out for that perfect man. And they meant not just perfect in our eyes but also theirs. To me that always seemed like an impossible task," Starlet shared.

"Why did it feel impossible to you?"

"It felt impossible because I never imagined there was someone like you out there. You are the man I have always seen in my dreams. And before I laid eyes on you this evening, I just felt a dream was a dream and dreams don't come true. But here you are standing before me, a real live person. Not just in my dreams but also in my reality," She folded her lips and smiled at him. "I'm probably not making any sense to you with my explanation."

"I would never say that. But you are definitely unlike any female that I have ever talked to; and I mean that in the kindest most profound way," he assured her.

"Thank you, Sydney."

"I should be thanking you," he said.

"Thanking me for what?"

"Thanking you for that huge compliment you just gave me," he said, smiling and winked at her. "Since I don't think I have ever been referred to as anyone's dream guy," he whispered near her ear. "But I'm exceedingly pleased that you think so." He grabbed two glasses of champagne from a passing waiter.

Starlet welcomed the idea of sharing a glass of champagne with Sydney. It would be her first glass for the evening. She wasn't much of a drinker but enjoyed a glass of champagne at certain events.

"Here you are." He passed her one of the glasses of champagne. "If I'm the man in your dreams I guess it won't take us as long to get acquainted since we have already sort of met in our dreams," he teased and paused in her eyes. "So, tell me, have you heard of Franklin Gas here in town?"

She shook her head. "I'm sorry but I haven't. We are still learning the area, why do you ask?"

"That's where I work," Sydney nodded.

"You work at a gas station?"

"It's not just a gas station. The name makes it sound that way. It's actually the family business and believe me, it's a money maker," he stressed.

"I'm sorry. I didn't mean to imply that it wasn't," she quickly said and touched his arm. "What do you do there?"

"I'm the COO," Sydney smiled. "I sort of over see the business and I usually hire and dismiss employees when we need to."

"Wow, that's a great position to have," Starlet smiled. "So, it's a family business and I take it, your other brothers probably work there as well?"

"That is correct," Sydney nodded. "Rome is CEO, Britain is the CFO and Paris is the CIO. Our father left the business to us."

"But I heard someone whisper in the crowd tonight that your father was a famous movie star," Starlet said.

"That is correct and my brothers and I are trying to live up to his name. We have done a lot to beautify the old company six-story building. We completely redone the landscaping and remodeled the entire interior of all the offices," he said with pride. "You'll have to drop by for a visit sometime," he said and then stopped himself. "That is if you want to get together sometime."

She nodded, smiling at him. "That would be great."

"I was just checking. I didn't want to assume you would say yes if I asked you out. But now since you have pretty much said yes, I'm going to put it out there and just ask you properly."

Starlet stared at him attentively with her heart pounding from anticipation, awaiting the precious words that she knew were probably coming from his lips next.

"Miss Starlet Taylor, would you like to have dinner with me tomorrow?"

Starlet was speechless again.

"Should I take your non-verbal response as a yes?" He smiled and touched the side of her face.

"Of course, I would love to have dinner with you tomorrow," she said with her excitement held back as not to appear too overly excited.

"Thank you, that's fantastic. Do you have a favorite restaurant in the area?" he asked.

"I'm not familiar with many restaurants in the area yet, but I would love to try that new Italian restaurant that everyone is raving about," she said.

"Okay, great. Now that we have decided when and where, what time I should pick you up?" He took a sip of champagne and held the glass to his lips.

"Six o'clock is fine with me."

"Okay, six o'clock it is." He took another sip of champagne. "So, I know you just graduated from college a few months ago, but are you working yet?" Sydney asked.

She nodded. "We are in a situation similar to you and your brothers. We all graduated with business degrees and we are all working at my fathers' company. My father is part owner and CEO of Taylor Investments of downtown Chicago. We are all part-time workers at the company. He wants us to learn the business inside and out, so in his old age he can turn the business over to us," Starlet explained.

"You have a smart father." Sydney nodded. "If his daughters know the business, he knows his business couldn't be in better hands if he's not around or not able to run things." He smoothed one curl back that had fallen near her eye. "The Taylor girls are not just beautiful, you are also smart."

"I feel the same about you and your brothers," Starlet said with conviction. "You are not just drop dead gorgeous. All of you are smart and very honorable to take over your father's business the way you have," she paused and smiled at him. "I'm sure your mother is very proud of what you all have done."

He grinned and took another sip of champagne.

"Did I say something funny?" she asked.

"The fact that Mother is proud of what we have done. Hearing you say it caught me off guard; and it's a tad bit funny to me."

"Why would it be funny?" Starlet mumbled, not sure what he meant. "I'm sure she's very proud of all of you and what you have accomplished with the business."

"Yes and no; my mother is always proud of us. She's the most wonderful mother in the world. We are all very blessed to have such a loving, devoted mother, but she also would like for us to literally follow in our father's footsteps by getting into acting."

"She wants the four of you to get into show business? Wow!" Starlet grabbed her left cheek. "That's amazing."

"Yes, it would be if that was what we wanted. We are actually happy at the family business, doing what we spent four years in college studying to do. Yes, we also took some drama classes during high school and college and we have done some acting. But we are not actors and have no desire or intentions of getting into that field," Sydney explained seriously.

"I guess it's hard to disappoint your mother if that's her dream for you and your brothers."

"Yes, it is hard to disappoint her, especially when she wants to give us the world." He paused for a long moment. "She actually asked me to persuade my brothers toward the idea of giving acting a shot. I told her I would talk to them and I did and now we are all onboard to give it a shot. Mother took us to the office of our father's old agent two weeks ago and he signed us up on the spot."

"That's amazing, Sydney, you're going to be in a movie?"

"It seems that way. According to Mother and our new agent, Mr. Coleman himself, he'll have us booked and signed to a movie deal before the year is out. So I guess we're slated to appear on the big screen just as Mother has always wanted for us since the time I have been old enough to remember."

"Now you'll get a feel for it and see what you think," she said excitedly. "How do you feel about the whole thing? Are you excited at all? I know it's what your mother wants for you and your brothers, but do you think you could fall for the business?"

Sydney looked at Starlet but didn't comment as he listened to her.

"Maybe performing in movies will be gratifying to you and your brothers and you'll enjoy making films and it will become something you really want to do?"

Sydney shook his head. "We promised to give it a shot for Mother, just one film. So my answer is no, I don't think it's something we'll ever want to do. On the surface it sounds exciting, but deep down we're doing it to please our mother. It's not because our hearts are in it," Sydney explained, and then glanced toward his mother and Rome who were standing near the front entrance as if they were ready to leave the party. He turned to Starlet and touched her shoulder. "Excuse me for awhile."

Sydney headed across the room toward his mother and Rome. Rome spotted him and met him halfway across the room. Rome informed him that he located their mother and they would be leaving in ten minutes. Sydney nodded and headed back toward the refreshment area. Starlet was at the refreshment table placing some fruit on a plate. He kept his eyes on her and how lovely she looked in the long blue feminine dress she was wearing. He was enthralled with the sight of her and how the dress complimented her slender figure, and how her soft black curls hung just below her shoulders, pulled back at the left side of her ear. He felt overwhelming chemistry for her. He could imagine kissing her in his mind. When she walked near him with the plate of fruit in her right hand, he looked at her and smiled with longing in his eyes.

"That looks delicious," he said.

"It is delicious, small chunks of pineapple and watermelon." She placed a chunk of watermelon in her mouth and stretched out the plate toward him.

Sydney took the dish and very calmly placed it on the table. He then took Starlet by the hand and swept her around the corner into a nearby dark room. He fell against the wall with her in his arms, and then brought his face down to hers, giving her an urgent, passionate tender kiss. Starlet was breathless and his willing participant.

After their long lingering kiss, Sydney pulled away and smiled down in her glowing brown eyes. "Whose room is this?" He asked.

"We're in the dinning room," she uttered breathless.

"Okay, I think it's safe to say no one will bother us here." He smiled and brought his mouth back down on hers, swallowing her up in a forceful, demanding, yet gentle kiss, this time massaging his fingers in her hair. When he pulled away from her lips slowly, he looked down at her and shook his head, smiling. "That was...simply indescribable, beyond description."

They stared at each other longingly with their faces just inches apart, and then suddenly as they were lost in each other's eyes, they noticed that the music stopped. Sydney glanced at his watch. "We should probably sneak back to the party. Rome had just informed me a few minutes ago that Mother was ready to take off." He winked at her. "But I'm glad we were able to sneak away from the crowd for a second. I had an incredible time and can't wait to see you for dinner tomorrow," he said assuredly and headed out of the room. "I should probably walk out of here alone so nobody will be the wiser to our secret get-away," he whispered and threw her a kiss; and then eased back into the party room without anyone noticing.

Seconds later, Sydney glanced over his shoulder and smiled at Starlet as she had made her way back to the refreshment table. She couldn't take her eyes off of Sydney. She watched him as he stood there and conversed with his mother and Rome. She knew he was about to leave and wondered if she should walk over. But her ladylike manners kept her put as she smiled to see Sabrina and Britain were still in separable. She had noticed from their first dance, that they had not left each other's side. She had also noticed how Samantha and Paris had been stuck like glue to each other all during the party. Now they were talking closely, looking attentively at each other as they stood against the wall near the patio entrance. Meanwhile, she was engrossed with the wonderful feelings that danced in her stomach from being in Sydney's arms.

Right before the party ended, Paris and Samantha found themselves out on the patio, standing there looking up at the stars as they held hands.

"This whole night seem like a dream to me," she mumbled softly. "We didn't even want to attend because we are so burned out over attending these dinner parties that our parents' host. We know how they turn out with just a middle age crowd. We only attended this evening because we were expected to; then the four of you walked in and we were shocked."

"That's funny," Paris spoke in a whisper. "My brothers and I didn't want to attend for the same reason. But just like your folks, our mother insisted with the motivation that the party would include young people: you and your sisters, "he explained.

"So, you live right next door. That's crazy how we had no idea," Samantha said. "We have mostly stayed inside of the house for the past month. It's a new area and we like it here, but most of our friends live in Chicago."

Paris looked in her light brown eyes and touched her cheek. "Well, you don't have to stay inside anymore. You have a new best friend who lives just next door."

Paris and Samantha had irresistible chemistry and wanted to fall into each other's arms but he merely asked for her number. They were exchanging cell numbers just as his mother and brothers were stepping outside to head home. The party had just ended at straight up mid-night. Starlet and Sabrina stood in the doorway and waved goodbye. Sydney glanced over his shoulder and winked at Starlet and beckoned for her. She walked over to him and he grabbed both of her hands and they took a seat on the front steps. Britain walked over and stood at the front door talking to Sabrina as she was sandwiched in. Paris and Rome had headed home with their mother. The three had come to the party in Veronica's black Bentley. Britain and Sydney had driven over in their cars.

Sydney held Starlet's hands and smiled at her. "I know it's late but I had a really swell time with you tonight and don't want our meeting to end yet. Would you like to take a drive?" He glanced at his solid gold Rolex watch. "I'll have you back home sometime before morning," he teased.

"I would love to but it is getting late, don't you think," she smiled.

"No, I don't think. Let's take drive." He stood to his feet and pulled her up by both hands.

"Okay, sure, why not?" She smiled.

As they headed down the driveway toward Sydney's car, they both waved goodbye to Britain and Sabrina who were still standing at the front door talking.

"We're taking a drive," Starlet said as she and Sydney hopped into his car and drove off the estate.

They drove to a concluded area out in the countryside and parked. The only light came from the full moon shining down through the windshield. They sat in silence until Sydney said. "I hope I didn't offend you or come on too strong earlier when I swept you away to that dark room and kissed you like that."

"I didn't think so. I wasn't offended," she smiled, feeling a bit nervous now that they were completely alone.

"Good, I'm glad," he nodded.

Then there was another bit of silence before Sydney asked her.

"How do you like the area and your new home?"

"I still don't know that many people in the area. All my friends live downtown. I'm trying to adjust and get used to our new home." She nodded. "So, I guess I can say I like it okay."

"Do you think you can adjust and get used to spending more time with me?" Sydney slightly touched the side of her face with the back of his hand.

Starlet felt another wave of butterflies running through her stomach just like she felt earlier when he kissed her. She didn't know quite how to answer his question without sounding too eager. Her insides were screaming with excitement. Then she calmly nodded with a smile. "I think I can get very used to spending time with you." She grabbed both cheeks. "Spending time with you at the party and now sitting here with you like this feels like some incredible fantasy or some kind of an illusion. It just doesn't feel like it's happening in real time." She looked in his eyes.

"And why is that?" He placed his left arm on the steering wheel.

"Because you are so out of this world; nobody looks like you and your brothers. When the four of you walked into the party tonight everybody mouth fell. The entire room was stunned by your good looks and how well you were dressed."

"Thanks for that assessment." He winked at her. "However, beauty is in the eye of the beholder; and from where I'm sitting, you are incredibly beautiful." He leaned in toward her face. "There's something about you that touches the depth of me unlike anything or anyone ever has."

Starlet kept her eyes on his and braced herself to keep her compose and not pass out as he placed his lips against hers softly and then more forceful and passionately. Then in the middle of the kiss, their lips slowly pulled away from each other. He glanced at his watch.

"I could look in your lovely eyes and how they are glowing from the moon up there for the rest of this night." He pointed through the windshield toward the moon. "But, now it is late. It's pass one o'clock and I need to be a gentleman and get you home if I expect for you to get your beauty sleep and keep our date for tomorrow," he smiled and winked at her.

Chapter Nine

When Paris and Samantha left the house for the drive downtown, Veronica and Catherine stood in the living room window smiling as they drove away.

"Catherine, the Taylor's party was a Godsend. I'm on top of the world that my boys are dating those lovely young ladies," Veronica uttered quite pleased.

"I meant to ask, but with all the excitement of the boys' new relationships with the Taylor girls, it slipped my mind," Catherine said.

"Okay, go ahead. What did you mean to ask?"

"What did you think of Charles and Candace Taylor?"

"I found Charles and Candace to be fantastic people. Their home looks like a showroom, even more elegant than the Sterlings. And get this; Charles Taylor is a lot better looking in person than that picture of him in the papers."

"I thought that was a great picture of the man. If he looks any damn better than that, he must be quite handsome."

"Yes, he is quite handsome and he also reminds me of Ryan in a way."

"What way is that?" Catherine asked. "He's a handsome guy, but he looks nothing like my brother."

"I wasn't referring that he looks like Ryan. I was referring to his similar manners and kindness. If I were ever going to look twice at another man since losing my husband, Charles Taylor would be the one." Veronica smiled, lost in thought for a moment. "But I'll scratch that notion. He's a married man; I'll just continue to be content living without a man in my life."

"I'm impressed with you, Veronica. You never cease to surprise me."

"What are you impressed about, Catherine? Are you impressed that I'm above throwing myself on a married man? You figured his bank book and status would cause me to throw my ethics out of the window?"

Catherine laughed. "Well, it did cross my mind. I know you quite well."

"Yes, you do know me quite well and I have never pretended to live up to Ryan's high moral standards, but I raised my sons with those values."

"Yes, I know, you don't waver when it comes to those boys," Catherine agreed.

"But I admit that I don't really march by the same beat. But, when it comes to relationships and marriage, that's where I draw the line. I admit that Charles Taylor is my type and out of the past twenty years I have never ran into another man that even came close to someone I would consider being with since Ryan. But as I said, the man is a moot subject since he's married. I respect the union of marriage."

Catherine nodded. "I respect the union of marriage as well. That's something we can agree on."

"I guess it is Catherine and I'm glad you can relate. That's why I have always been so protective of the boys, wanting them to get involve with the right girls," Veronica stressed. "That's why deep down in my soul I'm so pleased that they are dating the Taylor girls. You saw how happy Paris and Samantha looked when they left the house. They were holding hands and couldn't stop looking at each other. I do think they are in love," Veronica said excitedly.

"Yes, I saw how happy they looked. But please, Veronica, wake up and stop dreaming. He just met the girl a couple weeks ago. I highly doubt Paris has given his heart away so quickly. Plus, he doesn't seem like the type to fall that easily. None of them are. Have you looked at your sons lately? They are all drop dead gorgeous with females calling and screaming for their time. They may be into the Taylor girls at the moment, but the Taylor girls are only their flavor of the month and it to will pass."

Veronica threw Catherine a firm look. "Where do you get your reasoning from? My sons don't think of women as their flavor of the month. I raised them to be gentlemen and they respect females," she snapped. "I know what your problem is; you are confusing my sons with that miserable Casanova you were married to."

"I wouldn't call Antonio a casanova," Catherine stumbled with her words.

"That's exactly what he was," Veronica reminded her. "Antonio Armani was the biggest Casanova on this side of Barrington. Afterall what is a Casanova, some smooth-talker who seduces and uses women and then throw them away. Does that sound familiar? That's exactly what that louse did to you!"

"But the man did marry me," Catherine snapped.

"Yes, he married you and treated you badly. He only hung around because he figured you would be rolling in it after your folks passed, but the moment he found out you were left out of the will, he had no more use for you and took off."

"I have to say you are right. For the smart woman I think I am. I surely allowed that man to play me like a fiddle," Catherine admitted.

"Yes, you did, Catherine, and you still have a sour taste in your mouth from all of that. You still have all that bitterness inside of you. You experienced such a dreadful marriage with Antonio Armani that nobody should have to endure, but you need to let go of your bitter past and be more encouragement for my sons."

"I admit it; I'm sort of bitter about the past, yes. But I'm also trying to open your eyes so you can stop living in fantasy world thinking just because the boys are dating those girls that they will all end up tying the knot some day."

"But you didn't have to make that disrespectful statement about my sons. You know they do not think of women as their flavor of the month. You are projecting your bitter image of your sorry ex-husband upon them to say something like that."

"I'm sorry I misspoke. I shouldn't have said that about my fine nephews," Catherine humbly apologized. "Of course, you were right, I was reflecting back on my louse of an ex-husband, which our boys are nothing like. They are the most respectful young men around," Catherine said sincerely. "But I won't apology for saying you're living in a fantasy world to think they could end up marrying the Taylor girls."

Veronica waved her hand at Catherine. "What do you know? It could happen; and I rather think positive than not."

"Okay, just answer me one question," Catherine asked. "Why are you so on board with these young ladies? I can not recall during their teenage years or adulthood that you have ever approved of any of the girls that my nephews have shown interest in or dated."

"None of those girls were right for them."

"They all seemed okay to me, but they didn't measure up to the filthy rich test. Is that the qualifying piece of the puzzle? A girl is interested in one of the boys need to have dollar signs after their name?"

Veronica smiled. "Their bank account is important, I agreed. However, I love my sons more than my own life. Therefore, good looks and good manners are also just as important. They could have all the money in the world but if they had bad manners and a big mouth, I would have to pass and view them as unsuitable for my boys. But since they are all well mannered, soft spoken with good looks and the cash to boot, I'm all in and would welcome them into the family, hands down," Veronica said firmly.

"What about the one that Sydney is dating? She's cute and skinny as a pole, but she has a very big mouth," Catherine laughed.

"What's so funny? Besides, it was quite rude for you to say that about Starlet. She's a sweet young lady."

"Yes, but wouldn't you agree that she has a big mouth?" Catherine smiled. "And I don't mean that in a putdown way, I'm just saying she talks too much."

"Sydney's friend, Starlet, doesn't have the kind of big mouth I'm referring to when I say big mouth. She is well mannered but maybe a bit more inquisitive and talkative than her sisters, but she's quite innocent and refreshing," Veronica said kindly.

"You didn't seem that way or too pleased when she asked you if you would be throwing a dinner party soon. As a matter of fact, you completely ignored the question and didn't even answer her."

"That's because I didn't have an answer for her. There is no money in the budget for a big bash at Franklin Home of any kind at this time. Besides, that's not being a big mouth. She's just a curious young lady and that was a reasonable question," Veronica explained, headed toward the dinning area.

"Yes, it's a reasonable question because she has no idea how unreasonable it would be to throw a party here." Catherine laughed.

Veronica stopped in her tracks and leaned against the doorframe that separated the dinning room from the living room. She stared at Catherine in silence.

"So, what's up? Why are you looking at me like that?" Catherine asked. "What's going on in your mind? Just say whatever it is."

"I was just thinking, we could probably throw a small party," Veronica said.

"You have to be kidding, a small party for this community? If you tried to pull that off, everybody around here including your own sons would find out your secret that you are broke!"

"Why do you keep saying that? I'm not broke. I'm just not filthy rich anymore."

"Well, you would be a lot richer than you are if you wouldn't let those boys live like they are filthy rich. You allow them to take the salaries they earn and bank every dime while you bankroll their every desire with all the finest things in life along with the most expensive cars ever built. Why couldn't they buy an average car?"

"You're asking me why my sons couldn't buy an average car. Do I drive an average car, did your brother? The answer is no! So why should my sons?"

"I'm driving an average car," Catherine reminded her.

"Your Mercedes is anything but average," Veronica snapped.

"It may not be average, but it's old," Catherine strongly stressed.

"So, what if it's old, it's still running like new. Besides, there's no money to buy you a new Mercedes."

"Veronica, that's my point exactly. There's no money for a new Mercedes for me. Therefore, there's no money to allow your sons to live like kings. How long do you think the funds are going to hold out?

You want your sons to drive the kind of car that Ryan drove, but Jaguar wasn't even making the kind of car that the boys are driving when Ryan was alive."

"That might be true, nevertheless, Ryan only drove a Jaguar," Veronica stated.

"So what, Ryan could certainly afford his heart's desire, but the nine zeros left in his bank account twenty years ago have faded down to barely nothing! So you say, and with nothing coming in but the interest, you need to clue those boys in on your financial concerns so they can start pitching in!" Catherine suggested seriously.

"It's more than nothing," Veronica snapped.

"It's so close to nothing that those boys had no business purchasing cars that cost over $100,000 dollars in all different colors: silver, white, blue and black."

"It was their Christmas gift," Veronica said and waved her hand.

"It didn't start out that way as I recall. Three days before Christmas, Rome went out and purchased a brand new extravagant elaborate silver 2013 Jaguar, then the next morning Britain went to the same dealership and purchased one of the same in diamond white and by evening Paris ended up at the same dealership to match their purchase in metallic blue," she stressed. "Should I continue?"

"By all means, you have the floor," Veronica humored her.

"I guess we can look on the bright side and be thankful they didn't end up buying some toy car!"

"What's a toy car?" Veronica asked.

"One of those ridiculously pricey cars like a Lamborghini or a Ferrari and let's not forget those preposterous costly Aston Martin. So if anything good came out of their purchases at least they bought practical expensive cars, but the word Christmas gift only came out of your mouth the day before Christmas," Catherine reminded her.

"How do you figure that?"

"I know you can recall the day before Christmas when you encouraged Sydney that the cars were actually Christmas gifts and that he should feel free to go out to the same dealership and pick the color of his choice. That evening he drove home in a shiny black one. Those boys drained the account big time in less than a week. They are all driving 2013 Jaguars and living in the lap of luxury as if the well is overflowing," Catherine argued. "But I don't blame them for how they use their credit cards when you have given them a false sense of security."

"Don't tell me how to raise my sons. They may not be rich, but they should be rich and they would be rich if I hadn't carelessly spent too much of a fortune that should have been saved for them. Therefore, just because Ryan passed away when they were little doesn't mean they will miss out on any of the things in life they would have had if he was still alive! I will do whatever necessary to help stack the deck in their favor! And if I'm not clear, I'll repeat myself. I'll stack any deck and rig any game in my sons' favor so that they can have every advantage in life. If there's a block in the road hindering them, I'll use all of my resources to remove it," Veronica said firmly.

"Does that block in the road refer to a female you don't approve of?"

"That's a moot question, Catherine, since I do approve of their choice in women. The Taylor girls are perfect for my sons."

"Aren't you forgetting one thing?"

"And what one thing is that?"

"There are only three Taylor girls and you have four sons," Catherine brought to her attention. "And from what I hear, there's a very pretty young lady that works at Franklin Gas who has her eyes on Rome," Catherine relayed with a smirk on her face. "The last I heard, she's a Ross and not a Taylor."

"So, what if she is? Nothing will come of that crush that young lady has on Rome. Besides, if he does take to her, it won't last. I have spoken to Rome and he knows how I feel about that girl. Besides, he already knows that those young ladies at the business are not right for him," Veronica waved her hand. "And if he doesn't know it now, in time he will. I will see to that! Do I make myself clear?"

Chapter Ten

It was the twelfth of September, a cool and breezy day with blue skies that made everything seem perfect in Courtney's world. She had a song in her heart and a permanent smile on her face because it was her twenty-fourth birthday and she had high hopes that it would end up being one of the best days of her life. Britain had made her a promised three weeks prior that he would show her the best birthday ever. She had mentioned to him a few things that she thought would be fun to do and he had promised they would do whatever she desired. He wanted to make her birthday special because he thought of her as a special friend. And although, Courtney was a bit uneasy about socializing with Veronica after their first conversation at the company, Britain had discussed with her that she would warm up to his mother and his mother would warm up to her once they got to know each other better. He wanted to give them that opportunity by taking Courtney to Franklin House for a visit. He felt sharing an evening of coffee or tea with Veronica would be a good socializing start. He had promised to take her to Franklin House at the end of her birthday evening with him.

This day was also particularly special for Courtney, since it wasn't just her birthday, but the day she hoped would make a change in her relationship status with Britain. She hoped he would formally ask her out as a girlfriend instead of just a girl that he had befriended. She was anxious for the time to fly by, but all morning long during work, the morning seemed to drag. All the customers complimented her cheerfulness; and one customer even noticed her extra good mood.

"Miss Ross, you look sort of different this morning," Mrs. Belle Nestle smiled at Courtney when Courtney handed the old lady a get well card.

Mrs. Nestle was a regular who pulled into the station every Thursday morning around ten o'clock for gas and coffee. She had just had hip surgery a few weeks prior, and this was her first visit since the surgery. Courtney was pleased to see that the old lady looked well and seemed to be healing well.

"Yes, I'm in a really upbeat mood. Does it show?" Courtney asked.

"It shows a lot," Mrs. Nestle said as she opened the card and read it. "What a sweet card. You are always friendly and most helpful. One of the nicest attendants, but there's a special glow in your eyes today."

"It's my birthday and this cute fellow I have lunch with everyday has promised to show me an unforgettable evening," Courtney explained excitedly.

"Is his name Rome?" Mrs. Nestle asked.

"I guess I mentioned Rome to you," Courtney smiled.

"Yes, when you first started working here, you mentioned a young man by the name of Rome that you were hoping to go out with."

Mrs. Nestle recollection caught Courtney off guard. She had forgotten that she had confided in the old lady about her huge crush on Rome several months back. She smiled. "Yes, I recall. I did mention Rome to you."

"Is he the cute fellow you are referring to?"

Courtney was in a daze sort of preoccupied with her thoughts of the upcoming evening and didn't readily answer the little lady question. When the question registered and it dawned on her that the little lady was standing there waiting for her answer, she shook her head and smiled. "No, it's not him," she quickly said.

"I take it, you wish it was him?"

"Well, that's debatable now." She smiled. "He's adorable and indescribable good looking, but he sort of took too long to notice me."

"How was that possible?" Mrs. Nestle asked.

"It was possible for him and I couldn't wait around forever."

"So, you're with a new fellow?"

"I'm not with him yet, but after tonight, I hope to be," she said assuredly.

"I'm happy for you. You are a lovely young lady and you deserve to be with a special young man who can make you happy." She held up one finger. "But I'm afraid I won't get an opportunity to hear about your exciting evening anytime soon. I won't be in for awhile. I have to go back for another surgery tomorrow," Mrs. Nestle told her before she headed away from the counter.

Courtney waved at Mrs. Nestle as she slowly made her way out of the building. No other customers were at the counter and the other workers were busy with projects. Courtney was in thought and extra anxious about her luncheon with Britain. For all of July and August, he had constantly shared his lunch with her. But for the past two weeks, he had been preoccupied and hadn't talked to her except through passing. His routine for the past two weeks had been to come down to the cafeteria buy a tray and take it up to his office. But on this day, she was sure he wouldn't forget her birthday since he had promised her such an exciting evening. She could deal with the distance he had displayed over the past two weeks as long as he took her out as promised.

Vickie Simpson's well-dressed brother, Wally Simpson, was captivated by her and he had adored her since their college days when they dated each other for a whole year. However, Courtney broke off the relationship because Wally had expressed an interest in becoming a chef. Her father was a chef and never earned much money from the profession. She anticipated that the same fate would result for Wally. She wanted to date someone with a more promising future. And although they haven't dated since college, Wally hopes to get back the connection they once shared. Courtney was once attracted to his medium height, thick built and average looks. He had called a couple days ago and asked to take her out on her birthday, but she turned him down, proudly relaying that Britain Franklin was taking her out. Wally wrote her a birthday letter:

Dear Courtney, September 12, 2013

I asked Vickie to give you this letter because even though you didn't accept my invitation to take you out for your birthday, I hope you have a wonderful time with the person who does. I remember how much you love your birthdays. We are all pleased to reach another birthday, but I don't know anyone who treasure their birthdays more than you.

Vickie tells me that you are not dating anyone right now. I'm still single as well. I miss what we had back in college and I haven't given up on you that you'll give us another chance. Everyday, I find myself thinking about you and what we meant to each other. That's my daily custom to spend hours with you on my mind. Sometimes I can get through a day without thinking about your pretty face. I'll be coming along pretty well and just like that, you'll be in my thoughts again. After we both graduated college and went our separate ways, I tried with other relationships to put you out of my mind. But it seems, every time I do get over you, I find myself back in love with you. We had a great connection and I was never sure about what caused our breakup. Breaking up with you was never what I wanted. Don't you know that?

If I recall correctly you were turned off by my interest in becoming a chef. You never did like the profession because you felt it kept your household deprived. But I have to disagree with you, because I know for a fact that some chefs can make a better than average living. You probably shouldn't look down on the profession as a whole based on the results of your father status. But back to my point here, although I seriously considered becoming a chef, it didn't pan out and I ended up in the same educational field as you are in. I'm teaching tenth grade mathematics right now, but my father is retiring and I'll be taking over the Principal spot here at Barrington High. I know you are still at Franklin Gas and don't plan to leave until next year. But I just want you to know that if you decide to apply for a teaching position here, I'll be pleased to find a position for you.

It doesn't matter what I do or where I go, my thoughts are always on you. It's clear to me, that you are the only woman I want in my life. I feel we were destined to be together and one day when you realize the same, we will find our way back to each other.

Happy Birthday, Love always, Wally.

After reading Wally's letter, Courtney busied herself with her work but kept watching the clock. Then suddenly, she glanced at it and it was straight up twelve noon, the hour she had waited for. She grabbed her purse from beneath the counter and walked away from her station. She was leaving the counter in good hands with Trina and a couple other workers who were busy taking care of customers. She rushed toward the elevator, stepped on to it and excitedly pushed the second floor button. When the elevator opened to the second floor, she stepped out and hurried toward the cafeteria, finding herself almost running toward the area. Britain and she had lunch plans in the cafeteria and would discuss the rest of their plans for later.

When she walked into the cafeteria and scanned the crowded room she didn't spot Britain as she made her way over to their regular table; she slowly removed her white work jacket and draped it over her chair. She couldn't stop smiling as she kept surveying the medium size lunchroom trying to spot Britain. He wasn't standing at the food counter, she had arrived before him. Therefore, she took a seat and would wait for him to arrive before purchasing any other food or beverage. She had a can of Pepsi and a turkey breast sandwich wrapped in foil in her purse.

She sat there at the table and removed her sandwich and Pepsi from her purse, but wouldn't touch it until Britain joined her. She spent her time sending some text messages as she waited for him. Then five minutes into her wait, with phone in hand, she glanced up and spotted Britain walking into the lunchroom. She discreetly grabbed her mouth with both hands when she saw that he wasn't alone. He was walking alongside Sabrina Taylor. Seeing them together, suddenly Courtney felt a tight knot pulling in her stomach.

Sitting there stunned, she felt like someone had just given her a hard punch in the stomach and Trina's words came to thought. "Open your eyes and finally face the truth. Britain is not really interested in a real relationship with you. He is just hanging out at your table during his lunch hour as a friend it seems."

However, the truth that her sister was trying to get her to face, Courtney didn't want to accept. She had come to care a lot for Britain over the past couple months. When she first started working at Franklin

Gas she had hoped to catch Rome attention and eventually date him, and although Rome showed her some interest, and couldn't seem to keep his eyes off of her, he never asked her out. When Britain started socializing with her and sharing her lunch table every day, she felt just as lucky since she felt the Franklin guys were almost perfect.

For the past two out of eight and a half months since being hired as a counter assistant for their business, the tall, handsome, twenty-five-year-old, Britain, and the very pretty, smooth complexion, Courtney had shared lunches together in the cafeteria at the same table. But this particular day was the icing on the cake since not only would they share lunch but they would finally go out together socially.

Courtney anxiously dialed Trina's cell.

"Hello," Trina said. "If you are calling me, something must be wrong."

"Yes, something is wrong. Britain is having lunch with someone else."

"What do you mean; he's having lunch with someone else?" Trina asked with confusion pouring through her words. "But the two of you have special plans to celebrate your birthday today, right?"

"That was the plan, but he just walked into the cafeteria with someone else," Courtney said sadly. "Of all days, why stand me up on my birthday? Plus, three weeks ago he had given me so much hope that I was going to be a guest at his house and meet his mother."

"But you already met Mrs. Franklin."

"I know I have already met her, but not socially. He had promised to take me to his house and introduce me to her formally. Plus, he told me he had made so many wonderful plans for the two of us to do this evening. Did Britain out and out lie to me?" Courtney asked.

"I'm not sure, but it doesn't sound like Britain. You know how straight-laced the Franklin guys are. Are you sure he's with someone else?" Trina asked.

"Yes, I'm sure. I'm sitting here looking right at them. They're standing at the lunch counter ordering their food."

"Wow, that's a slap in the face! I'm sorry. I know how excited you were about today. What a letdown."

"Yes, what a letdown; for the past two months you know I have always kept the chair next to me reserved for Britain. No matter what, rain or shine I made sure he had a seat waiting," Courtney mumbled.

"Okay, but what's your point?"

"My point is that this is where he usually sits. The lunch hour is always crowded, and this cafeteria is always packed since it's also opened to outside workers. People are always in here looking for the first available seat they can grab; but as usual, I always save a spot for Britain. I either put my purse or jacket in the chair next to me to keep other employees from taking it."

"I'm sorry, Courtney. I don't know what to tell you, except what I have always said. Britain doesn't seem to be interested in you as more than a friend. It's a letdown I know, but maybe he forgot your birthday. It's not like you are his girlfriend," Trina pointed out. "And on that note, I need to get back to work."

Courtney ended her call with Trina and stuck her phone back in her purse. She never took her eyes off of Britain as she sat there at her table not touching the sandwich and Pepsi in front of her. She was too overwhelmed by the attractive young lady that was with him to eat a thing. Sabrina was visiting Britain's job for the first time and he had showed her around the offices and now they had stepped into the cafeteria to have lunch. Since the two weeks after the Taylor's party, the two of them had spent a lot of time together getting to know each other better. She had clear brown eyes with dark eyebrows and long lashes. Her warm smile complimented a smooth complexion. She was medium height, slender with extremely long brown hair styled in French curls hanging down to her waist. She was friendly, well mannered with exceptional looks.

Courtney grabbed her phone back out of her purse and was tempted to dial Trina again, but unable to refocus, she discreetly with a sick feeling dashing through her stomach, glanced back over at Britain and Sabrina as they took their lunch trays and took a seat at one of the two tables that were always reserved for members of his family. The two tables were toward the front of the cafeteria. They were seated a rather good distance from where she was seated. Britain looked in Courtney's direction but their eyes didn't meet, and then he turned his attention right back to face Sabrina. His glance was too quick to notice that Courtney was sitting there. Courtney kept wondering if he had really forgotten her birthday. Then she quickly dialed Trina's number again.

"What is it now? I'm trying to get some work done," Trina answered.

"Yes, I know and I'm sorry to bother you, but I was just sitting here thinking that he couldn't have forgotten it was my birthday since he had just mentioned my birthday and all the things he wanted us to do together when we talked last."

"Okay, but when was that last conversation?" Trina asked.

"It was the last time we talked about my birthday?"

"I heard that part, but when was this? You two have lunch everyday. Was it yesterday?"

"No, it was probably three weeks ago."

"Three weeks ago? And you think he should remember what he promised you three weeks ago?"

"Yes, I do, since he had made a point of talking about all the things we would do on my birthday. He told me to just think of what I wanted to do and let him know during lunch on the day of my birthday. He said we would do something special for my big day," he promised. "He told me since I had mentioned how much I wanted to see the inside of Franklin House that he would make sure to take me there."

"Maybe he'll still do something with you later," Trina encouraged her.

"Thanks for trying to lift my spirits, but I doubt that very seriously. Not the way he's looking at this other person, whoever she is? I'll see you after lunch."

Courtney ended her call to Trina and placed her phone back into her purse. She tried to keep her composure and for a moment she wondered if Britain was engaged in a business lunch. He was always meeting with a lot of executives; but none of them were usually female and pretty, dressed in such expensive attire. She got the sense that the women he was with were just as wealthy as he was.

She thought to herself, "If it was a business meeting, he would of course walk over to my table and let me know."

Five minutes went by and Britain continued to sit there with Sabrina, obviously enjoying his meal and her company. He was enthralled in her company and mesmerized looking into her eyes as she was his. The lunchroom was crowded but was sort of quiet. Therefore, Courtney could slightly hear their voices and laughter. Then, suddenly as the realization of what was really taking place hit her, a sharp pain ripped through her stomach. She collected herself as she scanned the room to see if anyone had noticed her obvious discomfort of watching Britain with another girl. It appeared that no one had noticed, she glanced back across the room at Britain and kept her eyes his way until he looked her way and their eyes caught. She flashed him a smile as to not give away how she was really feeling. He smiled back at her and gave her a ten second glance but didn't attempt to get out of his seat to go over to her table. Then a second later, he looked toward her again and smiled; and this time he waved, but quickly turned right back to look in Sabrina's eyes as well as the meal in front of him.

Courtney couldn't believe he had just smiled and waved at her but made no attempt to walk over to her table. She grabbed her phone out of her purse and dialed Trina's number again. "This is happening like a nightmare," Courtney uttered sadly. "How could he promise to have lunch with me today and now act as if I'm not even sitting here waiting for him to share his lunch with me? It doesn't make sense, but it's adding up in my head. He probably knew he was dumping me on my birthday."

"Stop second guessing the man and just walk over to his table if you need to know for sure," Trina suggested.

"Are you kidding? I'm not walking over to his table with Miss you-know-who sitting there with him."

"Maybe you should. Does he even know you're sitting there?"

"Yes, he knows. He just smiled and waved at me just a second ago."

"If he waved and smiled at you, at least he's not completely ignoring you."

"What good are smiles and waves when he's supposed to be at my table having lunch with me and not sitting there with Miss America? Like I said, he probably knew he was going to stand me up today. However, he failed to inform me that we were through because he had met someone new. It was as if he didn't even see me sitting there. But he did see me because he looked over and smiled and waved at me as if we had no plans. Plus, he out and out ignored coming over to the table to wish me happy birthday or even a hello since he was too preoccupied with this other woman."

"Courtney, do you hear yourself, you are still references everything as if Britain is your boyfriend. The guy only sat at your lunch table, period. He never said anything romantic to you and he never asked you out. So, just get over it and get over him already," Trina suggested.

Courtney paused with the phone to her ear as she scanned the room with her insides boiling with anger. She had the urge to walk over to Britain's table and pour his iced tea on his head. She felt in the spotlight with all eyes on her. She felt many different emotions all at once, especially embarrassment and humiliation. Suddenly it seemed as if her hearing had enhanced, and she could hear every word coming from everyone's mouth. Suddenly it seemed as if every whispering conversation was about her. It seemed as if everyone in the cafeteria was looking at her, chatting and laughing among themselves about her situation of sitting there alone as Britain, her usual lunch companion, was sitting and enjoying his lunch with someone else: a very stunning someone else. She took a deep breath and collected herself, realizing it was all just her mind conjuring up such thoughts of people chatting and laughing at her. Of course, nobody was paying her any attention.

"Are you still there?" Trina asked.

"Yes, I'm here. I was just sitting here thinking how everybody in here is probably whispering about me."

"Why would you think something like that?"

"It's easy to think that way. So don't try to convince me that no one is paying any attention. We both know how workers around here can gossip. Therefore, how far from the truth are my thoughts; after all, most of the workers are aware of my close connection with Britain and how we share our lunch together everyday. Now they can plainly see that he is boldly sitting in here with someone else, right in my face."

"It's all in your head, Courtney. I'm sure you are the only one focusing on your situation. You are upset about this because you are obviously hung up on Britain Franklin, but he isn't hung up on you. I always thought you were into Rome, but it's obvious to me that you are into them both," Trina pointed out.

"I'm not hung up on anyone," Courtney snapped. "I think I have a right to be upset after being stood up like this. The realization of this situation is giving me the nagging thought to walk across the room to where they are seated and enlighten him on just how upset he has made me. But I won't give him the satisfaction of knowing he has wounded my feelings," Courtney said. "If he can sit there with that girl and enjoy his lunch, pretending I'm not even in the room, I can do the same. Besides, I can already hear some workers whispering and talking in low voices. I know they are all watching and waiting to see how I react to Britain's bold behavior of having the audacity to lunch with another girl right in my face."

"Okay, I have to get back to work," Trina said and ended their call.

Courtney put her phone back in her purse and finally snatched her purse from the other chair and draped it on her chair. One minute after she removed her purse from the empty chair, dreamy eyes, slender built, drop dead gorgeous, twenty-six-year-old, Rome headed across the room with his lunch tray. When he walked toward Courtney's table, her eyes widened and her mouth fell open. She couldn't believe he was heading toward her table. Before she started sharing her lunch hour with Britain, she had secretly hoped Rome would sit at her table and share his lunch, but he never did. He had never joined her for lunch at her table before. Seeing him walking toward her table was suddenly the highlight of her day. He placed his tray on the table and smiled at her with a look that made her crushed inside feel alive again.

"Hi, Rome, you can sit here if you like," she said, smiling.

Rome smiled and narrowed his eyes as he looked at Courtney and then glanced over at Britain seated at the other table with Sabrina.

"So, I take it, this seat is not taken today?" Rome asked, smiling.

"No, it isn't," she mumbled up at him and waved her hand toward the chair. "Of course it's not taken. Please be seated."

He took a seat, still smiling. "Well, happy birthday, Courtney."

"Thanks, Rome," she blushed nervously.

"You are welcomed. I stopped at the counter and left your employee gift there for you. I wasn't sure I would get the opportunity to run into you today."

"Well, you did," she mumbled sadly.

"Plus, I wasn't sure about taking this seat, because I wasn't sure if Britain was coming back over after Sabrina leaves"

"No, he's not coming back over because he was never here in the first place," Courtney mumbled sadly and turned her can of Pepsi up to her mouth.

Then it dawned on her that Rome knew the woman's name. "So, do you know Sabrina?"

He nodded. "Yes, that's Sabrina Taylor, her family just moved into the old Sterling estate next door to us."

"She lives next door to you?" Courtney asked, surprised.

He nodded. "Yeah, they moved in a little better than a month ago; but we just meet them two weeks ago at an open house party their family threw. And ever since that night, Britain has spent all his time at her house. I really think she's the one who can steal my brother's heart." Rome smiled.

"Did I hear you correct that he has spent all his time at her house visiting her for the past two weeks?"

Rome nodded. "That's correct." He lifted his eyebrow. "Did I say something wrong?" He lifted his ham and cheese sandwich and took a bite.

"I'll say you said something wrong. I was under the impression that your brother liked me."

"He does like you, Courtney." He took his napkin and wiped his mouth.

"He has a funny way of showing it by spending his time with someone else."

"I'm sorry, but I think you just lost me." Rome leaned back stiff in his seat.

"Nevermind, let's not discuss a sudden Franklin, because as you can see, Britain is busy at the moment; and as far as I'm concern, he can just stay busy."

"Okay," Rome said, not realizing why Courtney was so out of sorts with Britain sharing his lunch with Sabrina. "I guess this is my lucky day, Miss Ross. Can I tell you a secret?" He winked at her. "I have wanted an opportunity to do lunch with you almost from the day you started here."

Her heart skipped a beat as she looked into his most stunning eyes. She was in a knot about Britain but quickly perked up after what Rome had just said to her. "I'm speechless," she said and stared. "Now, you get that chance, I guess."

"Yes, I guess so. But my timing could have been better, don't you think?"

"What do you mean by that?"

"I mean, you don't seem to be having a good day. I was hoping for a happier, friendlier you when we did," he said, smiling, as he bit into his sandwich again.

"I know, Rome. I know I'm not in the best mood. I'm sorry for my less than pleasant attitude, but I hope you can overlook it and bear with me because I think you know why I'm in such a rotten mood."

He nodded. "Yes, I have an idea."

"Then you know it doesn't reflect in any way of your company." She touched the top of his hand but quickly removed her hand. "I'm glad you have joined me."

"That makes two of us," he smiled.

"Your presence eases some of my stress," she said.

He smiled. "I don't know whether to take that as a compliment or what?"

"It's a compliment," she assured him.

"Are you sure you're not just pleased to have a substitute lunch partner since your regular lunch partner is sharing his lunch with his new dream girl?" he teased.

She stared into his eyes. "No, it's not that. You have no idea."

"I have no idea about what?" he whispered, pushed his plate aside and leaned toward her with both arms folded on the table in front of him.

"That I have wanted to share my lunch with you as well."

"Even though you have always saved a spot for my brother," he reminded her. "I guess you two are pretty good friends."

"Let's not talk about my friendship with your brother," she quickly said. "Because to be honest, I was in quite low spirits before you took your seat; but now, I must admit your company has really lifted my mood. I can hardly remember what had me in such a knot," she said laughingly.

"I can remind you," he teased, pointing toward Britain's table.

She smiled. "No, please don't remind me. Let's finish our lunch in peace without the mentioning of a certain Franklin guy." She lifted her turkey breast sandwich and took a small bite.

They sat and enjoyed their lunch, looking and smiling at each other but not talking much. Thirty minutes later, Courtney had finished her turkey breast sandwich and Rome had finished his ham and cheese sandwich, small garden salad and drained his coffee cup, Courtney was all smiles. They walked out of the lunchroom together and had to walk right pass Britain and Sabrina's table on their way out, but Courtney held her head high and didn't look in Britain's direction as they stepped out of the cafeteria and out into the hallway.

Headed down the hallway toward the elevator, Rome grabbed Courtney by the hand and stopped her.

"I hope this doesn't seem too forward, but would you have dinner with me tonight? It is your birthday."

Courtney looked up at Rome and stared in his dreamy eyes for a moment before she answered. "I'm going to say yes. Why not? I would love to have dinner with you."

He nodded and smiled. "Great, it's your birthday but I'm starting to feel like it's mine too." He smiled. "You have made my day and the day is early. So, where would you like to eat later?" he asked.

"What about that new steak house in town. I hear they have good specials on Thursdays," Courtney suggested.

"Well, the new steak house it is," he said, smiling; and then glanced at his watch as he waited for the elevator. "My workday ends at six."

"My shift ends at five-thirty, but I'll wait for you," Courtney said and headed down the one flight of stairs to the first floor.

"Sounds good, I'll pick you up in front of the building a little after six just as soon as it takes me to lock up my office and get my car out of the garage. How is that?"

"It sounds perfect." She glanced over her shoulder smiling.

"Okay, I'll see you then," he said, stepping on the elevator to the third floor conference room for a meeting..

When Rome stepped off the elevator and headed toward his office, he noticed that Britain's office door was closed. Britain was on a business call at the moment, but glanced down at his desk calendar and shifted in his chair when he noticed he had September twelfth circled in red with Courtney's name written next to the date. Shortly afterwards, he ended his call and hit his forehead with the back of his palm and thought to himself. "Damn, I completely forgot it was her birthday today. Plus, I made plans with Sabrina for this evening and I can not cancel. I'll have to apologize to Courtney and make it up to her somehow."

He hurried out of his office dressed in a chic blue business suit, white shirt and a blue tie. His blue leather shoes looked like they were made of glass as they shined like crystal from the reflection of the office lights. When he stepped into the elevator to head down to the first floor, it dawned on him that he hadn't thought to buy Courtney a birthday card. "I'll get her one later," he thought.

When the elevator stopped on the first floor, Britain stepped out and walked directly over to Courtney's work area. He leaned against the doorframe and folded his arms. He could see that she was busy with a few customers. She glanced over at him and he smiled and nodded. She figured he was waiting there for her, but she didn't want to talk to him at the moment, therefore she continued to wait on the customers and when she was done with the customers she busied herself with other work. He was pressed for time and couldn't wait there in the doorway any longer. He hopped the elevator back to the fourth floor and strolled back to his office, knowing she was most likely upset with him for completely forgetting her birthday and not even saying happy birthday when he saw her during lunch.

At the end of the work day while Courtney waited inside of the main entrance for Rome to pull his car around, she noticed Britain waiting outside of the building, leaning against his car with his arms folded, she wondered if he was waiting there to approach her when she walked out. She didn't want to talk to him and was pleased to see the surprised look on his face when Rome drove his car in front of the building and waited for her with his engine running. She stepped outside and didn't look in Britain's direction as she quickly opened the car door and hopped in Rome's car.

Rome and Courtney's evening together was everything she could have imagined a perfect evening to be and more! Rome didn't give her a chance to think about how Britain had stood her up and forgotten her birthday. His fascinating presence and magnetism overshadowed even the remote thought of his brother.

While seated at their dinner table, she smiled as she poked her fork in her garden salad. "You said something that I'm curious about."

"And what was that?" he asked.

"Well, you said you wanted to share your lunch with me from the first day I started working at your company. So if that's true. I was just wondering why you waited so long to ask me out?" she asked shyly.

"To be honest, I didn't ask you out sooner because my mother actually frowns on us dating our employees. It's a point that she always reminds us of," he explained as he sipped iced water from the delicate crystal glass.

"I see, so what made you change your mind and ask me today?"

"It wasn't planned or on my agenda. It just sort of happened. We were sharing our lunch together and it felt right," he told her.

"I'm sure your mother is not going to be too please to hear that we are spending time together, that you took me out on a date."

"You may have a point there." He smiled. "But I'm a big boy and my mother doesn't run my life," he said lightheartedly. "But you are probably right and mother will not be too pleased. But most importantly, in a few months you will no longer be my employee when you leave at the first of the year to seek a teaching job. And as far as my mother goes, I'll deal with her."

"You can't make her like me."

"No, I can not make her like you, but I'm sure she will fall for you all on her own. Besides, my mother is always polite to our friends whether she likes the person or not. Therefore, she will always be polite to you; and in time, she will grow to respect and admire what a lovely young lady you are." He reached out and gently touched the side of her face with the back of his hand. "You are quite special, and I have respected and admired you from the first day I laid eyes on you," Rome said in a whisper as he placed his hand on top of hers and held it there for a moment before he pulled it away.

The touch of his hand made her tingle; being with him felt heavenly. For a day that started out like a nightmare to Courtney, it was ending like an incredible dream.

"Rome, I didn't know you felt the way you do about me," she said breathless. "I have respected and admired you from the first day I laid eyes on you as well."

Their time together flew by quickly, and at the end of the evening as they stood on her parent's front porch, Rome wanted to kiss her on the lips but he didn't want to overstep and move too fast. He kissed her softly and quickly on the side of the face.

"Courtney, I hope you enjoyed yourself. I had an incredible time with you and hope we can do this again," he said sincerely, smiling at her.

"Of course," Courtney said, smiling and blurted out before she realized. "What about tomorrow?" She caught herself and grabbed her cheeks with both hands. "I can't believe I just asked you out."

"It's okay," Rome smiled. "Tomorrow is fine with me, starting with lunch at work, and then dinner afterward? How does that sound?" He reached out and softly touched the side of her face and massaged it slightly before me pulled it away.

"It sounds perfect."

"Okay, splendid. So we are on again," he said in a whisper and slowly turned and walked off of her porch, down the steps and across her yard.

As he headed across the street where his car was parked, he glanced over his shoulder and winked at Courtney, and then took his hand and threw her a kiss in the wind. All that night, she thought about his smile and his kiss in the wind. It was as if that kiss landed inside of her heart and stuck like glue.

Chapter Eleven

The next morning, when Courtney arrived at work, Britain was waiting at the assistant counter. He was standing there leaning against the counter with his arms folded. He looked at Courtney and smiled.

"Courtney, I'm sorry about yesterday. I completely forgot your birthday and the promise I made you. I wasn't trying to ignore you or stand you up. I just simply forgot it was your birthday. I feel pretty rotten about it and hope you can accept my apology because I really did want to show you a nice time for your big day as I had promised," he explained. "But I gather Rome took you somewhere really nice."

"You gathered right," she mumbled, hanging up her jacket on the coat stand.

"Well, that's good. It makes me feel better to know you got the opportunity to do something special on your birthday."

"But no thanks to you, right?" Courtney snapped. "Since you had better things to do with what's her name?" Courtney relayed in a not so friendly way.

"There's no reason to be impolite," Britain said. "Besides, it's not like you to be rude. That's not who you are."

"How do you know who I am? I think I have a right to be upset that you stood me up on my birthday for what's her name."

"Okay, maybe you do; and I'm trying to apology. But Courtney, rudeness doesn't become you. What's her name has a name and it's Sabrina Taylor. She's new in town. Her family just bought the estate next door to us," he explained. "She was here for a visit yesterday and I showed her around and treated her to lunch. When I made those plans with her, I had simply forgotten I already had plans with you."

"What made you remember?" she asked.

"After lunch, I noticed that I had the date circled in red on my desk calendar with your name written next to it. I stepped out of my office and came down here to wish you a happy birthday and to explain, but you were busy with customers." He held up both hands. "But all well that ends well, right? You ended up having a fantastic birthday after all. And that's all that matters." He smiled.

"How do you know I ended up having a fantastic birthday?"

"It's obvious how I know. Rome and I live in the same house. I saw when you left work with him yesterday; and besides that, he knows we are fairly close friends. He told me that he took you out for your birthday after I stood you up. It was just an oversight on my part. It wasn't intentional," he assured her.

"It sure felt like it was intentional to me."

"Well, I can assure you that your feelings are incorrect. You know, Courtney," Britain began with his dreamy eyes. "Let's forget about what happened yesterday. I'll make it up to you somehow. I honestly feel bad that you actually think that I purposely stood you up on your birthday," he said sincerely. "But why did you hop in the car with Rome and drive off with him in a heat like that," he said. "I think you may have done that just to show me that if I couldn't take you out on your birthday that my brother could. Is that correct?"

"It wasn't like that," she said, wiping the counter with a cloth.

"Okay, how was it?"

"I was upset with you, but I went out with Rome because I really wanted to and not because I was upset with you and wanted to show you that he would take me out on my birthday instead."

He nodded. "Okay, that's good. Now can we move past this?"

"Yes, we should move past this since it's not important to me anymore. But at the time, it was quite humiliating when you stood me up in front of everyone at work."

"Okay, I realize that, but I'm here apologizing. Do you accept my apology? We can continue to be friends and have our lunches together if you like."

"Are you kidding me? You want to resume our lunches together? What would Miss Taylor think?"

"I don't follow," he said.

"I know you don't follow, that's why we should probably end this discussion. Could we please not discuss this anymore," she mumbled sadly.

"Courtney, I think I'm missing something here. But we need to put this stuff behind us. What more can I say? I have apologized," he stressed.

"Don't let me hold you up. I see how you keep glancing at your phone. You're probably expecting a message from Sabrina. Don't let me keep you. You say you're sorry about yesterday, but you probably can't wait to see her again. Please concentrate on her since that's who you're thinking of."

"What are you trying to say, Courtney?" He had surprise in his eyes.

"I'm not trying to say anything; I'm just returning the favor of being rude to you the way you were to me."

"Courtney, it wasn't intentional!" he said with conviction.

"Just the same you left me high and dry for lunch when you had promised to take me out for my birthday. But I'm over that; go be with Sabrina if that's who you want. I'm sure you'll never forget that woman's birthday," Courtney snapped.

Britain shook his head and stared at Courtney with confused eyes.

"Why are you looking so confused as if you don't get why I'm upset with you?"

"No, I get that you are upset and you should be and that's why I'm trying to apology, but I'm thrown by your rudeness. It was a simple oversight," Britain said.

"I'm sorry if you think I'm being overly rude, but I feel you were overly rude when you so easily forgot the promise you made me as if you never made it; therefore, as far as I'm concerned I have a right to be ticked at you," she snapped.

Britain was about to say something, but Courtney held up one hand to stop his words. "Keep your explanations, Britain. It's clear where your thoughts are. Just let me do my job. I have finally opened my eyes to you and there is no need for us to share a lunch table together anymore," she said, placing her purse under the counter.

Britain lifted one eyebrow. "I don't even know what you meant by that. But it's obvious that we have a misunderstanding." Britain stood there with his arms folded. He was dressed in a pair of black pants, a chic blue shirt and black tie. His long black loose wavy hair which reached middle ways his back was pulled back in one ponytail secured by a black rubber-band. He looked as if he was ready to pose in a display window of some upscale men's clothing store. His appearance was the picture of perfection, right down to his black shiny leather shoes.

"Courtney, I don't get it. Why are you so upset with me the way you are? Is it because I forgot your birthday or is it because you saw me with Sabrina? I like you a lot but we are just friends," he reminded her. "I have enjoyed spending time with you and sharing our lunch hour together," he said and paused. "But we are just friends and that's all it has ever been to me. But based on your reaction and what you are saying, you have gotten the wrong impression somehow."

"Excuse me if I got the wrong impression after you promised to take me to Franklin House and introduce me to your mother after you had shown me my heart's desire! Those were your words, not mine," Courtney reminded him.

He nodded. "Yes, I said those words and I meant them. It was going to be part of your birthday treat. We would have a nice dinner and then off to Franklin House to show you the inside of our home. And yes, I was going to introduce you to my mother as one of my friends." He stuck his cell phone in his shirt pocket and glanced at his watch. "I need to head back upstairs to my office. Are we good?"

Courtney shook her head. "Yes, we are good. Good and finished," she snapped under her breath in a low voice that he couldn't hear as she walked away from him and headed toward the mini-mart section for a bottle of water.

She was surprised how easy it was for her to walk away from Britain after she had clearly gotten the wrong impression about his intentions toward her. She thought to herself. "Love is a funny thing. It happens unexpectedly. I had thought I was falling for Britain and rather suddenly I'm thinking of Rome again, which means maybe its Rome and not Britain I'm thinking of."

She anxiously waited for the lunch hour as she daydreamed about Rome. When the clock on the wall struck straight up noon, she hurried from her workstation toward the stairs to the second floor. Enroot up the one flight of stairs to the cafeteria, she was all smiles and excited about her lunch date with Rome. At the spur of the moment after she reached the second floor, she stepped over to the elevator and took it to the fourth floor. She paused outside of Rome's office, wondering if she should knock on his office door and wait for him; and then the two of them could go down to the lunchroom together. But as she stood there trying to decide whether to knock, his door was ajar and she could easily hear Rome talking to Paris.

"Did you end up doing what you had mentioned?" Paris asked.

"Yes, my brother, I sure did," Rome said. "It was a smart call. I actually had a terrific time last night?" Rome assured him.

Courtney was just about to step back over to the elevator and head on down to the cafeteria, but when Rome said the words last night; her heart skipped a beat. She had been with him last night.

"Well, big brother, I would say that's a good thing," Paris remarked.

"Damn right, it's a good thing," Rome agreed.

"Rome, before you head down to lunch, I should mention that I saw you having dinner at that new steak house with Courtney last night. Samantha and I had dinner there as well. We meant to stop over at your table but when we finished the two of you had left," Paris explained. "But tell me, is Courtney the girl you were referring to yesterday? You always had your eyes on her from the time I hired her."

"You think so," Rome laughed.

"Yes, I know so; and she had her eyes on you too. The grapevine here already has the two of you as an item except for one confusing fact."

"What one confusing fact?" Rome laughed. "I didn't think grapevine rumors cared about the facts." He laughed again. "What facts?"

"Well, I can only assume that the confusion lies with her connection with Britain. He started having his lunch at her table everyday. You know and I know that he's not into her in any remote romantic way; because if for no other reason, we all know she's into you. But he's usually at her table having his lunch. What's that all about?"

"It's about absolutely nothing. They were just lunch partners for awhile," Rome explained.

"So, tell me, Rome, what made you decide to defy mother and ask Courtney out? You know mother would have a fit if she knew. She is hell-bent against any of us dating our employees."

"Are you really asking me that question? You know I never let anything that mother has to say stop me from doing what I want."

"This is true. You stand up to mother a lot better than the rest of us. Therefore, you made up your mind to ask Courtney out and you did so. You followed your conscience and not that ridiculous non-sense on the books."

Courtney was about to step away, because she didn't feel comfortable eavesdropping on his conversation, but once her name was mentioned, she couldn't resist hearing what Rome would say about their date together.

Rome's voice answered, "Besides, yesterday was a special day for her. It was her birthday and she was really disappointed when Britain forgot and ended up standing her up for lunch."

"Is that right?" Paris asked. "I know Britain had lunch with Sabrina in the lunchroom yesterday."

"I know he had lunch with Sabrina and he told me that he just simply forgot Courtney's birthday," Rome explained. "Besides, I think it was a misinterpretation about where they stood with each other. Britain didn't see their connection as more than friends but she was starting to think differently. But nevertheless, she was hurt because it was her birthday. Long story short, Courtney Ross is a lovely young lady, and she was sitting there yesterday in the lunchroom alone. She looked as if she was about to cry, sitting there with no one to celebrate her twenty-four birthday with, so when I spotted Britain at one of the reserved tables with Sabrina, I figured he had forgotten her birthday and how he had promised to show her a good time. Therefore, it was the perfect opportunity and excuse for me to walk over to her table and get Britain got of a pickle by having lunch with her and asking her out myself."

Courtney didn't wait to hear anymore; she couldn't stomach another word. She hurried away from Rome's door and hopped on the elevator to the second floor. She was crushed by what she had heard and felt miserable.

"So it was all about getting his brother out of a pickle; empathy and concern motivated him. It wasn't his interest in me that had brought him over to my table," she thought, standing in the elevator holding back her tears. She felt all the sadness and heartbreak that was buried inside of her for Britain. Now she also felt disappointment and hurt over the thought that Rome wasn't really interested in her. The incident had forced her to realize that she hadn't felt the same kind of pull at her heart for Britain as she was now experiencing from the disappointment of Rome. She had daydreamed about Britain mostly for his status and good looks and the thought of being with one of the ever popular Franklin guys. Even though Rome fell into the same category as his brother, Courtney was more certain that she had much stronger feelings for Rome. She had convinced herself that Britain had just been a distraction to help her get over Rome since Rome hadn't shown any interest in her.

When the elevator opened to the second floor, Courtney stepped off the elevator with her heart in pieces. She walked into the lunchroom with her lunch pail in hand and took a seat at her regular table. It didn't even dawn on her that Britain had walked over and taken a seat at her table. He placed his tray on the table and took a seat as if all was back to normal.

He looked across the table at Courtney, who sat there unusually quiet, staring down at her white lunch pail. "Courtney, are you okay?" He smiled. "Are you going to eat your lunch or just stare at your lunch pail?" he said jokingly.

She looked across the table at him and after a moment of collecting herself, she asked. "Britain, what are you doing?"

"What do you mean?" he asked.

"You are going to take a seat here and have your lunch with me as if I'm okay with the fact that you stood me up and embarrassed me in a roomful of people yesterday? You ignored me and had lunch with Sabrina Taylor?"

"I thought after our talk that we were past that." He held up both hands. "I'll find another table if you want me to, but honestly, Courtney, I apologized and thought we cleared that up this morning," he said with a confused look on his face.

"What did we clear up?" she asked.

"We cleared up the fact that we are just friends and I didn't forget your birthday on purpose." He glanced down at the Greek salad on his plate and placed a grape tomato in his mouth. "Besides everything turned out splendid, you went out with Rome last night; and I know you have had your eyes on him for sometime now," he said firmly. "So what's with the attitude?"

"Everything is not about you Britain Franklin. You made it quite clear that we are just friends, so could this friend please be given a pass to be upset." She stared at him hard. "Besides, at the moment I don't want to talk to any of you Franklin guys," she blurted out from all her distraction and disappointment with Rome.

"No problem, I'll step over to another table." He smiled and nodded at her. "But Courtney, drop the hostility. We all think very highly of you around here," Britain said and walked away from her table.

He placed his uneaten Greek salad on another table and then headed toward the exit. She kept her eyes on his back until he stepped out of the double exit doors. She felt guilty that she had spoiled his appetite to the point of leaving his lunch on a table uneaten. But mostly she was stunned how her strong feelings for him had suddenly faded as she sat there and concentrated on her strong feelings which were centered on Rome. Then she glanced back toward the door and spotted her sister, Trina, who had just walked into the cafeteria along with a few other workers. She waved her hand to get Trina's attention. Trina noticed her and hurried over to her table.

Trina hurried across the room to her table and Courtney grabbed her arm the moment she walked up to her table.

"Sit, I have something to tell you," Courtney said, pointing to the chair next to her. "This can't wait," Courtney said anxiously.

Trina stood there without taking a seat. "Can it wait until I get a tray and grab some lunch? It will just take a second and I'll be back and we can talk."

Courtney shook her head. "It can't wait, please be seated," she insisted.

"Okay, I'll sit. This better be good if it can't wait until I grab some food," Trina mumbled with an irritated voice as she dropped in the chair. "So, what gives? What's so urgent that it couldn't wait until I grabbed some lunch?"

"Everything is going to hell it seems," Courtney said sadly.

"Everything like what, I'm looking at you but honestly I can't tell if you are happy or sad," Trina said.

"That's because I'm both." Courtney shook her head as she passed Trina half of her peanut butter and jelly sandwich.

"How can you be both happy and sad?" Trina asked as she bit into the sandwich. "Do you have anything else in that pail? I'm starving," she said.

"Yes, here's a bag of potato chips," Courtney mumbled.

"Okay, pass them over."

Courtney didn't pass the chips as she sat there staring down at the table as if her mind and thoughts were preoccupied.

"What is up with you already? You made me sit, now spill. Why are you sitting there so quiet as if your mind is on everything except the here and now?"

"I have a lot on my mind." Courtney pushed the bag of chips toward her.

"I can see you have a lot on your mind, but you didn't tell me to sit so you could keep whatever it is that's on your mind to yourself; now did you?"

"Britain just left the lunchroom."

"So he just left the lunchroom; what does that mean?"

"It means I realize now that my feelings for him are not as strong as I thought they were."

"Please tell me that's not your urgent news." Trina narrowed her eyes at Courtney as she placed a chip in her mouth.

"It's part of it, which is a big deal to me."

"I know it doesn't surprise you that you're not as into Britain as you thought," Trina stated seriously. "Really now, there's a simple reason for that."

"What simple reason is that?" Courtney asked.

"You are into Rome on a much deeper level and you have always wanted his attention. Having lunch with Britain for awhile just sort of clouded your mind for a minute. You fantasized about Britain asking you out but deep down Rome never left your heart."

"You are so right about that. My every thought is focused on Rome right now and how much I enjoyed being out with him last night and how much I can't get his stunning handsome face out of my mind. Every detail about the guy is glued in my thoughts, right down to the diamond Rolex watch on his right arm and the sparkling diamond ring on his right pinkie finger." Courtney reached across the table and took a potato chip from the bag that sat in front of Trina.

"I thought you had me sit so quickly because you had something of an urgent nature you were going to share with me. But if you want to sit here and tell me how much you are into Rome Franklin, I guess that works too, since I can hardly believe he finally asked you out."

"I'm definitely into Rome. I have never felt this comfortable and this connected to any guy, ever."

"I know you are into Rome, but I don't know if I quite believe what you just said, because just yesterday you were torn up over the fact that Britain had stood you up."

"That was yesterday, I'm thinking about Rome right now. But I do feel just awful over how I just treated Britain."

"And how was that?"

"I was so rude to him just now. I shouldn't have been and I didn't mean to be. But I was short with him because I was sitting here all in knots about Rome, thinking he thought of me as a charity case," Courtney sadly explained.

"Why would you think he thought of you as a charity case? You and Rome had a great time with each other last night and the two of you are getting together again this evening, right?" Trina asked, placing a chip in her mouth.

"I'm hoping all is well between us, but honestly I don't know. Before I came to lunch, I went up to the fourth floor to Rome's office to wait for him. While outside of his door, I heard him talking to Paris and he told Paris that he asked me out so I wouldn't be stood up on my birthday," Courtney told her sister.

"I'm sure it was more to it than that," Trina assured her. "He has always had his eyes on you and probably would have asked you out before now if his mother wasn't such a control freak about who they date."

"How do you know this about Mrs. Franklin? Rome mentioned to me last night that he would have asked me out sooner but his mother didn't want them to date their employees. But he decided to ask me anyway. But he also mentioned the fact that I'll be leaving the company at the first of the year and I believed that figured in his decision since I'm slated to end my employment with Franklin Gas in the near future."

"Okay, maybe the fact that you're leaving did motivate him, but all the same he asked you out. So, there you have it. He liked you enough to defy his mother. That says a lot and I think you should just cheer up and be happy that you and Rome are finally getting that chance you always wanted," Trina said, and grabbed her mouth, pointing toward the entrance door of the cafeteria. "Look who just walked in."

Rome had just walked into the cafeteria. He looked handsome dressed in a fashionable pinstripe grey suit with a white shirt and grey tie. He smiled as he looked across the room toward Courtney. He gave her a quick wave as he strolled over to the lunch counter to buy his food.

Courtney smiled at him and then turned to Trina and spoke in a low voice. "Could you please leave the table? I think he's coming over here once he gets his tray."

Trina hopped out of her seat. "Sure, I need to get back to work anyway. I hope everything works out," Trina whispered and headed out of the lunchroom.

The cafeteria was crowded and Courtney had placed her purse in the chair next to her to hold for Rome. He glanced over his shoulder and smiled at her again as the cafeteria attendant placed a small green salad and a turkey breast sandwich on his dish along with a chocolate milkshake and a bottle of water. And just then, Courtney glanced to her left and spotted Britain and Sabrina walking into the cafeteria. Sabrina was dressed in a fashionable blue dress with matching shoes and purse as if she was headed to an after five affair. She was carrying an Olive Garden bag in her hand. She and Britain were smiling and chatting as they took a seat at one of the reserved tables. Courtney just looked their way and then placed her sights back on Rome. She had no rude thoughts or jealousy in her heart toward Britain at the moment.

Rome waved toward Britain and Sabrina and they smiled and waved back as he headed across the floor toward Courtney's table. When he reached her table he smiled. "I'm sorry I'm running a bit behind. I ended up spending too much time talking with Paris." He placed his tray on the table as he dropped into the chair opposite her.

She looked in his face and lost her thought. No words would come out of her mouth as his presence affected her in such a beautiful way.

"You have almost finished your meal. I thought you were going to wait for me," he said in a whisper and winked at her. "Too starved, were you," he teased.

He took a knife and cut his turkey breast sandwich straight down the middle. And as he lifted one half of the sandwich and bit into it, Courtney found her voice and the thoughts that had made her sad. She realized she was upset with Rome for taking her out as his charity date.

"What are you doing here, Rome?"

He looked at her with confused eyes. "What am I doing here at your table?"

"Yes, what are you doing here at my table?" she mumbled sadly with her eyes staring down at the half eaten peanut butter and jelly sandwich lying on her napkin.

"I'm here at your table because I thought we had plans to meet for lunch," he said as he reached across the table to touch the top of her hand. "Is something the matter? You seem a tad sad or upset. I'm not sure which."

"That's because I'm both," she mumbled disappointedly as she stared in his eyes. "I'm so sad and upset."

Rome nodded as he pushed his plate aside to give her his full attention. "Do you care to share? Is this about Britain?"

"No, it's about you and your mission."

"It's about me and my mission?" He pulled his tray back in front of him, lifted his sandwich and bit into it and then placed it back on the dish. He took time to chew his food as he looked at her with confused eyes. "Courtney, I'm sorry but you have lost me. I don't follow." He wiped his mouth and hands with his napkin, and then pushed his tray aside, placing both elbows on the table, leaning toward her.

"Do you care to explain what you meant by that? You look quite troubled as if you are deeply saddened about something," he said with deep concern and pointed to his chest. "If I'm following you correctly, you are telling me that it's something I did that ticked you off and caused that sad look that's in your eyes?"

She nodded. "I guess you did, since I was your charity date."

"Why would you say or think such a thing?"

"I can say and think it because I know it's true. You asked me out last night just so you could help your brother out of a pickle. Is that not correct?" Courtney asked, looking into his eyes. "I got the message loud and clear. So please make sure you pass this on to Paris."

Rome leaned back and stiffened his back in his seat. He didn't comment as it dawned on him that she had most likely overheard his conversation with Paris earlier.

"I know you were talking to Paris earlier. I overheard the two of you talking when I came up to your office to fetch you for lunch." Courtney Pointed toward Britain and Sabrina. "And I know Britain is busy having lunch with Sabrina right now, but when I first got to lunch, he was under the assumption that our lunches together could pick up where they left off. So I guess your good deed worked."

Rome was thrown by her assumption as he listened anxious to speak.

"But no need to feel obligated, and as far as your brother goes, I don't want or need Britain at my lunch table if it's not where he wants to be. He ended up placing his tray on another table. Besides, I don't know why he was trying to sit at my table when he knew he had plans with his new girlfriend."

"No, he didn't know," Rome quickly relayed.

"He didn't know what?"

"He didn't know that he was having lunch with Sabrina. He was done with his lunch hour, but Sabrina surprised him with food from Olive Garden. I know this because she was just stepping into Britain's office when I was just heading out of my office to head to lunch. They asked me to join them, but of course, I had plans with you," Rome explained.

"I don't know why you bothered if I'm just your good deed for the day."

"Courtney, I'm sorry you overheard Paris and my conversation, but you can't draw conclusions about how I feel about you based on bits and pieces of a conversation that really wasn't meant for your ears," he said firmly.

"So you didn't ask me out because Britain had forgotten my birthday?"

"Yes, and no," he said, smiling. "When you mentioned how disappointed you were and I could see that Britain had forgotten; it gave me a perfect opportunity to do what I had always wanted to do, ask you out. It would kill two birds with one stone. You wouldn't be stood up on your special day and I would get the opportunity to take out the lovely Courtney Ross," he explained seriously and then pulled on the straw of his chocolate milkshake.

Right then, across the room, Britain stood up from his table and glanced around from the sound of someone at a nearby table accidentally knocking their chair over. He glanced at his watch. "We can have ice cream at that ice cream shop on the corner," he said, took Sabrina's hand and they walked out of the cafeteria.

Courtney smiled. "My goodness, I hope I didn't run them off. They didn't eat much. They left a lot of food on their trays."

"I'm sure you didn't run them off. Why would you think that?"

"What the difference a day makes. Yesterday all eyes were on me and how Britain had stood me up; and now all eyes were on him and how I had picked myself up and moved right on without losing any sleep over how he had traded one lunch partner for another," she explained.

"Courtney, I thought you were past that. Why are you still bothered by it?"

"I'm not still bothered by it," she quickly relayed.

Seeing Britain walk out of the cafeteria with Sabrina, suddenly Courtney thought back to a few months after she was hired at Franklin Gas. She and Britain was standing at the lunch counter waiting for their order when they struck up a conversation. She was inquiring about Rome and he extended his hand to her.

"Do you know if Rome Franklin is at work today?" she asked.

At the very moment she asked, someone was being paged over the intercom and he didn't hear her question. "Good afternoon, you're Courtney Ross?" he said, smiling. "It is Courtney, isn't it?"

She smiled and shook his hand. "Yes, its Courtney, and I see it's so crowded in here today with just one table available. I hope we get our food before someone else walks in and takes the last table and we won't have a place to sit."

He smiled. "Don't worry about that. If someone takes the last table, we can sit at one of the reserved tables," he assured her.

"That's right; you're Britain Franklin, one of the owners. Nice to formally meet you," Courtney said, smiling, staring deeply in his eyes.

"It's nice to formally meet you as well, Courtney."

"I'm glad to get the opportunity to talk to you as well. Rome Franklin is your brother. Your older brother, is he not?"

"That is correct. He's the oldest of the pack," Britain smiled.

"Is Rome at work today?" Courtney asked again.

"No, he's out today. Did you need him for something? I can give him a message." Britain smiled. "I have seen how you two look at each other. You sure you don't want me to give him a message?"

"No, nevermind, it's not important."

"Okay, but maybe we'll end up at the same lunch table again?" Britain smiled.

"Sure, I'll save a seat for you."

Courtney focused back on her lunch with Rome, and noticed that it was like dead silence in the lunchroom. A lot of workers had left to return to work. A few were still having lunch, busy chatting, eating, drinking and enjoying their meals.

Rome and Courtney exchanged looks and then he gave her an apologetic look. "So you heard what I was saying to Paris?" Rome asked in a deeply serious voice with his eyes intently looking in hers.

"Yes, I hear you." She nodded. "You are busted," she mumbled with a slight smile. "And I must say that's why I'm in a rather disappointed mood. It made me feel like a charity case to you," she said and pointed to his chocolate shake.

He passed her the milkshake and she took a couple pulls through the straw. "I had hoped you found me irresistible and that's what brought you to my table," she said, teasingly, trying not to show how crushed she really was.

"Courtney, as I said, I'm sorry you overheard that conversation and I wish you hadn't." Rome held up one finger. "But apparently you didn't hear our entire chat."

"Of course I didn't hear your entire discussion. I'm not an eavesdropper. I only heard a portion of it by accident, and then I went on after I heard you say it was basically to help Britain out of a pickle."

"So, is that all you heard, Courtney?"

She nodded looking straight across the table at his dreamboat face. "Yes, that's all I heard. Does it get worse than that?"

"No, it doesn't get worse," he took another bite from his sandwich, chewed his food and then took a swallow from his bottle of water. "I'm sorry you had to hear that part, but since you were already listening in, you should have waited and listened to the entire conversation. You would have heard that I told Paris my original intentions were to just help Britain out of a pickle by taking you out, but I had never enjoyed an evening with a woman as much as I enjoyed last night with you. Bottomline, I was helping Britain out of a pickle but it ended up my gain."

"It was your gain because...?"

He held up one finger and cut off her sentence. "Yes, it was my gain since I was attracted to you from the first day you were hired. But by the time I thought of asking you out, mother had already beaten me to the punch and stressed how we shouldn't date our employees; and I'll admit that I sort of allowed what she said to wear on me."

"And after that you couldn't open your mouth," Courtney teased.

"I guess I could have, but what you don't know, Courtney, is that there's a ridiculous policy around here that everyone pretty much abides by. None of the staff usually date each other."

"That's silly and I know it's not protocol," Courtney said, laughing.

"It is silly; and of course, it's not protocol that we enforce." He paused for a long second. "But it is a binding policy that's on the books and it appears enforced, since you will not find a worker anywhere onsite asking out another worker," he said.

"And I guess I already know why," Courtney grabbed his milkshake again and pulled through the straw a couple more times.

"I'm not sure if you do," Rome said. "I still could have asked you out, since as an owner that policy doesn't apply to me and my brothers. The four of us owns the business along with our mother, or maybe I should just say my mother owns it."

"You mean your mother owns Franklin Gas?"

Rome shook his head. "It's the same difference. She may own the place, but she lets us run the show anyway. So, nobody is willing to take a bold stand and step on any of our toes," Rome explained.

"I guess not, when you put it that way, you all are technically everyone's boss that works here."

"That is so," Rome agreed. "Therefore, I could have asked you out, but since that ridiculous policy is on the books we try to follow it as well."

"When you say we, I assume you are talking about you and your brothers."

"That is correct." He nodded.

Courtney flashed back to Britain, wondering if that was the reason he never asked her out. It was easier for her to entertain that possibility than to face the facts that he never was interested in her on a romantic level.

"Earth to Courtney," Rome said as he slightly tapped on the table.

She sat there with the milkshake in her hand, pulling through the straw with her mind preoccupied in thought. She didn't answer Rome.

Rome reached out and touched her hand. "Hey, where did you go just now?"

"I was just wondering if your no-date policy is what kept Britain from asking me out?" she mumbled.

Rome shifted in his chair. "Why would you wonder that? The two of you were never an item. He never thought of you in a romantic way, I thought you knew that."

"I do know that," she quickly said to make light of her reflection.

"Good," he said. "But speaking of Britain, it seems apparent that the two of you are not on friendly terms any longer?" Rome asked.

"No, not really," Courtney mumbled. "I'll probably get over it, but right now I'm still disappointed that he made a big deal about doing so much for me on my birthday, but went and totally forgot the day. I guess since he thinks he's the best looking thing that ever walked, that gives him a free pass to forget birthdays and let his brother get him out of a pickle."

"I have one question," Rome narrowed his eyes at her.

"Okay, what one question is that?"

"Do you think he's the best looking thing that ever walked?" Rome grinned.

"Why would you ask me that?"

"You brought it up, and I was under the impression that you thought I was the best looking thing that ever walked," he teased her.

"Stop joking around. I'm still disappointed with your brother for leading me on the way he did," she mumbled sadly.

"How is that? The two of you were lunch partners and nothing more. I don't think he can be held responsible if you read more into the friendship? Besides, you just said you knew he wasn't interested in you on a romantic level."

"Do you hear yourself?" Courtney asked.

"What do you mean?" Rome asked.

"I mean you are defending Britain after the way he ignored me and stood me up on my birthday. You Franklin brothers really have each other's back. If I wasn't so disappointed and upset by the incident, I would admire that trait." She paused. "But you're probably right, and he didn't really lead me on, but one thing for sure, Britain was inconsiderate to make plans with me on my birthday and then conveniently forget on the day of," Courtney pointed out. "Can you deny that?"

"I'm staying out of this verbal exchange and that way I won't have to confirm or deny anything by putting a label on Britain," Rome held up both hands.

"But it's not a label; it's just the way it ended up. He was very inconsiderate to make all those promises and not keep any of them. Therefore, in my eyes your brother Britain Franklin was inconsiderate."

"What's going on with you and Britain is complex to say the least, but what I know for sure is that the two of you had a huge misunderstanding. I could see that."

"But I guess I couldn't see it," Courtney mumbled.

"Don't beat yourself up. How could you have known he only wanted to be friends when you wanted more?"

"Maybe, if someone had given me a clue?" Courtney narrowed her eyes at him.

"Would you have listened? Plus, with this loud grapevine around here I'm sure you have heard that we are all gentlemen," Rome explained. "I'm sure you heard that talk when you first started working here."

"That is true. I heard how such gentlemen you all are. But still I wasn't about to listen to anyone at that time."

"Courtney, I make an effort of not butting into my brothers' personal affairs with females; and they give me the same respect. But I thought of you when I saw your name on the bulletin board."

"You saw my name on the bulletin board?" Courtney repeated.

"Yes, your name was on the bulletin board announcing: Thursday, September 12th was your twenty-fourth birthday. When I spotted that announcement it bothered me, because I realized Britain had promised to show Sabrina around the company and that he would probably end up being a no-show at your table."

"Why, has he stood up anyone else for lunch?" Courtney asked.

Rome nodded. "That's right, a couple business lunches a few times, but not purposely." He ate the last of his sandwich and gave her a ten second stare.

"You're staring at me as if you just had a thought."

"This is true. I was just thinking about what happened with you and Britain. I'm sure it was an oversight on his part. But deep down in his non-conscience thoughts, it probably dawned on him that to celebrate your birthday with you would make your relationship appear to be something that it wasn't," Rome explained. "But frankly, for a moment, it did cross my mind that maybe you would end up being more than just a casual lunch partner with Britain."

"Why do you say that?"

"Because he broke a record with you," Rome explained.

"What do you mean by he broke a record with me?"

"Sharing his lunch with you like that for the past two months. It doesn't take a rocket scientist to put together that apparently he enjoyed your company to have wanted to spend that much time with you." He took his napkin and wiped his mouth and hands and then placed the napkin back in his lap. "I might sound bias, but Britain is a good guy. He didn't intentionally stand you up and he likes and respects you as a person." Rome nodded. "Maybe you could cut him a break for his oversight."

Courtney had listened conscientiously to what Rome was saying about his brother. Now that she knew those things, she began to see the real picture and think differently of Britain. She realized that it was her who had gotten the wrong impression when he was just trying to be a friend. She silently wished she could take back all the rude remarks she had said to and about him. It was now obvious to her that he carried no animosity or hostility toward her but thought highly of her with a lot of respect.

After a bit of silence, Courtney looked at Rome and smiled. "So how does that story go? You decided to join me at my table to help out your brother and also to lift my spirits so I wouldn't feel so letdown. Have you ever done anything like that before and taken out any other lunch guests that Britain unintentionally stood up?"

Rome shook his head. "Never, you are it, Courtney. Just for you. I just didn't want his oversight to spoil your evening." Rome paused. "That was sort of the idea." He shook his head. "I felt you were too nice and too beautiful to be left alone on your birthday. But you're right, that's it in a nutshell; I figured he had forgotten so I imposed myself upon your company so you wouldn't think too poorly of Britain." He paused and stared deeply into her eyes. "But I think you sort of still do, am I correct?"

She shook her head. "No, you are not correct. I'm sorry for my childish behavior toward Britain," she uttered sincerely. "It was uncalled for. I was just too embarrassed to admit that we were just friends and that he had never had intentions toward me," she mumbled. "But I guess what I want to know is did you ask me out just to make an awful situation better, or did you sort of want to take me out?"

He reached across the table and gently placed one finger against her lips. "Ssssh," he whispered. "Allow me to enlighten you on something. I have wanted the opportunity to take you out from the moment Paris hired you, showing you around the building introducing you to all of us."

"Wow, I didn't know." She grabbed her left cheek stunned. "Rome, listen; I'm sorry that I overheard your conversation with Paris. I also apologize for jumping to the wrong conclusion. Please accept my apology for my less than polite attitude."

"No, apologies are necessary," he assured her and paused in her eyes. "I just want to know one thing from you," he said in a whisper and narrowed his eyes at her.

"And what's that?" she asked.

"Are we good; and still on for dinner tonight?" he asked.

Courtney was moved by the realization that she was going to have dinner with Rome again, sitting there staring in his mesmerizing clear brown eyes. She stumbled with her answer, "Oh, sure, we are better than good. We are perfect," she said excitedly. "Dinner with you this evening, yes we are still on? I can't wait," she managed to get the words out without tripping over them.

He smiled and nodded. "Okay, now that we have settled that. Let's go over to the dessert counter and pick out a dessert," Rome suggested.

"Okay, that sounds good." She got out of her seat.

They walked over to the dessert counter and Courtney was standing there looking at the desserts overflowing with excitement inside that Rome had asked her out to dinner for a second night in a row and he seemed enthusiastic about it. She now felt more secure about his interest in her. He had explained himself and convinced her that his interest in her was sincere and didn't stem from some good deed to help his brother out of a pickle.

She was smiling and wanted to reach out and touch him, and he was smiling and wanted to reach out and touch her, but they refrained from holding hands or attempting any other kind of physical contact while standing at the lunch counter. They were strongly aware that they needed to be discreet about their togetherness. But he did tap her on the shoulder when it seemed she was just staring into the dessert case without making a choice.

"Are you eyeing that slice of apple pie as well?" he asked.

She glanced at him and smiled. "How did you know?"

"Let's just say, you have that look in your eyes." Rome smiled.

They both wanted the same piece of apple pie. It was the only slice left as he stood next to her, politely teasing her out of taking the last piece.

"Don't tell me, you plan to take that last slice of apple pie?" He pointed through the dessert window.

"Maybe," she turned and looked up in the face. "I'm not quite convinced I want any of the other desserts."

He narrowed his eyes and winked at her. "I think I spotted it first."

Courtney nodded. "I was just kidding when I said I wasn't interested in the other desserts. You can go on and take the apple slice.

"No, look, I was just teasing to. You go on and take it," Rome insisted.

"No, you go on. I'll have something else. The lemon or cherry slice looks good."

"No, I insist; besides, ladies are first in America. So, please, go right ahead and take that slice of apple pie." He nodded.

"Okay, I will. But what are you having?"

"I'll take that blueberry slice," he said and winked at her.

Courtney and Rome ordered their desserts and coffee and took a seat back at their lunch table. Courtney had spent ten minutes past her lunch hour, but didn't mention it seem she was lunching with one of the bosses. They sat there and enjoyed their apple and blueberry pie and drank their coffee engrossed in each other's company. After they were finished, they headed back to work with the eager anticipation of their evening together. Which fell upon them quickly as Courtney excitedly fussed over her hair and makeup while getting dressed and fixed up for her date with Rome. She couldn't decide on what to wear, but ended up slipping into a long pale green dress that complemented her slender figure. The final touch was the delicate sterling silver necklace her parents had given her for her birthday. She stood in her bedroom mirror smiling at her reflection. She felt like Cinderella who had been blessed with the attention of a real live Prince. She was in awe of her newly relationship with Rome Franklin.

When Rome arrived at her house and rung the doorbell, she was waiting at the door and opened it immediately. When she looked at him she was breathless at how handsome he looked all dressed up in a chic black outfit complemented by a dark gray dinner jacket and shiny dark gray shoes.

"Wow, you look great," she said as she stepped out the door.

He took her arm in his as they walked off her porch, down the steps and headed toward his car. "You look quite lovely, yourself. So have you decided where you would like to have dinner?" he asked as he opened the car door for her.

"That new fancy Italian restaurant would be splendid," she suggested.

"Okay, Italian it is." He closed the passenger door.

They had a nice quiet dinner at the new Italian restaurant and after the meal Rome took her straight home.

Chapter Twelve

Courtney felt like her entire world was perfect as she and Rome dated regularly for the rest of September and late into October. It all felt like a dream to her. However, she had re-adjusted her expectations not to expect too much. She had promised herself to just savior and enjoy the time they spent with each other. Each date with him was like a special surprise as if she expected their new relationship not to last. She didn't want to be caught off guard with Rome as she had been with Britain.

It was a clear, cold day on that fourth Monday in October, but Courtney heart overflowed with warmth as she sat at her lunch table smiling inside and feeling like a princess. She kept her eyes glued to the entrance door, expecting Rome to walk into the Franklin Gas cafeteria to join her at any moment. She looked away for a second but glanced back in time to see him headed toward the food counter. He discreetly nodded and waved at her as he stood in line and waited to order his food.

She didn't tear her eyes from him as the lunchroom attendant placed food on his tray. Then she watched as he took his tray and headed across the room toward her table. He looked handsome and fashionably dressed as usual. He smiled at her and placed his tray on the table and took a seat.

"Where's your lunch?" he asked. "A cup of hot tea is not going to fill you up. Are we not eating today? On another diet," he teased.

"No, I'm not on another diet." She lifted her cup and sipped her tea. "Those diets never work for me anyway."

"There's a reason for that; I think dieting works better when the dieter has weight to lose," he teased. "What are you anyway, a size 2?" He narrowed his eyes at her, smiling. "So, where's your food?"

"It's not ready yet. I ordered a hamburger and fries," she said, and then looked toward the serving counter.

"Okay, I should probably wait for your meal before I start mine."

"Your tuna sub and fries look appetizing," Courtney reached across the table and grabbed one of his fries from the dish.

"Help yourself, of course. We can start on my lunch as we wait for yours if you like." He lifted his cup but before he could take a sip of hot tea, just then her number was called.

Courtney hopped out of her seat and hurried toward the serving counter for her lunch order. When she reached the table with her tray, she noticed a yellow greeting card lying on the table near her cup of hot tea. She placed the tray on the table and took her seat, smiling. "What's this?"

"Open it and see," he suggested.

She opened the card and read it. "Thank you, Rome. What a nice surprise: a birthday card better than a month after my birthday."

"I finally remembered to buy you one, but listen," he said seriously with a firm look in his eyes. "I have something that I would like to say to you."

She shifted in her seat. His serious words had caught her off guard. She braced her back against the chair, waiting for his bad news. She looked at him intently hoping he wasn't about to announce the end of their relationship or say what they had was never what she thought it was. She couldn't get over the blow of how Britain had never had feelings for her and had ended their friendship suddenly. She was insecure and kept thinking Rome would end their relationship when she least expected it.

"I'm listening," she said anxiously. "What would you like to say to me?"

"Okay, I'm getting to it," he said, smiling. "Not so quick because I want you to listen to me closely. I don't want any screaming or jumping out of your seat when I relay what I have to say," he whispered and smiled at her.

"No screaming or jumping out of my seat? That sounds serious; should I be nervous and anxious about what you have to say?" She asked curiously. "I can see you are smiling so that takes away my nervousness, but not my anxiousness. I hope your news isn't anything sad." She grabbed her face. "It's not about my customer, that little old lady; Mrs. Belle Nestle didn't pass away, did she?"

He shook his head. "Mrs. Nestle is fine. Just listen." He lifted his cup and took a sip of hot tea and then placed the cup back on the table. "What I'm about to say is going to sound incredible. You probably won't even believe me."

"Now, I'm really anxious. Why wouldn't I believe you?"

He reached across the table and placed his hand on top of hers but pulled it back quickly as he stared silently in her eyes for a moment; and within that second her heart skipped a beat. It dawned on her that he had a very serious warm look in his eyes. Suddenly, she was motionless and speechless as she stared into his eyes.

"Courtney, I woke up this morning and realized something that I couldn't keep quiet about," he whispered, keeping his composure, yet his voice was filled with glee. "I have feelings for you, Miss Courtney Ross." He smiled, holding out both arms.

Courtney was still sitting there speechless, looking into his eyes. She heard him but she couldn't believe him. What he had just said was too wonderful to be true. But she wasn't dreaming, so it had to be true.

"You said I wouldn't believe you, and you are right. I don't believe you, but I do believe you because I know you wouldn't say it if you didn't mean it." She stared across the table at him with a stunned look on her face. "I was just happy to know you, to be with you, to talk with you, to go out with you. I never allowed myself to hope for more. When did you know you were attractive to me?" she asked.

"I guess it happened between the first time you first smiled at me and that incredible first date that threw me for an incredible loop. Spending that first evening with you felt right. Somehow we fit. You get me and I get you. Just spending time with you and holding you in my arms feels better than anything I could have imagined. No drug or potion could come close to how incredible it feels just being in your presence like this and looking in your lovely brown eyes."

"Rome, I'm speechless. I had no idea." Courtney grabbed her cheeks with both hands. "I have feelings for you too and I have felt this way from almost the first day I laid eyes on you. I stepped off the elevator onto the fourth floor in search of Paris' office for my interview. I spotted his name plate on the door and just as I went to knock, I glanced to my left and noticed you standing there outside of your office. I smiled at you and you smiled back at me. I was stunned by your good looks. I couldn't believe one man could be so incredibly handsome."

"I remember that day just like it was yesterday," he said.

"Of course, at that time you had no idea that I was attractive to you since I didn't have the nerve to approach you and let you know. Then after working at the company for awhile, Britain and I became friends and started having lunch together in the cafeteria everyday. He was so polite and charming and also incredibly handsome. Since you hadn't asked me out, I felt special that your brother wanted to spend time with me during his lunch hour. But as we both know, I read the wrong thing into Britain's friendship; but realized what he probably already knew that I never had significant feelings for him. My real feelings were always for you. They were just hidden beneath the surface. Because initially when you first asked me out I felt like it was done out of pity, but when I realized it was done because you were attractive to me, all the feelings I had held inside of me for you came rushing to the surface. I have been on cloud nine just enjoying our times together ever since. I had no idea you had developed real feelings for me. This is the most amazing thing you could say to me," she cried, but quickly wiped her eyes with her fingers. "So, when did you realize you had feelings for me?" She asked.

"That I had feelings for you? The exact day, I'm not sure, it seems like forever. But all I know is that I woke up this morning with you heavy on my mind." He touched his chest. "It feels like you have lived here inside of me forever." He shook his head, smiling. "Do you think that's weird or what? Because I do; I have been asking myself all morning, how can I be this into a woman that I have only dated for a little better than a month?" He kept smiling at her. "But, you know what? It's not for me to figure out. It happened and I like it. Just sitting here looking in your eyes is calming."

Rome glanced about the lunchroom and could see that most of the workers had finished their meals and had headed back to work. He whispered. "So am I loony, wacky or what?"

"If you are loony or wacky, that makes two of us, because I also have feelings for you that I developed almost immediately; and when I thought you didn't want to be with me, I can't begin to put into words how crushed I felt," Courtney explained.

Rome reached out his hand and placed it on top of hers and held it there for a quick moment before pulling it away as they looked at each other lovingly.

Tuesday morning was cold enough that a small fire was simmering in the dinning room fireplace at Franklin House. Everyone had just left the breakfast table except Veronica and Rome. Veronica had a habit of staying an extra fifteen minutes at the breakfast table after each meal. She would usually linger there enjoying coffee while reading the daily paper. Her sons knew this and would stay behind after a meal if either one of them desired to speak to her in private.

"Mother, we need to talk," Rome said to his mother that morning after everyone else had finished their breakfast and left the table.

Veronica stared at her son with a curious look on her face. "I'm not sure I like that look in your eyes," she said casually as she held the morning paper with both hands, reading the local section. "It's a look I have noticed for awhile now. So what's the awful news you have to share?"

"Why do you assume its awful news to share?" he asked.

"That look in your eyes tells me that you dread sharing whatever it is that you have to say." She closed the newspaper and laid it aside. "Therefore, I can only imagine that it wouldn't be anything that I would take pleasure in hearing."

"You must be a mind-reader," Rome said under his breath."

"What was that, dear?"

"I said you have no idea what I'm about to say," he told her.

"Okay, if I'm off the mark, please enlighten me. What's on your mind, sweetheart? The last time you stayed over at the breakfast table was right after you graduated from college and you wanted to inform me that you had decided to turn down the vice president position you had been offered by some prestigious corporation downtown because you wanted to take over control of the family business. That was four years ago. Now, you are here with a similar look on your face, so let's have it." She nodded toward him.

"I want you to know that Courtney Ross and I are seeing each other," he said and paused for her reaction.

"That young lady that works for you, I suppose." She frowned.

He nodded. "Yes, the one you met and spoke to in my office."

Veronica lightly slapped her hand on the table and shook her head. "I was afraid of this. I had heard that she had her eyes on you. But I was pretty sure that you wouldn't cross that line between worker and employee."

"It's a line that I didn't want to cross," Rome assured her.

"But you did anyway, which is rather hypocritical of you, dear."

"Mother, I know it's not at all in good taste since she does works for me, but we are discreet."

"How discreet can you be? People are like blood hounds and can smell gossip the moment it happens. You should have thought of this. You are the head of the company, you know. You have a written policy in place at Franklin Gas that indicates a worker can be terminated from their position for dating each other." She lifted her coffee cup and took a sip, then lowered the cup in a heat that almost missed the saucer. "Sweetheart, my precious son, that's being hypocritical and you know it. You are the CEO and should set the example."

"Mother, I get it." He grabbed his face and dropped his elbows on the table. "That's why I held off with asking Courtney out. And by no means are we open with our relationship on the premises. During work hours we are both very professional, giving our best efforts not to give any of the workers a reason to raise an eyebrow."

"I take it she knows about this policy," Veronica inquired.

Rome nodded. "Yes, I mentioned to her that we have a ridiculous policy on the books that most of the employees abide by. But I also told her that it's not enforced."

"Why did you tell her it's not being enforced? It's a binding policy that's on the books and a Franklin Gas worker can be terminated for breaking it by dating another Franklin Gas worker," Veronica said firmly.

"Mother, I'm in charge and I do not plan to terminate any of my staff for dating each other. Therefore, it's a policy that's on the books that's not being enforced just as I told Courtney."

"Whether you would actually enforce the policy and terminate a worker doesn't matter, since all the workers follow the policy anyway. And since they are following it, they sure will not take well with you breaking it."

Rome held up one hand. "Mother, before you concern yourself thinking our relationship is going to be workplace gossip that all the workers are going to know about, Courtney knows and I have mentioned that we need to be very discreet since I don't want our affair to be rumored at my place of business."

Veronica eyes were filled with disappointment. "When did this relationship happen? As you can see I'm extremely disappointed. It really doesn't make for good business to date one of your employees," she stressed.

"Mother, I just agreed with you on the subject," he quickly stated.

"I gather, but you decided to date her anyway?"

"The thing is; Courtney will not be my employee for much longer. She's leaving at the first of the year, remember? " he reminded her. "Therefore, Mother, after January this little snag will be off the table."

"Yes, I remember that she did say that. But dear, that's a couple months from now. What will the other workers think and say?" She shook her head. "I don't want this for you. You are too considerate and above board to have nasty rumors floating around about you. I really don't like this."

"Mother, it should ease your stress to know that Courtney and I are extremely discreet at work. We do have lunch together in the cafeteria but other than that, we are professionals all the way."

"I'm sure there's talk already and the other workers assume or suspect that the two of you are in a relationship."

Rome nodded. "Yes, I have to admit this is the case. But I didn't make that policy and I don't really agree with it. It was in place when I took over, therefore, I have tried to follow it," he explained. "But it's not a good policy and I will definitely take it off the books."

"You just said it's not being enforced, so why bother removing it from the books?" Veronica lifted her coffee cup and her hand slightly shook.

"I'm going to remove it so I can announce the removal to my workers. I'm sure it will give them a peace of mind to hear the announcement. They won't have to fear termination if they happen to want to date each other."

Veronica shook her head. "All because of this girl, I assume," Veronica stated firmly. "You feel it's necessary to change company policies."

"It's not because of Courtney, it's because it's a bias policy. I don't feel we have the right to tell our workers who they can or shouldn't date. It's not a good policy and I will get it off the books as soon as possible."

"Do you really feel that is necessary?" Veronica asked.

"Mother, why do you ask if it's necessary? You can't possibly feel that policy does anyone any good?"

"Rome, look at the timing. For all of the four years that you have been in charge at the company, you have never considered changing any policies."

"I admit, I never really looked into the policies because I had my plate full with remodeling and another host of projects; but now that it has come up and it has hit home, I'm staring it right in the face and I have the power to make it disappear so Franklin workers will not have to abide by something that goes against a person's basic rights." He shook his head. "The more I think about this, the more it really bothers me that we, of all companies would have such a policy on the books. My father was too caring and compassionate about all people to have executed such a company policy. This policy goes against what he stood for. I'm sure he didn't ink such a policy." Rome looked toward his mother who was looking down in her coffee cup. "I know the business was inherited from his folks and it could have been on the books when they left it to him," Rome wondered as his mother seemed rather quiet.

He narrowed his eyes suspiciously at his mother. "Mother," he called her name to get her attention.

She lifted her head and looked toward him. "Yes, dear," she said, bracing her back against her chair for the question that she figured would be coming next.

"I was just wondering about that employee policy that indicates they can not date each other."

"The way you and Courtney are doing," she managed to quickly say.

"Mother, did you put that policy in place?"

Her stomach tightened and suddenly she felt uneasy with anxiety of telling him the truth. It would be easy for her to lie, but she didn't make a habit of ever being untruthful to her sons if they asked her something straight out.

She nodded. "Yes, I put that policy on the books long after we lost your father. He never would have allowed it while he was alive," she admitted.

"But why, Mother? You know he wouldn't have gone for such a policy, why did you?" Rome asked.

"I'm not your father. He had his beliefs and they were remarkable. But I'm not as trusting as your father was."

"But Mother, why put a policy on the books to control your workers, telling them who they can or can not date?"

"I didn't put it on the books for the workers," she admitted.

"I don't follow you, Mother. If you didn't put it there for the workers, why did you put it there?"

"I did it for you and your brothers," she admitted.

"You did it for us, and why is that, Mother?" Rome asked irritated.

"After you graduated from college and informed me that you were taking over the business, I had that policy placed on the books. I wanted to ward off the workers from you and your brothers. That was my sole reason. I couldn't care less about what the rest of the workers do, or who they date. If they want to date each other that's their business. My concern and only concern was you boys."

After a long pause, Rome looked at his mother. "Mother, thanks for being on the level with me, but just so you know, I will be removing that policy immediately."

Veronica nodded. "Suit yourself. It's your company to run as you please." She waved her hand. "Besides, it didn't do me any good to put that policy on the books anyway; you ended up dating one of your workers just the same."

"Yes, I'm dating Courtney; and this is the real deal, Mother. I happen to care about her. I'm dating this woman and it's not just casually. I would like your blessings. She'll be coming here and I would like for the two of you to get to know each other," he stressed. "As a matter of fact, I'm bringing her here for dinner this evening. So, please tell Natalie there'll be one more at the table. I want you two to get acquainted and there's no time like the present."

"Well, if you insist in bringing the young lady here for dinner, I'll be polite to her, of course; and I'll make sure Natalie gets your memo about an extra plate at the table," Veronica assured him. "But we are not going to make a fuss or change the menu for your last minute dinner guest."

"No fuss is needed. I just want to bring her over. She hasn't been here before and really wants to see the inside of this house for some insane reason. Rumor has it, and this is what she told me that Franklin House is some kind of palace," he smiled at his mother. "She'll be disappointed to see it's just an average big house."

"I'm sure she won't be disappointed. Franklin House is on a grand scale compared to her humble home," Veronica said snobbishly, but Rome didn't comment.

"So, you didn't tell me how long the two of you have been going out?"

"It's been over a month now."

"Over a month, thanks for letting me know. I'm sure all your brothers have known about your relationship with this Courtney all along; but you have dated her all this time and didn't see the need to mention it to me. I'm slightly hurt and offended that you felt you couldn't share this information with me. I raised you boys to feel at ease to be able to share anything with me."

"Mother, I just wanted to spare you the distress because I know how you feel about the situation of Courtney being an employee." He paused. "But as I said, her status is going to change the first of the year when she leaves the company. Plus, I'm removing that policy from the books immediately and there'll be no reason for you to think of our relationship as a breach of protocol."

"Sweetheart, you need to realize that we think differently on this matter. You are not against employer, employee dating, but followed it because it was on the books. I'm sure you will remove it just as soon as you can, but I am somewhat against an employer dating an employee; although when I put that policy in place it had nothing to do with the idea of regular employees dating each other, I just wanted to keep the employees out of your hair and your brothers hair. With that being said, an employer dating his employee is not my only objection toward your relationship with this young woman. I'm just simply against your pairing with her. I merely think she isn't the right girl for you. I want you to be with a young lady with a decent background like the Taylor girls, and not some loose female who has been with every Joe and Harry and looking to get on the gravy train with the first Franklin guy that will let her!" Veronica argued.

"Mother, what are you talking about?" Rome asked.

"How she went after Britain first and now she's after you!"

"Mother, you have your facts wrong. It wasn't like that. It was a big misunderstanding with Britain and Courtney. They were just having lunch together. He never said anything out of the way to her."

"It's not because she didn't want him to."

"My understanding is that she befriended Britain only to inquire about me."

"I tell you, she isn't the right young lady for you."

"Mother, I happen to believe she is. You don't really know anything about Courtney. She's sweet and warm and kind."

Veronica interrupted her son. "And she's quite good looking, I know. I'm sure that's why you are so infatuated with this young lady. I don't know why you couldn't have gone after one of the Taylor girls. Britain,

Paris and Sydney are happy with those girls. Why didn't you take one of them out?"

"Mother, what are you saying? You do realize that it's only three Taylor girls, and they are all taken my your other sons." He held up both arms. "Besides, I had my eyes on Courtney from the moment we hired her. I resisted asking her out for months and I just got to the point where I just couldn't resist any longer."

Veronica wiped a tear and Rome shook his head. "Mother, please get a grip on yourself. I know you want the best for us, but you can't live our lives for us and you can't pick who we decide to care about."

"So, you care about this young lady?"

"Mother, that's not the point."

"It may not be the point, but I'm still pleased you didn't come right out and say you're in love with her."

"Mother, the point is, I'm a twenty-six year old man and I'm going to make my own choices when it comes to women. I appreciate your opinion toward my love life, but the bottomline is always going to be the same. I'm going to date who I choose."

"Whether she's a gold digger or a little slut? You are going to dishonor your father by cheapening yourself with someone beneath you in that way. Your father wanted his sons to be with decent girls with a good heart and a decent background. He told me this was what he wanted for all of you. It's also what I want for all of you."

"Mother, I understand and I'm not trying to dishonor father. I would never do that. Father was a one of a kind incredible human being. We all strive to follow in his footsteps in so many ways; although it's not easy to fill his shoes. From the stories we have heard, he was almost perfect in his generosity and how he cared for others. He donated his money to help toward many causes and heavily tried to stop world hunger. He donated lots of money for food and shelter for the homeless. He was totally opposed to racial discrimination and he promoted civic rights and equal rights for women. If it made sense and it was a good cause, I heard my father would support it one hundred percent with his actions and his bankbook. And even though he was an extremely wealthy man, he lived by and encouraged traditional moral values."

"That is all true about your father. He was a remarkable human being and traditional values meant a lot to him. That's why I do not think he would approve of this girl you are dating," Veronica pointed out.

"I disagree; I think Father would like Courtney. She's not what you have made her out to be. Mother, you really have the wrong assumption about her. She's a nice young lady. She's smart and funny and she's by no means some slut," Rome explained. "Think about it, Mother, at my age, how many girlfriends have I introduced to you?"

"So, she's your girlfriend now?"

"Yes, Mother, she's my girlfriend. But you haven't answered my question. How many girlfriends have I introduced to you?"

"Give me a moment to think," she stumbled with her words.

"Well, how many? You can't answer because the answer is zero."

"You have had young women here before." She stared curiously.

He nodded. "Yes, I have, many times." He lifted his glass and finished off his ice water. "But they were just dates, Mother. Just girls that I liked and wanted to take out once or twice," he explained seriously. "What I feel for Courtney is different. It's so different, Mother. This girl is different."

"I agree that she's different, but not necessarily in a good way," she said firmly.

"Just listen for a moment, Mother, if you will. I have a comment for you," he said sincerely. "You raised very selective sons and that's for sure. But Courtney is different and that's why she is my girlfriend."

"Okay, but I'm not convinced that she isn't a little slut. I can't get over how she was cozying up to Britain."

"Mother, you know that was a misunderstanding with Britain; and stop calling her a slut because she's a respectful nice young lady."

"How do you know this? Is that what she told you?"

"Mother, I just know, okay; and I also know she isn't a gold digger. Besides, those are such harsh words. What's a gold digger anyway?"

"It's someone who's after your money," she quickly said.

"I know that, but everybody likes money and nice things. Who decided to call a woman a gold digger for that reason? Now that I think of it, I don't think that's a nice thing to call anyone," he said seriously.

"Sweetheart, you may not like the words aimed at women, but there's a lot of gold digging females out there who's looking to latch on to unsuspecting guys."

"What you have to stop to realize, Mother, is that I didn't just start dating. I have been dating for a number of years now, and I can tell the difference between a nice young woman and one that's not so nice; and I can also tell the difference between a decent young lady and someone who is just after money. Believe me, I know the type and it's not Courtney Ross."

"Okay, maybe not, but she's not right for you either way. I know you are not going to listen to me, but in time you'll see."

Rome thought about his conversation with his mother all morning, and during lunch with Courtney in the Franklin Gas cafeteria, he dreaded sharing with her the conversation that he had had with his mother after breakfast. His mother had made it clear that she was not onboard with his new relationship and felt Courtney was not the right girl for him. He wanted to share his mother's opinion to Courtney in the least hurtful manner as they sat at the table across from each other. They had both just finished up their veggie subs and were finishing off their strawberry milkshakes. Courtney was anxiously awaiting his news about his discussion with his mother.

"Our lunch hour is almost over." She glanced at the clock on the cafeteria wall. "Are you going to tell me about that talk you had with your mother or not? I'm assuming you did have your talk with her as you mentioned you would."

Rome nodded and smiled at her. "Yes, I had that talk with Mother this morning," he said with no perkiness in his voice.

"Okay, based on the sound of your voice, the talk didn't go too well."

"That would be an understatement," he said. "However, I would like to relay what she had to say in the best possible light."

"I'm sorry, Rome, but there's no best possible light for the word "hate." Just go on and tell me what I already know," Courtney said with anxiety. "I know she hates me I just want to know how deep her wrath is. Just how bad is it?"

"Calm down already." He glanced about the lunchroom, and then reached across the table and quickly touched the top of her hand and then pulled his hand back. "I can tell this is really bothering you and you're letting yourself get worked up over nothing."

"You would get worked up to if you were in my spot. My parents think you're the best thing ever. When I had you over they treated you like you were the president of the United States or something. You have no idea how I feel inside knowing your mother looks down on me as if I'm too common or not good enough for you," she said sadly. "I know you don't want to hear this, but there's no way to sugar coat hate. Therefore, I wouldn't call the fact that your mother hates me, nothing," Courtney explained, keeping her voice low.

"Okay, tell me how you really feel." Rome smiled. "You're shooting the messenger here. But just listen. It wasn't that bad."

"Okay, if it wasn't that bad, let me have it. How awful was it?"

"Let's just say, the important thing is that my mother knows all about us." He lifted his glass and pulled a few sips of his milkshake through the straw.

"She knows about us, but does she hate me a lot or just a little?" Courtney asked.

He shook his head. "It's not that she hates you. She doesn't really hate you. How could anyone hate someone as sweet as you?"

"Your mother does."

"She doesn't hate you. She just doesn't like the idea that we are dating."

"What's the difference?"

"The difference is that it doesn't matter."

"It matters to me, Rome. Your mother just doesn't care about me. I could see it in her eyes and sense it when I first met her," Courtney uttered sadly. "She doesn't think I'm good enough for you; and you know as well that she doesn't think I'm good enough for you, does she?"

"That's correct, she doesn't. But don't take it personal," he said seriously.

"How can I not take it personal?"

"Courtney, because it's who she is and she doesn't feel any female is good enough for her first born," he joked. "I can't think of a single girl that I have dated that met my mother's approval. Therefore, if I lived my life and scheduled my affairs based on my mother's approval, I would still be waiting for my first date," he assured her.

"You are joking about this, but I wished you could show more empathy. This is a big deal to me."

"I know it's a big deal to you, but it doesn't need to be. I know my mother and you just have to stand your ground with her. I don't live my life around her wishes and wants," he stressed. "I won't get into all that right now but one case in point is her constant push to get us into the movie business."

"To follow in your father's footsteps I assume."

"That's it exactly, but we stand our ground regardless to her constant urging."

"You mean you stood your ground for awhile, because she finally persuaded the four of you to get into acting, you told me," Courtney reminded him.

"She didn't really persuade us. She talked to Sydney and asked him to persuade us. After Sydney encouraged us to give it a shot, the four of us made up our minds and agreed to a one movie deal to make her happy. It's a one time thing, which means after we shoot the one movie we'll be done with acting and movies no matter how much she wants that kind of career for us."

"I'm not sure I get your point," Courtney mumbled.

"The point is, hold your ground; and I'm telling you this so you can see that I do understand how you feel. But you can't waste your energy over how my mother feels about you. All you can do is stand your ground and not allow it to affect you."

"I hear what you are saying and my head tells me you are right, but my heart tells me something different. I really wished your mother liked me. Instead of standing my ground as if it doesn't hurt me that she hates me, I wish I could think of a way to win her over to the point that she could at least tolerate me as the woman in your life."

"Courtney, you don't have to worry about my mother tolerating you. She'll tolerate you. You are in my life and therefore my mother will treat you with respect."

"She'll treat me with respect, but inside she will still hate me. You know your mother and you need to help me think of some way to improve her opinion of me."

"If you don't have an extra million hanging around, you can scratch that thought," he said jokingly.

"Are you saying what I think you are?"

Rome nodded. "Yes, I'm not proud to admit this, but my mother is a tad bit snobbish. Just a tad bit. As far as she's concerned, you don't have enough zeros in your bank account to be fit for me."

"Did she say that?" Courtney asked, stunned.

"I'm not trying to make you feel uncomfortable, and of course my mother would never actually say something like that to me regarding you. But I know my mother pretty well and if you were filthy rich she would probably sing you praises."

"I'm not sure if that makes me feel any better," Courtney said.

"I'm sure it doesn't, but the good thing is that I have told her about us and she expects you to join us for dinner tonight."

"Dinner at your house tonight, so soon after you just told her about us."

"Yes, why not; I figured it's a perfect time. You are the one who constantly talked about how you wanted to see the inside of Franklin House, now you'll get your chance tonight at dinner."

"I do want to visit your home, but I'm not sure if I'm ready to socialize with your mother. What would I say to her?"

"Discreetly tell her you have a million dollars in your purse," he joked.

"Will you stop joking and be serious. I have no idea what to say to your mother since her opinion is so low of me."

"Look at it like this, with her opinion being so low of you; it can only go up, right?" He grinned. "But seriously, you will be just fine. Just as I told her, it's time for the two of you to get to know each other," he said sincerely.

Courtney held her milkshake with both hands and pulled through the straw. "Okay, it will be nice to see inside of Franklin House. But I'm sure your mother and I will not socialize much. I will probably stay stuck to your side like glue."

Chapter Thirteen

Veronica was seated on the living room sofa with a cup of coffee in her hand but she placed the cup on the coffee table when Catherine walked into the room. Catherine was dressed professionally in a dark blue two piece dress. She was headed to the local library where she volunteered every Tuesday afternoon. She was due at the library at two-thirty. It was only twelve-thirty but she had decided to go in early.

"You are off to the library rather early, aren't you?" Veronica mumbled with no perkiness to her voice.

"Yes, I know. Just figured I would give them a little extra time today," she said heading toward the door.

"I wish you would hold off. I really could use an ear," Veronica said sadly.

Catherine stopped in her tracks. She knew that sad voice all too well. It meant Veronica was upset about something. "What's the matter now?" Catherine placed both hands on her hips. "You have everything my brother left you and four healthy good looking sons but you still find something to sit here and sulk about. So let's have it. What is so earthshaking that I need to listen to you and not go volunteer my time at a facility that needs the help?"

Veronica waved her hand. "Don't let me stop you. Where is my brain to think you would ever be concerned about anything I had to say? By all means run on to the library! I'll figure it out on my own."

"Figure what out on your own?"

"It's my business and not yours!"

"It was my business just a second ago when you asked me to stay and hear whatever sad story you're sulking about. Now suddenly it's not my business," Catherine said and took a seat on the opposite sofa facing her. "Give it a rest and tell me what's eating you. It must be an earth-shaking problem to have you tied in knots this early in the day?"

Veronica lifted her coffee cup and took a sip of coffee. She held the cup up to her lips and her hand slightly shook with nerves as she lowered the cup. "It's your stubborn nephew," she uttered sadly.

"I assume you are speaking about Rome."

"As a matter-of-fact I am, but how did you figure?"

"He had a serious look on his face when he stayed seated with you after breakfast. So I'm assuming it has something to do with what he may have said."

"You are right; of course, it does have something to do with some news he relayed to me. If he wasn't so stubborn I might be able to get through to him."

"In your eyes he's stubborn since he has real backbone to stand up to you. Actually, none of the boys are putty in your hands, but I must say, Sydney does want to please you."

"And what's wrong with that?"

"I just think he feels protective of you and wants to make you happy. After all, he is your baby," Catherine stated.

"I'm glad my youngest son wants to make me happy, because right now I'm not happy with my oldest son."

"What has Rome done that has you in such a blue mood? Did he run off with some girl that is too common for your blood?" Catherine joked.

Veronica stared with a solid face and Catherine quickly realized that she was closer to the truth than she knew.

"Based on how you're looking at me, I guess it would be safe to say, Rome is dating someone that doesn't meet your approval."

"You are correct. He stayed at his seat after breakfast and told me he's dating Courtney Ross, that young lady that works for him." Veronica shook her head in despair. "He made it exceedingly clear that she's not just a casual date, but his girlfriend. He has painted me into a corner."

Veronica eyes were filled with tears that didn't fall. "He has been seeing this young lady for over a month now. If I had known about their affair sooner, maybe…"

"There is no maybe; you would still be pouting just as you are right now. What else can you do? Rome is a grown man and he's going to date who he chooses. You can't pick and choose his women. Just leave it alone," Catherine suggested.

"Never, he's my first born and I will not allow him to fall through the cracks with some female that's not right for him while his other brothers end up with decent women in their lives. I will have to find away to convince him that Courtney Ross is not the right young woman for him, because deep down I don't believe she is," Veronica said with conviction.

Catherine glanced at her gold Gucci watch and still had plenty of time to get to the library before two-thirty. "There's nothing you can do, Veronica. You need to let those kids be. If this Courtney is who he wants then support him and accept her. What's so hard about just accepting the young lady? If she's not right for him, trust Rome's judgment that he'll figure it out on his own."

"I do trust my son's judgment. I'm so proud of my sons and sometimes I can't believe they are my boys. In spite of me and my shortcomings, they are just about perfect gentlemen just as their father. And with their hearts being as trusting as they are, they can easily be fooled by some young woman who's only after their good looks and money."

"And in your eyes, Courtney Ross is that kind of woman?"

"Yes, I happen to think this about Courtney Ross. I'm not convinced that she has Rome best interest at heart." Veronica wiped a tear that rolled down her face.

"My goodness, you are really torn up over this. But I think you are borrowing trouble. After all, they have only dated for a little better than a month. It's not like they are engaged. Give it some time and Rome may decide that Courtney isn't the one for him," Catherine said to try and lift her spirits.

"Do you really think so?"

Catherine stared at Veronica and shook her head. "I'm sorry, but I don't really think so. I was just trying to lighten your burden of worry. But listen, Rome is a strong minded young man, as the rest of his brothers. If he is seriously dating Courtney Ross, he sees something in her that's special. You need to try to allow yourself to see that same something so you can get over your reluctant and be more accepting of this girl."

"I agree that he does see something special in her," Veronica nodded toward Catherine with sad eyes.

"Okay and you see the same thing? You did meet this young lady a few months ago. What did you think of her? I hear she's soft spoken and quite pretty."

"Who did you hear that from?" Veronica asked.

"I just heard it. Word gets around. Just like the word that she has been into Rome since Paris first hired her," Catherine pointed out.

"That much is true, and yes, she has good looks. But she's still not the right young lady for Rome."

"But you just said there's something special about her that has grabbed Rome's attention. Is her beauty the special thing you were referring to?"

Veronica shook her head. "Not her beauty, her body. The special something that he sees in that girl is sex appeal. I'm sure he sees her as someone who can give him endless sex around the clock."

Catherine was stunned at her words. "Veronica, what are you trying to imply about the young lady?"

"I'm not trying to imply anything, I'm just stating it the way I see it. I'm sure this Courtney has blinded Rome of his good senses with unlimited trips to her bed," she stressed strongly. "She'll lure him with sex and then end up being unfaithful to my son. With all my shortcomings, being unfaithful to your brother was not one of them. I will not sit by and let some loose girl lure Rome with sex."

"Veronica, what you think and assume about this young lady is all speculation. My money is on Rome and his good sense not to fall for some female that is loose and about town. That's not who he is. Don't you know your own son?"

"Yes, I know my own son and that look in his eyes this morning told me how he has fallen for this girl."

"I have to admit, I didn't think he would have chosen one of his employees to date. That part doesn't look good, otherwise it's his business."

"Well, he's going to take that policy off the books," Veronica shared.

"He is?" Catherine smiled. "Good for him. I can't imagine who placed such a policy on the books in the first place," she said with a smirk on her face. "When my brother was alive, he never would have approved of such a policy."

"We all know Ryan was perfect," Veronica snapped.

"Do I detect a tad of jealousy because you are not?" Catherine snapped back.

Veronica gave Catherine a ten second stare. "In your old age, you have not mellowed! You are a rude bitch, do you know that?"

"It's take one to know one!" Catherine snapped.

Veronica held up both hands. "Okay, look, this snapping back and forth isn't getting us anything. The point is, Rome told me that Courtney Ross is leaving the company in January and will no longer be his employee and therefore, he feels that makes it okay to date her."

After a moment of silence, Catherine who was looking down toward the carpet furious that Veronica had called her a rude bitch, collected herself and stared at Veronica. "That's good that she's leaving the company. January is right around the corner; therefore, she won't be his employee that much longer. Maybe after that, you'll be more open to their relationship."

Veronica shook her head and frowned. "I don't think that day will ever come. Because as much as I dislike the fact that he's dating this woman who happens to be one of his employees, after she no longer works for Franklin Gas, she still won't be fit for my son. I will do everything in my power to convince him of that," Veronica assured her. "I might not be twenty-five any more, but my powers of persuasion are still sharp as ever. One way or another I'll get Rome to see the light about Miss Courtney Ross."

Catherine glanced at her watch and stood up to leave. "When you are this determined about something nobody can stop you, but a word to the wise. While you are trying to get Rome to see the light, don't be surprised if you end up seeing the light first," Catherine stated firmly and headed toward the front door to leave.

Chapter Fourteen

By Friday, Rome had brought Courtney by the mansion for dinner a total of three times. Veronica was beside herself with concern with worry that he was getting too involved with her. She desperately wanted to put an end to the relationship but couldn't think of a way to get her results without alienating her son. She never wanted her conniving to hurt her sons. She wanted to make their worlds better by her schemes, but didn't want her sons affected in a negative way by them.

She was standing in the living room window looking out when Sabrina's red Mercedes and another white Mercedes right behind her pulled into the Taylor's driveway. Sabrina stepped out of her car and then assisted the other young lady with two toddlers. Veronica stared keenly, recognizing Sabrina's guest. It was Amber Taylor-Dumont, Sabrina's twenty-six year-old first cousin who was widowed with two-year-old twin girls. She was the only child and heir of the multi-billionaire Don and Angela Taylor, Charles Taylor's older brother.

Veronica staring was interrupted when Catherine walked over and pulled the curtains back and stared with her.

"What's so interesting about the Taylor's front yard? You have been staring toward it for a long while now. I was standing over by the fireplace watching you watch whoever you are watching."

Veronica waved her hand for Catherine to mind her own business. "Do you have anything better to do than worry about my business? Why don't you head to the library or something? Don't they need someone to volunteer today?"

Catherine shook her head. "I'm afraid not. I would be there if they needed me. I might start donating a little of my time to the hospital as well."

"Fine, why not start today?" Veronica suggested.

"Hold your horses. It will happen but not this minute. Besides, you're too anxious to get rid of me. You're not getting me out of your hair that easily. I think you're up to something."

"You always think I'm up to something." Veronica threw her a hard stare and then focused back toward the Taylor's. "What could I possibly be up to just standing here looking out the window?"

"You aren't just standing here looking out; you are looking toward the Taylor estate at Sabrina and her cousin."

"So, what if I am; this is a free country. There's no harm in watching two people exit their cars."

"Maybe not, but I think you're looking for a love interest for Rome."

Veronica mumbled with no perkiness to her voice. "He has a love interest, remember? She has shared our dinner table for three evening in a row."

"Yes, a young lady that you don't feel is fit for him. But on the other hand, Sabrina's cousin who is heir to a billion dollar estate, I'm sure is more suitable and acceptable for Rome in your eyes."

"She does seem like a lovely girl," Veronica admitted.

"Yes, I'm sure she is a lovely young lady. But what can I tell you, other than the fact that Rome isn't interested in her because he's interested in Courtney Ross. Besides, you wouldn't want your son to start a relationship with a widower with two kids would you? I know you don't care for the Ross girl, but you wouldn't want Rome to jump into a relationship with someone who has kids would you?" Catherine asked. "Nothing against young single women with kids, but that's a lot of extra responsibility for a young man to deal with if it can be avoided," Catherine pointed out. "So, tell me, would you want Rome to start out in a relationship with a female with kids?"

"Well, of course not, but I do sympathize with young women who are widowed with small children. You know that was me once upon a time. I was quite young when I lost Ryan. But I didn't have to concern myself with finding a stepfather for my sons, because I was too devastated over losing Ryan to even consider the possibility of another relationship. My sons were my only concern. A new relationship was never my focus. Yet, when you're that young and lose the love of your life, it's hard. Because as you mentioned, nobody wants a ready made family."

"Veronica, you need to try and accept Courtney. She seems like a lovely young lady. And most importantly, Rome seems to care about her. Just get over yourself about her background and bank account and cut her a break. Besides, three out of four isn't bad."

"What are you getting at?" Veronica stared at Catherine as if she had just stabbed her in the stomach.

"Why are you giving me such a heated look?" Catherine asked.

"What did you mean by three out of four isn't bad?" Veronica snapped angrily, dropped the curtains and stepped away from the window.

"No need to take my head off. I just meant three girls of your choice for your sons, isn't bad. You are so happy that Britain, Paris and Sydney are with those Taylor girls. Just count your blessings with those three and let Rome have Miss Ross in peace," Catherine suggested.

"Catherine, you fool! When will you ever figure me out? My mind doesn't work like that. I'm not going to leave Rome be just because my other sons had the good sense to fall for proper, decent young ladies."

"You might as well leave him be. He's not going to listen to you and stop seeing Courtney."

"He might not listen to me, but maybe he'll listen to someone else."

"Someone else, like who? Is this person someone who can get him to think in your favor and stop seeing Courtney Ross?"

Veronica stared into space for a moment and then nodded. "Just maybe."

"Who is this person?"

"It's his father."

"You're not making any sense. My brother is dead, remember?"

"I know he's dead, but he left letters for his sons. You know, Ryan envisioned how he wanted their lives to turn out."

"Okay, if he envisioned how he wanted their lives to turn out, did he mention anything about show business in his letters?" Catherine curiously asked.

Veronica shook her head. "Not really and I'm confused by that. I'm not sure why he didn't mention it, but I'm not convinced he didn't want them to follow in his footsteps toward the entertainment world."

"Veronica, this is where you really need to get a clue. If he didn't mention it in his letters, that should tell you something, don't you think?"

"Tell me what?" Veronica snapped.

"You know what? If he didn't mention anything about his desire for the boys to follow in his footsteps into the movie industry, why are you so convinced that's what he wanted for them?"

"I just feel it in my gut he would be proud to see them on the big screen doing what he loved so."

"Just because you feel it in your gut doesn't make it so. Just admit, it's what you want for them and my brother probably just wanted them to be happy at whatever they decided to pursue. That's who he was. Besides, you know how straightforward Ryan was about everything."

Veronica gave Catherine an annoyed look.

Catherine held up both hands. "Okay, I'll drop it. So, anyway, you have a letter from Ryan that you think will convince Rome to walk away from Courtney Ross?"

"Yes, I have a letter from Ryan that just might do the trick."

"Okay, but you could be setting yourself up for a letdown," Catherine suggested. "He could read the letter and still decide not to end his relationship with that girl."

"It's a chance I have to take. Right now I'm desperate and will try anything. I know you think I'm being petty and not accepting in regards to Courtney Ross because of her questionable background. But seriously, it's more to it than that. I honestly believe Courtney Ross would have settled for Britain if he had hit on her. That means to her, any Franklin man will do. I don't want my sons to be an interchangeable consolation prize for some materialistic, conning female."

"What are you saying? You already know that situation with Courtney and Britain was a big misunderstanding."

"That's what we have heard from Rome and Britain both. But think about it, why was this young lady so annoyed with Britain for forgetting her birthday?"

"He had promised to take her out and then blew her off or forgot," Catherine reminded her. "I think that was something to be annoyed about."

"I agree it was something to be annoyed about, but not bitter. I heard she was over the top upset with him about the incident as if he was her man," Veronica relayed.

"Maybe she took it too personal, but I think I would have been a bit disappointed if some guy had blown me off or forgotten my birthday after promising to show me a good time," Catherine argued in Courtney's favor.

"Yes, being disappointed is understandable, but if she thought of him as just a friend, why did she take it so personal?"

"Veronica that's water under the bridge and you need to stop fishing for a reason to have an aversion to this young woman. Can you do that for your son's sake?" Catherine firmly asked. "Besides, Courtney Ross is only human, for goodness sake. What if she did have a brief crush on Britain? Who wouldn't develop a crush on such a handsome man as Britain or any of your gorgeous sons for that matter? The issue at hand that you are not dealing with is her relationship with Rome. Once you accept that relationship, your life will be a lot less stressful."

"Well, I guess stress will follow me because I have no intentions of ever being okay with Courtney Ross pulling the wool over Rome eyes. Someway, somehow I will open his eyes to that young woman."

"I'm not going to hold my breath," Catherine said and headed toward the kitchen.

Chapter Fifteen

Autumn showers had fallen earlier in the day, but now it was a clear night as stars lit up the sky. The night air was breezy and quite cool, but Courtney had chosen to dress in a sleeveless summer outfit beneath her spring jacket. She wanted to entice Rome with her appeal in an effort to try and secure his continued interest in her. She was concerned about their relationship and didn't want it to slip through her fingers as it had with Britain. Even though, Rome had confessed that he had feelings for her, she wasn't certain his feelings were strong enough to survive up against his mother's constant disapproval of her.

Rome stood up from the small black sofa but Courtney remained seated not sure where he was headed. He grabbed their glasses of wine from the coffee table and then beckoned for Courtney to follow him out of the crowded house. They stepped outside onto the patio into the cool night air. The music could be heard outside and they were not the only couples that had wondered outside. They noticed a few other couples sitting on benches holding hands and some standing closely talking.

"It's nice out here," Courtney said, looking around at the large backyard.

"Let's sit at that table." Rome pointed to a small picnic table at the far end of the patio where the lights were dimmer. "It's a bit too crowded in there. We could have gone somewhere else other than here, but a Friday night after Halloween, every house and club in town is having a Halloween bash."

He placed the drinks on the table and before they were seated, Courtney pulled off her black jacket and placed it over the back of the chair. She was wearing a feminine somewhat revealing short low-cut sleeveless black dress that hugged her slender figure. Rome did a double take and accidentally swore. "Damn, you look magnificent tonight. I had no idea you were wearing something so damn sexy beneath your jacket."

"I hope it's not too much," she said, pleased with his approval.

"Are you kidding me? Come here," he whispered and pulled Courtney in his arms and gave her a lingering passionate kiss.

When he pulled away from her lips, he looked at her and smiled. "Seeing you dressed so enticingly has caused a situation," he whispered.

"And what situation is that?"

"It's a very serious situation where I want to be alone with you, Miss Courtney Ross." He glanced about the backyard. "This house party is too crowded and I would much rather be somewhere quiet and alone with you." He grabbed her jacket and handed it to her. "As lovely as you look, I think you should slip this back on before you end up sick. It's quite chilly out tonight."

She nodded. "I think you are right. It is quite chilly," she said, slipping back into her jacket.

"So, what you say? You want to take off and go somewhere quiet where we can be alone?" he asked.

"We're leaving the party already?" she asked.

"I would like to, but only if it's okay with you," he said as he took a sip from his wine glass and frowned. "I see why you didn't finish your wine. The wine they are serving is pretty dreadful as far as wine goes."

"You're probably only used to fine wine."

"I have had my share of both during college; and this is about the worst."

"I guess all the money went to the Disc Jockey. The music is excellent, don't you think so?" Courtney smiled.

Rome nodded. "I do think so, but you didn't answer me," he said. "You don't mind if we take off, do you? The music isn't so great that it could hold you here, is it? Maybe we can think of a way to make our own music," he whispered close to her neck.

She laughed. "You are not getting fresh with me, are you Mr. Franklin?" she smiled. "I thought you were too much of a gentleman for that."

"A gentleman, I am; but too much of a gentleman for that, no," he whispered against her neck again. "So, are you going to answer me? Do you mind taking off?"

"I guess not, but it is still early and we did just arrive an hour ago. But here's an idea, we can go to the party my sister is throwing at my house if you like," she suggested. "We probably have better wine there I'm sure. Or better yet, we can go to the Taylor's party you were telling me about. I would love to see the inside of that big house. I'm sure it's a magnificent sight just like Franklin House. "

"Yes, the Taylor's home is on a grand scale and quite a sight to see, but I wasn't thinking about going to another party. I was hoping we could just go somewhere and be alone together." Rome reached out and touched her face. "I'm not that keen about finding better wine or another party. I just thought we could be alone. So do you mind leaving this party and not heading to another one?"

"Sure, but shouldn't we say good night to your friend first?"

"What friend are you referring to?" he asked.

"I'm referring to your friend that invited us here?"

"Oh, that friend," he smiled.

"Yes, shouldn't you find him and let him know we're leaving?"

"I think that would be rather hard to do since he's not here." Rome smiled.

"He's not in attendance at his own party?" she asked.

"This is not his party. He doesn't live here," he announced.

"So, we are at some house party and either one of us knows the host?"

"That's about the scope of it, but although I don't know the people who live here, a friend from work knows them and told me about the party. Besides, they throw it every Halloween and it's open to the public. I dropped by last year and was pleased with the music and the fact that you don't have to wear a costume," he explained.

"I guess that's why I only noticed a few people wearing costumes."

"Yes, that's why." he nodded.

"You mentioned the Taylor's party, but they would have turned us around at the door," Rome said.

"Who are they and why would they turn us around at the door?"

"They are the Taylor's cook; Mrs. Carrie Westwood, who is hosting the party."

"And she would turn us around why?"

"We are not dressed in costumes." Rome smiled. "Mrs. Westwood is a dear lady and she loves Halloween, but if you show up, you need to be dressed in something that makes you look like anything other than who you are."

"You talk as if you know their maid quite well."

Rome nodded. "Yes, I do know her quite well. From the time I can remember, she always lived and worked next door. She used to work for the elderly couple that the Taylor's bought the estate from. She, her husband and the rest of the staff stayed on to work for the Taylors because they didn't want to be out of a job or relocate to Jupiter, Florida where the Sterlings moved to."

"Wow, Jupiter, Florida. I hear the scenery is beautiful there," Courtney said.

"I have heard the same, but I'm looking at a beautiful sight right now," he said softly. "That I would much rather look at in a more private setting, so shall we go?" he asked, reached for her hand.

She smiled and nodded and then placed her hand in his. He gentled squeezed her hand and then they headed across the backyard toward the street.

"So where are we headed?" she asked, laughing.

"We are headed to Franklin House."

"We're going to your house? I thought you wanted to be alone with me?"

"That's why we're headed to Franklin House. I know there's nobody home." He glanced at his watch. "And it should be that way for the next two hours."

"So, we'll have your house all to ourselves for the next two hours?"

"That's the idea, and I can't wait to get you home so I can hold and kiss you the way I have wanted to all night," he said as they headed quickly across the grounds toward the street corner where he had parked his car.

When Rome and Courtney arrived at Franklin House, he took Courtney straight upstairs to his bedroom. She had never visited his room before and was in awe of the enormous room and how neatly it was decorated in four shades of gray. She noticed that the expensive furniture and décor was traditionally elegant with dark gray furniture, light gray walls and carpeting offset with pale gray window treatments and bedding. Silver gray fireplace mantle, picture frames and accessories along with an entertainment stand across one wall.

She was slightly nervous about being alone with him in his bedroom, but she was still in awe of his beautiful bedroom. Before she could remove her jacket, Rome grabbed her in his arms, leaned down and kissed her urgently for a moment before he pulled away and looked her in the eyes with desire pouring through his veins.

"Courtney, I hope I'm not jumping the gun, but these feelings I have for you have sort of taken over. I need to feel you next to me tonight, in my arms all to myself."

"You do have me all to yourself right now," she said.

"I think you know what I mean. I want to make love to you," he whispered, bringing his mouth back down on hers to swallow her up in a quick urgent kiss.

Courtney was stunned at first. She hadn't expected him to say that, but then her surprise quickly turned to longing and she realized how much she wanted to be alone with him in that way as well because she wanted their bond to strengthen. But she thought better of it and didn't want to hop in bed with him too soon to give his mother another reason to discourage him away from her. In her mind, she was sure his mother would find out and consider her a tramp.

"So, what do you say?" he whispered a kiss against her neck. "I don't want to rush you if you're not ready, but something tells me you are."

"You are right. I am ready to be with you in that way, but not tonight. I told you awhile back that I have waited because of my religious beliefs.

Therefore, the same reason I waited in the past is why I'm waiting now. It's not because I'm not ready."

"Okay, what is your belief that is holding you back?" he asked.

"That a step so important should feel right when it happens."

"And now you are ready, but it doesn't feel right?"

"Rome that is exactly how I feel. Besides, you told me yourself that everybody will be back in a couple hours. I feel like we are rushing and I don't want our first time to be like this," she explained.

"Okay, I understand. Maybe tonight isn't the best time," he agreed.

"Plus, Rome, I'm a bit surprised that you want to take me to bed so soon in our relationship. Do you think of me as someone who is easy? If you were dating one of the Taylor girls would you try to get them in bed so fast?" Courtney said from her insecurities of feeling their relationship would slip between her fingers.

"I can't believe you just said that to me." He held her shoulders and looked her in the eyes. "I have feelings for you and want to show you how much. That's why I want you in my bed. It's that simple. Where is this coming from?" he asked with a tad of confusion in his voice.

"You and your brothers have a reputation for being gentlemen. We have only dated for a month and a half; so with that in mind, I guess I didn't expect you to bring me up to your room and try to get me in bed," she mumbled as he helped her slip out of her jacket.

"Yes, we have a reputation for being gentlemen and I would like to think that we are. However, we are as red-blooded as the next guy. Did you think we were not?" He winked at her. "Seeing you dressed the way you are this evening in that sexy black dress weighed heavy toward facilitating the situation that drove me to this point." He threw her jacket across the settee to his left and then quickly slipped out of his jacket and threw it across the settee on top of hers.

She thought for a second how she had purposely wore the little black dress to appeal to him. But she hadn't expected that he would have wanted to go all the way. She stiffen as he took her hand and led her over to his king size bed where they both stood at the side of the bed looking longingly into each other's eyes.

"But Rome," she managed breathless.

"But what?" he asked.

"But I thought you understood that I feel it's too soon. We are still getting to know each other and I don't want to spoil things."

"That is true, we are still getting to know each other, but how do you figure this could spoil things?" he whispered, kissing the side of her neck and on her hair. "I know you feel it's too soon, but it doesn't feel like it's too soon to me."

Courtney stepped back from his grasp. "But it is. Your mother already has a very low opinion of me. I'm not going to hop in bed with you too soon to prove her point that I'm some loose female that you shouldn't waste your time with."

Rome held out both arms and shook his head. "Courtney, I respect you and if you're not ready, okay you are not ready. But please do not bring my mother's name into our romantic moment. That's one sure way to kill the moment."

"I won't bring up your mother's name again, but I think I'm right."

"Maybe you are and I know we have only dated for a short time, but I have dreamed of you and held you in my thoughts a lot longer than that, pretty much from the moment I laid eyes on you." He stepped toward her and pulled her in his arms again, kissing her throat and neck. "But you were always the one I couldn't talk to or the one I couldn't be with. Now, we are together and something is still keeping us apart," he said with a touch of disappointment in his voice as he pulled away from her and dropped down on the side of the bed.

He grabbed his face for a second and then looked toward the ceiling before he looked at her and smiled.

Courtney took a seat on the bed beside him and looked at him longingly; and suddenly he grabbed her face with both hands and swallowed her up in a passionate kiss. Her head fell back on the pillow and they continued to kiss until he forced himself to pull back. He sat up and pulled her up. "I can't blame it on the wine since I couldn't stomach the darn stuff that they were serving; but I do have something to blame for losing my head this evening." He smiled.

"And what is that something that you can blame?"

He touched her stomach with his finger. "It's you, of course; wearing that sexy black dress to drive me crazy. Are you sure you weren't trying to drive me wild tonight?" He softly caressed the side of her neck. "I'm just teasing you, of course. I'm sure when you slipped on that dress, driving me crazy was not your intentions. I just have to get used to how irresistible you are." He looked longingly into her eyes.

She kissed the side of his face, thinking how he was joking, but he was dead on the money when he mentioned that she had worn the dress to entice him. "How can I help if I'm so irresistible?" she said, jokingly.

"You're joking, but it's very true. You are an irresistible female after my own heart. I can barely keep my hands off of you when we are together. But of course, you are right. This isn't the right time." He glanced about his room. "It's not the least bit romantic here in my bedroom." He held out both arms. "What was I thinking, don't answer that. I know what I was thinking." He grinned. "But apparently I wasn't thinking straight." He turned to her and gave her a tender kiss on the lips, and then he glanced at his watch. "We need to get out of this room and out of this house before my family returns and think you and I have done what we both know we haven't." He caressed her left cheek tenderly for a quick moment and then hopped off the bed.

Courtney was still seated on the edge of the bed as Rome stepped over to the settee and grabbed their jackets and passed Courtney hers.

"So, you're not too disappointed, are you?" Courtney looked at Rome as she stood up and slipped into her jacket.

"No, I'm not disappointed at all." Rome threw on his jacket and nodded. "I'm the one who overstepped and got a bit out of hand. I should be asking you if you're disappointed with me for acting like some wild animal in heat." He winked at her, and then strolled over to his bedroom door and held it open.

She walked toward the door smiling. "I'm not disappointed at all either. I'm glad we came here to be alone with each other. It was perfect, even if it was just for a short time. Being in your room alone with you and in your arms like that was nice. I had an incredible time tonight," she said as she walked out of his room.

In the hallway, he pulled his door shut and then grabbed Courtney in his arms and fell his back against the closed door. He lifted her off the floor, wrapped in his arms in a passionate kiss that lingered for a few minutes. When they pulled away, he looked at her and smiled. "I know sleep will not be on my agenda for this evening." He winked at her. "I'm going to be too preoccupied thinking about you and this." He touched her lips."

"So you're not disappointed that I thought we should wait?"

He shook his head. "No, I'm not disappointed," he assured her. "I want you badly, but I'm not disappointed that tonight wasn't our first time. Our first time is going to be a very special event that takes place on a yacht or maybe in a penthouse at some luxury hotel, but not my bedroom," he said.

Chapter Sixteen

Meanwhile the Taylor's Halloween party was going strong. Rihanna song, Yellow Diamonds In the Sky, was playing on the stereo while Samantha danced with Paris along with a roomful of other guests dressed in costumes. Samantha had her shoulder length hair styled in french rolls, dressed as Cinderella in a long white dress with a pink sash around the waist. Paris was dressed as the Prince in all white, which suited his princely appearance. They were slow dancing as she was smiling up at Paris and he was smiling down at her. Then suddenly in the middle of their dance, someone tapped Samantha on the shoulder. She glanced around and was stunned to see that someone was Kenny Ross. She stop dancing and faced him as he stood there smiling at her. Then she had a quick flash back to their college days. She anxiously stumbled with her words. "Kenny," she said as she took a deep breath.

The smile on Kenny's face was as vain as Samantha remembered, but they were once friends in college and she always overlooked his absurdity attitude. He was average height with average looks and his family had no wealth but he had somehow charmed her back in college to the point that she thought he had it together and was someone she wanted to go out with. Samantha dated him briefly in college and never heard from him after college. They had graduated at the same time and she knew he lived in the area but they never ran into each other because they didn't run in the same circles. She never mentioned Kenny to her parents because she knew deep down that he wasn't the right fellow for her. Not because he was poor in wealth but because he seemed poor in his treatment toward himself. When she knew him in college he was into non-stop partying. He stayed up late every night hanging out at the clubs, drinking heavy and smoking constantly. She had no idea that he would show up at one of their family parties.

"Miss Samantha Taylor." He smiled. "I know you are standing in for Cinderella tonight, but even without that outfit, you would still look like a princess," he grinned. "You are still a knock-out. The past year has served you well." He glanced around the room. "Your home is a page out of a book. They almost didn't let me in until I showed the gateman a picture of the two of us."

Paris stood calm and polite, listening and discreetly observing Kenny and Samantha's reaction to each other.

"My goodness, I can't believe it's you." Samantha grabbed her mouth.

"It's me, but that look in your eyes tell me I'm the last person you expected to see at your Halloween party," he grinned. "I must admit that I have an inside track since my sister is dating a guy who lives next door to you; and his brother is dating you; and that's how I found out that you lives here and was throwing this big bash."

"You haven't changed that much have you? You always could find a party with free drinks and food," Samantha reminded him.

"That didn't sound much like a compliment. But you never had much of a sense of humor," he laughed.

Kenny was dressed in a Chicago White Socks baseball costume, right down to the shoes and the cap. And without waiting for Samantha to introduce them, he extended his hand to Paris and said, "You must be Prince Charming. I'm Kenny Ross."

Paris nodded his head with a curious look in his eyes. "Paris Franklin."

Kenny pointed his finger at Paris. "Are you the famous Paris Franklin? Your father was that famous movie star, Ryan Franklin, right?"

Paris nodded. "That is correct, but I..."

Before Paris could finish his sentence, Kenny cut him off and slapped his shoulder. "Samantha and I knew each other quite well back in college."

Paris discreetly exchanged looks with Samantha and could see from the surprise in her eyes that Kenny's presence still affected her in some way. He placed his arm around Samantha waist and pulled her in closer. "My college days seem like another lifetime ago." Paris smiled. "In case you were wondering, Samantha and I know each other quite well now."

Samantha stared nervously at Kenny hoping he had not showed up to make a scene. She remembered how loud he could sometime get out at parties during their college days. Then he pointed at Paris again and smiled. "Hey, I do know you. You own that service station in town "Franklin Gas."

Paris smiled. "Yes; do we have your business?"

"I can't say that you do. But two of my sisters works there. I've picked one of them up from the station a few times. I didn't see you, but probably one of your brothers. You all look alike with that wave in your hair. This dude I spotted when I picked up my sister had hair down his back."

"That would be Britain."

"Do you mean Great Britain, that weird combination of England, Scotland and Wales?" Kenny laughed and exchanged looks with Samantha.

Samantha gave Kenny a hard stare that showed she was not pleased with his behavior. She figured he was being comical to get under Paris skin. "Britain is his brother's name," she enlighened him.

"What's that look for? How did I know his brother was named after an island or whatever Great Britain is supposed to be! Give me a break. I'm not a mindreader, but I think I see a pattern here. Your brother is named Britain and you're Paris," Kenny laughed. "Is your father named after some foreign city too? Scratch that, your father was the famous Ryan Franklin. That we both know." He held out his glass to them and took a big swallow from his glass of red wine.

"I know you both probably think I'm wasted out of my mind here, but I'll tell you two something. I wanted to meet your new fellow." He nodded at Samantha. "That's right, I wanted to meet prince charming here." He stared at Paris. "But now that I have, you two make me laugh." He paused. "Yeah, you heard me right, you make me laugh. And if you're listen I'll tell you why. Here goes, because you make a perfect pair. You are both like two damn plastic dolls living in a fantasy world." He took another swallow from his glass. "No kidding, you two have no clue what it's like to cope in the real world," Kenny snapped loudly.

Paris and Samantha exchanged appalled looks with each other, and then Paris stuck both hands in the pockets of his prince cape and turned his back to Kenny. He was floored by Kenny's detestable behavior and felt it didn't dignify a response as he stared up at the ceiling and counted to ten before he turned to face a beard face offensive Kenny. Kenny smelled like a wine factory as he stood before them talking loud with red eyes. Paris emotions raged inside of him but he wasn't going to allow Kenny's obnoxious rudeness to push his buttons.

"What's the matter? I guess the truth hurts," Kenny laughed.

"Kenny, why are you laughing as if something is funny?" Samantha asked calmly, holding back her emotions of anger. "Besides, why are you here in my home being so disrespectful? Nobody here invited you."

"You're right, nobody here invited me because I guess I'm too common for your invitations," Kenny roared. "Just like back in college. I wasn't good enough to meet your folks, remember that? But I'm here now and if you don't like what I have to say, then too bad!" he fussed. "We don't all live with our heads in the sand looking at the world through rose-colored glasses." He pointed at Paris and then at Samantha. "You two need to open your eyes and see the real world for what it is! Life is a bitch and then you die!"

Paris and Samantha stood there listening to him as they held back their heated emotions. They figured if they just allowed him to speak his mind then soon he would walk away.

"It must be grand to be born with a silver spoon in your mouth, looking down on me like I'm something to throw out with the trash," he argued.

Samantha couldn't hold her words any longer. "Kenny, I'm not going to ask you why you are carrrying on like this and saying all these unkind things to us because I know it's not you. It's all that alcohol you have consumed. But if you can't hold your liquor you need to leave my house."

Kenny held up both arms and backed a couple steps away. "Don't make me leave your party. This is my watering hole. All this free booze, why would I want to leave. Besides, I'm done preaching. You two are too dense to catch on. You're happy in your fairytale world so I'll leave you be. My lips are sealed." He sealed his lips with his fingers. "I got it all off my chest! You two lovebirds carry on," he said, but continued to stand there.

Paris swallowed hard discreetly, not showing an ounce of the raging emotions that wanted to pour out of him toward Kenny. He stood straight and tried to ignore Kenny's rude remarks and drunken state. But it dawned on him to change the subject in an effort to alter Kenny's vulgar mood. Therefore, after a brief silence of the two of them standing there hoping Kenny would walk away, Paris calmly asked. "What's your sister's name that works for us?"

Kenny turned his glass of wine up to his mouth and drank it in one swallow. He lowered the glass and stared at Paris grinning. "Get your facts straight, dude; you mean sisters," Kenny pointed out, holding up two fingers. "I have two sisters and they both work for you, Courtney and Trina."

Paris shook his head and smiled. "What a small world."

"Why is it so small?" Kenny asked as he stood there with an unsteady balance. "Is it because my sisters work for my ex-girlfriend new boyfriend? So tell me, is that why you call it a small world?"

"The small world remark is more about the fact that you had mentioned that your sister is dating a guy who lives next door to Samantha. That's my brother, Rome, that's dating your sister, Courtney," Paris said.

"You have lost me, man. Who is Rome and what about my sister?"

Paris didn't comment. It registered in his mind that it was useless to hold a rational conversation with Kenny, who was falling down intoxicated.

Samantha stood there beside Paris with her heart in her throat, hoping Kenny would walk away from them. She wasn't sure how much longer she could hold her emotions and she didn't want to make a scene by having their bulter escort him out. Besides, she wanted him out of their faces so she could talk to Paris in privacy. She could detect how bothered Paris was by Kenny's presence and drunken manners and she could also sense how standoffish he seemed toward her since Kenny's arrival.

Finally Kenny turned to walk away but made only three steps away from them before he glanced over his shoulder and smiled at Paris and Samantha. "Take good care of her, you hear. She was my girl first." He tipped his baseball cap. "I think you know what I mean," he said loudly. "Otherwise, I can paint you a picture. Do you need me to paint you a picture?" He stumbled with his words and almost lost his balance. "I wish the two of you much happiness," he kept blinking his eyes as if the booze was putting him to sleep.

Paris nodded. "The same to you and yours."

"That's right, you just reminded me that I have a date somewhere in this house," Kenny added, "I want you two to meet Vickie."

Samantha grabbed her stomach with her left hand and collected herself. She was all nerves due to Kenny's unexpected appearance. As Kenny walked across the floor to the other side of the large party room in search of his date, Samantha held Paris's arm tight. Paris stiffened; he knew the reason behind her sudden nerves and the serious expression in his eyes were a clear indication that he was disturbed by the nervous behavior she had displayed in Kenny's presence. But before he could voice his disturbance, Kenny and his date had made their way across the room to stand before the two of them.

Samantha held on to Paris's arm even tighter when an average looking young woman stood at Kenny's side. "Paris and Samantha," he said, smiling, slightly rocking back and forth from intoxication. "This is Vickie Simpson. She's my date and my driver and right now also my wallet." He laughed.

Paris stared up at the ceiling and then back at Kenny's date. He recognized her right away as one of his workers. "Good evening, Vickie."

"Good evening, Mr. Franklin," she said, and then glanced toward the floor as if she was embarrassed to be seen with Kenny in his drunken state.

Kenny exchanged looks with Samantha and Samantha looked at Paris. "So I take it that the two of you know each other because she works for you."

"That is correct; Vickie works for us," Paris smiled.

Kenny glanced around the room for one of the Taylor's hired waiters before he stared at Paris. "Is there anybody in this town that doesn't work for you? I need another drink." He grabbed Vickie by the hand and they headed across the room in search of a waiter.

"I think another drink is the last thing he needs," Paris mumbled, dropped Samantha hand and headed toward the door.

"You're just leaving without saying goodbye," Samantha mumbled sadly.

He stopped in his tracks and looked at Samantha with a solemn look on his face, "Yes, it's late. I think I'll take off."

"But you were leaving without saying goodbye. Besides, it's not that late. We have stayed out a lot later than this many times. So, why are you really leaving?"

He turned and headed toward the door. "I think you know."

She caught up with him and grabbed his arm. "I don't know. I know you can't be jealous of Kenny Ross." She followed him outside.

Paris looked down at her. "You are right, jealous I'm not."

Samantha followed him to his car and jumped in on the passenger side as he got in on the driver's side. He looked at her. "I'm not headed home."

She stared at him with sad eyes. "So, I guess I'll go with you wherever you are headed."

"Samantha, you need to get out of this car and head back inside. I'm not in the mood to have a discussion with you right now," he said firmly.

"I'm not getting out until we talk. I'm not going to let you leave like this," she stated strongly.

"Okay, fine, suit yourself. Don't get out." He started up the engine and headed out of the driveway.

They were both silent as he drove toward downtown Barrington. The only sound they could hear was the slight wind against the windows of the car on that cool, breezy night. He was looking straight ahead through the windsheild and Samantha kept glancing at him every few seconds until he finally glanced toward her and their eyes met. However, he quicky looked right back toward the road in front of him.

"Paris, I really wish you would talk to me and tell me what's going on. Why are you sore with me? You have no need to be jealous of Kenny."

Samantha statement didn't set well with Paris, but he calmly pulled into the twenty-four hour Walgreens and parked in a stall. He turned the engine off and propped his left arm on the steering wheel and looked at Samantha.

"Let's get one thing clear," he said with complete confident. "I don't do the jealous thing, and I'm halfway offended that you would think that I would be jealous of another man, especially someone like Kenny Ross who has a drinking problem."

"I didn't mean to offend you. I just want to know what's the matter."

"It's obvious to me that you were once into Kenny Ross, is that not correct?"

Looking at Paris, she frowned and mumbled. "Are you serious?"

"Yes, Samantha, I'm very serious. Just answer me, were you once into Kenny Ross or not?"

"Paris, I can't believe you are so serious about this," Samantha stressed. "But I'll answer your question. I dated the guy in college and liked him at the time, but we were never in a real relationship. We dated for a short while and then it was over. Believe me, he wasn't the one. We didn't have anything in common. I'm sure you can see what a drunk he is," she stressed. "And believe me, he was the same way in college."

"Samantha, your behavior was a give-away. His presence still affects you in someway," Paris pointed out.

"Yes, he affects me in a discussing way. If you thought I still sort of liked him because of my nerves around him; I can assure you that it had nothing to do with like. It had all to do with shock. My nerves took over immediately when I saw that he was at the party. I was extremely surprise to see him, especially at a party given at my home."

"I see," Paris said and started up the engine.

Five minutes later Paris was pulling back into Samantha's driveway. She looked at him. "I thought we were going somewhere, to another party maybe?"

Paris shook his head. "No, it's late. The bewitching hour is over. We are back home." He turned off the engine and rested his left arm on the steering wheel. "Samantha, we need to have a serious talk and now isn't the best time." He glanced at his diamond rolex watch. "It's far past midnight and you should head inside. We can talk over brunch tomorrow. How is that?" He gave her a slight smile.

"Sure brunch would be great," she mumbled with no excited to her voice. "What time should I expect you?"

"I'll pick you up at ten. I'm partial to Red Skillet Saturday morning brunch. If you haven't eaten there I'm sure you'll love it," he said getting out of the car to walk around and open the door for Samantha.

She stepped out of the car slowly feeling anxious about their situation. He walked her to her front door. She stood there looking up at him. They were a sight out of a fairytale as they looked at each other dressed as prince and princess, but he didn't kiss her on the lips. He merely grabbed her hands, lifted them and kissed them both. "We'll talk tomorrow," he said and then he was gone.

Samantha went inside and headed straight up the staircase to her room. The party crowd had left and the house was quiet with nobody stirring. When she got to her room she dropped on the bed still dressed in her beautiful white gown. She stared at the wall for a moment before the tears started to roll down her face. Suddenly she looked up and there stood Starlet in her doorway.

"What's the matter? Why are you sitting here in the dark crying?" She smiled. "Your Prince Charming didn't kiss you goodnight." She teased.

Samantha shook her head. "No he didn't and now he probably never will," she wiped her tears with her fingers.

Starlet mouth fell open and she ran to Samantha's side. "What happened with you and Paris? You two left the party and we figured you went to another one." Starlet hopped off the bed after she realized she was sitting on the gown.

"We didn't go to another party. Paris was leaving and I hopped in the car with him because I could sense he was sort of ticked at me or disappointed in me or something."

"I don't understand what you are getting at. What was he ticked or disappointed about?"

"I'm sure it was Kenny Ross?"

"Kenny Ross, I saw him falling all over some girl who had the misfortune of being his date. What does that drunk have to do with anything?" Starlet asked.

"He came to the party uninvited and stunned me. I hadn't seen Kenny since college and he made it a point of telling Paris that we knew each other quite well in college."

"So what if you knew him well in college, what does that have to do with anything?"

"It caught Paris by surprise and I think he thinks that something happened between Kenny and I back then."

"You think he thinks that? Why would he, anybody can see that Kenny Ross is a loser and you would never waste your time with some guy like that," Starlet grinned. "You have to let Paris know that you knew him in college but you never went out with him."

"That's not true, Starlet. I did go out with Kenny and he and I dated for awhile. I told this to Paris."

"You what?" Starlet grabbed both cheeks as she leaned against the dresser wearing a short white night gown. "Oh my goodness, I had no idea that you had dated that guy. What were you thinking? It was all over campus how he drunk like a fish and smoked even worst. I saw him in your face a lot but figured he was just one of many who never had a chance with my smart straight-A sister."

"That's why I'm crying. I think Paris is going to break up with me."

"Why do you think that? Did he say that to you?"

"No, but he didn't kiss me goodnight and he wants to have a talk with me tomorrow over brunch."

"He wants to have a talk." Starlet paused and nodded. "Well, that's never good when a guy wants to have a talk."

"I know that's never good. He's going to break up with me. I can't believe I blew it with Paris Franklin. He's perfect and too good to be true. I should have known something would come between us," Samantha cried.

"I know it doesn't look promising if he wants to have a talk. However, look on the bright side. He didn't dump you on the spot."

Samantha stared at Starlet and shook her head. "You're not helping with your comments."

"I know but it's crazy how Kenny Ross showed up here tonight and put you on the spot like that. Paris could see he's a loser and should know Kenny doesn't pose a threat to what you feel for him."

"It's not about that. Paris is not the least bit jealous. You think some hunk like Paris would be jealous of any guy? I think he's disappointed because I never mentioned Kenny. He was completely thrown for a loop when Kenny introduced himself and said he and I knew each other well in college," Samantha explained.

"Okay, maybe he was but Paris can't expect to have known about every guy you ever dated before he met you."

"But that's actually what he expected."

"Why would he expect that?"

"Because when we first started dating we shared all of this information with each other. He believe in being very open and honest and told me that he never stays in a relationship with someone if they are not completely open and honest with him."

"And you feel you haven't been completely open and honest with him because you didn't tell him about Kenny?"

"That's correct; I never mentioned that I dated Kenny."

"Why didn't you?"

"Well, I just told him that I had dated a few guys in college and mentioned their names but I didn't mention Kenny's name because I was ashamed to mention that I had dated such a loser of a guy. I didn't want him to think less of me. Besides, I figured I would never see Kenny Ross again. I took a gamble and held the truth from him and now he may never trust me again. How could I have been so stupid to blow my chance with him? I'm well aware that the Franklin boys were raised a certain way. They are straightlaced pretty boys with good manners and can have any female at the drop of a hat. They don't play games and they don't tolerate lies."

"I'll second that. Sydney and I sort of had a similar conversation. He knows about every fellow I ever dated in college and after. We have no secrets between us. I know how lucky I am to have him in my life.

I wouldn't mess that up for anything." Starlet walked over and touched Samantha shoulder. "I'm heading to bed but I'm so sorry about what happened. All you can do now is just be honest with Paris about why you didn't mention Kenny Ross and hope he'll understand."

"Hope who will understand what?" Sabrina asked, standing in the doorway dressed in a short beige night gown. "I thought I heard voices."

Starlet walked past her. "Samantha will fill you in. Goodnight you two. I need to jump in bed."

"Why are you still dressed in your Halloween outfit with traces of tears on your face? Oh my, did you and Paris have a fight?"

Samantha nodded. "Something like that. I think he's going to break up with me and I really don't want to lose him. I love him so much, more than anything else I can think of."

"You need to tell me why you think he's going to break up with you. You appeared to be having a good time together at the party tonight. Britain and I commented on how the two of you looked so cute together in your costumes. So, what did we miss? After two months of dating and spending all your time together and staring at each other like there's no tomorrow, what makes you think Paris is going to break up with you?"

"Kenny Ross showing up here like that. It caught me off guard and now Paris knows I used to date him."

"And he wants to break up with you because of some guy you used to date before he met you? That doesn't sound like Paris Franklin. If he's anything like Britain he's understanding and will listen to reason. Just explain how Kenny Ross meant nothing to you back then."

"It's not about what Kenny meant to me or not, it's about how I kept this information from Paris. I never told him about my relationship with Kenny."

"I know you went out with Kenny Ross but had no idea that you had an actual relationship going on with him at anytime. So, spill; did you have a real relationship with Kenny Ross; and if you did, what were you thinking? And why should this ancient information break you and Paris up?"

"We dated for awhile but it never turned into a real relationship thanks to his drinking and smoking that turned me off. And what was I thinking? I was thinking how he seemed okay until I got to really know him," Samantha explained stepping out of the princess gown.

"Okay," Sabrina nodded. She was now seated on the settee in Samantha's room. "Now you can answer my last question. Why do you think this information that you used to go out with Kenny Ross will cause Paris to break up with you?"

"It's like I told Starlet, Paris and I had an understanding that we would be completely open and honest with each other. You know how the Franklin guys are about being transparent and honest in relationships."

"Okay, I do, go on."

"Well, I completely blindsided Paris at the party when Kenny showed up uninvited and informed Paris that we knew each other quite well in college. I had to then tell Paris that Kenny and I dated in college. This was information that I should have relayed to him back when we first started dating and he was under the impression that I had mentioned all the guys that I had dated in college. The bottomline is how I kept that relationship from him because I didn't want him to know how I had made such a lousy choice in dating some loser like Kenny."

"Did you and Kenny ever…?"

"Don't be silly, of course not." Samantha waved her hand as she stepped into a short blue nightie. "I was a fool back then, but not that big of a fool to ever go to bed with Kenny Ross."

"Well, if you didn't go to bed with him maybe Paris will understand."

"Understand what, how I lied to him? I don't think there's any way to make him understand how I misheld the truth from him. The bottomline is that I wasn't truthful with him. I don't think I can make this right. Why should he forgive and forget when he doesn't have too. He can have any woman of his choice and he doesn't have to put up with someone who lied to him. I wish I could start over and correct this stupid mistake that I made but right now I'm at his mercy and can only hope that Paris will not pull the plug on what we have."

"When are you supposed to see him again? Did he invite you to the dinner party at their house tomorrow night?"

Samantha stared at Sabrina with surprise in her eyes. "There's my proof that he's done with me. He didn't mention a dinner party to me."

"It's just a family dinner, but Britain mentioned that Mrs. Franklin had extended invitations to their significant others."

"Well, I must no longer be a significant other to Paris. He didn't invite me. He never mentioned a dinner party."

"I'm surprise he didn't. Starlet mentioned that Sydney invited her," Sabrina relayed.

"Why should it surprise you after what I just told you? I just told you that Paris isn't pleased with me and will probably break up with me."

"So, he'll probably break up with you, but he hasn't broken up with you yet. When is this pending doom supposed to happened?"

"It will probably happen tomorrow morning at brunch. He said we needed to talk and suggested brunch." Samantha threw back the covers and hopped in bed.

"I don't think all is lost. Brunch tomorrow will be your chance to be completely open with Paris and put your cards on the table and let him know your reasons for not telling him about Kenny and convince him how sorry you are and that you'll never withhold anything else from him."

"I'll try but I think I blew it for good with him, goodnight," Samantha reached over and turned off her bedside lamp.

Chapter Seventeen

Paris parked his car in the driveway and killed the engine but he didn't readily get out and head inside. He remained in his car for awhile, reached in his glove compartment and pulled out a photo of Samantha. He looked at the picture in thought and then put the photo back in the glove compartment and rushed out of his car.

Veronica was stirring about as always until all her sons were accounted for. She usually stayed put in her bedroom reading, talking on the phone or watching television until her sons were in for the night. They had no idea of her routine and that she waited up for them because she usually never came downstairs. However, five minutes after Paris quietly took his key, unlocked the front door and stepped inside, Veronica flipped off the television in her room and threw on her robe. She was thirsty for a glass of water and she welcomed the oportunity to inquire how Paris enjoyed his evening at Samantha's house.

As Paris stepped across the large living room floor toward the sofa, he immediately pulled the prince's cape from his shoulders and threw it on the sofa. The living room was dark except for the light of the moon shinning through the window. He dropped down on the sofa, threw both feet on the coffee table and threw both arms behind his head. He was in deep thought about his disappointment with Samantha. However, just moments after staring up at the ceiling in stressful thought about the evening, on went the lights as his mother headed down the long staircase.

"Mother, what are you doing up this time of night? I hope I didn't wake you when I came in," Paris slightly smiled at her.

"I assure you, sweetheart, you did not wake me. I haven't been in bed yet," she said, smiling. "I got caught up in some movie and then noticed it was after one o'clock. I heard Rome come in about five minutes before you." She headed toward the kitchen.

"Rome just got home? I didn't know," Paris mumbled. He thought how his brother would be a good sounding broad to discuss his situation about Samantha.

"Yes, dear, and he's still awake. When I passed his room just now I noticed his light was still on," Veronica said, still in route toward the kitchen.

"Goodnight, Mother; I'm headed upstairs," he said.

"Goodnight, dear," she answered.

Paris hurried up the staircase and down the hallway to Rome's room. He knocked once on his door.

"Come in," Rome said.

Paris cracked the door and peeked his head in. "I know it's late but since you're still burning the midnight oil, do you have a minute?"

"Sure I do," Rome beckoned for him to step inside.

Rome's bedroom was large and spacious just as all the bedrooms. He was sitting in a chair near the fireplace with both feet on a ottoman. It was cool outside and the low fire that crackled in his fireplace felt and sounded soothing.

"What are you doing?" Paris asked as he took a seat in front of the fire.

Rome waved a stack of papers in the air. "Don't' ask me why I'm bothering to look through these job applications at one in the morning." He smiled.

"Okay, I won't ask," Paris grinned. "But you'll probably tell me."

"They ended up in my briefcase by accident and because I can't seem to fall asleep, I just decided to read some of them. I'll take them back to the office on Monday and give them to Sydney." Rome placed the stack of applications on a nearby table as he sat there looking like a rich king wearing a pair of posh navy silk pajamas.

"When did you start having problems falling to sleep?" Paris asked.

Rome glanced at him and smiled. "Since I started dating Courtney. After an evening with her I'm so energized until it's not easy to fall asleep. But usually a nice glass of wine will put me right to sleep, but Courtney and I ended up having an early dinner and we chose not to have wine with dinner; and as you know we didn't show up at the Taylor's Halloween party. We ended up at another house party where they were only serving a dreadfully cheap wine that I couldn't stomach. I didn't get a chance to down one nice glass of wine. Now, I'm still wide awake." He looked at Paris. "But no worries, I'll fall asleep soon. What's on your mind? Usually when you knock on my door this time of night it's usually serious. Last time was a year ago when you were trying to make up your mind about dismissing a worker that you felt you had given enough chances to improve."

"You are right, it is serious, but it's not about work. It's personal." Paris nodded.

"Personal?" Rome paused. "How personal? You have never talked to me about a personal issue. So I know this isn't about some female!" Rome smiled.

"It sort of is about a female." Paris looked at Rome with a serious stare.

"Okay, I can see that you are serious. What's up?" Rome asked.

"It's about Samantha. Something happened tonight that bothered me a lot and I'm not sure I can get past it," Paris stressed.

"What happened? You two have been glued to each other's hip for the past two months. You seemed liked you were hitting it off damn good. She's a beautiful young woman." Rome nodded. "All the Taylor girls are. So, what gives? Did the two of you have your first fight?" Rome asked. "I'm surprised because as I said, the two of you appeared to be getting along well."

"We were; and don't get me wrong. I'm still into her just as much. But I found out tonight at their party that she lied to me about something quite important." Paris shook his head with deep disappointment in his eyes.

"Damn, I was hoping it was anything but a lie," Rome said. "I know a lie is the ultimate betrayal to you."

"Why do you say it's the ultimate betrayal to me? None of us tolerate lies. Britain doesn't, Sydney doesn't and I know you stop dating a few girls because of lies," Paris reminded him.

"That's true, but I think out of the four of us, you stick to your guns more and put up with lies less. I'm not saying I would tolerate a lie from any female, but with you, that's the finish," Rome explained.

"Damn right, that's the finish. One lie is too much as far as I'm concerned."

"Okay, one lie is too much. But what was that one lie? I can't believe Samantha Taylor lied to you. She doesn't seem like the type. What did she lie about, if I can be so bold to ask you again."

"She lied by omission when she didn't tell me about some guy who was and still is a problem drinker that she used to date back in college. I was totally blindsided by this dude when he showed up at the party. This guy is a complete mess and he purposedly quite rudely showed me up in front of a roomful of people. He made my supposedly special girlfriend appear cheap with little respect for herself," Paris stressed. "How am I supposed to process this and look at Samantha in the same way?" Paris held up one finger. "And get this, his name is Kenny Ross; and it turns out he's Courtney's brother. Go figure. Courtney is a beautiful, smart young woman but her brother is a complete idiot as far as I can see."

Rome took both hands and grabbed the back of his neck and stared toward the ceiling for a quick second. "Courtney has a brother who used to date Samantha?" Rome was surprised to hear. He was unaware of this information. He knew Courtney had a brother but had no idea he had dated Samantha.

"What a small universe we are living in," Rome said.

"Too small for me and that drunk!" Paris said sharply.

Rome rubbed his chin and looked at Paris. "I know you are ticked and I would be as well, but remember what Mother said Father said about drunks?"

"There are no drunks?" Paris mumbled and took a deep breath.

"That's right, just individuals with drinking problems."

"And we should hate the disease but sympathize with the disease carrier," Paris said, shaking his head.

"That's right, but I don't expect you to sympathize with some guy who was that disrespectful toward you and Samantha," Rome said. "But as far as his drinking goes that's a disease he's struggling with."

"Yeah, sure, I get that he has a drinking problem, a disease he's dealing with. But it doesn't lessen my disappointment toward Samantha," Paris admitted.

Rome nodded. "Well, I have to admit it is a shocker that Samantha would have been involved with someone so not together. But you need to think long and hard about this," Rome suggested. "Is this a reason enough to break up with her?"

"It's reason enough for me beause she lied to me about it. When we had our talk about who we had dated, she mentioned a few guys from college but Kenny Ross name was never mentioned. She only mentioned it tonight because Kenny showed up at her house uninvited and introduced himself to me," Paris explained. "He was smashed, of course, but seemed pleased about his little announcement."

"What announcement did he make?" Rome asked.

"His announcement to me that Samantha was his girl first," Paris said with deep disappointment in his eyes.

Rome was speechless for a moment, then asked. "Do you think he meant?"

"I'm sure he did, why else would he say that to me in front of Samantha other than to make himself look bigger than the idiot that he is?"

"You are right, that guy is an idiot. To say the least, what he said was totally disrespectful toward Samantha and a low blow to you," Rome frowned. "And if he was as loud and as offensive as I suspect, a few other ears heard him as well."

"I'm sure others heard him. He wasn't the least bit discreet and seemed quite proud to be on display as a wasted loud mouth!"

"He sounds like a real piece of work," Rome said. "Because who walks up to a woman while she's standing with her boyfriend and say something like that? This guy really needs to get back on the wagon before he meets with some man and his fist!"

"I can see him meeting with a fist sooner than later if he keeps making a habit of vulgar rudeness," Paris stated. "He's lucky it wasn't my fist. It took everything in me to keep my composure. I wasn't about to dignify his repulsive behavior with a response of emotions."

"I'm proud of you and I'm sure Father would be to," Rome said. "I know it couldn't have been easy to just stand there and listen to his insults and rudeness. Especially how he slammed Samantha's honor, giving you a low blow along with it."

"Yes, it was a low blow and it came from a falling down drunk! And with all due respect to Father for not referring to someone as a drunk, but in this case I think he would give me a pass," Paris said sharply. "Afterall, that's exactly how Mr. Ross carried on at the party! And that's exactly what I think of him!"

Rome nodded. "I'm sure it is."

Paris shook his head. "You bet, he was so wasted on his ass until he couldn't even walk straight." Paris grabbed his face and paused down at the carpet for a moment. Then he looked at Rome with sad eyes. "It really threw me for a loop because I thought Samantha valued herself more than that, to date someone with no respect for women or himself. I don't need or want to be with someone like that."

"So, your mind is made up? You plan to break up with Samantha?"

After a moment of silence, Paris mumbled in a disappointed voice. "I guess my mind is made up. I'm not pleased about my decision but I feel It's the only one I can make. I don't want my woman to be some female that some jerk refers to as his first. Besides, I thought she hadn't."

Rome nodded. "I think we all thought they hadn't. According to Aunt Catherine and Mother, the Taylor girls are all still virgins, even twenty-four-year-old Sabrina. Its an honorable stance to be commended, but even if a female has not waited it really doesn't matter as long as she's honest and you know what you're getting into. When Courtney and I had a talk about protection I found out about her stance in that department. We haven't gotten to that point in our relationship because of her religious belief; and that's why she's still a virgin. But as far as the

Taylor girls are concerned, Aunt Catherine and Mother read a spread about the Taylor family and the article stated that the Taylor girls are saving themselves for the right fellow. I'm incline to believe the article. Newspaper don't set out to print lies."

Paris took a deep breath. "Well, I guess Kenny Ross was the right fellow in her eyes." He rasied both hands. "I'm done! I'm through! I don't need this headache! Since Samantha isn't who I thought she was. It's best that I found out sooner in this relationship than later," Paris said sadly as he slowly got out of his seat and headed across the room toward the door.

"That's a tough break that the two of you couldn't make a go of it. She's super beautiful and a nice girl. Everybody can see how crazy she is about you," Rome smiled.

Paris stood at the door with his hand on the doorknob. "I know she's beautiful with the face of angel and her eyes are the most beautiful pair I have ever looked into. But if she'll lie about some old boyfriend from college, what else will she lie about? I don't want to be that guy who is lied to by any female."

Chapter Eighteen

Paris pulled into Samantha's driveway that Saturday morning at straight up ten o'clock. He was dressed devinely in a burgundy designer pullover sweater and black dress slacks. He killed his engine, inhaled sharply and slowly got out of the car. As he headed toward the front door, he glanced up to the third level at Samantha window. However, just as he looked up the certains at her windows were pulled closed. He figured Samantha had saw him and was headed downstairs to greet him at the door. He paused at the doorbell before he hit the buzzer. He was nervous and anxious about how he was going to find the right words to break up with Samantha. But as he stood there on her front porch awaiting her beautiful face to greet him, he was surprised when Sabrina answered the door and stepped outside to greet him. She was smiling, dressed neatly in a pair of black leggings and a chic maroon top with delicate lace along the hem line and collar that hung just below her hips.

"Hi Paris, you look real nice this morning," she smiled.

"Thank you; but so do you," he smiled with a curious look in her eyes.

"I know you are wondering why did I come out and not Samantha, but Samantha won't be joining you for brunch this morning. She asked me to come out and give you this." She handed him a letter.

"I see," Paris nodded and held his emotions inside as he politely took the letter.

He didn't ask any questions because he didn't want to make an awkward situation more awkward. "Thanks, Sabrina. Enjoy your day," he said and merely turned and walked away.

Since he was dressed and was looking forward to a Red Skillet meal, he drove to the restaurant anyway. Once he was seated at a table and had drank a cup and a half of coffee, he slowly opened the letter:

Dear Paris, Saturday, November 2, 2013

I'm sorry I didn't have the courage to meet you this morning. I thought about it all night and got up early thinking about it. I couldn't face you telling me goodbye. I could see it in your eyes last night that you were disappointed beyond words with me. I know I was wrong to keep the truth from you about Kenny Ross. I didn't mention that I had dated him because I was too ashamed to admit that I had gone out with such a mess of a guy. But at the time when I first met Kenny he didn't seem such a mess and disrespectful. Otherwise, I never would have gone out with him. We only dated for three weeks and when I saw his true colors I never went out with him again. He lied when he told you I was his girl first. I was never his girlfriend. We went on three dates, to the movies twice and to dinner once. I allowed him to kiss me twice, but only on the side of my face.

I'm so sorry that I didn't tell you about Kenny because I realize now what a huge mistake I made. Especially how he showed up and caught you and me off guard. I was beside myself with nerves and embarrassment when he brought himself to our attention at the party. He was the last person I expected and thought I would never see him again. I can imagine how that made you feel. I wish I could go back and not be a fool to have ever given Kenny the time of day, but it was a huge, foolish mistake that I made; and the biggest mistake was not telling you the truth when I had the opportunity to. You asked me about my ex-boyfriends and I purposedly omitted mentioning Kenny and therefore I lied to you. But I don't want you to think it was easy for me to lie or that it was a casual thing for me. However, the bottomline is that I did lie. But I know as surely as I know the sun will rise, I'll never withhold the truth from you again.

I miss you so much until I'm just sick about the whole thing. We have only dated for a couple months, but I love you so deeply with everything within me. You are everything I have ever wanted in a man. You are the most handsome man I have ever laid eyes on, and your dreamy eyes are out of this world. But besides from your good looks and good manners, there are so many wonderful things about you that make you so uniquely you.

I know I messed up and you probably never want to see me again, but please remember how much you mean to me and how you will be in my heart until the end of time.

I will always love you, Samantha.

After Paris read Samantha letter, he folded the letter and stuck it inside of his wallet. He glanced at his cell phone that sat on the table in front of him and he was tempted to dial Samantha's number. The letter proved that there had been a misunderstanding with Kenny. Samantha had not had a real relationship with him, yet he was still upset that she had lied to him in the first place. Therefore, he sat there and drank his coffee, had a meal and left the restaurant without calling Samantha. When he arrived home around eleven-fifteen that morning Veronica was waiting for him as he walked through the door.

"I wanted to catch you before I left the house," she smiled.

"Sorry I was out of the house so early and missed cook's famous Saturday morning breakfast, but I had plans to meet Samantha for brunch," he said as he walked over and kissed his mother on the cheek.

Veronica smiled at the mention of Samantha's name. "I'm so pleased that you and Sydney and Britain are dating those sweet young ladies. Now, if only Rome would come to his senses and see through that Courtney Ross. She is not the right young lady for him." She shook her head. "But he won't listen to reason as far as that girl is concerned. Besides, he is so stubborn and hardly listens to anything I say. He thinks she's the one." She waved her hand. "But just for my own peace of mind, I checked into Miss Courtney's family background," Veronica shared.

Paris gave her a serious stare. "Mother was that really necessary?"

"Yes, it was necessary to find out a little bit about that young lady's family. I figured I should since your brother is so taken with her," Veronica dropped on the sofa and Paris took a seat on the opposite sofa facing her.

"Okay, what did you find out if anything?" He asked.

"Not much, just that her father, Raymond Ross is a recovering alcoholic. He works as a chef at some Chicago restaurant. Her mother, Mildred, is a high school history teacher in the area. They own an average four-bedroom home here in town."

"Mother, how did you find out all this information about Courtney's family. Who's your source?" Paris asked. "And besides from that have you considered how Rome is going to feel about you checking into Courtney's background?"

"He already knows. I told him and everybody else over breakfast. He wasn't too pleased about it, but he never is pleased about anything I do. However, since he insists on continuing his relationship with the young woman I felt I had no other choice but to find out more about her family background."

"Well, they sound okay from what you have told me. Her father is a chef and her mother is a teacher. That sounds like the average American family. Wouldn't you agree?" Paris asked.

Veronica nodded. "Yes, they are an average American family, but I want more than average for you guys."

"Well, Mother," Paris smiled. "I know you pride yourself in having a say in who we date and go out with. But it's not your call. I know I'm not going to date someone just because you think that person is right for me, if I don't feel that person is right for me," Paris stressed.

"I'm listening, sweetheart and you have a point, but you are my sons and I want the best for you and do not want any of you, especially Rome since he's dating that Courtney, to end up in a relationship with someone that's not worthy of you," Veronica explained.

"Mother, you can not control other people's emotions. You can want the best for us, but in the end we have to decide what that is."

"Look, a great example of jumping into a relationship with the wrong person, is what happened to your Aunt Catherine. Her bad marriage that ended in divorce scarred her for life."

Paris leaned back on the sofa and propped both feet on the coffee table. "So was that it?" he asked.

"Was what it?" she looked at her son.

"So, was that it on the Ross family? You discovered he's a chef and she's a teacher. Are you pleased now? Did you satisfy your curiousity and will now welcome Courtney into our home?" Paris smiled.

"That young lady is welcome here. She has been here a number of times, you know that."

"Yes, she has been here a number of times, but you don't really say that much to her as you do with Sabrina, Samantha and Starlet. Why is that, Mother?" Paris looked inquisitively at his mother.

Veronica glanced at Paris and then fussed with the hem of her suit jacket. "Maybe I don't say as much to Courtney as I do the other girls, but…"

"Mother, I haven't heard you say anything other than hello to Courtney."

Veronica shifted in her seat before she answered. "I'm sure I have said more than that. I just find myself more drawn to the Taylor girls. I guess I just don't have that much in common with Courtney." She paused. "By the way, she has a younger sister by the name of Trina who works at the station and an older brother by the name of Kenny who waits tables at the restaurant where his father works. Apparently Kenny drinks like a fish and in less than a year has racked up two DUI's. I guess it runs in the family," she hopped off the sofa and grabbed her purse that sat beside her and headed toward the front door. "I'm headed to the supermarket to pick up a few things for this evening dinner."

When she reached the front door, she grabbed the doorknob and then looked around at Paris. "You will be at dinner this evening?" she hollered across the room.

Paris nodded. "I'll be there."

"Good, it's always a pleasure to see you and Samantha together so happy," Veronica said, stepping out the door.

Chapter Nineteen

Later that morning just past noon, a slight breeze stirred in the air with the bright sun lending a bit of warmth overhead, Britain and Sabrina were walking along the grounds behind the Taylor estate. They were dressed warmly, holding hands, headed toward the clearwater pond at the edge of the property. The little duck pond was surrounded by tall evergreens and along the banks were small bush evergreens. Two steel silver benches sat a slight distant beneath a tall tree and Sabrina and Britain leisurely headed toward the seats.

Britain looked especially stylish in a short grey exclusive windbreaker, grey slacks and black shirt. Sabrina was dressed in a long below the knees auburn print skirt and tan pullover sweater, finished off with a short rust jacket.

"Mother said dinner will be served at six. Is it okay if I pick you up at 5:30?"

"Sure, I'll be ready. Should I dress up for dinner or is it a casual dinner?"

Britain smiled. "There's no such thing as a casual dinner at my house."

"So, I should dress up just as I would if we were going out to dinner?"

"Well, sure, why not?"

"Why not, based on what you just said I figured it was required."

He held out both arms. "You should probably dress up since my mother is hosting this meal. Believe me, she will most likely expect everyone to be dressed for dinner as usual." He gave her a long stare as he nodded, smiling. "Seriously, you don't want to risk it." He smiled.

"Risk what?"

"Risk my mother giving you the eye."

Sabrina smiled. "I don't get what you're getting at."

"I'm just simply saying, please dress for the occasion."

"Which is a meal at your house?"

"Yes, it's a meal at my house, but its a special dinner party that my mother is hosting. When a project is hers, she expect everything to be just so." He grinned. "You'll have to get to know my mother, and once you do, you'll see how particular she is about almost everything. It's just the way she is. We all try to accommodate her since we realize it hasn't been easy on her all these years raising us on her own."

Suddenly Sebrina thought of the dinner and the dinner guests and became a bit distracted as she thought how much she didn't want to run into Courtney at Britain's house. She stared out across the grounds as Britain talked. He noticed that she was suddenly rather quiet. He looked down to find her looking out across the grounds as if she hadn't heard anything he had just said about his mother. He leaned down and kissed the side of her face. Then he stopped in his tracks and she stopped and looked at him. They faced each other. He smiled at her and she half smiled at him with a preoccupied look in her eyes.

"Is anything the matter? You seem a bit quiet," Britain pushed aside one hanging curl that the wind had blew covering her right eye. "I hope you are not bothered about dressing for dinner. Of course, you can wear whatever you want. Besides, you could wear a plastic bag and still be the prettiest girl in the room."

"You wouldn't be a little bias would you?" She looked at him and smiled.

"Maybe just a little, but don't fret about what to wear to my house for dinner."

"I'm not fretting about that. I actually like dressing up for dinner. We dress up at my house for some meals. So it's not about that, but it is about the dinner."

"What about the dinner?" Britain asked inquiringly.

Sabrina nodded. "Rome's girlfriend, Courtney, will probably be there, right?"

"Most likely she will. Is that the what you wanted to say?"

She nodded. "Yes, it is. After you brought up the subject of your mother's dinner party, it dawned on me that Courtney Ross would be there."

"Courtney being there is troubling you for some reason?" he asked.

"I guess it is sort of," she answered.

"Why does the thought of Courtney's presence trouble you?" he asked curiously. "Besides, why are you thinking about that dinner and its guests?" He held out his arms. "When you have something a lot nicer to think about like your present company."

"I know it's silly," she said. "But I get the feeling that Rome's girlfriend just doesn't like me," Sabrina explained.

"What makes you say that?" Britain asked concernly.

"She doesn't talk to me."

"What do you mean by that," he asked.

"I mean when we are in the same room at different functions, she doesn't talk to me. She'll say hello but nothing more. She doesn't talk to Samantha or Starlet either."

Britain nodded in her eyes. "I'm sorry. I wasn't aware that Courtney wasn't socializing with you."

"Britain, why do you make it sound like your problem? She just doesn't want to talk to me, I guess," Sabrina mumbled. "There's no law that says she has to talk to me just because she and I are dating brothers. It just feels a little uncomfortable being around her when she gives me the impression that she's awkward being around me as if she hates me for some reason."

Britain leaned against a tall tree with his arms folded. "Sabrina, again, I'm sorry if Courtney is giving you the cold shoulder. However, I seriously doubt that she hates you. Believe me, Courtney Ross is a nice person and I seriously doubt that she could ever hate anyone," he said sincerely.

"I know she works for your business and I agree, she does seem nice; but am I missing something? You seem to know her quite well to praise her so assuredly."

"This is true. I do know her quite well." He paused and stared at Sabrina for a moment. "I should tell you something." He inhaled sharply.

"Tell me what?"

"It's about a huge misunderstanding that took place between me and Courtney before I met you. But, I think now is a good time for me to tell you about what happened. It's not that it's really significant, but since you have brought up the fact that you feel awkward around Courtney, sensing that she feels awkward around you, that's why I'm going to tell you," he said seriously.

"You don't mean you and she used to date?" She grabbed her mouth.

"No, we never dated. We were just friends," he said casually.

"If you were just friends, what was the misunderstanding?" Sabrina asked.

"That we were just friends," he said. "We started out that we would sit and talk in the work cafeteria sometimes. Then she started saving a seat for me and when I would walk into the lunchroom she would wave for me letting me know she had a seat waiting for me. I didn't mind. She was very attractive and good company. Then I looked around and we were having lunch together nearly everyday."

"What would the two of you talk about?" Sabrina narrowed her eyes at Britain.

"Nothing in particular. Maybe work stuff. We were just friends but she read more into it." Britain shook his head. "Long story short, she felt I led her on and when she saw me having lunch with you on the first day you visited me at work, she felt I had stood her up on her birthday," he said regretfully.

"That day you invited me over for a tour and lunch, you already had a luncheon date with her? Her birthday no doubt."

"Yes, it was. However, when I invited you it had completely slipped my mind that I had already made lunch plans with her," he said apologetically. "What can I say in my own defense of being absence minded?"

"I don't know, what can you say?" Sabrina smiled.

He held out both arms. "I was so pleased that you had agreed to drop by until I probably would have gotten my own name," he teased.

"Thanks for the compliment," she blushed, looking in his eyes.

"But seriously, it completely slipped my mind that it was Courtney's birthday and that I had promised to take her out and show her a nice time," he explained. "I was going to take her to Franklin House and the works." He nodded. "And get this, while you and I were sitting there having lunch it felt like she was sort of looking our way; but I was enjoying your company too much for any distraction. Never-the-less, I tore my sights off of you for a second and I looked at her. I waved at her and we exchanged smiles but it still didn't register that she was sitting there expecting me to have lunch with her. Besides, I was already having lunch with you, but if it had crossed my mind I could have walked over and apologized or asked her to join us," he explained remorsefully. "It only dawned on me after lunch when I noticed the date circled on my desk calendar. But still I had made plans with you for the evening. So, as the gentleman that I am, I went downstairs to explain and apologize but she was in a mood and didn't want to talk to me."

"If you were just friends, why were you going to do all of that with her and take her to your house?" Sabrina asked curiously.

"She had mentioned how she always wanted to see the inside of Franklin House so I was going to do the honors of showing it to her as a birthday gift, along with introducing her to my mother as one of my friends. She was excited about it when I told her all of this, but later I found out that she took it all to mean something that it didn't," he explained regrettably. "Long story short, having lunch at her table, oblivious to her real feelings, for two months straight was not the best idea. She was livid with me for forgetting her birthday and not taking her out as I had promised. It caused a major headache at the workplace for a quick second."

"I can see how she could have gotten the wrong impression. Some gorgeous guy spending his time at her lunch table everyday, and then decides to take her out on her birthday to introduce to his mother. I would have gotten the wrong idea as well."

"Maybe, but I never said anything the least bit romantic to her, but nevertheless, that incident caused a lot of tension between us at work for awhile. It wasn't pretty and quite awkward, until Courtney finally realized it was all just a big misconception. I was her friend and not her boyfriend."

"Okay, based on what you have said, Courtney was under the impression the whole time that you two were more than friends. Of course, you thought you were just friends but she thought the two of you were more than friends?"

"That's the scope of it," Britain nodded. "So, if she's not talking to you, she most likely feels awkward."

"But why would I make her feel awkward, you're the one she was ticked at?"

"But she probably thought you knew about the misunderstanding that happened between us. Courtney is probably more embarrassed about it than anything elsle," he pointed out. "She probably thinks you don't want to talk to her."

"She seems nice and I wouldn't mind getting to know her better," Sabrina said. "It would make gatherings a lot less awkward for us."

"That's for sure," he agreed.

"But something seems out of sorts here," Sabrina said and stared at Britain curiously. "Courtney is quite attractive and I know you know that." She paused and narrowed her eyes at him. "So, seriously, why didn't you ask her out?"

Britain smiled. "She is pretty, I agree. However, when she was first hired the grapevine was loud with rumors about how she had a crush on Rome. And when we first started talking I could tell she was into Rome." Britain nodded. "Plus, Rome made no secret of his attraction toward her. He didn't approach her at that time or ask her out, but it was obvious to us that she was into him and he was into her."

"So, what you are saying is Courtney liked Rome when she first started having lunch with you?"

"That's right." He nodded. "We actually started conversing because she would walk up to me from time to time and ask about Rome. I actually think she initially wanted to talk to me just to get closer to him."

"That's hard to believe that she was into Rome when she got so upset with you for not being into her when you forgot her birthday?"

"I guess by then she thought she was into me," he mumbled. "I'm not a shrink but what she thought she felt for me was what she actually felt for Rome, because when he ran to her rescue they connected instantly." He nodded. "All well that ends well."

Sabrina shook her head. "I beg to differ that what she felt for you was actually what she felt for Rome. No, I think she really liked you for awhile. Otherwise, she wouldn't have been so upset that you forgot her birthday. Maybe she had stronger feelings for Rome, but she had fallen for you for awhile as well," Sabrina explained.

"Maybe she did for awhile, but it was probably no more than a crush since she was pinning away for Rome. As I said, from day one on the job, it was obvious that she was into Rome. She was always asking about him when he wasn't around and when he was around she was constantly finding a reason to be in his office," Britain explained.

Sabrina smiled. "Well, Rome is very good-looking. But so are you and all of your brothers." She held up one finger. "So you are telling me that you didn't ask Courtney ask because she was into Rome? But you shared your lunch with her nearly every day and you promised to take her out on her birthday. You are rich."

"I have been called that a few times." He smiled.

"I don't mean rich with wealth, which I know you are, I'm referring to your overwhelming compassion," Sabrina said in awe of his empathy.

Britain smiled. "Thanks for that compliment. But if I was as compassionate as my father was then that would be something. But back to the point of why I continued to have lunch with Courtney." He rubbed his chin and paused. "At the time, I figured why not? She seemed so pleased whenever I would. It especially seemed to make her happy. Besides, she was easy to look at and I was not attached then. But honestly, I never entertained the thought of her in a romantic way. But the biggest hinder of all."

She interrupted and finished his sentence. "You thought she was into Rome?"

"That's correct, I knew how much she was infatuated with Rome and pinning away for him. I guess somewhere in the back of my mind, I wanted to show her that at least one Franklin guy could make her happy." He held up both hands. "Not as a boyfriend but as a friend," he explained. "I was going to show her a birthday that she would never forget, and then I forgot; some good deeder I turned out to be."

"I'm still a bit confused over this would be triangle," Sabrina mumbled.

"What are you confused about?"

"Confused about how you were not interested in Courtney Ross. She is very attractive and even though she liked Rome and he liked her, apparently she wasn't aware of his attraction. You could have easily dated her since she really wasn't dating or even talking to your brother on any non-professional level at that time."

Britain nodded and stared into Sabrina's eyes. "Yes, this is true. But all else aside, as lovely as Courtney Ross is, she's not really my type."

Sabrina eyes wided and she smiled up at him. His six foot frame towering over her five foot four frame. "You have a type? What type is that?"

"I'm looking at her." He leaned down and kissed her softly and then pulled her in his arms and swallowed her up in a passionate kiss before their lips parted.

"So, what is it about me that makes me your type?" she asked.

He narrowed his charming eyes at her. "Are you putting me on the spot?"

"No, I just would like to know. If a pretty girl like Courtney Ross isn't your type, but I am, I would like to know why. I'm not trying to put you on the spot."

"Yes, you are," he teased. "You want me to tell you all the different ways I find you irresistible." He smiled and winked at her.

"Okay, maybe I am putting you on the spot a little, but I would like to know mainly because you mentioned that I'm your first real girlfriend. Besides, how could some gorgeous man like you not get roped in by some man killer female?" She laughed.

"I just did and I'm looking at her," he teasted.

She hit his arm in a playful manner. "Stop teasing and just tell me what it is about me that makes me your type, and someone as pretty as Courtney not your type?"

He leaned down and placed his lips over hers and swallowed her up in a demanding passionate kiss. When he pulled away she was breathless and unsteady.

"What was that for?" She smiled.

"That was to get you ready for the next step."

"What next step?"

"What I'm about to say." He massaged the side of her neck. "You still want to know why you are my type, right?"

"Yes, tell me already," she insisted with love pouring from her eyes.

"For one, just for argument sake, Courtney is a pretty young lady; and not that looks are everything, but you are more than pretty, Sabrina." He held her face with both hands as he looked down in her eyes. "You are beaming in here." He pointed to her chest. "And all that shines through to make you radiant. Have you ever really looked in the mirror at yourself?"

"So, I'm your type because I'm radiant, whatever that means?" She gave him a quick kiss on the side of the face.

"It means you are one complete package." He took his hands and held out two of her long black curls on either side. "I'm also partial to long hair," he whispered.

"Any girl can let her hair grow out," Sabrina answered.

"I have a thing for long hair, but my type is the type who actually love wearing their hair long, not just to please me but to please herself."

"And you think I wear my hair long just to please myself?"

"I think that exactly." He grabbed her face again with both hands and kissed her forehead and then her neck and back up to her lips, where he lingered.

"You are right," she mumbled between kisses. "I have always worn my hair long. Starlet and Samantha never let their hair grow much past their shoulders, but I just never let the stylish cut more than an inch each time I visit. I usually like to keep it right above my waist." She reached out and touched one of his waves. "I love your hair too. It's nice and almost as long as mine."

"I have always worn it this way. I figured once I finished college that I would probably cut it, but it's sort of my trademark. I like wearing it this way." Britain smiled.

"You and your brothers have such beautiful hair in those natural waves."

Britain nodded. "Yes, we all have the big loose waves in our hair, which is bascially a gift from our father. But if you have noticed, my mother hair is also slightly wavy." He reached out and grabbed her hand and pulled her in his arms. "You feel perfect right here next to me." He kissed her neck. "Now let's get back to why you are my type. Do you really want to hear more?" he whispered against her neck.

She stared up in his eyes and smiled. "Yes, I'm curious."

"Why are you curious?" He winked at her.

"Because you're so…"

"I'm so what?"

"You're so indescribably good-looking and also…," she said laughingly.

"And also what?" he whispered, gently carassing her left cheek with the back of his hand as he brought his face down to hers, giving her a passionate kiss and then pulled away leaving her breathless in his arms as she stood there looking up in his eyes.

"So, are you going to finish your sentence?" He teased. "And also what…?"

"Also sexy, smart and fun to be with," she said in a whisper.

"Okay, since I'm all that to you, I think the least I can do is to tell you why you are my type," he whispered. "You are my type because you are a promise I made to myself when I was twenty-one."

"I'm a promise you made to yourself, how so?" she asked.

"While we were all in college, me and my brothers, we dated a lot. But frankly, none of us ever had an official girlfriend. Then one of my college buddies asked me one day was I ever going to go steady with someone." He paused and gave her a long stare.

"Well, what did you say to him?"

"My exact words to him were, when I meet the most beautiful girl in the world I'll make her mine. It was a joke at the time, but now you are here and it's not a joke. It's a reality. You are simply the most beautiful woman I have ever laid eyes on."

"You think so, do you?"

"No, I do not think so, I know so," he whispered, covering her mouth with his in a hungry lingering kiss that left them breathless before he walked her back to her door.

Chapter Twenty

At dinner that evening while gathered at the dinning room table, Veronica looked toward Paris and smiled. "Where's Samantha, is she not feeling well?"

Paris exchanged looks with Rome and Starlet and Sabrina exchanged looks with each other and then glanced down at the table.

"Dear, why are you looking at your brother?" She smiled. "I'm the one who asked that question. Where's Samantha this evening? Why isn't she joining us?"

"I didn't ask her to join us," Paris mumbled just as their cook, Natalie, was placing a salad on the dish in front of him.

Veronica frowned and kept her comment until the cook had placed salads on everyone plates. The moment she headed out of the dinning room, Veronica placed her eyes on Paris again. "I specifically asked all of you to invite your dates here this evening. I see your brothers complied. Maybe you didn't hear me," she said as everyone was busy eating their salads.

Rome glanced toward his mother. He hoped to change the subject to give Paris a break and he didn't want Courtney to feel more uneasiness than what she already felt.

"Mother, this salad is tasty." He took his fork and lifted a chunk of apple from the salad and placed in his mouth. "The chopped apples really enhances the flavor."

"You can thank Natalie for that," Veronica solemnly said as she wasn't pleased that Paris wasn't talking. She could sense something wasn't quite right. But she didn't say anything else to Paris at the dinner table. She didn't want to appear so inquisitive in the presence of the other three dates.

After dinner, while they were all gathered in the family room, Britain, Sydney, Sabrina and Starlet were seated on one of the sofas looking through photo albums. Rome and Courtney were standing at the bar mixing a cocktail: seven-up with red wine. Paris was busy across the large room at the stereo stand. He had a handful of music CDs trying to decide which one to play. Rome glanced across the room, spotted him and touched Courtney on the shoulder.

"I'll be right back. I need to talk to Paris for a second." He took a sip from his mixed drink of red wine and seven-up. "This isn't half bad. Actually it's pretty good. Good idea." He winked at Courtney, placed the glass back on the counter and headed across the room toward Paris.

By the time Rome reached Paris on the other side of the room, Paris had just popped a CD in the stereo and the song "Locked Out of Heaven" by Bruno Mars was playing smoothly and balanced through the room.

Rome tapped Paris on the shoulder just as he placed the other stack of CDs on the shelf. Paris looked over his shoulder with a grave look on his face. "What's up? Is the music okay?" He asked as he continued to orderly stack the CDs back on the shelf.

"Yes, the music is okay, but what about you?" Rome asked.

Paris turned and faced Rome with his arms folded and before he could answer, Britain and Sydney were both standing on either side of Rome.

"Yeah, man, what's up with you and Samantha?" Britain asked. "I know something is up because I asked Sabrina and she nodded that something was the matter but she didn't feel it was her place to say what it was."

"But you felt it was your place to ask her?" Paris snapped.

Britain smiled. "Yes, I did after how you clammed up with Mother when she asked about Samantha at dinner. It's obvious there's a problem."

"Yeah, yeah, I know I did clam up; and excuse my rudeness, but no way did I want to get into my business with Mother at dinner." Paris shook his head.

Britain held up both hands. "Whatever it is, I hope it works out; but look, I get it if you don't want to talk about it."

"I get it to," Sydney glanced over his shoulder and spotted Veronica chatting with Sabrina and Starlet. "But listen, man, whatever is going on with you and Samantha, you can bet Mother is not going to let it go until she knows every detail."

Rome shook his head. "That's the truth."

"So good luck with what's going on with you and Samantha." Sydney nodded. "And you'll need even more luck trying to keep it from Mother." Sydney winked at Paris, and then he and Britain headed back across the room to rescue Sabrina and Starlet from Veronica.

Rome stayed behind with Paris but winked and waved across the room toward Courtney who was still standing at the bar nursing her mixed red wine and seven-up cocktail. She felt out of place and alone as Rome was busy with Paris. Sabrina and Starlet wasn't communicating or socializing with her and she felt awkward and didn't know what to say or how to approach them. Although she still somewhat blamed Sabrina for destroying her friendship with Britain, she wanted to move on beyond her hostility and make an attempt at becoming friends with Sabrina and her sisters. She had decided that if they didn't make the effort to be social with her, she was going to make the effort to be social with them. She was too pleased to have Rome in her life to feel any resentment or hostility toward Sabrina or anyone else.

"Did you meet Samantha for brunch as you had planned?" Rome cautiously asked, hoping Paris would open up.

Paris nodded. "As planned I went to pick her up but she didn't end up joining me after all. When I arrived at her door to pick her up, she sent Sabrina out of the house with a note for me."

"A note?" Rome asked.

"Yes, a note." Paris reached inside of his back pocket and pulled out his wallet and romoved the note. He handed it to Rome.

After Rome read the note he handed it back to Paris. "Sounds like a big misunderstanding to me."

"Yeah, I think so," Paris agreed.

"Okay, if you feel that way have you called Samantha?"

"No, I haven't called her yet."

"So, I guess you will. She's really into you, you know." Rome encouraged him. "And since she really didn't have a relationship or go to bed with Kenny Ross the two of you can pick up where you left off. You can sit around and stare at each other playing kissy face all while you're together," Rome teased.

"That's not what we do." Paris smiled for the first time during the evening.

"I beg to differ. It is what you two do. You can't keep your hands off of each other," Rome laughed.

"Speak for yourself. I see how you and Courtney are all over each other. Besides, you probably got me and Samantha confused with Sydney and Starlet. They are the ones who are always showing affection in public," Paris said.

"Maybe they do, but I'm not confused. Everybody knows how you and Samantha stares into each other eyes all while you're together," Rome kept teasing.

"Whatever; it still doesn't change the facts," Paris stated seriously.

"What facts?"

"The fact that she lied to me. I get that she didn't have a relationship with Kenny Ross or go to bed with the guy, but she still lied by omission. How am I supposed to get pass that and trust her as if it never happened?"

"You just do; you start with a clean slate."

Paris nodded. "I supposed you're right; a clean slate from this day on and hope we never run into another snag of this magnitude in our relationship."

Rome smiled. "I'm sure you won't. She made a mistake. Samantha is a very lovely young woman who's miserable without you and you're miserable without her. You need to fix this before too much time goes by," Rome suggested strongly.

They both glanced around and spotted their mother headed across the room toward them. Paris glanced at his watch and it was seven-thirty on the nose. "Mother is headed this way. You deal with her, there's somewhere I need to be and something I need to do." He nodded and smiled at Rome, and then turned on his shiny black Louis Vuitton shoe heels and hurried toward the back entrance.

Paris didn't dial Samantha's phone number to inform her that he was headed over, he just jumped in his car and drove next door to her house. Samantha was lying across the bed trying to read a fashion magazine to pass the time, but she only managed to read a few pages before she closed the book and dropped it to the side of the bed. She was too saturated with misery over her fight with Paris to concentrate on reading.

She was home alone. Her parents and grandparents were out and Sabrina and Starlet were at Franklin House. She quickly hopped off the bed at the sound of a car engine pulling into her driveway. She ran to her bedroom window and pulled the curtains back and her heart skipped a beat when she saw Paris shiny blue car outside. The engine was still running and he was still seated inside of his car. She wondered if he would get out and ring the doorbell to visit her. She ran to the dresser and looked at herself and she felt she looked presentable in the long peach skirt and peach top that she was wearing. She had cried most of the evening, but her eyes didn't look puffy. She had felt miserable being home alone thinking about Paris and the disarray she had caused in their relationship while they were all having a nice dinner at Franklin House. She wasn't invited because she had disappointed Paris. She was praying and hoping that they could get pass their problem and make up.

Although he had not rung the doorbell, Samantha ran down the staircase to be near the door just in case he did. She paced anxiously in front of the fireplace wondering why he had pulled into her driveway if it wasn't to get out of the car and see her. She thought that maybe he was writing her a letter to leave in the mailbox, but just as she headed toward the living room window to lookout, the doorbell sounded. She rushed to the door to open it.

She slowly pulled opened the door to his tall, slender, handsome frame.

"Hello, Samantha," he said with a straight face. "You look beautiful."

"Hi, Paris, thank you, you do too," she uttered with a smile. "Please come in."

He stepped inside and she closed the door. He didn't walk into the body of the living room; he stayed at the entrance of the room with his hands in his jacket pocket.

"We need to talk," he said to her.

She nodded. "I know we do and I'm glad you came over so we can." She stretched out her hand toward the sofa. "Would you like to have a seat?"

Without answering, he headed toward the long white sofa. He took a seat on the sofa and she took a seat on the opposite sofa facing him; and after a bit of silence with the two of them looking at each other, Paris said.

"I read your letter and realize I owe you an apology."

"I'm sorry too," Samantha cried, but quickly wiped her tears with her fingers. "What I kept from you was foolish and made no sense to do. I'm ashamed of myself for not being completely open with you about something so petty. I'll never do something like that again. I love you with all my heart and I have been so miserable without you. You are the man I have waited for all my life. It's you, Paris," she cried.

"To be completely frank, I have been miserable without you as well. But I'm still not over your deception," he said with sad eyes.

"But you just said you owe me an apology."

"Yes, I owe you an apology for jumping to the wrong conclusion. But one fact is the same. You chose to lie to me when you had the opportunity to be truthful. I don't know how to get past that one lie. I know it shouldn't matter so much because nobody is perfect and we all make mistakes, but its right in the pit of my stomach and I can't seem to shake it."

"Where does that leave us? I love you so much and I don't want to lose you," Samantha uttered sadly. "If I do lose you I will hate myself forever and I won't think I'm worth that much of anything. If I lose you on my own accord I'll never forgive myself," she cried.

"Why are you saying something like that?" he asked. "I'm the one who needs to get a grip. Samantha, I blame myself for putting you up so high on a pedestal. You were that one special dream girl in my mind that had lived a sheltered life and untouched by the average things like lies and secrets. You were the girl of my dreams that I had always wanted to meet but didn't think anyone like you existed. I put you up so high and that vision I carried of you were my reality of you. Then Kenny Ross showed up and said you were his girl first. That shattered my illusion and the illusion that I fell in love with doesn't really seem to exist. Now I have to try to fit you in my heart along with the illusion I thought you were. I have never felt instant chemistry and emotion for a female the way I felt for you on the first night we met. In my eyes you are an angel and now that I know you are not I'm having a problem with accepting you as a regular person as the rest of us."

As Paris was talking, they heard a car pull into the driveway. They stayed seated, figuring it was probably her parents arriving home. But minutes later the doorbell rung and their cook, Carrie Westwood, appeared in the room and rushed to answer the door. Moments after answering the door she stepped across the enormous living room where Samantha and Paris were seated.

"Excuse me, Miss Samantha, there's a Kenny Ross at the door to see you."

Samantha was stunned as her heart reached up to her throat with anxiety of what Kenny could want. He had already caused a problem between Paris and her, but she kept her composure in their cook's presence.

"Thanks Carrie, I'll take it from here," she said to Carrie and exchanged looks with Paris.

After Carrie exited the room, Samantha looked at Paris. "I have no idea why he has showed up here like this. I'll send him away."

Paris stood as she stood. "No, don't send him away. Invite him in. I would like to hear what he has to say." He nodded.

Samantha went to the door and asked Kenny to come in. Kenny stepped into the living room and he seemed completely different from the falling down drunk he had been the night before. He was clean shaven and he was wearing a pair of neatly pressed blue jeans and a neatly pressed black shirt. However, when he spotted Paris standing there he didn't seem surprise. And after Samantha closed the door, before she could say a word to Kenny he raised both arms.

"I'm here to apologize to you both. I knew you were here, man. I wanted to face you both and say how sorry I am about my drunken rude disgusting behavior last night. I didn't mean to cause a problem. Courtney told me what trouble I caused for you two," he said regretfully.

Samantha exchanged looks with Paris and stared with confusion in her eyes. "Courtney Ross, your brother's girlfriend is…?"

"She's his sister," Paris answered, looking straight at Kenny. "I had a talk with Rome last night and he most likely shared it with Courtney what an appalling scene you caused at the party."

Kenny looked at Samantha. "Please accept my apology. It was appalling. I was out of line to say you were mine before you were his. Because the truth is, you were never mine. You went out to dinner with me once and to the movies with me twice when we were in college, but only after I told you a boatload of lies just to get your attention. And although you let me kiss you goodnight twice, it was just a kiss on the cheek. That is hardly considered a real kiss. I'm sorry my liquor made me show up and show out!" He stepped across the room to the fireplace and stared into the low flames for a moment. Then he stepped back across the room to face them. "The truth is I'm an alcoholic and I was on top of the world at that party, filled with every kind of booze I could get my hands on. I purposely crashed your party to show you both up because I was feeling sorry for myself that I was never worthy of a special girl as yourself," he said sincerely and paused.

Samantha stood there with both hands covering her cheeks. Paris stood there with his arms folded. They were both engrossed and surprised by Kenny's confession as Kenny continued.

"Samantha, you are the most beautiful woman I have ever met and I know I'm not worthy of you. And, the way I see you, I don't feel there's a man alive that is worthy of a woman like you. You are the type of woman that is an illusion in most men's dreams. We dare to hope or seek for someone like you because we know that person doesn't exist.

But in reality you do exist. You were the most precious girl at college, but you took pity on me and allowed me to take you out to the movies twice. Deep down I think you did that because you felt sorry for me and you care so deeply for others. You stood up in class and read a paper on the kindness of others and how it can help heal the world. Your beliefs and causes are things I believe in too and to listen to you read that back in college touched me. Your essay consisted of your belief system and all the causes you wanted to help and make a different with. You spoke about how you wanted to donate your efforts and money to feed the hungry and help world peace. You recited to the class how you wanted to make a difference and help promote civil rights and equal rights for women. After you read your essay, you stood in front of the class and asked us all to do our share in an effort to help feed and shelter those who needed it. Miss Samantha Taylor, you left a remarkable profound awareness on my heart and I have never forgotten you because I have endless respect for you. I have such respect for you that the rude, heartless, drunken incident that hurt you last night has prompted me to seek help for my drinking. I have vowed to never take another drink. If my drinking can cause me to hurt someone like you, I don't want it," he said with conviction, took his finger and made a cross on his chest.

By now, Samantha and Paris were standing side by side facing Kenny as Kenny continued.

"Paris, you are a lucky man to have been blessed with a woman like Samantha Taylor. And to see her for the truly angel that she is; and you probably think she's an illusion but she's not an illusion she's real. She's out of this world and she has chosen you which means she sees something in you that no other man could ever see in another's eyes that would hold the heart of a woman like Samantha," he said seriously and turned and headed toward the door. He glanced over his shoulder. "That's it. That's what I came to say."

Paris and Samantha were stunned and didn't know what to say to Kenny. He had proven to be a bigger man than they had thought he was. He walked across the living room to let himself out. As he gripped the doorknob Paris and Samantha exchanged looks and hurried across the room to follow him out. When they stepped outside Kenny had both hands propped on his car leaning face down at the driver's door. His 2010 black Mustang was parked behind Paris's car. He was leaning there trying to collect himself after his emotional confession, and when he grabbed the door handle, Paris tapped him on the shoulder.

"Thank you, Kenny, for coming here today and talking to us, in the respectful thoughtful manner that you did. Your talk really helped us and cleared up a lot of things. I realize I was wrong about you. I can tell you are a decent guy who is fighting a disease that overtook you last night; and now you are giving it up. I want you to know that you have my support." Paris gave him his business card. "The things that you believe in that touched you because Samantha believes in them; those are values and causes that I believe in as well. They are also the kind of values and causes that my father lived by. So, if you ever find yourself out of work, don't hesitate to come to Franklin Gas and ask for me."

"Thank you, man. That means a lot." Kenny took the business card and looked at it for a second and then placed it in his shirt pocket.

Paris stepped away from the car as Kenny hopped in and started the engine.

"Thank you, Kenny," Samantha said.

Kenny nodded. "You both are welcomed. I should be thanking you for making me realize that drinking was destroying my life. I plan to go to my first AA alcoholics anonymous meeting tomorrow. Vickie has agreed to help me through this. She's a good woman and now with the lack of booze I'll be able to appreciate her more."

After Kenny drove away, Samantha and Paris stood in the driveway and stared at each other smiling, basking in the glow of surprised satisfaction of Kenny Ross's visit.

"Should we go inside and finish our talk?" Samantha asked.

Paris shook his head. "No need for that. I think it's all been said," he said seriously without giving her an indication where they stood.

"Okay," she uttered nervously. "Where does that leave us?"

He smiled at her. "It leaves us right where we are, standing here looking at each other, thinking about how crazy we are about each other." He glanced at his watch. "Now there's only one thing left to do," he stated and headed toward his car.

Samantha stood there with her heart in her throat wondering if he was leaving her for good. She wanted to say something but the words wouldn't come out.

He reached for his door handle and glanced over his shoulder. "Why are you standing there? Come hop in."

She hurried toward the car and stopped at the front of the hood. "But I thought you were…"

"You thought I was what?" he asked.

"I thought you were leaving after you said there's only one thing left to do."

"And you thought that one thing was to walk away from you?"

"It did cross my mind."

He stepped over to her and grabbed her face with both hands and looked down at her. "The one thing I'm referring to is food. We need to find a place that's still serving dinner. I couldn't eat my meal earlier and I'm sure you probably couldn't eat as well. So, what do you say? You want to go grab something to eat?"

"Yes, I would love too," she said lost in his eyes. "So does this mean we are good and you can get over how I didn't tell you about going out with Kenny in college?"

He brought his mouth down on hers and kissed her urgently as if he had never kissed her before. His kiss reached the depth of her as if he needed her kiss to breathe. When he pulled away from her lips, he smiled. "Yes, we are good; as a matter of a fact we are perfect. As of this moment on, there's nothing to forgive. You did nothing wrong, and I had my head in the clouds. I'm back down to earth and hope you can forgive me for being such a stubborn bastard about the whole big misunderstanding. It took a guy struggling with alcoholism to come over here and set me straight about what a treasure I have in you."

Samantha touched his smooth face. "I know I was pleasantly shocked by Kenny's visit and his beautiful words. It was as if God sent him to my door to show us both how to look inside of our hearts to see how blessed we are to have each other," she said heartfelt. "But sweetheart, all the same, you didn't know if what he was saying was lies when he was drunk and saying them."

Paris kissed her forehead and then he kissed the side of her face and then swallowed her up in a quick passionate kiss before he pulled away from her lips and looked at her with deep desire in his eyes. "But I should have known. My heart knew but deep down in my soul I was hanging on to the possibility because that's the kind of world we live in and I figured you couldn't be who I thought you were because who I thought you were was an illusion. But you are not an illusion, you are who you are; and who you are is who I thought you were."

"Paris you are everything to me. When I said I loved you when we were talking inside. I meant that. I do love you so much." She gazed lovingly up in his eyes as he held her face with both hands gazing lovingly in hers.

"So, you think you are in love, do you?" he teased her. "And do you think you are the only one." He winked at her.

"I'm not sure, am I?" she asked.

"No, you're not alone in that emotion." He patted his chest. "This is where you live," he said and wrapped her in another passionate kiss before the sound of a passing car in the distant broke their kiss.

He glanced at his watch. "We should probably find some food before everything closes its doors."

"I just remembered all that party food from last night. Let's go inside and raid the refrigerator." She ran toward the door. "The last one in is a rotten egg."

He ran and caught her right at the front door, grabbed her in his arms and they fell inside against the closed door, wrapped in each other's arms kissing.

They finally journey into the kitchen, still holding and kissing each other.

"I'm starved," Paris admitted.

"Me too," she laughed.

"I think we have worked up an appetite, don't you think?"

She glanced up in his face and he winked at her and a flood of warmth rushed through her at his sexual undertone; and suddenly she felt weak, but kept her composure and pulled opened the refrigerator door. She glanced up at him and they both shook their heads when they found no leftover party food in the refrigerator.

"I can't believe all that party food is gone. Then again I can believe it; Mrs. Westwood probably took it to a homeless shelter per my mother's instructions. Leftovers have a very short shelf life in this house."

Paris laughed. "Are you sure this isn't Franklin House?"

"It's the same at your house, I take it," she laughed.

He nodded. "Leftovers don't even exist at my house. It's sort of an unspoken rule that nobody eats leftovers. I think it had something to do with the fact that my father didn't like leftover pizza. Plus, he didn't believe in leftovers because that meant wasting food. Our cook has strict instructions to prepare what's going to be consumed at that meal. Strangely enough, Mrs. Madden does just that. Therefore, there's usually nothing leftover to be leftovers," Paris explained.

"I'm not sure what's the deal regarding regular leftovers with us," Samantha said. "But I know after dinner parties and parties like the one we had last night, the food is usually donated to a soup kitchen or a homeless shelter."

Paris closed the refrigerator door and glanced at his watch. "Here's the deal, it's still fairly early. It's only eight-thirty, but too late for a full course dinner. So, let's go out and have dessert and coffee. That should work for your hunger pains for now? What do you say? Do you think that will work for your hunger pains?" he smiled and winked at her and pulled her in his arms.

She looked up at him and smiled. "Dessert and coffee will hit the spot," she agreed. "I'm thinking a slice of chocolate cake from Olive Garden."

He covered her lips and swallowed her up in passionate, lingering kiss before they headed to Olive Garden for chocolate cake and coffee.

Chapter Twenty-One

"So, Ryan's old buddy, Jack, is the boys new agent and manager?" Catherine said as she walked across the living room floor toward the staircase.

Veronica was lying on the sofa reading a National Geographic magazine when she dropped it on her chest and smiled toward Catherine.

"That's right. How did you find out?"

"I read about it in the paper awhile ago. You didn't mention it, but the boys have brought it up."

"I wasn't trying to keep it from you, but I didn't bring it up because I didn't want to jinxed it. I promised myself that I wouldn't breathe a word about it to anyone until I saw with my own eyes the four of them on location filming."

"Jack Coleman, I wonder if he's still full of himself," Catherine commented.

"He didn't seem that way when he signed the boys up back in August. He is still slender, but now he is completely bald. But didn't seem anything like that cocky boy that we remember back in high school."

"I suppose you didn't try to find another agent?" Catherine asked.

"I wasn't about to waste my time looking for another agent. Jack has a good track record. My sons couldn't be in better hands and now they are on their way. If anyone can get them in a hit movie with an excellent contract, Jack can," Veronica said.

Catherine nodded with her back leaned against the staircase railing. "That's probably true. He was a great asset in Ryan's career. I'm sure he'll be the same for my nephews." Catherine smiled and glanced into space for awhile.

"What's that look for?" Veronica asked. "You don't have any doubts about Jack giving his all for the boys do you?"

Catherine laughed. "It's not that. My mind just took me back for a moment."

"Back where?"

"Back to a time when Jack Coleman was a crazy wild kid who thought rules were made for everyone else and not him," Catherine said.

"That was around the time when you had such a big crush on him."

Catherine waved her hand. "Don't remind me of that. Back then it seemed as if I couldn't pick a decent boy; if he was bad luck I usually ended up with him. And my choices didn't improve as I got older, especially when the guy I married was just as bad or worse as the boys I had dated during high school. I'm so much better off today not concerning myself with any entanglements," she said seriously.

"I won't disagree with you," Veronica mumbled in a low voice.

"What was that you just said?" Catherine asked.

"Something awful just dawned on me," Veronica said.

"That's not what you just said," Catherine paused against the staircase railing with her arms folded. "You said something in a low voice regarding me, didn't you? Something about disagreeing?"

"I was just agreeing with you that you are better off without any entanglements."

"Okay, got it; now tell me what just dawned on you?" Catherine asked.

"That scary mess we ended up in at the hands of Jack back in high school. I know you remember how we ended up in that jam with Jack?" Veronica reminded her. "Jack was so cocky back then. It's incredible how he turned out to be a successful business man."

"You mean it's a miracle," Catherine shook her head. "He was walking on the wild side back then."

"All the way on the wild side, I'm sure you remember when he was arrested for striking Terrie Armani. Her folks filed charges against him and he spent a week behind bars," Veronica reminded her.

"I remember that, of course." Catherine nodded and stepped back into the living room and took a seat on the sofa facing the one Veronica was lying on.

"That seems like a lifetime ago. Our high school days. We were all kids back then and everybody sort of looked over the fact that Jack was an arrogant jerk with a loud mouth and a mean streak. I think most of the students put up with him because my brother was so popular. Jack Coleman was always with Ryan. He was Ryan's best friend and his folks were loaded too." Catherine shook her head. "What a small world that he is now in charge of the boys' career. But I got to hand it to him. It's impressive how he turned his life around to be such an important well-known business man who has made millions from the movie industry," Catherine stressed.

"That's weird," Veronica mumbled.

"What's weird," Catherine asked.

"That you and I are actually in agreement about Jack. Because I'm quite impressed with Jack Coleman."

"That's obvious, how you have given the man so much praise to the boys. It's hard to believe he's the same person that beat up a girl when he was eighteen," Catherine shook her head.

"That's because he's nothing like that now. Do you honesty think Ryan would have stayed friends with Jack if he hadn't straighten himself out?" Veronica said.

"Probably not, but who knows? Maybe Ryan didn't see the real side of Jack. Some people only show the side they want you to see," Catherine pointed out. "But I have to admit I'm convinced that Jack doesn't seem anything the way he was back in high school when he beat up Terrie Armani. He hit her just because she refused to let him have his way with her; and it's funny how cold chills still run through me all these years later when I allow myself to think of those days and what happened to Terrie. I realize all too well how that could have been me beaten just as easily as Terrie."

"You are the one who had your folks to call the cops on him, is that correct?" Veronica asked.

Catherine nodded, staring into space thinking of that painful memory. "That is correct. I had no other choice when I saw what he was doing to Terrie Armani. I remember that day so clearly when she jumped in the car with him after school. I knew she was in for trouble."

"Terrie was real sweet and nice back then," Veronica quickly said. "She was nothing like her brother."

"I second that hundred percent. Antonio was just as different as night is to day from his sister," Catherine agreed, grabbed her face and stared up at the ceiling. "That's why I knew she was headed for trouble when I spotted her with Jack that afternoon. Especially the very polite, kindhearted Terric Armani, barely sixteen and I knew as well as mostly everybody at school that Antonio's parents didn't allow Terrie to date because he had mentioned this to me. That's why I was sure smooth talking, loud mouth Jack had lied and tricked her to go home with him. When I saw the two of them walk inside of the Colemans' house, I got worried just as I had every time I saw Jack bring home some girl to his house, especially after the incident that took place there with you and I."

"I recall how it was all over school that Mr. and Mrs. Armani didn't allow Terrie to date. We all thought it was absurd since we were allowed to date at that time," Veronica smiled.

"They were really strict on Terrie and both Peter and Ellen Armani died hating Jack for what he had done to Terrie. Afterall, Terrie never got over that incident and ended up joining a convent and becoming a nun at the age of 21," Catherine relayed.

"Even though he's nothing like that now, that was a nightmare he put us through and we never told a soul. If we had, Ryan probably would have never spoken to his best friend again," Veronica mumbled.

"That would have likely changed the course of Ryan's future. If Ryan had written Jack off, Ryan wouldn't have gotten his big start in the movie industry which was singledhandled jumpstarted by Jack when Jack managed to get him signed up for his first movie and kept him rolling in movies up until Ryan's death," Catherine said.

"We have a different perspective as far as that goes," Veronica said. "Jack may have done all of that, but Ryan was a born star and if Jack hadn't been his agent and manager someone else would have be there for Ryan."

"Maybe, but the past is what it is. Jack Coleman was the air beneath Ryan's famous wings; and now he's going to get the boys on the big screen. And that's all good, but it still doesn't erase the past of what he did to Antonio sister, Terrie, and what he did to us when we were all in high school together," Catherine remined her.

"Catherine it doesn't erase the past, but the past is the past and now the man is larger than life in my eyes. He helped jumpstart my husband's career and now he's going to do the same for my boys. Can we just drop what happened all those years ago when we were all too young and too silly to know what was what."

"Jack wasn't too young and silly to know what was what. He knew exactly what he was doing when he took Terrie Armani to his house," Catherine snapped. "And I get it; I know you don't want to hear about the past and how Jack was. But I'm going to tell it to you so it can be refreshed in our minds."

"And why do we need that awful night to be refreshed in our minds?"

"So we won't lose sight of who Jack is now and what he was once capable of."

Veronica waved her hand, not interested in Catherine reliving and revisiting the past. "If that's what you need to do to get it out of your system, have at it. I'll listen because I have no plans to leave this sofa for the next ten minutes; so go ahead and pour your heart out about that afternoon that you saw Terrie at Jack's house; and that awful evening that we ended up in that jam at his house."

"I think it will help to tell the incident out loud, since we never told a soul about what Jack did to us. The trauma we experienced at his hands was awful. It started like this: After dinner, concerned about Terrie, I walked across the grounds and sneaked over to his house and tiptoed across their long porch, and peeked inside the living room window. As you know, Jack and his parents lived next door to us at the time at 604 Academy Place. We were sandwiched in a half of a block apart from each estate with the Colemans on the right and the Sterlings on the left of us. I had to see if Terrie was okay after Jack had driven off the school grounds with her. I arrived at his living room window just in time to see him arguing with her. He was standing a couple yards from her with his arms folded yelling angrily.

"You are wasting my time little girl! Why is it taking you so long to get undress?" That's what he said to her.

"Who said anything about getting undressed? I don't even know you that well, Jack," Terrie snapped.

"You know me well enough for what I have in mind. So don't play dumb with me now that we're alone. I read your signals loud and clear. Always willing to talk to me in the hall and sharing your lunch with me on the school grounds. You wanted to be alone with me and now you are. So, I don't buy it that you don't understand our reasons for coming here!" he yelled.

"No, Jack, it wasn't clear. You have another thought coming if you think I'm going to undress for you, inspite of the way you are yelling at me," Terrie said sadly.

"I don't have to yell," he said calmly. "Now, pretty please will you get undress the way we planned," Jack encouraged her.

Terrie shook her head. "It doesn't manner how nicely you ask, I'm not about to get undress and get in bed with you, Jack. I'm sorry if I gave you that impression. Now will you please take me home."

"Who do you think I am? I'm not some chump you can get to haul you around and spend money on, and you pull a fast one on me. I said get undress!" He yelled angrily. "Do it now! Can you manage that or do you want me to rip that dress off! One way or another, it's coming off!" Jack yelled.

It's cemented in my brain. As Jack yelled in Terrie's face, she stood there staring up at him with a stunned look on her face. It was as if at that moment her voice had vanished. She took her hands and covered both cheeks and tears poured from her eyes as she shook her head. I looked at Jack again and I could see incredible rage in his eyes. She had really rubbed him the wrong way. He looked as if he was ready to punch three people. Her rejection had the all time, school campus, Mr. Cocky boiling. He drew back his left arm and slapped her across the face with his left hand and then a second time with his right hand. She tried to cover her face with her arms, but he grabbed her by the shoulders and threw her on the sofa and held both of her arms back as he forced her to kiss him. Her tears were falling down her face like water from a roof top, but she only screamed once. She was probably too afraid to actually make much of a sound. Then suddenly she managed to push him away. He rolled off of her just long enough for her to hop off the sofa and run toward the wall.

"I know you have had too much to drink, Jack. You need to stop right now before you end up doing something that you'll be sorry about tomorrow," Terrie cried.

"This is not about tomorrow. This is about today, right now!" Jack rushed toward her and slammed her against the wall with both arms above her head. He argued at the top of his voice as he released her arms and slapped her again. "You haven't done one single thing I have asked of you! Who do you think you are, Miss Terrie Armani? You are supposed to do what I ask you. Just answer me one question: why do you think I wasted my time taking you for a burger and ice cream? Do you really think I sat there in that little nosy café chatting with you about your history teacher just because I wanted to spend time with you?"

He stepped away from her and walked toward the window as if he had heard a noise. I was anxious and nervous hoping he wouldn't find me standing on his porch spying on him. I stood very still and didn't make a move. He never opened the door to peek out. He started in on Terrie again.

Terrie dropped down on the sofa and grabbed her face in her hands. "Jack, I can't believe you are treating me like this. You have everybody at school fooled. Nobody knows you are such a cruel jerk who hits girls. I'm sure Ryan Franklin doesn't know this about you. He's nice and his parents are rich. Why would he even waste his time with a jerk like you for a friend? But as I said, I'm sure he doesn't know you are such a damn bastard!"

"Blah, blah, blah, nobody is listening to your crap. For an innocent, you have a nasty mouth little girl." He grabbed his cigarettes from the coffee table and stuck one in his mouth. He grabbed a book of matches from the coffee table and lit his cigarette and then blew his smoke right in Terrie's face. "You can give Ryan all the praise if you like, but his folks don't have anything that my folks don't have and more!" Jack shouted angrily. "Plus, if you want to leave here in one piece you better zip up your big mouth before I really let you have it!" Jack threatened her.

Terrie shook her head. "You have slapped me around and still threatening me. Now I know you were lying when you said you liked me," she snapped. "You probably don't even know what the word like mean."

"You are right about one thing." He nodded. "You are the last girl I would attach the word like to. The sole and only reason why I asked you out after school and spent a dime on you was to get you in my bed. I knew my folks wouldn't be home and this would be the perfect opportunity. Why else would I have invited you here? So, if you think I slapped you around and you don't like it, too bad. This is what you get for wasting my time!" He slapped her so hard across the face until she fell over on the floor.

"That was it. I couldn't just stand out on his porch and watch him beat her up without trying to help or get help. That's when I ran home and told my mother. She looked at me with concerned eyes. "Is Robert and Patrica there?" I was too upset to answer and then she answered herself. "No they are out of town on business. I better call Terry parents." Then my mother called Mr. and Mrs. Armani and ten minutes later, they showed up at the Colemans' mansion with the cops. Ryan was upset with me for telling on Jack. He was never convinced that Jack had actually really hurt Terrie."

"Listening to how heartless Jack was at that time, it's hard to believe he's a completely different person now," Veronica said. "But people can change and he's proof of that. Besides, that was over forty years ago. He was only eighteen."

"It's been all those years, but it still bugs me that I was once blinded by his bull shit and lies," Catherine stated. "For some reason at that time, I just couldn't see beyond his boatload of garbage and fake charm. Of course, the fact that I couldn't is incredible to me now. But at the time I had a crush on the guy and everything about him seemed exciting to me. The way he wore his hair slicked back on his head and his fast talk.

And the fact that he was Ryan's best friend automatically put him high on my list. It made me feel more mature to have my brother's best friend interested in me."

"You kept that crush a secret," Veronica reminded her.

"Yes, I know I did. It's just that we had sort of grew up together and he was just always my brother's best friend, then suddenly as we grew older I realized I had developed a huge crush on Jack. And because he was Ryan's best friend, my folks actually approved of him. If I had married Jack Coleman, I wouldn't have gotten cut out of their will. Little did they know that he was just as big of a jerk or more so than Antonio. But it didn't matter, because Jack was not into me. Many days I walked around in a daze daydreaming about being his girlfriend. However, he never tried to talk to me. He was just interested in hanging out with Ryan. He worshipped Ryan and tried to copy him by dressing like him and convinced his folks to buy him a car like the one Ryan was driving. He wanted to go and do whatever Ryan was doing."

"I do recall how Jack started dressing like Ryan, which made him appear more attractive. Although, he wasn't that cute," Veronica said.

"I agree that he wasn't that cute, but nobody could convince him that he wasn't that cute. He thought he was the second handsome boy on the school grounds next to my brother. Where did he ever get that idea is a mystery to me." Catherine laughed. "He was so full of himself until he probably thought by hanging out with Ryan it somehow made him just as handsome." Catherine stared into space for a moment. "But I think his overwhelming confidence, no matter how misguided, was the very trait about him that made him appear so irresistible to me at that time," Catherine admitted.

Catherine and Veronica was still discussing Jack when Natalie walked into the living room carrying a silver serving tray with a pot of hot mint tea. She placed the tray on the coffee table and poured a cup of tea for Veronica and Catherine. Veronica sat up on the sofa as Natalie passed her the cup of tea.

"Thank you, Natalie. This is just what I needed."

"Me too," Catherine said as Natalie headed out of the room.

"Okay, where were we?" Veronica sipped her tea, looking toward Catherine.

"We had just discussed how Jack was trying to imitate Ryan during high school. He thought Ryan was some kind of idol and stuck with him like glue. And even though he never said anything to me that would have hinted any romantic interest, I was still hopeful that he would ask me out."

"As I said before, that was one crush you kept secretly," Veronica pointed out.

"Yes, I did for awhile. Mostly, because I felt deep down inside that he didn't share my feelings. I didn't want to be that girl that was chasing after a boy who didn't want her. Then it got to the point that I liked him too much and couldn't hold my feelings to myself any longer," Catherine recalled.

"Is that the Friday you told me about him during lunch?" Veronica asked.

"Yes, that was the day," Catherine said.

"At the time, I didn't know he was Ryan's best friend," Veronica said. "I liked Ryan and he liked me then, but we didn't seriously start dating until a couple months after that incident. Besides, after the way Jack scared us, I'm glad I didn't know he was Ryan's friend. It might have negatively influenced how I felt about Ryan. But I'm sure Ryan never knew how much of a jerk Jack was back then."

"I'm sure he didn't know. I surely didn't know when I poured my heart out to you in the lunchroom that day. As soon as you walked through the cafeteria door and strutted over to my table, I pulled you by the arm," Catherine said.

"You had an excited look on your face. I had no idea what you were about to tell me. You had gotten me all excited too," Veronica recalled.

"Sit, what took you so long? I have something to tell you. It's about Ryan's friend, Jack Coleman. I have fallen hard for that boy. I think I'm in love with him."

"If you're in love with Jack, what about Antonio Armani?" Veronica asked.

"What about Antonio?"

"Well, he likes you and I thought you liked him."

"Yes, he does like me; and I do like Antonio, but I think I'm in love with Jack. I know I am. He has somehow managed without even knowing it, to turn my world upside down. I can't seen to stop thinking about him. I have hoped and prayed for him to say something to me," Catherine explained.

"Why bother with some boy who hasn't said anything to you?"

"He will, I'm sure. Plus, it's an advantage that he's friends with Ryan. He is bound to notice me soon. He's always at my house visiting Ryan and we have had a chance to talk some. Just regular small talk but last week was different."

"How was it different?"

"When he dropped over to see Ryan, we had an opportunity to spend a little time together visiting with each other. Get this, he's no silly boy. He's a mature eighteen-year-old. In my opinion, he is certainly a Mr. Right. Remember, we said we wouldn't date any silly boys, that we would wait for the right boy that knew how to treat a girl. Most of these boys at school don't know the first thing about how to treat a girl," Catherine said.

"You've got to introduce me. I can't wait to meet Jack. He sounds perfect."

"Don't worry, I'll introduce you just as soon as I get a chance. Maybe during lunch one day."

"Is he at school today?"

"I'm not sure. I haven't seen him around today."

"Is he in any of your classes?"

"No, but he's in all of Ryan's classes."

"Okay, let's find Ryan and ask him if Jack is at school today and then you can introduce me and I can get a chance to see who this boy is," Veronica said.

"You and I looked for Ryan after lunch but we didn't find him nor Jack. And just when I had somewhat given up hope of Jack ever asking me out, I ran into him after school the following week and he invited me to a supposedly party he was giving. His invitation rekindled all my hope. I never will foget how windy and cold it was the night of his fake party. You and I were so thrilled we had been invited that we were beside ourselves giggling and smiling all evening. I had sneaked on one of my mother's dresses and a pair of her high heels. I wanted to look as grown up as I could," Catherine recalled.

"Now is your chance to get to meet this boy. You'll see for yourself just what I have told you. I know you're going to think he's all that, but just keep in mind, he's mine! You'll have to find your own fellow. Besides, you're into Ryan."

"What kind of party is it? Do you think he'll mind me tagging along?"

"Don't worry, he's not going to mind. Besides, he asked me specifically to bring a friend if I liked."

"So what's with you two, if anything? Has he asked you out yet or what?"

"Nothing yet. The only contact we have had is when he drops by to see Ryan or running into each other coming and going. That's how he invited me to his party. I had just hopped off the school bus and he had just pulled into his driveway. He got out of his car and waved to me. I waved back and by the time I walked to the front steps, he called out my name."

"Catherine, Catherine, Miss Catherine Franklin."

"When he called your name, did you go running to him?" Veronica asked.

"No, I didn't go running to him. I was only seventeen and too shy to show how much I liked the boy. I just glanced around and waved at him again. But when he beckoned for me, I headed across the grounds toward him where he stood. He was leaning against his car and when I reached him we talked just long enough for him to invite me to his party," Catherine explained.

"Catherine, it's incredible that he invited you to his party."

"Oh, don't I know it. I'm so excited. I'm hoping to get a chance to talk to him and be alone with him for awhile," Catherine recalled.

"This happened forty years ago, but it seems just like yesterday in my mind when we showed up at Jack's house that afternoon around four-thirty," Catherine said. "His car was the only car parked in their driveway.

He had mentioned that his folks were out of town on business for a few days."

"I remember it well too," Veronica said. "When we got to his house, I looked at you and said, I guess we're the first ones here."

"I told you I was nervous and asked if you were nervous?" Catherine said.

"No, I'm not nervous. I'm just dying to finally meet Jack Coleman. Everybody at school says he's Ryan's shadow but I have yet to see who Jack Coleman is. I guess once I do, I'll recognize him. Why haven't you pointed him out to me at school? You have felt this way about this boy all this time and never mentioned it; that's not like you," Veronica recalled. "I was blowing in my hands trying to keep warm. It was very cold that evening and I remember how Jack made us wait so long on his porch. I think he purposedly made us wait, don't you?" Veronica asked.

"Yes, that's how I remember. I'm sure he saw us and heard us when we first walked across the porch and knocked on his door. He waited until we had given up and were walking away before he stuck his head out of the door and smiled.

"Hello, girls, please come in," Jack said.

Veronica raised one finger, still seated on the sofa. "The moment I saw his face, I recognized him. I just never knew his name and the way you had described him I thought he was some good looking fellow. I had no idea your dreamboy was the plain looking boy that was always at Ryan's side," Veronica relayed.

"He wasn't plain looking to me at that time. I thought he was it. Thinking back I should have been smarter than I was. I have lots of smarts for other stuff but when it come to choosing a decent man, I'm dumb as they come. I seem to have a flare for choosing the rotten apple among men. I did it with Jack and then turned around and did it with Antonio," Catherine explained.

"We all have our strong points and picking a good guy wasn't one of yours," Veronica laughed.

"You'll get no argument from me on that," Catherine agreed. "But back to the story about Jack. We rushed inside of his house trembling from the cold. We had stood on his porch for at least five minutes before he answered the door."

"I told him we were glad he was home and that we were just about to head off the porch. Because we thought maybe he had canceled his party," Veronica said. "When I stared him straight in the face I thought I had seen a ghost. But I was only staring at him like that because I was stunned that he was your mystery fellow. You had built him up and it never dawned on me that it could be someone that I had actually seen at school," Veronica explained.

"I know I had built him up and for the first ten or fifteen minutes at his party, even though he was just an average looking fellow, I thought he was the finest boy who ever walked. I was consumed with anxiousness as he showed us over to the sofa. Headed across the floor, we looked all about the room giving him compliments and admiring the lovely party decorations. We could see it took a lot of work for him to decorate the room," Catherine explained.

"Well, as you can both see, I am here. My party hasn't been cancelled and the two of you are my very first guests. So take off your coats and just relax."

"Jack, this is Veronica Parker. Veroncia, this is Jack Coleman."

"Hi, Jack. I have seen you at school with Ryan but never knew your name."

"Yes, I have seen you too." Jack nodded. "It's good to formally meet you. So, you two just help yourself to the punch or whatever you want. I'm going to run and change. I'll be right back," he said anxiously as he rushed out of the room.

Veronica shook her head. "That anxious look in his eyes should have raised a red flag for us. But we didn't have a clue at the time as we walked over to the long table in the middle of the room. We were both hungry but rather disappointed when we saw he was only serving punch, carrots and celery sticks. We had missed dinner to save our appetite for his party. So when we grabbed a plate and grabbed for the celery and carrot sticks, I laughed. It was too funny that what had happened was something that your parents had told us could happen. But of course, we didn't listen to them," Veronica grinned. "I remembered when we were walking out of the door, your folks had tried to get us to at least eat a sandwich before we left for his party. They said he might not be serving any food. It turned out that they were right. Carrots and celery sticks didn't do the trick for us," Veronica recalled.

"Yes, my folks were right, but I was too hung up on Jack at the time and when he walked back into the room, smiling. We both were speechless to see him dressed so nice in an all black outfit," Catherine said.

"I'm glad the two of you ate some of the food," he said, smiling.

"What food?" Catherine asked in a low voice that he didn't hear.

"Now you both can join me in a cocktail." He winked.

"I knew we shouldn't drink anything because we were not of legal age and neither of us had tried booze before. We knew better, but since Jack had offered, and just the fact that he had offered made us feel grown up," Catherine recalled. "We weren't about to make ourselves look like the kids we were by saying no. However, after just a couple drinks, neither you or myself could even stand. Jack sat across from us smiling. He got up and walked over to lock his front door. He dimmed the living room lights, then he sat between you and me. He put both arms around me and started kissing my face and my head. I didn't respond at all. I was out of it. I felt him sweeping me up in his arms. He carried me to his bedroom and sat me on the edge of the bed. My head felt like it was spinning, but I somehow managed to sit there without falling over. My eyes were glued to his body, admiring his perfect figure, as he stood before me, taking his clothes off piece by piece. My heart was in overdrive, beating out of control. The boy that I liked so much was pulling off all his clothes right in front of me. I figured I was having a dream, and if it wasn't a dream, I wondered why was Jack undressing before me? I knew I had had too much to drink, and figured that was why I couldn't remember what had happened at the party. But in my mind, unaware of the facts, I felt I had made a lot of progress with Jack, because the last thing I could remember was sitting on the sofa hoping he would want to kiss me goodbye. I was unaware at the moment, that no party had taken place," Catherine explained.

"You are right, no party had taken place except for the sick party that he had conjured up in his mind," Veronica quickly relayed.

"That's true, and after he undressed down to his black bikini shorts, he sat on the bed next to me. He looked at me long and hard before grabbing me up in his arms, giving me a tender kiss on the forehead; running his fingers through my short black curls, softly moving his mouth to my neck; kissing me tenderly from my neck to my shoulders and all down my arms. Now I thought for sure I was dreaming. I wrapped my arms around his back, as he kissed me in a wild passionate manner. I had never been kissed that way in all my seventeen years," Catherine said.

"Your lovely brown eyes tell me you're having fun. I'm having fun too, and I can't wait to have more fun with you," Jack said. "I also can't wait to see you without those clothes you're wearing." He stood to his feet and headed out of the room. "I'll be right back, Catherine, don't move."

"I wasn't about to move because I was in awe of Jack Coleman. He stood in the doorway and blew me a kiss with one finger. I sat there trying to sober up because I figured I needed to pull myself together if I expected to enjoy the rest of the evening with Jack. I felt sick to my stomach and I was afraid to walk to the bathroom. It seemed as if that entire room was spinning."

"You were feeling sick and I was also feeling sick. He had spiked our drinks or something," Veronica said.

"Yes, he probably had. But finally, I managed to pull myself from the bed, and managed to walk to the bathroom, which was directly across the hall from his bedroom. But as soon as I wobbled back into his room, Jack arrived in the bedroom carrying you in his arms. I could tell you were half asleep. He stood you up and slipped off your skirt, then threw you on the bed. The heavy fall completely awakened you. You was so filled with wine, and was in worse shape than I was. You had no idea what was going on until Jack jumped in bed with you and started pulling on your sweater top, trying to get it over your head," Catherine recalled.

"I had never felt so awful," Veronica uttered. "My head was pounding and spinning. I asked what's going on? Where is Catherine and why are we in bed together? Then I managed to pull away from him and took my hands and rubbed my eyes to get a grip on my senses."

"It's okay Veronica. We are only going to play a game," Jack said.

"I had just stepped back into the room and I was stunned to see him in bed with you. I was wearing only a short slip." Catherine lifted her cup and took a sip of tea. "I yelled at him and asked what was he doing? And then I threw both hands over my mouth frozen in shock. And before I could say another word, Jack jumped out of the bed with a white towel wrapped around him. He took me by the hand and led me back over to the bed. I didn't say a word as I sat there on the side of the bed next to him. I was waiting to see what he had to say. I could see how you were still out of it from all the wine. I knew we had to get out of his house someway. It was obvious by now that he was up to no-good. I had put it together that he had fooled me and wasn't interested in me. Because if he had been, he wouldn't have had you in his bed. He had given us that wine on purpose just to take advantage of us."

"It's okay, Catherine, I was just telling Veronica we're going to play a game."

"I was burning mad and wanted to know what kind of game?" Catherine asked.

"It's called making love, and there's no need to scream. I'm not deaf," Jack yelled as he grabbed Catherine up in his arms and slammed her down on the bed."

"I asked him why did he slam me on the bed?" Catherine said.

"It was to show you I'm not kidding around. We are going to play a game, and the two of you are not leaving until we do. So you might as well relax and let me be in charge! You really have no other choice. Refusing to cooperate will only make matters worse!" Jack warned us.

"I begged Jack to let us go. Can't you see, Veronica is in no condition to play a game. Neither am I," Catherine pleaded to no avail. "And by this time, you had completely pulled herself together. You heard what we had said. You knew that the two of us were in big trouble. When Jack walked out of the room slamming the door hard behind him, I started crying, feeling like such a fool. I was sorry that I had gotten us into such a mess with a crazy jerk."

"I told you to calm down and told you it wasn't your fault," Veronica said. "I pointed out to you that we both could see how big of a jerk Jack Coleman was. I figured we could pull ourselves together and play along with him. I explained how we knew what he wanted. That he wanted to have sex with us both. And even though we didn't want him to touch us, that we should let him, since if we did, he would then let us go. I was afraid that if we made him mad, he would beat us. We had no idea what he was capable of. But I figured by going along with him, he would let us leave."

"I can't believe you considered sleeping with that jerk," Catherine remarked.

"I wouldn't have, of course, not. But at the time I was trying to convince myself as well as you that we should play along with Jack and do whatever he wanted us to," Veronica recalled.

"Yes, I know you were but that was a bad call and I wasn't about to give in to that bastard," Catherine stated.

"It was a crazy evening. The evening begin with Jack Coleman as your dream guy but by the end of the evening, we both hated that boy," Veronica recalled. "And I was out of my mind for suggesting we give in to him. But I wasn't thinking straight and had only suggested it because I was so afraid of him."

"I know you were afraid and I was afraid to, but it upset me that you suggested we give in to him," Catherine stated. "I pointed out that I hadn't did it and either had you; and our first time was not going to be with some calculating bastard who was under the false impression that he could have whatever girl he wanted. I'm sure he has confused his exsistence with that of my brother's. Our first time should be with a boy that we are in love with. Just think, Veronica, I wanted him so badly at one time. I dreamed about being alone with Jack Coleman. I thought he was the one, and I dreamed about him so much. Now, I was finally alone with him, and I was seated afraid to move. I figured we didn't know what he was up to. But he felt he was something special to females. I wondered where did he come off treating us like we were toys that he could operate at his demand," Catherine recalled.

Jack walked back into the room, pulling the door shut behind him. He was carrying a bottle of wine under his arm and two glasses in his left hand.

"Here we are, girls, more wine," he announced and threw us both a wink.

"Seeing that wine bottle under his arm made my blood boil," Veronica said. "I told him that we didn't need more wine. That we had drunk enough. I pretended we didn't need wine to get in the mood since we were ready to play his game."

"Is that right, Catherine?" Jack asked, walked over and kissed my shoulders.

"I crossed my fingers and lied to Jack and told him yes that you and I were ready to play his game," Catherine mumbled. "But Jack sat next to me rubbing his hand up and down my back and with each rub, I tensed."

"What's the matter? You don't seem ready," Jack said angrily. "Do you need me to help loosen you up, or what? This is just a simple game. It won't hurt. It will bring lots of pleasure. Once this game is over, you're free to leave. There's nothing to fear."

"I shouted at him to please spare us his garbage," Catherine recalled. "I told him how did he expect for us to loosen up? You know we are afraid. Who wouldn't be? You are keeping us here against our will. Just wait until I tell Ryan about your sick game! My brother is going to drop you like a bad habit. Did you think you could treat us like this and we wouldn't tell on you?"

"Talking to Jack back then was like talking to the air," Veronica said. "Nothing we said caused him any concern."

"You are right, my words about telling Ryan didn't move him. He strutted across the room to check the lock, glanced back at me and winked, then started to laugh. He informed us that he didn't believe that the two of us were going to tell anybody about what had happened at his house," Catherine said.

"I don't think you want anybody to know how wasted the two of you ended up and half naked at that," Jack said. "I'm sure Ryan is the last person you'll tell about this incident. Actually, I think you are both glad to be here and I'm sure this won't be your first time, Catherine. You are very much a woman at seventeen. All you seventeen-year-old girls have done it at least once. But I'm not sure about your friend, Veronica. I can't get a good read on her. She seems innocence and I know Ryan is sort of into her. But she is so tiny. How much do you weigh, anyway? 90 pounds, I bet." Jack asked.

"I told that bastard not to worry about my weight. Let's just get this game over with. Which one of us do you want to do it with first?" Veronica asked.

"He started to laugh as if you had said something funny," Catherine recalled.

"What do you mean? Why ask which one of you do I want first? I'm going to have fun with both of you at the same time. Just the way I like it, a girl lying on each side of me. And as if you didn't hear me, I asked you a question. But never mind, if you only weigh seventy pounds and skinny as a noodle, I would still have sex with you. But how old are you? That's where I draw the line! I only go to bed with girls over fifteen and under twenty," Jack explained with a smirk on his face.

"I told him I was over twenty and asked him to let me go," Veronica recalled. "But he walked over and stood before me where I was seated on the edge of the bed. He grabbed my face with both hands, lifted it up and stared down at me without cracking a smile and then yelled in my face asking my age!"

"I was all nerves. I was hoping you would just tell him; because I had a feeling he might slap your face if you didn't. But you stuck to your bones," Catherine said.

"I said I'm over twenty," Veronica said.

"Okay! You could be over eighty and I would still take you to bed! Get real! I already know your age. You're both seniors, if you're not eighteen, you will be soon. I figured you would try to lie. Did you really think you could lie about your age and turn me off? You both are goners. When I'm finished with the two of you, you'll be knocking on my door every evening, but you'll probably have to take a number," he laughed. "But if I'm too busy, I'll be happy to make time. You can ring my bell anytime, any hour of the day. I'll keep all you little seniors happy as long as you come in two's," Jack bragged.

"I asked him what kind of game was that? Wanting two girls in your bed at the same time?" Veronica mumbled.

"It's the only kind of game I play. I do it because I love it. Nothing can top it." Jack smiled. "Just sit down, Catherine, next to Veronica.

"I flopped down stiff as a board next to you. Then we glanced at each other with sad eyes. We had no other choice but to do what he asked. Then he walked over and pushed me over on my back, rubbing his hands up and down my thighs. I laid there flat on my back, afraid to breathe. He pushed you aside, bringing his face down to mine, and his mouth covered my mouth. He pushed his forceful lips against mine and within seconds he had pushed his burning tongue down my throat. I was being suffocated by his unwanted kiss with his lips wrapped around my mouth. I could barely breathe as I thought I would throw up from the feel of his hands all over me; then he grabbed my head with both hands, winding his fingers in my hair, propping my head back with my hair as he kissed my throat, dropping lower to my shoudlers, and lower to my chest and even lower to my stomach. His mouth was on fire as he kissed me all over my stomach. And by the time his face reached the bottom of my stomach, his hands were busy pushing my slip up around my waist. I laid there beneath him, soaking wet from the sweat that was rolling from his face, I trembled in disgust of his kisses. And as he began to breathe harder, making passionate sounds, I began to cry more. Then I heard you crying on the other side of the bed, and then suddenly his face moved up to my face and crushed me next to him. He pressed himself hard against me, forcefully covering my mouth, forcing his tongue between my lips and within seconds, pulled his lips from mine and turned to you and grabbed you, pushing you beneath him as he gripped a handful of your long black hair, yanked your head and I could see the torture in your scare brown eyes. And as you opened your mouth to scream, he covered your mouth with an urgent grip, kissing you forcefully as if he would swallow up your whole face. When he finally released his lips, you struggled to catch your breath. He gripped your shoulders, burying his face in your chest and mumbled somewhat to himself. You closed your water-filled eyes trying to force yourself not to feel. He kissed your closed eyelids and gripped and ripped your long red slip. He had almost ripped it off when suddenly you kicked Jack with full force right in the mid-section. He screamed out in pain and fell to his knees. That wasn't the soaring ecstasy he had sought," Catherine explained.

"We were shaky and crying, but we quickly threw on our clothes and got out of that creep's house," Veronica laughed.

"Yes, a creep he was. But he was in so much discomfort until he didn't even look toward us as we quickly dressed, grabbed our things and ran out of his bedroom through his big house and out of the front door," Catherine said, smiling.

Veronica poured herself another cup of tea and took the pot over to Catherine and filled her cup as well. She placed the tea pot back on the silver tray and took her seat back on the sofa. She then lifted her cup from the coffee table and took a long sip with the cup to her mouth as she looked toward Catherine.

"That was not a pleasant memory. I think I could have done without reliving that awful tale about Jack Coleman, especially since Jack is nothing like that now," Veronica pointed out.

"Maybe, but I remember how shaken we were when we got back to my house. The house was dark as we quietly let ourselves in and softly hurried up the staircase to my room. Your folks had given you permission to stay overnight."

Veronica nodded. "Yes, I had some wonderful parents. They always wanted to make me happy and they knew staying over at your house at that time made me happy. They were the best parents ever. I try to live up to their standards by being the best mother I can to my sons."

Catherine took a sip of tea. "I think you got that covered," she said, smiling. "But I agree, Jordon and Naomi were wonderful parents to you. I use to pray that my folks would treat me the way yours treated you."

"I recall how strict and controlling they were with you, more so than they were with Ryan," Veronica said.

"But your parents were nearly perfect. You were their only child and they treated you like a queen. I can't believe you would lose them less than five years later right after your college graduation. Your folks died young just like Ryan died young. And to think the three of them all died from the results of an automobile crash," Catherine said sadly.

"Stop it already," Veronica insisted. "One sad story at a time is enough. If you don't mind, I really don't like to think about how my parents and my husband died all in the same sentence," Veronica firmly said. "Besides, listening to you tell the revolting story about how Jack tricked and mistreated us during our senior year has turned my stomach enough. As I can recall, we cried all night when we got back to your house."

"Maybe it wasn't the best idea to relive that incident about Jack. It didn't help my comfort level about him being involved in our lives again," Catherine mumbled.

Veronica rolled her eyes toward the ceiling and rose from the sofa slowly and headed toward the dinning area. "Snap out of it Catherine. I agree that it wasn't a pleasant memory to relive that awful incident, but there's no need to feel uncomfortable as far as Jack is concerned. He's over the hill and harmless, nothing like that wild teenager he used to be." Veronica waved her hand. "He's a different person now; and I thought you thought so as well."

"I agree that I thought so as well, but reliving how disrespectful he treated us have given me my doubts." She followed Veronica out the front door onto the porch.

They looked across the grounds to their far right and stood there staring at the old mansion where Jack and his family had lived for many years. Jack sold the property shortly after Ryan's death. He couldn't bear to live next door to Franklin House after he said goodbye to Ryan at Ryan's funeral. Veronica and Catherine both noticed how the old estate looked just as it did twenty years earlier when the Colemans still resided there. The only difference was the sign at the gate that read: London House that was owned by an elderly, unfriendly grouchy couple that stayed to themselves. They hardly ever peeked out or left the premises. The only traffic moving in and out of their doors was their workers and caregivers.

"Catherine, don't let the teenage jerk that used to be Jack cloud your judgment about the upstanding man that he is now. He worked wonders for Ryan and he'll do the same for the boys. You know me." She pointed to her chest. "There is no way on God's green earth that I would have introduced my sons to Jack Coleman if I didn't absolutely think he was completely above board."

"I hope you are right, but I'm still not hundred percent convinced that he's so much different than he used to be. He was crude at that time and thought the law couldn't touch him. He's older now, yes! But what he did to us all those years ago was criminal. He held us against our wills and tried to make us do some sick stuff. He was one sick bastard then, but as you pointed out. He was young and foolish back then and now he's an established businessman."

"I'm glad you finally get that," Veronica sighed.

"Yes, I get it, but I'm not necessary buying his nice guy act. But I'm hoping he's not still the same sick bastard he was as a teenager, because now that Sydney has convinced his brothers to give this movie deal a shot, I want everything to go smoothly and work out for them," Catherine humbly uttered.

"Who told you Sydney convinced his brothers to take the movie deal?" Veronica asked with surprise in her eyes.

"Sydney mentioned it. Why do you ask?" Catherine narrowed her eyes at Veronica. "Is it supposed to be some kind of secret from even me?"

"It's not a secret, but..."

Catherine drew an attitude. "But what, Veronica; do I have a stupid sign written across my forehead? Even if Sydney hadn't casually mentioned how he convinced his brothers for you, I still would have figured he did. Besides, we both know it's not really what they want. They are giving up what they enjoy doing to get into a career that they promised not to."

"I know it looks that way now, but once they start shooting the movie they'll get into it and enjoy the glamour and attention of the work. Not to mention the incredible pay that will come along with the work," Veronica stressed with a gleam in her eyes.

"Veronica, I know you mean well; but when are you going to realize that you can't go back."

"What do you mean I can't go back?"

"I mean you can not go back to the past. You are trying to relive the past you had with Ryan through your sons instead of allowing them to just be and chose their own path. It's their life and they should live it in whatever way that makes them happy," Catherine stressed firmly.

"What do you know, Catherine? They are my sons and I believe they'll be happy doing what their father loved. Ryan was so incredibly happy making movies and I know that once, Rome, Britain, Paris and Sydney get their feet far in the door and start making movies they'll be incredible happy doing the work as well. They'll be following in their father's footsteps and honoring his name. They never got a chance to really know their father and by doing what he loved, it will give them an opportunity to experience something that made their father very happy," Veronica stressed.

"I get how you would want that for them. But it shouldn't be at their expensive of giving up what they really want in life. And I know you think that at some point after they start shooting the movie that they'll realize that doing movies are their dream, but I don't think so."

"Of course, you don't think so, Catherine, because that would mean that I would have to be right."

"It's not about being right! It's about being realistic and considerate."

"Therefore, you are telling me that I'm not being realistic and considerate of my own sons."

"Well, if the shoe fits. Think about it, Veronica. If you were realistic and considerate you would realize that acting and making movies isn't either of your son's lifelong dreams!"

"I don't know what my own sons' dreams are, but you do?"

"I don't claim to know what their dreams are, I just don't think it's making movies like their father," Catherine stressed firmly.

"Well, we have a difference of opinion because I happen to believe it is their lifelong dream and birthright. Ryan paved the way for them and I'll be damn if I don't do all I can to see them fulfill it."

"Whether it's what they want or not, right?" Catherine snapped. "Here's my point Veronica; if simply making movies were their lifelong dream, I think one of them out of four would have perused it or talked about it with you or even myself. I have never heard Rome, Britain, Paris or Sydney mention the movie industry other than how much they are appalled by the thought."

"I don't buy that they are appalled. They think they are disgusted with the business because of all that garbage they read. For some insane reason you couldn't stop buying all that garbage after Ryan died. You did my sons a huge misfortune when you saved all those tabloids about Ryan's death. Most of those stories were twisted lies about how he died from depression because no one would hire him after his accident. Hyped up stories about how the movie industry washed their hands of him; it was all lies and my sons think his career is what killed their father. I know better and you know better. Ryan died from an injury resulting from his accident," Veronica argued.

"That is probably true, but all trash articles have some aliment of truth to them. My brother may not have died from depression, but he was extremely depressed. And yes, calls were coming through but he didn't want to work because he didn't like his looks anymore after the accident. So maybe the movie industry didn't wash their hands of him but he washed his hands of them because he knew all too well how it worked. You were as good as you looked and Ryan knew he no longer had the looks and didn't want to step down in parts, therefore he didn't accept any," Catherine fussed. "And another thing, I will not apologize for saving those tabloids. I wanted whatever I could find in print about my brother after his death. It didn't matter to me at the time whether it was good print or bad, just that it was," she keenly explained.

"I'm not asking you to apologize but reading all those lies is the main reason why my sons are so against getting into acting and making movies, which I do feel is their lifelong dream as a career," Veronica said firmly.

"You still think it's their lifelong dream as a career but you still can't answer me why either of them has expressed this love for the business. For one, whether it was lies they read or not, they do blame the movie industry for their father's death. On the other hand, I think I know what a lifetime dream looks like. Growing up in a household with Ryan, I knew from the time we were little that he wanted to be a movie star. It was his constant talk. He lived a short life losing it at 38, but he lived a life fulfilled and filled with happiness because he was doing what he wanted to do. Ever since he was twelve he loved the idea of the movie industry and knew he wanted to be a movie star when he grew up. For extra credits in high school he didn't play any sports. He spent all his time studying drama and acting in all the school plays. Then he went on to a four year drama school and graduated at the top of his class, achieving that honor allowed him a rapid introduction and quick transition over into the industry."

"How did Jack happen to take charge of Ryan's career?" Veronica asked.

"I'm surprised Ryan didn't mention to you how Jack was his shadow and where-ever he went so did Jack."

"He did sort of mention that, but it still doesn't tell me how Jack ended up in charge of his career."

"Jack attended the same drama school and not because he wanted to be an actor but for the sole purpose that he wanted to be at the same college with Ryan. Long story short, Jack had no interest in being an actor, but knew it was Ryan's passion. Therefore, after graduation, Ryan decided that Jack would be his agent and manage his career. And with breakneck speed, Jack put all his efforts into being the best agent and manager he could. I guess my point here, is how Ryan was happy from the start with his chosen career," she explained sincerely. "I want the same and think Ryan would want the same for his sons."

"If you paid attention, you would notice how excited Sydney is about starring in a movie," Veronica pointed out.

Catherine looked at Veronica with heartfelt eyes. "I don't see the excitement that you see. I will admit that Sydney seems more into this movie deal than his brothers but his heart and soul is not in it," Catherine stressed strongly. "His persuasion toward his brothers to do the movie came from his desire to please you. If following in his father's footsteps will bring happiness to you, he wants to achieve that goal of making you happy. He was only three years of age when Ryan died and doesn't share the same sad memories of his father's death as his older brothers. And for all the persuading his brothers tried to influence him away from the movie business, she constantly had his ear encouraging him to follow in his father's footsteps into the movie industry," Catherine explained seriously. "So, no matter what you say, Veronica. We both know it's all for you. Even as a little boy Sydney couldn't bear to see you unhappy. He persuaded his brothers and he's doing this movie to makes you happy."

Chapter Twenty-Two

Veronica was almost content by the end of the first week of November. Most of her plans had folded out just as she wanted. Britain, Paris and Sydney seemed content and happy in their relationships with the Taylor girls. And although she wasn't pleased in Rome's choice to date Courtney, she had slowly adjusted to the idea until she could figure out some way to convince Rome how strongly she felt that Courtney was not the right girl for him. She was raking her brain overtime to figure out a way to discourage the relationship and succeed. She hoped her persuasion would sway Rome from Courtney as it had worked in persuading Sydney back in August to convince his brothers to give acting a shot. She was beside herself with good cheer knowing she had lined her sons up with their father's old agent, Jack Coleman, and although they were all still working at the family business, and had no readily plans to resign their positions, they were scheduled to start shooting their first movie in January. Sydney had the leading role in the film titled: Four Brothers In Love.

It was Friday, November 8th, the sun was pouring in through all six floor-to-ceiling windows in the spacious dinning room at Franklin House. It was a quiet afternoon as Veronica and Sabrina was gathered at the dinning room table sharing hot tea and lemon drop cookies.

"Thanks for joining me for tea," Veronica said.

"Thanks for inviting me. Today works out perfect since I didn't have to drive into the office," Sabrina lifted her cup and sauce and sipped her tea.

"That's right; you and your sisters work at your father's company in the city. I think it's honorable that you young ladies are working at your family business. I'm so impressed with all of you girls. Plus, that cousin of yours that Britain mentioned."

Sabrina was chewing on a cookie but stopped, lifted her cup and took a long sip of tea. "You must be referring to Amber?"

"Yes, Amber. Britain tells me that she's your best friend. And he mentioned that she's widowed with two kids."

"That's right, she is. I told Britain about her but they haven't met yet. I talk about her often because she has faced some pretty sad times in the past couple years."

"What happened to her husband and how long has she been widowed?"

"Austin was killed in a plane crash two years ago. He was on a business trip from Europe when his plane went down killing the two hundred and eighteen people aboard," she said sadly.

Veronica shook her head as she could see the hurt in Sabrina's eyes from just recalling the devastating accident.

"Amber gave birth to Holly and Dolly just one month after she buried her husband. Austin never got a chance to meet his daughters."

"What a pity. She seems like such a lovely young lady. I haven't met her, but I have seen her come and go by you. I have noticed that she visits you at least once a week, usually during a weekday in the middle of the day. I'm not prying, just happen to see her car when she pulls into your driveway."

"She does try to drop by once week at the moment. It's usually on my day off. She recently purchased a condo in the area and doesn't readily know anyone in the area just as we don't know that many people in the area yet."

"Is she dating anyone?" Veronica asked with subdued interest.

Sabrina shook her head. "She hasn't gone on a date since she lost Austin. I'm not sure if she's interested in dating."

Veronica quickly changed the subject after finding out the piece of information that she was searching to obtain. "What is she doing with her time? I guess she has her hands full with the two toddlers."

"She's not volunteering or working anywhere. Right now she's just taking care of her kids, with the help of two nannies, of course. I think she wants to work if the right opportunity represents itself."

"What was her major in college?"

"She majored in business management like the rest of us."

"I see." Veronica bit into a cookie and placed the uneaten portion back on the dish. "Sydney was telling me just a couple days ago that they are looking for someone to take a position in the business office at Franklin Gas."

"What kind of position?" Sabrina asked.

"They are looking for a bookkeeper, someone to process payroll, accounts payables and receivables," Veronica explained.

"I'm sure Amber would know how to do all of that; and she might just jump at the opportunity," Sabrina said, smiling.

"I'm sure Sydney would be pleased to interview her and give her the job. And since she has the two kids, I'm sure they could work around her schedule."

Sabrina smiled. "That just might work. She just bought a place to live out here, and now she could also end up with a job all in the span of one month," Sabrina said excitedly. "I will call her when I leave here and tell her about the job."

Veronica held up one finger. "Here's an idea. Give her a text and see if she can join us for tea. I'll tell her about the position and if she likes what she hears, the three of us can drive over to the business and she can interview for the job. One recommendation from me and I can assure you Sydney will hire Amber on the spot."

"That sounds very encouraging Mrs. Franklin. I will text her now."

Thirty minutes later Amber was at Veronica's front door. She was dressed very professional in a fashionable two piece maroon pantsuit, displaying a striking white blouse. Her shoulder length dark brown hair was a head of tight French curls that she wore parted on the side.

Natalie showed her to the dinning room where Veronica and Sabrina were seated. Veronica and Sabrina stood up from their seats to greet Amber, and Sabrina walked over and hugged her.

"I'm glad you could come right over," Sabrina said. "I would like for you to meet Britain's mother, Mrs. Veronica Franklin. She's the one who thought you might be interested in the position that's available at Britain's job."

"It's nice to meet you, Mrs. Franklin. Thanks for asking Sabrina to contact me and have me come over," Amber smiled, looking toward Veronica as she took a seat at the table. "I'm quite anxious and excited to hear about the bookkeeper position at your son's company."

"It's my pleasure to meet you as well, Amber." Veronica smiled, very pleased to finally meet Amber and hopefully secure her a spot at their family business. "From all the wonderful things I have heard about you from your cousin here, you will be a great asset to my sons' business."

After the three of them finished a cup of hot tea, Veronica had told Amber all about the position.

"Mrs. Franklin, thank you for this opportunity. Based on what you have told me, I would love the job if your son offers it to me," Amber said and picked up a cookie from the dish.

"Would you like to go in today and talk to Sydney and apply for the position?" Veronica asked.

"Today would be fine." Amber smiled.

Veronica exchanged looks with Sabrina and then Amber. "Okay, let's go talk to my son and see what he says about giving you that job." She smiled.

They all took one last sip from their tea cups, and then got up from the table with smiles on their faces. They gathered their coats and purses and headed out of the house. When they stepped outside, they all gathered in Veronica's black Bentley and headed into town. When they arrived at Franklin Gas Veronica took Amber up to Sydney's office and recommended her for the job. Sydney gave Amber a thirty minute interview and hired her on the spot.

The three of them left Franklin Gas quite excited that Amber had been hired. When they arrived back at Franklin House, Sabrina had mentioned that she had an appointment with her hair stylist. She said her goodbyes and hopped in her red Mercedes and headed to the beauty salon. And for no particular reason, Veronica and Amber stood in the driveway and watched Sabrina as she drove away. Amber didn't readily get in her white Mercedes and leave. Veronica invited her inside. And while sitting on the living room sofa, Amber quickly noticed the 16x20 paintings in exclusive pearl white frames of six men. All six paintings were lined on the wall above the fireplace. She hopped off the sofa and walked across the room near the fireplace to get a closer look. Veronica was seated there and smiling that Amber seemed intrigued by the paintings on the wall.

Amber pointed to the painting of Sydney. "That's your son, Sydney, who just interviewed and hired me." She glanced over her shoulder and smiled. "So, who are the other five?"

"Those are the Franklin men," Veronica said with delight. "That's my husband at the far right, and my husband's father at the far left and my four sons in between: Sydney, who you met, Rome, Britain and Paris."

"Wow, they are all very good looking, even your husband's father. I'm sure that's a younger picture of him, but he looks just like Sydney. And wow, from the names listed below the pictures, that's Britain, Sabrina's boyfriend," Amber said excitedly pointing to Britain's portrait. "She had mentioned how handsome he was but I had no idea he was an incredible good looking man. And my goodness, Rome and Paris are also drop dead gorgeous." Amber grabbed her face with both hands. "They should all be models in commercials and in the movies."

"I knew there was a reason why I was so drawn to you," Veronica smiled. "We think a like. I also think my sons should be in movies."

Amber heard Veronica but she was still enthralled in the paintings as she stood there with her back to Veronica admiring the paintings.

"I would love to take credit for their good looks, but that honor goes to their father and their father's father. They come from a long line of pretty genes. When I first laid eyes on their father, Ryan, he was the best looking boy in the world to me and I knew I would love him forever. That was forty years ago and he has been deceased for twenty, but he still has my heart," Veronica said.

Amber nodded, "That's beautiful, Mrs. Franklin," she said, but still standing admiring the six paintings as Veronica continued.

"Yes, I have to admit I do have good looking sons, but I also have to admit how it can be a curse as well as a blessing."

Those words caught Amber attention. She glanced around at Veronica and then walked back across the room to be seated. "Why do you say it can be a curse?"

"Because my life mission has been to make sure the wrong type of female doesn't hurt one of my sons."

"How can you prevent something like that?"

"The problem is that I can't. I just want the best for them. And I want all of them with young women who are worthy of them; and who will love them for who they are and not for how they look or what they have. I don't want them with women who are trying to make themselves feel better by being attached with someone who makes them feel complete. I want them with women who are already complete and can love them with their whole heart and soul," Veronica said sincerely.

"I know how you feel, Mrs. Franklin. I felt that way about my late husband. I loved him with my whole heart and when I lost him I didn't think I would be able to feel that way about another man. But I'm still very young at twenty-six and now I realize that I would like to feel what I felt for Austin with someone else one day," she said earnestly and paused. "That is, if the right person comes along."

"I'm going to tell you something that I probably shouldn't," Veronica said slowly and paused. "But for some reason I feel very close to you even though we just met. And what I have to tell you is about my oldest son."

"Is your oldest son named Rome?" she asked.

She smiled. "I figured you had the pictures lined up in age order."

"You guess right. Rome is my oldest, and he's the one I'm worried sick about."

"Is he sick?" Amber asked.

Veronica shook her head. "No, he's not physical ill, but in my humble opinion his mind could use some doctoring."

"I beg you pardon," Amber said.

"I'm just kidding, of course." Veronica smiled. "But what I'm not kidding about is his infatuation with a young woman that is totally unsuited for him. She works at the company and I'm just sick about their connection." Veronica took a deep breath as if the thought brought her great anxiety. "I tell you; with my whole heart I feel this young lady isn't right for Rome."

"What makes you feel that way, if you don't mind me asking?"

"It's just a mother's intuition. A feeling I have that I can not shake. At first I tried to reason with myself because I felt I was being too hard on the young lady because of her less than perfect background, but figured I could get past that."

"But you don't think you can? I'm not sure I follow your reasons for not wanting him with her. Is she not a nice person?" Amber asked.

"I think she's probably nice and I think she cares about Rome. But I don't believe she cares about him for the right reasons," Veronica explained.

Amber stared with confused eyes. "I guess I'm not getting it."

"I'm sure you're not getting it, but my instincts tell me that Courtney Ross is not the right girl for my son. I think she's more fascinated by his looks and his status."

"Mrs. Franklin, with all due respect, what female wouldn't be fascinated by his looks? Rome is an exceptionally handsome guy," Amber said. "And since you think she's a nice person, maybe she is," Amber suggested.

Veronica shook her head. "I would love to think better of Miss Ross since Rome has made it clear that he's quite fond of her, but that one had her eyes on my son from the moment they hired her. Everybody at the company knows this. But after Rome didn't ask her out, she somehow figured out a way to cozy up to Britain."

Amber shifted in her seat. Britain was Sabrina's boyfriend and she was waiting on the edge of her seat to hear what Veronica had to say about Britain and Courtney.

"Are you saying this Courtney used to date Britain?" Amber asked.

"No, they never dated because Britain was never interested in the young lady, but she befriended him anyway and shared a lunch table with him for two months. Then Britain forgot her birthday and she made a big deal about it." Veronica held up one finger. "Bear in mind, he wasn't her boyfriend but she acted as if forgetting her birthday was like leaving her on the side of the road bleeding."

"If she was that upset because he forgot her birthday, she probably liked him as more than just a friend," Amber said.

"That's my thought exactly." Veronica nodded. "And although she had her eyes on Rome in the beginning and is probably pleased to be with him now, she was willing to be with Britain if she couldn't be with Rome," Veronica stressed. "So what does that tell you? Just be candid and say what you think."

"I think she's fascinated by the Franklin guys. But they are very fascinating."

"I agree. But you seem like such a lovely young lady so I'll ask you this." Veronica pointed toward the pictures on the wall. "You are fascinated by how good looking my sons are, is that correct?"

Amber nodded, listening carefully to see where her question was headed.

"So, let's say, you are fascinated by Rome, fall for him and hope for a relationship with him, would you decide to date one of his other brothers if he wasn't interested in talking you out?"

Amber shook her head. "That's not me. I don't want to date the brother of someone I care for."

"That's how I feel exactly, therefore, that's why I can not accept Courtney Ross as the right young lady for my son," Veronica said firmly. "Now, someone like you I would welcome with open arms." She smiled and held out both arms.

"Thank you, Mrs. Franklin for that compliment. I'm sorry to hear that you are troubled by your son's affair with this woman of his choice."

"I don't think she is the woman of his choice. I just think that he thinks so. He only asked her out to keep his brother from looking like less of a gentleman."

"What do you mean?"

"Back in September, on the 14th to be exact was her birthday. That's the day Britain forgot it was her birthday. After all, he was a bit preoccupied in his new relationship with Sabrina and was having lunch with Sabrina in the company's cafeteria. Long story short, Rome realized

Britain had forgotten that he promised to have lunch with Courtney and take her out for her birthday. Therefore, Rome being the gentleman that all my sons are, he joined Courtney at her lunch table. He proceeded to have lunch with her and took her out that same evening." Veronica nodded. "If that incident hadn't occurred maybe Rome wouldn't be seeing that young lady today."

"But they have been seeing each other ever since, is that correct?"

"Yes, that is correct, but the jury is still out on how long that relationship is going to last. Rome needs to open his eyes and see this girl for who she is. She is going to break his heart once he realizes she's not who he thinks she is."

"You feel rather strongly that she's going to deceive or hurt Rome in some way," Amber said. "I hope that doesn't happen. He sounds like a fantastic guy.

"He's every bit of that," Veronica smiled. "He's handsome, of course, but he has many other decent qualities, like thoughtfulness and compassion."

"I'm sure he does and I bet all your sons are that way. Sabrina is always telling me how thoughtful and compassionate Britain is."

Veronica paused and smiled at Amber for a moment before saying. "I got an idea. Why don't you hang around and have dinner with us. It will give you an opportunity to meet all of my sons. I know you met Sydney on a professional level. But stick around and meet the family."

"I'm sorry; Mrs. Franklin, but I'll feel awkward."

"Why would you feel awkward?" You'll be my dinner guest," she said and then hit her forehead with the palm of her hand. "What am I thinking? You probably need to get back to your kids."

"No, that isn't it. I have two nannies taking care of my daughters." She glanced at her solid gold and diamond Gucci watch. "I could actual hang around and stay for dinner and the kids would be fine with the nannies."

"Okay, hang around and stay for dinner. "I'll show you around this big house and I have more than one hundred photo albums of the family to keep you entertained until my sons arrive and dinner is served."

"Okay, I'll stay for dinner. And just so you are aware that I know you're hoping your son, Rome, will find me attractive," Amber said, smiling. "I have to admit that looking at his picture and hearing about how wonderful he is and how strongly you sense that the girl he's dating could be wrong for him and break his heart, it makes my heart goes out to him," she explained. "And Mrs. Franklin, I have to admit that Rome is the kind of man that I could love again. But although, you may think I'm right for him, it's not going to make him think I'm right for him if he has his heart set on being with the person he's dating."

"I realize you are right and you are such a proper and sweet young lady. I'm hoping that just being around you will make him fall for you."

"Well, I guess he'll see me at work sometime, but other than that I'm not sure when I'll ever run into your son."

"You will run into him more than you think," Veronica said quickly.

"How is that, Mrs. Franklin?"

"As of today, you are my new best friend. I liked you from the moment I spotted you from afar visiting your cousin Sabrina. When I heard about your tragedy of losing your husband at such a young age with two small children to raise on your own, I had empathy for you. Your situation reminded me of my own tragic past. You remind me of myself. To be frank with you, before I laid eyes on you, I never figured I would have approved of a young woman as you for my son."

Amber stared curiously at Veronica since she wasn't sure what Veronica meant by those words.

"I'm referring to the fact that you already have been married and you have two kids. I have nothing against either, just never wanted any of my sons thrown into a ready made family."

"What changed your mind?"

"Mostly your beauty as a person which makes all the other stuff seems invisible. Then there's this current situation that Rome is in with Courtney. She is a single young woman with no kids but if he continues that affair she will hurt my son. I'm not sure how, but I can feel it in my bones. And I'll do just about anything to protect him from a pending doom that I'm so certain will fall on his head."

"But how does he feel about dating someone who has been married with kids?"

"He doesn't care at all. My sons are gentlemen. Their hearts control a big part of them. They are like the average guy and wouldn't fall for a loose female with little respect for herself, and of course, like any fellow, they are into good looks. But marital status and kids would not be something that would sway any of my boys. I'm more uptight about that kind of stuff than they are."

Amber nodded. "Okay, so I guess I'm having dinner here. But what else do you expect from me? Rome is handsome and I would love to go out with him but he already has a girlfriend. I know you don't care for the lady, but I won't come between him and the person he's dating."

"Amber, I would never expect that of you. That's not who you are. That's why I'm hoping with my whole heart that Rome will fall for someone like you." She paused and stared at Amber with serious eyes. "To answer your question, all I want from you is just for you to be Rome's friend. Do you think I'm asking too much?"

Amber stared with sincere eyes. "Of course not, I would love to be his friend. Having a male friend in my life is something I welcome. It will give me an opportunity to have conversations with more than females and two year olds." She laughed.

"I'm hoping that after being friends with you, he'll be able to tell the difference in a genuine connection, compared to someone who's just out to get what she can get," Veronica said strongly. "I know she seems nice on the surface but in time her true colors will show. And the thing about my sons, they are sweet and trusting, but if a female ever deceive or double-cross one of them, that's the finish," she said with conviction.

Chapter Twenty-Three

Snow was lightly falling against the windshield on that cold Tuesday afternoon the 3rd of December as Charles Taylor drove his white Rolls-Royce cautiously down the street toward Leo's, the new Italian restaurant for lunch. His wife Candace sat on the passenger's side very quiet as he looked straight ahead with sorrow on his face. They had just left the doctors' office for Candace scheduled nine o'clock appointment. The doctor had shared with them some unexpected news that would be life altering.

After they arrived at Leo's and were seated at a table, Candace appeared lost in thought looking down at the table when the waiter asked for their order.

"Please give us a moment," Charles said to the waiter.

The waiter walked away and Charles reached across the table and touched his wife's hand. "Candace, we both feel lost in despair right now, but we need to try to collect ourselves so we can be strong for the girls," he uttered with care. "We really need to decide when we are going to tell the girls."

Candace looked at her husband and shook her head. She was too choked up to utter a word. She took the white cloth napkin that was sticking out of the glass next to her silverware and dried the tears that were falling from her sad eyes. At that time the waiter arrived at their table again.

"Can I get you something to drink while you decide what you would like to have?" he asked.

"I'll take a glass of white wine," Charles said and looked at his wife. "Would you like a glass of wine as well," he asked her.

Candace nodded, but never looked toward her husband or the waiter. She kept the napkin to her eyes as she kept looking down toward the table.

Charles nodded at the waiter. "We'll take two glasses of white wine."

"Two white wines coming up," the waiter said and hurried away from their table.

"You need to eat something," Charles said. "I think I'll have the soup and salad special. I don't think I can stomach much else."

"That sounds fine with me," Candace mumbled as she finally lifted her head and looked across the table at her husband. "I don't know if I'll be able to eat a bite but I know I need to."

"Did you take your medicine? The doctor said you should take it before or with food," Charles reminded her.

"I'll take it now. They want me to take these pills four times a day." She pulled the bottle of little pink pills from her purse and poured one into her palm. "I can't believe this tiny pill is mandatory for my pure existence."

The waiter arrived at their table again with two glasses of white wine, which he placed in front of each of them. He had his order pad in hand. "What can I get you for lunch?" He looked toward Mrs. Taylor and smiled.

She looked up at the tall thin waiter and forced a smiled to show on her deeply sadden face. "We are both having your lunch special, the soup and salad. I'll have French dressing and ranch dressing for him."

When the waiter walked away Charles eyes watered up as he placed his napkin in his lap. "Candace, before we leave this restaurant we need to decide when we are going to share what the doctor told us with the girls."

"Charles, I really do not want to worry the girls. If it's okay with you I would like to keep this information from them. After all, it serves no purpose except to break their spirits; and that's the last thing I want to do."

"I agree," he nodded. "But it's something we can't get around. They need to know. We can't keep them in the dark about something this important," he stated.

"I don't want to discuss it." She waved her hand. "Please excuse me as I find their ladies room," Candace said and wheeled her wheelchair in the direction of the ladies room at the entrance of the restaurant.

Candace was away from the table for nearly ten minutes. When she returned her lunch was waiting on the table for her. "Sweetheart, coming here was a waste of time and money. I'm afraid I can't eat a bite," she sadly mumbled.

"I can't stomach any food either," Charles lifted his glass and took a sip of wine. "But I'm glad we are here so we can decide on what we are going to tell the girls."

"I thought I made it clear before I went to the ladies room that I don't want to worry Sabrina, Samantha and Starlet. Please Charles, let's keep this information to ourselves," Candace stressed.

Charles shook his head. "I'm so sorry, sweetheart. But I think they should be told," Charles said, poking his fork into his salad but not eating it.

"Charles, I would agree if it would serve a purpose. It will only serve an unwanted purpose to keep them worried about me all the time. We need to agree on keeping my condition to ourselves before we head home," Mrs. Taylor said as she unsteady lifted her wine glass and took a small sip and shaky place the glass back on the table.

"Candace, I sympathize, but I will not keep something of this magnitude from the girls. They are adults and need to know what your doctor just told us. Your doctor has given you a maximum of one year to live and I just don't see any way around not telling them," Mr. Taylor explained seriously, and then took a big swallow from his wine glass. His eyes were sad and filled with water. "Besides, they will take one look at me and figure out something is wrong."

"Charles, I'm begging you," Mrs. Taylor reached across the table and held both of his hands. "Please, do this for me. It's my life that's being cut short. This is my way of giving them one last gift. I want to spare them the agony and worry of thinking about my fate. I know you can recall how devastated they were when we shared with them that I would never be able to walk again. That news knocked them off track for a long while. Their college studies suffered along with their social life. This news would shatter them. It's a lot more life changing than being permanently stuck in a wheelchair. This news would destroy their livelihood. I don't want to disrupt their lives. When the time comes it will be hard enough on them. I want to spare them a year of pain. They are going to have the rest of their lives to grieve me and I don't want to suffer while I'm still with them." She slowly removed her hands from his, took her napkin and dried her falling tears. "Besides, if we tell them they will treat me differently and our lives will be one big depression zone. It won't resemble any regularity. All normality will be sucked out of our lives and that is not what I want. I do not want to live my final days depressed and worried that my girls are sad and fussing over me." She glanced about the restaurant and smiled at the elegant Christmas tree and decorations, and then she looked at her husband. "You know, that reminds me. I know it's just the first week of the month but I think we should put up the tree and decorate it early this year." She turned to her side and continued to admire the tall Christmas tree, which was elegantly decorated in all silver and blue lights and trimmings. After staring at the tree as if she was lost in thought, Charles reached out and touched her hand.

"Sure, my lady love, if that's what you want to do."

She looked at him and smiled. "You haven't called me your lady love since I was pregnant with Starlet. I always wanted ice cream in the middle of the night when we had none and you would drive to a twenty-four hour seven-eleven and buy me ice cream. You would deliver the ice cream and say anything for my lady love."

Charles smiled. "Those days were so precious and you are still my lady love." He touched his chest. "And you always will be." He paused. "I like the idea of putting up the tree and we can all decorate it," he assured her.

"Can we do it this evening?" she looked at her husband with a solemn face.

He nodded. "Sure, why not? If the girls are up to it with no other plans I think this evening would be perfect."

"I think it would be perfect as well." She lifted her wine glass and finished all of the drink before she lowered the glass. "Charles, I know you are broken over this news just like I am. But we need to keep our composure for our daughters. I'm determined to be strong for them and get through this period with as much regularity as possible. I want our household to be as normal as possible for the time I have left. So, Charles, please tell me you won't tell the girls."

"That you will only be with them for one more year," he said sadly. "Candace, I have listened to your reasons and I understand why you don't want them to know, but it's not inside of me to keep this from them." He touched his chest. "We didn't raise them that way. We have never kept them in the dark about anything."

"Charles, I know all of this and it rips at my heart to withhold this information, but it also rips me more to have to deal with the chaos of sharing this news and tearing their worlds. So, I beg of you with everything I have to grant me this one last wish."

After a long pause, Charles Taylor pushed his salad plate aside and placed his elbows on the table and nodded at his wife as he dried a tear before it fell.

"Okay, Candace, after all these years I have never been able to say no to you. I'll keep your secret from the girls. I'll do it for you. It won't be easy but I will grant you this wish. You are the love of my life and I never thought we would be having this conversation. And now that we are, it seems unreal. A thought I would have a lifetime to be with you. One more year isn't enough time to spend with you."

"Charles, I'm sad yes. But before the doctor told us I sort of had a sense that this was coming. The agony and sadness consumes me, but I'm also so very grateful for all the wonderful years that we have spent together. And I'm so very thankful and proud of the three lovely girls we have raised. Their caring and thoughtful ways move me. Just like your caring and thoughtful ways moved me all those years ago back in high school when we met during our senior year and fell in love."

Charles nodded and smiled. "I try my best, but those girls are something special. You and I can pat ourselves on the back. Raising our daughters to be the caring individuals that they are has been our greatest achievement." He lifted his wine glass to his mouth and swallowed the last drop of wine. "I can't even imagine my life without you," he said as he placed the empty wine glass back on the table.

"I know you can't. However, we have to be strong and not think of the gloom that awaits us. We'll lean on each other during this next year as we always have. After all, we have been with each other most of our lives. You were my high school sweetheart and the first and only boy I have ever loved. But I'm not sure if I can say the same about you." She smiled. "I think you were into that redhead cheerleader before you asked me out." She laughed.

Charles smiled. "For the one hundredth time, I was not into that cheerleader, she was into me. Of course, you already know that you were the only girl at school that caught my interest." He stared into her eyes. "Where did the time go? If we could set back the clock I would value and treasure our time together even more, if that's possible," he said with a deeply sadden voice.

"Charles, you are still basically a young man. You are only sixty-one."

Charles threw up both hands and stopped her words. "I can see where your conversation is headed. Please, don't go there. You are the only woman I have ever loved and will ever love. When you are gone, I plan to stay single for the rest of my life. No other woman could ever replace you in my heart," he said with conviction."

"I just don't want you to be alone. Sabrina, Samantha and Starlet will no doubt all marry and move out within the next few years; and you'll be left alone in that big house. You need to think of a companion after I'm gone. I really want that for you."

"Candace, you might as well let it go. I'm not going to have this conversation with you. Besides, sixty-one is not that young and women in my age group are either married, sick or not interested; so even if the thought of a companion would cross my mind after I have lost you, I'm sure the picking would be slim and next to none."

"Charles, you don't realize what a fine man you are. You are a very rich man and good looking to boot. I saw how Veronica Franklin couldn't stay out of your face at our house warming party."

"She was just trying to get acquainted with us. She was in your face as well." He pointed out.

"Yes, she was, but she couldn't stop smiling at you while you two talked."

"And because she couldn't stop smiling, I'm to assume she found me attractive?"

"Of course, she found you attractive. What woman wouldn't find you attractive? Charles you are still a very good looking fellow. Not to mention how kind and smart you are," she said sincerely. "And did I mention filthy rich with high moral values." She smiled. "You are almost a carbon copy of the late Ryan Franklin."

"Thanks for the compliment, but I wouldn't go that far. Ryan Franklin was above broad and almost perfect in every aspect of his life. The guy was almost a saint. I try my best but I can only strive to achieve his level of benevolent."

"Well, in my eyes you already have; and I'm sure it has probably crossed Veronica's mind as well."

"Now, I'm not just attractive to her, I also remind her of her late husband?"

"I'm sure you do. Besides, you know the girls are dating her sons; her very respectful, well mannered sons."

"Candace, could we please change the subject. You are still with us and I can't imagine my life without you; and I definitely can't concentrate on ever being with someone else," he stressed firmly.

"Charles, it makes me feel helpful and makes me feel as if I have a hand in your future. I will be able to accept my fate easier if I know you will not be left alone for the rest of your life. And since our daughters are dating the Franklin boys why can't you date Veronica Franklin after I'm gone?"

"For one, if you insist on this ridiculous conversation, Veronica Franklin probably isn't interested in a relationship with me or any other man. That woman buried her husband twenty years ago. She has been single all these years, which means single is what she wants. So if you are set on picking out a potential mate for me before you leave me, you should probably mark Veronica Franklin from your list."

Chapter Twenty-Four

While Amber and Rome were working late that Tuesday evening, he knocked on her office door.

"Come in," she said.

He peeped in and smiled. "I thought you were still here." He glanced at his watch. "It's six-thirty. I think we should take off."

She smiled at him. "I wanted to finish those reports. I called my nannies and told them I wouldn't make it home for dinner." She stacked the papers on her desk.

"I called home as well and informed my mother not to hold dinner which sounds like we both missed dinner," he smiled and held up one finger. "So here's the deal, you're going to follow me to that new Italian restaurant up town."

"You mean "Leo Fine Eatery" that everybody is raving about?"

"That's the place, and dinner is on me." He held out both arms. "I'm not taking no for an answer."

"I hear the place is quite nice." She stood up from her chair and looked down at the shoes and outfit she was wearing. "Do you think I'm dressed okay?"

"Sure, we are dressed fine," he answered.

"Thanks, but I'm not so sure about my outfit," she said. "But of course, you are dressed wonderful. You and your brothers dress beautifully every single work day. But tell me honestly, do you think my outfit looks appropriate. My skirt has gotten quite wrinkled."

"Believe me, Amber, your skirt and you looks just fine. I can't imagine you not looking fine in whatever you wear." He glanced quickly at her skirt and then locked eyes with her. "You are quite beautiful, Amber."

His compliment caught her off guard and she blushed. "Okay, if you say so." She turned and headed toward the coat stand in the corner of the office. Looking in his eyes made her weak and she needed to keep her composure around him. "You have yourself a dinner partner," she said over her shoulder as she grabbed her coat and purse off the coat stand.

When she turned around with her coat and purse in her arms, Rome had stepped into her office and was headed toward her. Her heart skipped a beat as she had a quick glimpse of romance. Was he going to grab her in his arms and kiss her?

"Let me help you with that." He took her coat from her arms and helped her slip into it. The closest of his presence filled her with warmth.

"Okay, you are all bundled up," he said and patted her shoulders. "Are you ready for some dinner at the nicest Italian restaurant in town?" He looked at her and smiled as he held the office door open for her.

She draped her Louis Vuitton purse on her shoulder, flicked off the light, and then they headed out of her office together.

In the few weeks that Amber had worked closely with Rome on different work projects, they had become quite good friends and worked well together. Now sitting at a small round table in the upscale Leo's waiting for their meals to be served, Amber noticed how her heart had continued to beat faster in Rome's presence. He was by far the most striking man she had ever seen; and she was enormously impressed with his polite manners and charismatic personality. Sitting across from him, the burning candle in the center of the table flickered and highlighted his radiant beautiful eyes and every time she glanced at his face, his eyes left her mesmerized. She lifted her glass and took a sip of water just so her anxious hands would have something to do. But she placed the glass back on the table just as the waiter placed a fresh garden salad in front of her and one in front of Rome.

"Amber, if I haven't told you, I'm telling you now how blessed we are to have you onboard at the company. As long as you want to be apart of our team we are glad to have you." He took his knife and fork and chopped the whole small tomato on his plate into four quarters and popped one quarter into his mouth. "We want to be as flexible as you need us to be so we won't keep you away from your kids for too many hours. Plus, we don't want Mr. Taylor to convince you to quit."

"You don't have to worry about my father trying to talk me into quitting," she grinned. "He has already done that and failed. Besides, I enjoy working for your company. And of course, my folks don't agree, but working at Franklin Gas is just what I needed. I'm finding it very rewarding." She lifted her fork and her hand slightly shook to the point that she placed the fork back down and lifted her glass of ice tea and took a quick sip.

"Amber, is anything the matter?" Rome asked with concern.

She looked at him. "Why do you ask?"

"It just seems that after you mentioned your father not being pleased about you working for us, you seem bothered. Maybe it's just my imagination, but you also seem a bit nervous. If you need to give the job up for any reason, as much as we love having you, we'll understand." He reached across the table and gave her a quick touch on the top of her hand.

"Rome, I am a bit nervous but it has nothing to do with my father or either of my parents or how they feel about me working full time." She paused and stared down at the table for a moment and then looked across the table at him. "It has nothing to do with me thinking about giving up my job," she said sincerely.

He nodded with a solemn look on his face. "Okay, that's good to hear so far. But I guess you're going to tell me what the problem is, because something is bothering you, am I correct?"

She nodded. "You are correct," she mumbled in a low voice, staring him in the eyes. "There's no easy way to tell you this."

"What is it, Amber? You have assured me that you are not quitting and there's no issue with your folks, but whatever it is you seem torn up about it. Otherwise, you wouldn't look so sad."

"I'm not sad; it's just that what I have to tell you isn't easy."

"Well, if you would rather not tell me. There's no law that says you have to," he said in a teasing manner to lighten her up.

"I know I don't have to tell you, but it's something that I want to tell you. I just don't know how to say it. I don't want to offend you or make you feel uncomfortable."

"I don't think you could ever do that. Just tell me, I'm sure it can't be anything that dreadful coming from you." Rome lifted his glass of ice tea to his mouth and before he could take a sip he put the glass back on the table when he noticed Amber take her napkin and wipe a tear from her left eye.

"Amber, I'm quite concerned now to see you cry. Please share your news with me and let me know if there's any thing I can do to help," he urged her.

She slowly placed her napkin in her lap and locked eyes with him. She had deep emotions pouring from her eyes when she quickly said. "I'm falling in love with you."

Rome stared at her motionless for a moment. Her confession had completely stunned him. "Did I hear you correctly? Did you just say you are falling in love with me?" he said in a low voice.

"Yes, Rome, you heard me correctly. It's true." She took her fingers and dried her tears. "I know this puts you in an awkward position telling you this. But I think it's only right to be completely on the level with you."

Rome was speechless for a moment. He stopped chewing his salad, swallowed hard and then lifted his glass of ice tea and took a long swallow. "I'm deeply flattered, but is it possible that I could have misunderstood?" He stared with appreciated eyes.

She shook her head. "It's not possible that you misunderstood me. It's true; I have fallen in love with you, Rome."

"Amber, I had no idea you were even interested in me."

"I know, and I thought long and hard whether to tell you. But decided to tell you because I feel being open and honest is the best policy. My late husband and I lived by those rules."

"Amber, I'm overwhelmed and extremely honored. You are such a beautiful stunning lady. But you're more than just beautiful, you are remarkably unique. There's something quite special about you, Amber." He paused and stared in her eyes for a lingering moment. "I'm sort of lost for words; because I know you are already aware of my relationship with Courtney."

"Rome, yes, I'm aware of your relationship with Courtney and I know the two of you are happy and I'm not trying to come between you two," she explained.

"That thought never crossed my mind," he quickly relayed.

"Just the same, I want you to know that I respect the fact that you are in a relationship," she explained. "My reason for telling you has nothing to do with trying to win you over from the person you are with. And I just hope telling you this will not make you feel awkward about being around me," she said softly, looking across the table at him.

"No worries there." He smiled. "I could never feel awkward around someone as lovely and incredible as you. I'm just so flattered by what you have told me."

She smiled. "I'm glad you are flattered."

"I'm very flattered," Rome assured her.

"It means something to me that you said that." She lifted her water glass and took a sip of water. "I decided to tell you my feelings because I wanted you to know how you have made such a wonderful difference in my life. My feelings for you are strong and real."

"Amber, I'm moved by your confession, but how did I make a difference?"

"Just being you," she said softly, looking in his eyes. "I never thought I could feel again what I'm feeling for you. And even though you are in a relationship with someone else, just being around you, you have given me the most precious gift of all. You have given me back the gift of love." She touched her chest. "After all this time since I lost Austin, I can finally feel love again and know I want to be loved again."

Chapter Twenty-Five

The snow covered the grounds and trees like the scenery on a postcard. No wind was stirring and it was a cold, still night before Christmas. Rome and Courtney had just gotten to Franklin House from a Christmas party. They had both had their share of Christmas cheer and too much champagne, although Rome had only drunk three glasses to her six and he was surprised by her indulgence. He pulled into the driveway at Franklin House around one o'clock in the morning. Everyone in the house was asleep. He and Courtney kept quiet heading up the staircase to his room. The moment they reached his room and closed the door, Courtney fell into his arms and he kissed her passionately. When he pulled away from her she dropped on the bed and fell over smiling at him as he slipped out of his coat and threw it on the settee.

"What are you doing?" she asked.

"I'm getting out of my clothes," he said unbuttoning his white shirt.

"I guess I should do the same," she said with blurred language. She then sat up, hopped off the bed, removed her coat and threw it on the settee on top of Rome's coat. After which she was spellbound by the paintings above his fireplace.

He was smiling at her and couldn't undress swiftly enough. "Why are you standing there looking at those paintings over the fireplace?" He asked.

"Because I just noticed that they are the same paintings above the fireplace downstairs in the living room."

"Yes, they are, and the same paintings above every fireplace in this house and before you ask, no, I can't tell you how many fireplaces are in this big house."

She continued to stand there looking at the paintings and her heart melted as she felt enthralled by the beautiful painting of Britain.

"Hey, you; are you going to keep staring at those paintings or get undressed?" Rome said playfully. "You're giving me my Christmas gift tonight, right?" He winked at her as he stepped out of his chic black slacks and threw them on the settee with the rest of the clothing he had shed.

She stepped away from the fireplace and staggered slightly. "Of course; I'm going to unwrap it now." She started unbuttoning her cranberry top. She slipped it off her shoulders to reveal a bright white lacy bra. Then she stood up and slipped out of her cranberry skirt and white slip. By this time Rome stood there in just his black silk shorts, Courtney was standing there in just her bra and panties and stockings.

Rome grabbed her in his arms and they fell on the bed wrapped in each other's arms. "You feel better than anything I could have imagined. It's more unreal than anything. Feeling your body next to mine is like being wide awake in an incredible dream," he whispered before he placed his mouth over hers in a hungry kiss.

He held her next to him and moved his hands all over her back and down her shoulders. He wanted to savior the irresistible feeling of touching her skin for the first time. He kissed her deeply and passionately to the point that he had to pull away so they both could catch their breath.

"Courtney, you feel sensational in my arms," he whispered against her neck. "No, I should rephrase that because you feel better than sensational if that's possible. You are so incredible. I can't seem to get enough of holding you and kissing you. Your lips are perfect," he said softly, as he brought his mouth closer to hers, swallowing her up once more before he rolled over on his back with her in his arms.

With Courtney lying on top of him looking down smiling, he leaned toward her and kissed her. "Courtney, I'm sure I can get used to this. I can't think of anywhere I would rather be than right here with you like this."

"I'm happy to be here with you too," Courtney managed.

"You can't possibly be as thrilled as I am right now." He smiled and rolled back over on top of her. "I'm crazy about you and I think you know that."

Rome placed one pillows under Courtney's head and then rubbed his perfect shaped nose across her throat; bringing his mouth up to kiss her face repeatedly. He kissed her nose, both cheeks, her chin, and then dropped down to the side of her neck before ripping up to press his mouth over hers in a wild passionate kiss that left them both breathless. Then he pulled away from her and smiled.

"You are driving me out of my head here. You are so irresistible, I don't know if I'm going to be able to stop holding you and kissing you. What part of you can I kiss next? I think I'll start with the bottom of your feet and work my way up. How does that sound?" He whispered in a soft sexy voice.

"It sounds out of this world," she moaned, reaching out to touch his face.

"Out of this world is a good answer. That's exactly how it feels, somewhere between here and heaven," he uttered breathless.

She laid flat on her back smiling up at him as he took both hands and slowly removed her stockings from each leg and hung them across his neck. He then held her right leg in his hands, bringing his face down to her leg, placing his lips against it. He kissed his way down her leg to the bottom of her foot. He then caressed and massaged her right foot with both of his hands until she couldn't bear the overwhelming sensations any longer.

Courtney wrapped her fingers in his loose wavy hair and guided him to kiss her again. He moved from the foot of the bed quicker than a flash of light to cover her lips with his. He gripped her in his demanding arms and every part of him was silently overflowing for her as he made urgent passionate love to her.

By 2:00 a.m., Rome was fast asleep laying there beside Courtney. She was alert and wide awake. She hadn't fallen asleep at all. She had waited patiently for him to close his eyes. When she sensed that he was fully asleep, she sat up in bed and looked down at him and could tell that he was completely asleep. She then threw the covers back and eased her way out of Rome's king size bed. She grabbed her underwear off the carpet and stepped into them. She located her bra at the foot of the bed and threw it on. She then quickly threw on her skirt and top and sneaked across the room to the door. She eased the door open and sneaked out of bedroom and down the hallway in search of Britain's room. She recalled that all the rooms had a gold initial of the occupant's name displayed on the upper left side of the occupant's door. She passed two doors, one with the initial P and one with the initial S and then the third door were open and she couldn't see the initial but could see that it was Britain's room. The dim light from the moon shining through his window highlighted him lying in his bed fast asleep under the covers. Courtney walked into his room and slowly with great ease closed his bedroom door and then walked across the room toward his bed. The only light in the room came from the bright moonlight pouring through the windows of his very spacious room. His room was decorated in all white, from the floral white walls, right down to the floral white carpeting on the floor. She remembered that he had told her that his favorite color was white. From the dim lighting she could see that his room was decorated in four shades of white. Long snow white curtains hung at his windows and the two lamps on either side of his bed were displayed with snow white lamp shades and a snow white comforter covered his bed. His traditional posh five piece bedroom set was displayed in vanilla white as well as the small sofa in the corner of the room. The fireplace mantle and the frames of all the paintings on his bedroom wall were all showcased in magnolia white. His room was an absolute delight she thought as she stood at his bedside glancing about the room before she collected herself and stared down at him. She watched him sleep for a few minutes before she reached out and lightly touched the side of his face. He opened his eyes and looked at her. At first he was calm lying there looking up at her, then it dawned on him that he wasn't dreaming. He sat right up, yawned and wiped his eyes with both hands. He was startled at the sight of her standing in the dark in his room.

"Courtney, what are you doing in my room? What's going on?" He reached over to the night stand and clicked on the lamp light and grabbed his gold Rolex watch and glanced at the time. He placed the watch down and stared at her. "Is anything the matter? Is Rome okay? Where is Rome? When we left the party the two of you were still there. Did something happen?" he asked with concern.

"Nothing happened, Rome is in his room. I came in here to talk to you."

"You what, you came in here to talk to me?" Britain was confused, still trying to get a grip and wake up. "Why would you do something like that at two in the morning?" He grabbed his satiny white robe from the foot of the bed and threw it on.

"I just need to talk to you," Courtney mumbled and stumbled as she took a seat in a nearby white comfortable chair.

Britain could see that she had been drinking heavy. "This isn't a good time to talk. You need to get back to Rome's room before he misses you and come looking for you. I know you have been drinking, but if he finds you here in my room at two a.m. your relationship will be over," Britain assured her.

He stepped into his connecting bathroom, wet a towel and then walked over to her where she was seated in the chair and handed her the towel. "You need to get a grip and get out of here quick."

"I just said we need to discuss something." She wiped her face and threw the towel on the carpet.

He stood with his arms folded and nodded at her. "Okay, Courtney, what is it?"

"I have one question for you. Why did you dump me like that? For two months I waited and thought you were going to ask me out, but you never did. Just answer me why! Can you please do that?"

Britain shook his head. "Why are you bringing this up now? That happened months ago; and besides, I didn't dump you. We were not in a relationship, remember? You were into my brother and I was being a friend."

"That's a lie!" she hopped out of the chair and threw her arms round him. But he quickly, yet gently pushed her away and she dropped back in the chair.

"Courtney, you need to leave my room now. I don't know what's up with you, but whatever it is, I don't like it," Britain said firmly.

"Why do you keep rejecting me? Why do you feel you're so above me?"

Britain stepped across the room and stretched opened his bedroom door. He extended his arm toward the door. "You need to leave," he stressed firmly. "Do you want Rome to find you here in my bedroom in a drunken state? If he does, it won't end well. He will not put up with his kind of behavior," Britain explained anxiously in a low voice. "You better snap out of it otherwise your relationship with Rome is going to be in big trouble. Don't you care about that?"

"No, I don't care about that," Courtney snapped.

"You don't mean that. I know how much you care about my brother. You just had too much to drink and you don't know what you are saying."

"I have been drinking but I know what I'm saying. Yes, in the beginning I had my eyes on Rome; and then you showed me kindness and you were so nice to me. Sitting there having lunch with you every day meant so much to me."

Britain nodded. "It was cool hanging out with you at lunch. But we were just two friends sharing a lunch table."

"I know it started out that way, but we had lunch together for nearly everyday for two months. Spending an hour with you everyday like that was like magic and I fell for you, then you dumped me and Rome took a notice. By then, I was already into you too deeply, but I convinced myself that I was glad to be with Rome." She paused and wiped a tear. "I was happy with Rome until I wasn't. It was like little by little and day by day I just couldn't shake you out of my system."

Britain grabbed his head and stared up at the ceiling. He looked at Courtney and shook his head. "So, what are you saying?"

"I'm saying I love you and wish we could start over and have a real relationship?"

Britain was motionless and stunned as he stared with shocked eyes into her sad ones. Her confession of love had thrown him. "That's not going to happen. I'm in a relationship with the woman I want to be with; and what about Rome?"

"Stop asking me about Rome. I'm trying to tell you how I feel. I haven't been able to get over how you swept me aside and never asked me out, and then the one date we planned, you blew me off."

"Courtney, I'm not sure if the booze has clouded your mind and has you saying all of this, but either way it's not good."

"Stop talking to me as if I don't know what I'm saying! The booze isn't making me say what I'm saying. I know how I feel in my heart. I know exactly what I'm saying." She bent over to pick up the towel off the floor, but stumbled against his nightstand and accidentally knocked a tall thirty inch crystal vase and a stack of CDs to the floor. The delicate vase cracked and broke and shattered into many pieces when it hit the corner of the nightstand. It made a loud crashing loud.

Minutes later, Veronica, Paris, Sydney, Catherine and Rome were standing at Britain's bedroom door. They were all gathered there showcasing fine silks robes in an array of colors as if they were dressed to do a commercial selling a stylish assortment of robes for an upscale bouquet. Veronica matching robe and gown set was lavender and white, Catherine robe and gown set was deep purple, Sydney robe was black and Paris was wearing a royal blue robe.

They were all speechless to see Courtney in Britain's bedroom. Rome pushed past the rest and stepped into the room wearing a pair of silk gray pajamas with a matching long robe that hung open. He had a surprise look in his eyes and a slight frown on his face. He was the first to speak.

"I noticed you had left the room. I thought you went downstairs to the kitchen for a bottle of water or something." He walked near Courtney. "What are you doing here in Britain's room? And what was that loud noise that we all heard?"

Britain pointed to the broken vase and CDs on the floor. "The vase and CDs fell to the floor after she bumped against the nightstand."

She bumped against the nightstand?" Rome asked with confusion in his eyes. "Why is she in your room this time of night?"

Britain raised both arms. "I think you need to ask her."

Room looked at Courtney who was staring toward the floor. He lifted her face to look at him. "Did you get lost looking for the kitchen? I know you had had too much to drink. But how did you end up in my brother's room?"

"It's no big deal." She looked at Rome and waved her hand.

"Courtney, I think it is a big deal that you end up in my brother's room this time of time. After all you knocked over a vase and we were all startled and didn't know what had happened," Rome explained.

"I'm sorry about that vase, I bet it was worth a small fortune, but it was an accident. You can take the cost out of my pay if you want too."

"Courtney, I'm not concerned with the broken vase and nobody is going to take any money out of your pay to replace it. I'm just concerned to how you ended up here in my brother's bedroom?"

"There's nothing to be concerned about. I just came in here to talk to Britain. We needed to discuss something," she mumbled.

Rome stared at her and took a deep breath. "You mean you intentionally came to his room this time of night?"

"Don't ask me if I intentionally came to his room or how I ended up in Britain's room. I found his room and that's what counts."

"Why did you need to find my brother's room?" Rome asked anxiously with an irritated tone.

Courtney pulled her face away from his grip and stumbled away from Rome and started walking toward Britain. "Leave me alone." She waved her hand. "I told you already that Britain and I needed to discuss something."

Rome grabbed Courtney by the shoulders and turned her facing him. She almost lost her balance. She stared at him. "What are you doing? Can't you see I need to discuss something with Britain," she yelled angrily at him.

"No, you are not discussing anything this time of night in the condition you are in. You are coming with me now," he insisted. "I had no idea you were this wasted when we left that party. You don't seem to know what you are doing or what you're talking about. So, come with me now. You have awakened everybody in the house." Rome glanced toward the doorway at everybody and shook his head as if head; giving them a silent "I'm sorry." His eyes connected with his mother and he noticed the concerned disappointed look on her face.

Courtney pulled her arm from his grip. "Stop saying I don't know what I'm saying. I know exactly what I'm saying. I want to discuss something with Britain; and I'm not leaving this room until I do."

"What do you need to discuss with my brother? Tell me, better yet, if it will get you to leave this room so everybody can get back to bed, go on and discuss what you need to discuss. There he is." Rome pointed to Britain who was propped against the frame of the door with his arms folded, shaking his head. "Go to him and discuss whatever you need to discuss so I can get you out of here," Rome said with a voice filled with frustration.

Courtney stepped across the room to where Britain was propped but he didn't look toward her. He kept looking toward the floor. "Britain will you answer my question?" She asked.

He looked at her and shook his head. "What question is that?"

"Why did you forget my birthday and blow me off the way you did?"

"Courtney, that happened months ago. I apologized, why isn't that enough?"

"It's not enough because you broke my heart. I was in love with you then and I'm still in love with you now," she confessed.

When Courtney said those words, Rome grabbed the back of his head with both hands. He exchanged stunned looks with his mother and then stared up at the ceiling for a moment before rushing toward Courtney. He grabbed her by the arm. "I don't care if you are wasted you just told my brother that you are in love with him, therefore, we are done! You can sleep off your drunk in one of the guestrooms, but tomorrow morning I want you out of my house and out of my life! Do you get that?" Rome said firmly as he pulled her gently out of Britain's room.

They all looked on with surprise looks on their faces as Rome pulled Courtney fussing at him, down the hallway and into one of the guestrooms.

It was like the calm after a storm; they all exchanged looks with each other with stunned looks on their faces at what had just occurred. The scene Courtney had just displayed had shocked and disappointed them all, especially Britain. He felt a tad guilty for her behavior, although he wasn't at fault for her conduct. He humbly glanced at Paris and Sydney who stood at the entrance of his bedroom door with empathy in their eyes. But his sad eyes never connected with his mother and aunt as he stepped across the room and dropped down on the foot of his bed. He grabbed his face in wonderment of what he could have done differently that would have avoided the incredible scene that Courtney had showcased.

Across the large room still standing at Britain's door, Catherine exchanged looks with Veronica and shook her head. "Well, I'll be damn. You hit this one right on the head. If I was a gambling person, I would have lost this bet," she stated and headed down the hallway toward her room.

Veronica hurried down the hallway behind Catherine. She caught up with her and grabbed her by the arm, stopping Catherine in her tracks.

"Catherine, I agree that what happened here tonight proves my point about that little slut," Veronica said angrily. "But believe me when I say, I'm not pleased that she has hurt both Rome and Britain with her drunken disrespectful actions."

"By no means did I think otherwise," Catherine answered. "I'm sure you are not pleased how Courtney managed to hurt Rome and Britain, and how she also managed to disrupt the entire house by causing that shameful scene here in the middle of the night. But at least, if nothing else, her lack of ethics and poor manners have wiped her off of Rome and Britain's radar," Catherine said assuredly.

"From your lips to God's ears, I pray you are right," Veronica stressed. "But I would not have wished this hurt on my sons in order to have obtained this result."

"I know you would have prevented it if you could have."

"Yes, I would have. I'm outraged at that young lady; and my heart is burden with sadness to imagine how Rome and Britain is broken up over this!"

"I'm sure you are outraged. Those boys are at the top of your list."

"They are not just at the top of my list, they are my main priority! I'm sick inside that I didn't see this tragedy coming!"

"Well, you sort of did. You had a talk with Rome and me and informed us both of your misgivings about that girl. You said she would hurt Rome."

"I know I said it, but I didn't lift a finger to prevent this disaster. I should have tried harder to spare Rome and Britain of this distress that Courtney Ross has just put them through," Veronica cried.

"It was out of your hands, Veronica," Catherine said compassionately. "As much as I sympathize, your sons are grown men and they make their own choices in women. There was nothing you could do but voice your misgivings, which you did. And you were right to try and steer Rome away from that one. I have to admit that before all this fallout, I thought she was a decent girl."

"By no means did I think she was decent, but it turns out that she has fewer morals than I had pegged her for. I never felt she was right for Rome, but based on how he and Britain voiced how respectable she was, I thought she had some principles in place," Veronica admitted. "But to run from one brother's bed to the next while one is asleep in the next room. It doesn't take much of a leap to figure out that Courtney Ross lacks good manners and ethics. Her behavior in his house has been appalling to say the least." Veronica wiped her tears with the back of her hands.

"I agree, she disrupted the entire household," Catherine said. "But in her defense, not that I excuse her inexcusable conduct, but we could all see how boozed up she was. She was so intoxicated that she could barely stand up straight," Catherine pointed out.

"You are right her behavior was inexcusable. But I always heard that a drunken person does what a sober one thinks," Veronica roared with anger.

"That is what they say, but maybe you should keep your voice down. We have an audience," Catherine mumbled and motioned toward the other end of the hallway.

Veronica glanced over her shoulder down the hallway and noticed Paris and Sydney still standing at Britain's doorway looking in their direction. "They are still there. I thought they went back to their rooms and hopped back in bed. I need to check on Britain."

"Sure, go ahead; I'm sure either of them will have anything else to do with Miss Ross. The picture she painted here tonight is not about to fade out of their minds anytime soon."

"Thank you, Catherine." Veronica patted Catherine on the shoulder and then turned her back to her and headed down the hallway toward Britain's room.

When Veronica made it down the hallway to Britain's bedroom door, Paris and Sydney exchanged looks with each other and then looked at their mother with curious eyes. "What was Aunt Catherine talking about?" Sydney asked.

"What do you mean, dear?" She patted Sydney on the shoulder. She was so pleased that other than disappointment and empathy for their brothers, Sydney and Paris had not been affected by Courtney's behavior.

"I mean what she said to you before she walked away from the door," Sydney explained. "She said you hit something right on the head."

"Oh that, it was just a little something I told her." Veronica nodded at Sydney and Paris, and patted Sydney on the shoulder before she turned and headed across the room toward Britain.

Paris and Sydney looked at each other and shook their heads. "What just happened here?" Sydney asked.

"One thing that happened, is the end of a relationship," Paris said regrettably.

"Yeah, what a big mess, Courtney Ross getting wasted like that," Sydney yawned. "I didn't see something like that coming from Courtney."

"Yeah, what a mess, but maybe it runs in the family," Paris mumbled under his breath.

"What was that?" Sydney asked.

"It's nothing worth repeating. I just wish we had waited around for them or tried to get them to leave the party when we all left," Paris said.

"Yeah, me too," Sydney agreed.

Paris and Sydney both yawned a couple times, and then left Britain's room and headed down the hallway to their own.

Veronica tapped Britain on the shoulder. "Are you okay?"

"Mother, how can I be okay after what just happened here in my room with Courtney? It was a train wreck that I couldn't stop," he said regrettably.

"It wasn't your place to stop it. She's a grown woman and she made the choice to make that scene. Granted, she had too much to drink and that's for sure. Would she have made the scene otherwise, probably not, but what's done is done; and she did it. That young lady will get no sympathy from me. I just feel bad for you and your brother that she made that scene like that in front of everybody, but it was bound to happen."

"What do you mean it was bound to happen? How can you say that, Mother? Rome and Courtney were getting along well."

"It appeared like that to all of us and maybe to your brother as well. However, sweetheart, it's obvious after what happened here tonight that Courtney wasn't happy with your brother. If she had half of a brain she would have been. The gall of that young woman to stand there in front of all of us, especially Rome, and announce she's in love with you. Well, she cooked her own goose because your brother is done with her now," Veronica assured him. "And as far as I'm concerned it didn't happen soon enough. Good riddance to Miss Courtney Ross." She waved her hand toward the door. "Rome has no business with some female who has such little respect for herself. I'm surprised by her conduct to go out and drank herself blind. I guess alcoholism runs in her family. I'm just glad Rome finally got a chance to see her true colors. Now he can get his life back on track and find someone who's worthy of him," she said with anger boiling in her stomach at the thought of Rome's disappointment and hurt at the hands of Courtney's betrayal. "Spending time with one brother when she knew she wanted to be with the other one. The nerve of that little tramp! Did you have any idea that Courtney was in love with you?"

"Of course not, Mother."

"Well, sweetheart, I'm sure you noticed a few months back, how she was throwing herself at you."

"No, Mother, I didn't notice it. How can you ask me that?"

"You're right; I shouldn't have asked you that."

Britain looked at his mother and nodded. "Maybe you should have asked me that. Even though I had no idea that she was actually in love with me, and she never threw herself at me the way you were referring, but I should have paid attention to the red flags in my head about her. I had a hunch that she sort of liked me. But that was doing the time when we were having lunch together."

"And if I got this right, you thought she was having lunch with you to get closer to your brother?"

Britain nodded. "Yes, Mother, that is correct. I want you to know that I never led her on or gave her the slightest reason to believe I had any feelings for her," he explained. "Besides, just as you mentioned. I thought and pretty much everyone at the company thought she was always into Rome."

"She was always into Rome so you thought. She led all of us to believe she was into your brother, but tonight proved differently. It's quite obvious that she misled your brother so she could get close to you."

"Mother, I don't think it was that way in the beginning. I'm almost positive that she started having lunch with me so she could get close to Rome."

"What possessed you to start having lunch with her like that for all that time? I'm sure that's what gave her the wrong impression and apparently made her believe there could be something between the two of you."

"Mother, you are right, I'm sure. But I respected Courtney as a person and a worker at that time. I would have my lunch at her table mostly because it seemed to please her that I sat there. Besides, as I mentioned, I thought she wanted me at her table so she could eventually build a rapport with Rome. I had no idea she had feelings for me. I'm blown away by what just took place here tonight. I never would have believed she would have carried on this way to disrespect Rome in the manner that she did." He shook his head. "That she would have ended up in my room in the middle of the night to behave as she did in front of a houseful of people. I can't help for thinking that some of the blame should fall on my shoulders," Britain stated seriously.

"Sweetheart, do not second guess yourself because of that girl. She was no good for your brother and she just proved it by trying to throw herself on you. There was nothing you could have done to have changed her behavior. She is who she is, an unethical female unfit for your brother. "

"Maybe, but if I had acknowledged her possible feelings and communicated with her that I had no feelings for her. Then just maybe things wouldn't have turned out this way," Britain stressed.

"Britain, you listen to me. I will not allow you to sit here and blame yourself for that young woman's behavior. She was a train wreck waiting to happen. It was just a matter of time before she showed her true colors. Nothing you could have done or said would have made any difference," Veronica assured him. "So, please just drop the notion that it's somehow your fault for what happened here. None of this was your fault. Put the blame where it should be, right on Courtney's shoulders. We can all be pleased that such an unscrupulous awful young lady is out of Rome's life."

"Mother, I'm not trying to make excuses for Courtney, and I have washed my hands of her because of her disrespect toward Rome. I also agree that she's not the right person for Rome. But we have to look at all the facts. She had clearly had too much to drink and wasn't thinking clearly."

"What's your point, sweetheart?" Veronica asked.

"I don't think she's an awful person. What she did here tonight was awful, but she's not awful."

"Do you think your brother will feel this way and take back up with her?"

"No, Mother, I don't think Rome will take back up with Courtney or forget her disrespectful behavior of tonight."

"Let me get this straight, you don't think she's awful; but you're sure your brother won't take back up with her. Sweetheart, I'm not sure I follow what you're trying to say."

"Mother, I'm merely saying that she's not an awful person. Is she misguided with questionable behavior? Yes, I do think so. But that doesn't make her an awful person, and even though Rome will most likely end his relationship with her, I'm sure he wouldn't consider her as an awful person," Britain pointed out.

"You are too good for your own good. This girl comes here and turns the house upside down in the middle of the night with her drunken demeanor. But you find it important to point out that you don't think she's awful." Veronica rubbed his shoulder. "I admire your compassion, which also poured from your father the same way. However, I do not share your sentiment. In my firm opinion, Courtney Ross is a disgraceful little gold digging tramp who Rome never should have taken up with in the first place."

"Mother, please!" Britain stared at his mother, not pleased by her choice of words. "We are all taken aback by Courtney's behavior, but Mother, isn't that pouring it on overly harsh?"

Veronica rubbed his shoulder. "Sweetheart, I know it sounds as if I'm coming over a bit harsh, but I'm just being frank."

"But, Mother, Courtney isn't as bad as you are making her out to be."

Veronica paused for a moment in his eyes. "Britain, my son, after what just happened in this room with that girl, how can you defend her honor? Can't you see that she simply doesn't have any?" Veronica said firmly. "I know you are a gentleman and I realize you do not want to hear what I have to say, but you need to open your eyes to the reality that Miss Ross may not be an awful person in your eyes, but she's definitely a little slut."

"Mother, she's not like that," Britain mumbled.

"That's the way it seems to me. The first day I laid eyes on Miss Ross I could see that gleam in her eyes."

"What gleam was that, Mother?" he asked.

"That gleam that she couldn't wait to snag one of you. She was too friendly and too available. My instincts told me that she was lurching around just hoping one of you would take to her. That's why I warned you boys that she was not the right girl for any of you. But needless to say, your brother can be stubborn, therefore, went out and hooked up with her inspite of my warning. That's water under the bridge and she's out of his hair now, but I knew she wasn't right for your brother."

"Mother, I know Courtney made a huge shocking error in conduct here tonight, or should I say morning, but she's not what you are making her out to be. Rome never would have started up with her if she was the awful person you think."

"He took up with her, but your brother is too trusting and he allowed that one to pull the wool over his eyes. She would have done the same to you, you know." She nodded. "But good for you, you didn't give her a chance to get her hooks in you. She's not like the Taylor girls. I think she's a promiscuous little tramp."

"Mother, please, she's not that way. You don't know, Courtney," Britain mumbled in a low voice.

"Sweetheart, I don't think you know her either," Veronica stated firmly. "You didn't expect her to behave the way she just did here in your room."

"You're right, Mother, I didn't expect that of Courtney, but she was intoxicated."

"Yes, she was intoxicated, but the drunkenness only gave her the courage to do what she didn't have the nerve to do while sober. Just think about what went on here tonight," Veronica paused for a moment as she considered whether to say what she wanted to say to her son. "Sweetheart, I don't mean to be so bold and blunt, but what I'm about to say needs to be said."

"Mother, what's your point? What needs to be said?" Britain looked his mother in the face with curious eyes.

"That young woman had a purpose for showing up in your room. She knows it and you know it, and your brother knows it, but because you are such a gentleman, you won't allow yourself to reflect on that truth."

"Mother, I'm afraid I don't know what you're referring to."

"I'm referring to Miss Ross and her intentions of hopping in bed with you. It's a bold statement on my part, but I would bet money that it's true. By no means did that young lady make her way to your room in the middle of the night just to small talk. She wanted you to have your way with her."

Britain grabbed the back of his neck with both hands and stared toward the ceiling for a moment as Veronica continued.

"But she over played her hand and wrote her fate in stone with your brother when she left his room in search of yours. I'm sure Rome has washed his hands of her and her shameful intentions. The only reason nothing happened is because you never would have allowed it. You are a gentleman and a very respectful young man, but if it had been left up to that little slut, I'm sure she would have hopped in your bed while your brother slept unsuspectingly in the room down the hall."

Britain turned to his mother who sat on the foot of his bed next to him. But he didn't comment as she continued.

"With that said, I think what she did was just despicable."

"Mother, can we not have this conversation any longer." He stood to his feet and stretched while yawning. "Thanks for talking and I know you are trying to comfort me, but this discussion has gotten to the point where it's not making me feel any better."

"Sure, sweetheart." She stood to her feet and gave him a hug. "I'll get out of your hair. I'm sure you're exhausted."

He walked over to the head of his bed and looked at his mother with tired eyes. "I can barely keep my eyes open." He turned back the covers and looked at his mother standing at the foot of his bed. "I would like to get a few more hours of sleep before I face Christmas morning and the fallout of this evening."

"Sure, sweetheart, hop back in bed and try to fall back to sleep," she said and then turned and headed across the floor toward his open door. "Do you want your door closed?" she asked.

"Sure, please close it," he answered as he reached over and turned off the lamp that sat on his left nightstand.

Chapter Twenty-Six

Charismas morning found three inches of snow on the ground to an overcast sky and twenty-five degree temperatures. It also found Courtney opening her eyes in the middle of a strange bed. She sat up in bed, rubbed her eyes with both hands and then threw the lemon yellow bedspread off of her. She scanned the bedroom and nothing about the room looked familiar. Then she had a memory of being taken to a guestroom by Rome. She thought to herself. "I'm in a guestroom. I started out in Rome's room. Why would he put me in a guestroom?" She looked at herself and realized she had fallen to sleep in her clothes. She sat there on the edge of the bed and grabbed her face with both hands. She tried to remember the last thing she remembered. Then bit by bit it all came flooding back. Her night out with Rome was charming and romantic. She recalled how they had danced and had lots of sparkling champagne at a Christmas Eve party at some upscale banquet hall in town. She also remembered making love with Rome and then sneaking out of his room after he had fallen to sleep. She grabbed her stomach with both hands when it dawned on her that she had sneaked into Britain's room and spilled her feelings to him. Heart began to race even faster when she remembered announcing to everyone in the house, including Rome that she was in love with Britain. After recalling that memory, she hopped off the edge of the big bed, rushed into the connecting bathroom, undressed and took a quick shower. Then she dressed, grabbed her purse off the nightstand and left the room.

It was nine o'clock in the morning. She headed straight downstairs and the house was empty except for Rome. He was seated on the living room sofa with a cup of coffee in his hands. He placed the cup on the coffee table when she walked in the room.

"Good morning, Courtney," he said to her with a solemn look on his face.

"Good morning," she said, glancing about the room. "Where is everybody?"

"This is Christmas morning and everybody is out delivering gifts. Is there anyone in particular you were looking for?" Rome asked, keeping his composure.

"Why would you ask me that?"

"I asked you because I would like to know if you're looking for anyone in particular, like maybe my brother?"

She nodded and held it together. "I guess I deserved that. But I was just asking because I was dreading coming downstairs to face everyone."

"Well, now you can see you don't have to fret. There's no one here but us."

"That's a relief, because facing you is hard enough. I just don't think I have the stomach to face your mother and the rest of your family. I'm glad they are all out," she mumbled humbly.

"Yes, they are all out, but you still have to contend with me; and no matter how cool and collected I appear. I'm highly not pleased with your stunt."

"What stunt are you referring to?" she asked.

"Courtney, I know it's early and I know you had too much to drink last night, but I'm sure you know what happened here last night and the scene you made. That's the stunt I'm referring to."

Courtney took a seat on the sofa opposite Rome and grabbed her face and began to cry. "I'm so sorry for what happened here last night. My behavior was inexcusable. Can you ever forgive me?"

"Courtney, there's nothing to forgive," Rome lifted his cup and took a sip of coffee, and then he pointed to the serving tray on the coffee table. "That's a fresh pot of coffee. Please help yourself. I'm sure you could use a few cups of coffee."

"Yes, that sounds splendid." She stepped over to the coffee table and poured herself a cup of coffee. She lifted the cup and sauce, and then took her seat back on the sofa facing Rome.

"Thank you for forgiving my drunken behavior last night. I didn't share this with you before, but I should have because then you could have monitored my intake of champagne." She took a sip of the hot coffee. "Because of the alcoholic gene that runs in my family, I can not tolerate more than two drinks. I usually lose control if I have more than that."

Rome stared at her, and thought how that piece of information about her somehow seemed irrelevant since he had cut all ties with her in his mind.

"No comment about what I just said? I had mentioned to you that my father and brother are both recovering alcoholics, but I failed to tell you that I'm one as well." She sipped her coffee slowly and kept glancing back and forth at Rome who wasn't looking toward her. He was sending text messages of Christmas greetings to associates, workers and friends. Then he placed the phone down, because although he wasn't pleased with her it wasn't in the nature to be completely rude.

"I have no comment, because as far as I'm concerned it's not my problem to deal with. You chose not to tell me this important piece of information about yourself when we were together; and now since we are not, what the point of telling me, Courtney? If you are looking for sympathy or excuses for your behavior it won't come from me," he said with no warmth in his voice.

"I feel awkward and I'm really sorry about last night," she apologized.

"What are you sorry about?" Rome asked, reached out and lifted his coffee cup from the coffee table and took a sip and then placed the cup back on the table.

"I'm sorry for everything; how I left your room in search of Britain's room and ended up making a scene like that waking up your whole family," she said sincerely.

"Are you sorry about anything else?" he asked.

She stared at Rome and nodded. "Yes, I'm sorry I hurt you."

"And how did you hurt me?"

"I said in front of everybody that I loved Britain."

"Yes that is what you said, Courtney, so I'm going to ask you in the light of day. Did you mean it, or was it just the booze talking?"

After a long pause of staring at Rome, she nodded. "Yes, I did mean it. But it doesn't mean that I don't care about you, because I do."

He held up one finger and then lifted his coffee cup again and took a sip. He then placed the cup back on the table and gave Courtney a serious stare. "We are done with this conversation." He pointed toward the two large green bags of Christmas gifts that sat at the corner of the tree. "Those are your gifts from me and the family. Please take your gifts and leave. Whatever was going on between us?" He pointed to her and then touched his chest. "It's over and it makes no sense to discuss what we are discussing. Besides, I'm not sure what one can call what we had, since the whole time you were with me, you were pinning away for my brother." He paused and stared into space for a second with disappointment pouring from his eyes. "I didn't see it coming. All I could see was how I felt and I was convinced that you felt the same. But now I know that was a bunch of garbage."

"Rome, in the beginning it was you, but you never showed me any interest and then I started sharing my lunch with Britain and I developed feelings for him. I thought when he blew me off that I could pick up my old feelings for you, but I could never get Britain out of my head."

"Why didn't you tell me this or just break off the relationship instead of leading me on making me believe you felt the same for me as I felt for you. That's called deception, which I thought was beneath you, Courtney," he said with great disappointment. "I guess I didn't know you at all."

"You know me, Rome, but I'm only human. Falling for your brother doesn't make me an awful person," she snapped.

"No, it doesn't make you an awful person. The fact that you deceived me and kept this from me makes you a deceptive person."

"Okay, I get it. But I thought the feelings for Britain would fade."

"But when they didn't fade, why did you keep up the pretense?"

"I wanted to keep my relationship with you. I wanted to stay with you since I couldn't patch things up with Britain."

Rome shook his head and stared at her disappointedly. "So, you're sitting here telling me that I was your consolation prize! You couldn't have one brother so the other would do? I have to hand it to you; you really pulled one over on me. I was treating you like a queen and all along you wanted to be in my brother's bed. If I must be so bold. Do you have any idea how this makes me feel? I was warned that you were not the right woman for me." Rome held up both hands. "Take your gifts and leave. There's a car and a driver waiting in the driveway to drop you at your destination. I think you understand if I'm not in the mood to do the honors."

Courtney stood up with sad eyes. She walked across the room to the Christmas tree, grabbed the two large green bags and headed toward the front door to leave, Rome said. "Wait for a second. There's one more piece of business left between us."

She glanced over her shoulder. "What's that?"

"You're fired. I know you only had a couple weeks left before leaving the company, but I don't want you back on the premises. I don't want to see your face and be reminded of how you swallowed me up in your deception."

She dropped the two bags and stood there crying. She wiped a tear with the back of both hands. "So, you are going to dismiss me from my job?"

"Yes, I'm dismissing you, but you won't lose any pay. I just want to be spared the agony of all this deception that has happened. The gossip and everybody else's spin on what happened is going to be saturated at work. I don't need you there to add fuel to the fire that you started. Can you understand my viewpoint?"

"Yes, I guess I can understand your viewpoint, but I have to say, I have never seen you this upset; but I can understand why you are. I know you are disappointed in me and I'm sure you probably hate me and think I'm an awful person," Courtney wiped another tear.

"No, I do not hate you, Courtney, and I do not think you are an awful person. I just know that you are not the person for me. I have no desire to be in a relationship with a woman who has a divided heart. I'm only interested in someone who is totally into me. Your feelings are divided between me and my own brother. That's a mess that I want nothing to do with," he said firmly. "And concerning the fact of being upset; I'm not pleased to admit, but this incident has totally upset me." He nodded, looking toward her. "Your duplicity threw me for a loop and I think I'm entitled to be upset and highly disappointed."

"Yes, you are entitled to be upset, but I'm sure your mother will not be upset. She'll be rather pleased that we are over."

"Why are you bringing up my mother? I think it's rude of you to do so. She warned me about you, but this incident was not of her making. It's all on you."

"Maybe, but your mother warned you against me because she always hated me for no good reason."

"My mother never hated you; she just had a hunch that you weren't the right woman for me. She felt you would somehow hurt me. I didn't take her serious, but it turns out that she was right."

"Let's be honest," Courtney snapped with fire in her voice as she walked back over to the opposite sofa facing him and took a seat. "Your mother never liked me! I don't have the right address or enough zeros in my bank account. She was waiting for me to make a mistake!"

"What are you trying to say, Courtney? My mother was waiting for you to make a mistake; therefore, you went out and made one? Don't insult me with your attempt to throw the blame off yourself. Don't sit here and somehow try to blame my mother. She is not to blame for what happened in this house last night."

"Maybe she isn't, but she never liked me and we both know that."

"My mother had her misgivings about you, yes; but I didn't let that bother me. I never paid her any attention and you know that. I always chalked it up to be about your lack of status and money since my mother has a tendency to put a tad too much importance on those things."

"No disrespect meant, but your mother puts a lot more than a tad of importance on those things," Courtney firmly stated.

Rome held up one finger. "Please, do not sit here in my home and insult my mother by saying something unkind about her. I know the two of you had your issues, but my mother opened her home to you and was always respectful to you. But you highly disrespected her home and were anything but respectful last night. She could have said, I told you so, or requested that you not even stay overnight, but she didn't say any of those things to me."

"I'm sure she said something," Courtney mumbled.

Rome nodded. "Yes, she said something this morning: Merry Christmas and how are you this morning? Those are the words my mother said to me. She didn't even mention your name or what happened here last night."

"She probably figured she didn't need to mention my name since things had already worked out in her favor. She knew you would probably break up with me. She was happy inside and there was nothing for her to say. She had gotten her wish, since she never wanted you with me from the beginning."

"Maybe she didn't want me with you, but as I said, she was always respectful and polite to you."

"Maybe she was respectful and polite in my face, but inside she hated me and I know she did," Courtney argued.

"How many times do I have to tell you that my mother did not hate you? Besides, this conversation shouldn't be about my mother. It's about your behavior and not my mother's. But just so you can know, when my mother warned me about you, she just simply said she didn't think you were the right woman for me," he said sincerely and held up one finger. "And she never bought that you only thought of Britain as a friend. Hell, I'm not sure if I bought it. But I convinced myself that if you had a little crush on my brother at the time, what harm that was in view of the fact that we had found our way to each other and it was me you loved. But it was all a lie," he stressed regrettably.

"It wasn't all a lie. I do care so much for you, Rome. We had some wonderful times together," she reminded him.

"I can't see the good times in my head." He pointed to his head. "All I can see is your presence and a lie. I can't believe I'm saying this, but as I said before, my mother was right about you. You are not the right woman for me. If you were, you would have never deceived me in the manner that you did. You say you care about me, but if your care were genuine, you would have been honest with me. If you had been honest with me from the start and explained that you had feelings for Britain, but wanted to give us a chance to see if it worked. It would have given me a choice whether to start a relationship with you, knowing the possibility that you may not get over my brother," he said, staring at her with regret pouring from his eyes. "Most likely I would have opted out. But I would have respected you for being honest. Now, the way things have ended between us, all the feelings that I once felt for you, they have all been crushed under your lies," he said firmly.

Later that afternoon, Franklin House was quiet and still. Britain, Paris and Sydney were having dinner with the Taylors. Veronica and Catherine were both out. All the staff was in their quarters. They had made a meal for Rome, which he asked to be taken to his room. And when he walked into his room to have his Christmas dinner alone, after he closed the door, he noticed a small red six by four inch box sitting at the foot of his bed. He lifted the box and shook it, and then he ripped the paper off and opened the gift. Enclosed was an expensive solid gold ink pen. He read the enclosed card and saw that it was a gift from Amber:

What do you get a man who has everything and yet if he had nothing would still be the wealthiest man in my universe because of his rich heart.
Merry Christmas, Amber!

Rome smiled as he sat on the bed and read the note from Amber a second time, and then he glanced around the room for his phone, which he spotted lying on one of the nightstands. He hopped off the bed and stepped over to the nightstand for his phone. He quickly sent a text to Amber:

Thanks for the gift and note. Merry Christmas, to you and your girls!

An hour later Rome was dressed in a chic black jacket, black slacks and a silk red shirt. He left Franklin House with two large red bags filled with Christmas gifts. Ten minutes after he pulled out of his driveway, he was pulling into the driveway of Amber's condo. He parked in a visitors stall, killed the engine of his shiny silver Jaguar, grabbed the two bags from the passenger's seat and hurried out of the car. He glanced at his watch to check the time. It was straight up six o'clock as he headed up the walkway toward the red brick complex, but before he reached the six-story building to ring her bell, his phone began to ring. He placed the bags on the walkway and answered his phone without checking the caller identity to see who was calling.

"Hello," he said.

"Hi, Rome, it's me," Courtney answered sadly.

"Hi, Courtney, what can I do for you?"

"Do you have a moment to talk?" she asked.

"I don't mean to be rude, but as far as I'm concerned, we said everything we needed to say to each other this morning."

"I know, I'm not going to hold you, I just called to thank you for the gifts. Everything is so nice, especially the gold and diamond bracelet. It looks so expensive with all those diamonds. I know you bought all these things when we were still together. I'll understand if you want me to give them back and you can get a refund for what you paid for them."

"Courtney, I appreciate your gesture, but I purchased those things for you. It doesn't matter that we are no longer together and how much I spent for them, they are yours," he assured her. "Now if that's it, I'm really not that comfortable talking to you, which only reminds me of unpleasant thoughts."

"I know, I'm about to let you go, but before I hang up I would like to ask if there's a possibility that we might could try again after some time has gone by?"

"Try what again, Courtney?"

"Try our relationship again."

"Which relationship is that?" he asked. "The one where I think you're into me but you're secretly carrying a torch for my brother? No thanks, I think I'll pass."

"Rome, I know you are sore with me. But we were good together and I think in time we could get past this and try again."

"Courtney, please believe me when I say we are done! There will never be a you and me! That ship has sailed and crashed. We are finished. I'm asking you to please delete my phone number from your contacts and move on, because I have."

Courtney stomach tightened with sadness and anger. "Who have you moved on with, probably that skinny Amber Taylor? She couldn't stay out of your office. She was always looking at you as if you were the only man on earth," she snapped angrily.

"I'm not discussing this with you, but I'll leave you with one thought."

"What thought is that?"

"Maybe we would still be together if you had thought of me as the only man on earth," he said and ended the call.

By the time he placed his phone in his jacket pocket and grabbed the bags from the sidewalk, Amber had stepped outside. She walked toward him smiling.

"I thought that was your car when I looked out. No one else I know drives a silver Jaguar as nice as yours." She glanced at the bags in his hands. "What are you doing here, delivering gifts I guess?"

"Yes, you caught me. Just a few things I picked up for you and your girls."

"I'm honored. Thank you. But this is a surprise. I didn't expect to see you on Christmas. I figured you would be with Courtney," she said, smiling.

Rome looked at her and didn't answer. He didn't feel her walkway was the appropriated place to explain his breakup.

"Please come inside." She led the way.

Once they were settled in her sixth floor condo, Rome relaxed back on her small tan sofa and glanced about her cozy little living room. She handed him a glass of sparkling wine and took a seat on the sofa beside him. The room was dimmed with only the lighting from her small Christmas tree.

"I know my place is small, but it will do for now." She took a sip of the wine.

"No, it's cozy and cute. I wasn't thinking about the size, I was looking for those toddlers." He turned the glass up to his lips and finished a fourth of his drink.

"Holly and Dolly are in Europe with Marcus and Bailey Dumont. They flew in and picked them up two days ago."

"Marcus and Bailey Dumont are Austin's folks?"

"Yes, they are Austin's parents and I promised them that the girls could spend this Christmas with them."

"Cool, but Europe is a lot of miles from home. I know you miss your girls, but I'm sure Mr. and Mrs. Dumont is quite happy to have their grand kids for a visit." He took another swallow from his wine glass. "Where about in Europe do they live?"

"Dijon, France is their home."

Rome smiled. "We were all conceived in Europe while our parents were jet setting and traveling during their marriage. That's how we all ended up with our names: Rome, Italy, the British Isles, Paris, France and Sydney, Australia. So, three of us were conceived in Europe and Sydney was conceived in Australia." He smiled.

"How fascinating to have such a unique background, to know your life spanned two continents. It started out in a distant country to settle in your parents' native country," she said with her voice filled with perkiness.

"Were the Dumonts born in Europe?"

"Yes, Dijon is their native home. Austin was also born there as well. We met at a corporate party. He was recruited from my father's headquarters in Europe and given a vice president position at my father's company in Chicago. His plane crashed just one year after our marriage while he was in route to a business meeting in Europe."

"How sad, Amber. I'm sorry for your loss."

"Me too, but I have accepted it and my heart has moved on now." She slowly took a sip from her drink and sneaked a warm glance at Rome.

Rome didn't notice her looking at him, since he was looking across the small room at her Christmas tree. He smiled at all the white angels hanging because he knew too well what those ornaments represented. "I see you have also been a busy little Santa this year." He pointed to the tree. You have almost as many white angels hanging on your little tree as we have on our tall tree."

She smiled and nodded. "I always try to pick at least four names from church to donate Christmas gifts to. But this year the church had less people who could afford to help those in need and many names were left. I didn't have the stomach to take four angels and leave the other sixteen hanging on the church tree; therefore, I took all twenty names and donated money so those families could have a Merry Christmas with gifts and food for themselves and their kids."

"You had the same idea as me and my brothers. Every year, we usually take all the angels that are left hanging and donate money to those families to have a good Christmas. It's usually a total of about a hundred families. We want to do it and it's also a tradition that my father started, so we also feel good to know that we are following in his footsteps with that custom," Rome explained eagerly. "When he was alive, every year at Christmas he would choose hundred needy families to donate five hundred dollars a piece so they could have a good Christmas."

"Wow, I have heard so many wonderful things about your father."

"He was all those wonderful things and more." Rome nodded.

Rome and Amber smiled at each other and then touched their glasses together and toasted each other.

"Merry Christmas, Amber, my Christmas is turning out a lot merrier than I thought it would," he said and took a sip of wine, and then placed his glass on the end table to his right.

"Merry Christmas, Rome," she said and slowly took a sip of wine, holding her glass near her mouth as she smiled at him.

Rome smiled. "Before I forget, you look mighty lovely in that green dress. The color is exquisite on you. It's a unique shade between cedar and teal and that long pearl necklace really set it off."

"Thank you," Amber said as she kept smiling at him and then asked what had been nagging at the back of her neck. "I'm so pleased you're here but I thought you would have spent Christmas Day and evening with Courtney."

Rome looked at Amber and smiled. "Yes, that was the plan. However, those plans were cancelled at the last minute."

"Is she out of town?" Amber asked, hoping to get some kind of explanation.

Rome lifted his glass from the end table and finished the wine in one swallow. He held the long stem crystal glass out and looked at it. "This is the best sparkling wine I have had. We don't stock sparkling bottles in our wine cellar, but this is really good."

"It should be good; I think my father drops a couple hundred for each bottle. He gave me a dozen for Christmas."

Rome looked at her and smiled as she got out of her seat, lifted the bottle from the coffee table and poured more wine in his glass. Then she placed the bottle back on the coffee table and took her seat back on the sofa beside him.

"A dozen bottles, I guess you'll have good wine for awhile."

"Yes, I will. I love it to. If you would like I can give you a bottle to share with Courtney when she gets back in town."

Rome placed one finger against Amber's lips to stop her inquiring about Courtney. "I'm just going to tell you. Courtney and I ended our relationship last night and officially today. We are no longer seeing each other. That's why I'm spending Christmas with you right now and not with her," he explained, and then shook his head and stared up at the ceiling for a moment.

Amber was shocked. She could sense that the subject made him uncomfortable. "Rome, I'm sorry. I had no idea," she said softly and touched his shoulder. "You don't have to talk about it and tell me what happened unless you want to."

He took a long swallow from his wine glass and then stared in her warm eyes. "You are like an angel sitting here beside me: an angel that I didn't even completely notice until now. It's like God brought you into my life to cushion my fall." He stretched out his arm and placed his drink on the coffee table and then touched the side of her face with the palm of his right hand. "Your skin is so soft and your eyes are so beautiful, but it's not just your beauty that draws me to you, it's who you are inside." He leaned in and kissed her hungrily.

She closed her eyes as every nerve and cell in her body wanted him to grab her and never let go. She loved him more than she thought possible to love anyone. She melted from his tender kiss, but when he pulled from her lips and held her face with both hands, he noticed the tears on her face. He wiped her tears with his fingers.

"What's the matter? I hope I didn't over step by kissing you without any warning, but I find you irresistible. And I have always found you irresistible, but being the gentleman that I am I would have never allowed myself to give you false hope or touched you in any way while I was in a relationship. And I'm deeply disappointed in Courtney but being here with you right now feels rights," he said assuredly. "I feel as if you are completely here with me."

Amber pulled away and grabbed the box of facial tissues from the end table. She removed a couple tissues and dried her tears. "I'm sorry about the tears."

"You have nothing to be sorry about. I should apologize for causing you to cry."

"They are not tears of pain, they are tears of joy. I never thought you would look at me and say these things you just said to me."

"Why would you think that way? Granted, I probably wouldn't have said them if Courtney and I hadn't broken up. But it didn't mean I wasn't thinking them and that I couldn't see what a beautiful, wonderful and sweet woman you are."

"But I didn't think I was your type. I know you like me as a friend, but I didn't think there could ever be anything more between you and me."

"I know this is all quite sudden. I just broke off with Courtney and now I'm sitting here in your living room telling you how beautiful and wonderful you are." He touched his chest. "But this is how I feel about you. I see something genuine when I look into your eyes." He paused. "I'm not trying to brush away what I had with Courtney as if it didn't matter, because it did matter. She's a beautiful, decent girl but she's not the one for me. All while we were together I felt a distant from her. I couldn't put my finger on it, but it all came out in the wash last night. I was stunned and not pleased, but another part of me felt relieved. It was like an inkling, an intuition of a pending train crash. After the crash, although painful I can now move on to my rightful destination."
He leaned in and kissed Amber again, and this time he grabbed her and

wrapped her in his arms and kissed her urgently as if kissing her was all he needed.

Her head fell over on the arm of the sofa and they were so passionately into kissing and touching, until he stopped himself. "This isn't proper." He grabbed his wine glass from the coffee table and took a quick swallow of the sparkling clear liquid. "Being alone with you like this is causing me to lose my composure. As tempting as it is to sit this close to you, I can't continue kissing and holding you the way I'm doing. I want to make love to you with the utmost extreme. But now isn't the time. You'll think it's to numb the pain of sad thoughts of another woman. But frankly, that pain left the moment I kissed you. I just feel at home with you, Amber."

"What are you saying, Rome?"

He smiled. "I think it's obvious that I'm very attractive to you and would like to see where this can take us." He touched her chest and then his.

"Are you saying what I think you are?"

"Yes, I would like for you to be that special someone in my life."

"Rome, being with you is all I have thought of for the longest time, but are you sure this is what you want? After all, you did just break up with Courtney. You're upset with her right now, but after a little bit of time you might feel differently and want to get back with her. I'm just trying to protect my heart."

"Amber, all the time in the world would not convince me to get back together with Courtney. She crossed a line and burned a bridge that can not be rebuilt. Courtney Ross and I are done for good."

"How can you be sure?"

"I can be sure because what she did was unforgettable. I have the compassion for forgiveness, and I will forgive her in time. But I'll never forget," he assured her.

"Rome, I don't like putting you on the spot like this, and I wouldn't ask if you hadn't just asked me to be apart of your life. Besides, if it's unforgettable it must be unspeakable," she said humbly. "But is it possible to share with me what caused your breakup with Courtney?"

He stared into space motionless for a moment and then took a deep breath. He turned to face her and nodded. "Yes, it's possible. It's not pretty and it's down right shocking and I would rather not say, but I feel close enough to you and trust you completely. However, it's something that I would never share with anyone else."

"Rome, are you sure you want to share it. I sort of put you on the spot. I want to know, of course, but I'll understand if you're not comfortable sharing it," she said sincerely and placed her hand on top of his. "I guess I just wanted to know because couples breakup all the time, but after they cool down they some time get back together." She grabbed her stomach and held it. "I love you so much and to get together with you only to lose you to Courtney again would shatter my heart."

He took her glass of wine and placed it on the coffee table and then smoothed one of her tight curls away from her left eye. After which, he stood up and removed his jacket and threw it over the arm of the sofa and then took his seat back beside her. He held both of her hands while facing her. "Amber, the reason I'm so sure that Courtney and I will never start again is because I'll never trust her or forget why we broke up." He paused and glanced toward the ceiling for a moment. When he looked at her, he leaned in and gave her a quick kiss on the lips. "I'm sorry, I just can't help myself, but I promise to try and behave until I share this with you."

"I'm listening," Amber whispered.

"Okay, here goes. Last night after Courtney and I arrived at Franklin House from a party, we made love for the first time. And moments after making love with me, she went in search of my brother's room to tell him she loved him."

Amber pulled her hands from his and grabbed her face. "Oh, my goodness, that's incredible. Rome, I had no idea it was something so unbelievable."

"That's not all of it. Apparently she had carried this torch for Britain long before we started seeing each other, and to top it off, the entire household other than the servants, whose quarters are all on the first level, heard her confession. At that moment, I felt shock, humiliation, embarrassment and all kind of emotions. But the next morning my head was clear and I just felt absolutely nothing for her that resembled romantic feelings."

"All my goodness, I have never heard anything so unreal. She doesn't seem like someone who would make a scene like that."

"In all fairness, she was wasted, but it doesn't excuse her behavior and the lie of wanting my brother all while the two of us were together. But listen, Amber, that's behind me now. Just like the pending train crash. It's over and now out of the wreckage comes, beautiful, mesmerizing you. I care about you, Amber, and I think I always have from that evening at dinner when you poured your heart out to me in that fancy Italian restaurant. You stole my heart today but I just didn't know it then."

She stood and slowly stepped over to the Christmas tree and stared at the blinking green and red lights. "But can you love me?" she mumbled sadly.

He stood and stepped over to the tree and held her shoulders and gently turned her to face him. He looked down at her beautiful face and shook his head with warmth pouring from his eyes. "How can you ask me if I can love you?"

"I don't feel I'm your type," she uttered softly looking up in his eyes.

"Why would you say something like that? What's not to like? You're stunning and sexy as hell; you're compassionate, thoughtful, kind and caring," he said with conviction. "And it doesn't hurt that you are an heir to a billion dollar estate," he said jokingly and playfully touched her nose and laughed. "I just figured I would throw that in to make you smile. And it worked, look at that beautiful smile."

"Thank you for your compliment but you left a few things out."

"I'm sure I left more than a few things out. You are a lot more special things than just the few I mentioned."

"What about the not so special things: like being widowed with two kids. I'm sure that's not the future you saw for yourself. How can I ask you to give your heart to me when I feel you deserve someone who doesn't come with all my baggage?"

"Amber, I don't think of you as someone with baggage. You are a lovely young woman who experienced a train crash that got you to this point. Granted, I always felt that special woman would be someone who

I could share all our first things with together. And in a perfect world maybe, but this is real life and I have walked away from my crashed relationship and found you. You are all that I want and need: a woman who loves me for me; a woman who loves only me and a woman that I feel I can walk with through life with. Amber Taylor-Dumont, will you marry me?"

His proposal stunned himself and Amber as they both stood there facing each other. She grabbed her face with both hands as her mouth fell open. But she was speechless for a moment as he took a deep breath.

"Rome, I'm beautifully stunned. I didn't expect your proposal. I was trying to get comfortable with the fact that you could really be over Courtney and could actually want a widowed woman with two kids. Now you have asked for my hand in marriage and those were the ultimate beautiful words that I wanted to hear, but never thought I would hear them coming from your mouth."

He took her hand and led her back over to the sofa and they both were seated side by side facing each other.

"Amber, I can understand your shock. I'm shocked too. I had no idea those words were going to come from my mouth. When I decided to visit you this evening, it was because I wanted to see you and be in your calming, comfortable presence. I hadn't realized my feelings for you were at this point, but they are. I'm in love with you, Amber. I have never told another woman that I love her. But I'm telling you because it's what I feel. I get that the timing is a mess. I just broke off one relationship today, and before we can officially go on one date, I'm asking you to marry me."

"Rome, my heart is screaming, yes, to your proposal. But my good sense is telling me to wait."

"What are you waiting for?

"It's like you said, it's the timing. Up until tonight I didn't even know you were attractive to me. Now, you are in love with me and want to marry me? Rome it's a lot to take in," she uttered as they held hands. "My heart is overflowing with love for you and I want nothing more than to hold you and kiss you for hours and to have a future with you. But are you sure you are not just trying to mask the hurt from Courtney?"

"Amber, I'm not masking my hurt by being with you; I was masking my love for you by being with her. Working closely with you, I fell for you. I couldn't help myself. Although I didn't realize it at the time, I was captivated by you. When you poured your heart out to me at Leo's, I knew then that I had feelings for you, but I was with Courtney so I pushed aside the feelings I felt in my heart for you. At the time I thought it was gratitude and admiration. But now I know it was love. So, what do you say, will you make this my merriest Christmas ever by accepting my proposal?" He lifted her right hand and kissed the back of it. "Will you be my wife?"

"How could my answer be anything but yes? I love you immensely and can not wait to be your wife and share my life with you. Now I know prayers are answered and miracles can happen at Christmas," she whispered as tears flooded her eyes.

He held her face with both hands as his mouth over hers and swallowed her up in a hungry passionate lingering kiss.

Chapter Twenty-Seven

That evening around nine o'clock, Rome arrived home from visiting Amber. When he stepped inside smiling and in a happy mood, he found his family gathered in the living room chatting and enjoying Christmas snacks and drinking eggnog. The moment he stepped into the room everyone paused and looked at him with solemn faces. Britain and Sydney were seated on one sofa, Paris was standing with his arm propped on the fireplace mantle with a glass of eggnog in his hand, Veronica was seated on the other sofa and Catherine was standing at the serving tray in the corner of the room pouring herself a glass of eggnog. She was the first to speak.

"I'm just pouring myself a glass of eggnog; can I pour you one?" She smiled.

He nodded. "Sure, Aunt Catherine, that sounds good," he said, removed his jacket and threw it across the back of the sofa as he took a seat next to his mother.

Catherine walked over and passed him the drink and she took a seat on the sofa beside him. He took a sip from the delicate crystal glass and looked at his Aunt who sat there looking at him with concerned eyes.

"Aunt Catherine, why are looking at me with such gloom in your eyes?"

"We are all so sorry about what happened here last night and I hope you had a nice Christmas inspite of all that chaos." She patted his shoulder.

"Thank you, Aunt Catherine, but there's no need to feel down because of me. I must admit that my Christmas turned out surprising great," Rome said assuredly.

His good mood made Veronica blood boil at the thought of him making up with Courtney and forgiving her. "What did you do today?" Veronica asked. "I had just assumed you would be in all day and evening, that's why I left instructions for Natalie to prepare a meal for you."

"Thanks, Mother, she did just that and the food was wonderful, although I was a quite surprise to find Natalie and also Fred working, considering it was Christmas day. I didn't think any of the staff would be on duty. Although, it did come in handy when our Butler/chauffer was available to drive someone home," he said and looked at his mother. "But seriously, Mother, why would you have them working on Christmas?"

"I gave them all the time off, but Natalie and Fred asked for the extra hours. They are paid double time when they work on a holiday and they asked Catherine for the extra hours, and of course I granted them the opportunity to make a few extra dollars," Veronica explained.

"Thanks for that explanation, Mother. We don't want to do anything regarding the staff that is not above board. I want to treat them the way we would want to be treated," Rome suggested, and he got three nods from his brothers.

"Yes, I know dear, that's what your father used to say to me all the time," Veronica uttered in agreement.

Rome sipped his drink and noticed that everyone seemed a bit quiet; however, when he first walked into the room they all seemed to be chatting away.

"What's going on here?" he asked. "You all seem a tad too quiet." He smiled. "I'm sure it's because of me. You don't know what to say to me because of the incident that happened last night. Well, I have news for you, I'm over it."

Veronica exchanged looks with Catherine and then looked at Rome. "Dear, you never did say what you did today," Veronica asked casually, yet anxiously. "Based on your good mood, can I assume you found away to patch things up with Courtney?"

Britain, Paris and Sydney all looked toward their mother and shook their heads.

"Why are you boys shaking your heads? It's possible that your brother could have patched things up with that young lady. He seems in a good mood and he was definitely gone from here a few hours. Therefore, it sounds like they may have patched things up." She paused and looked back toward Rome. "Although that would be my worst nightmare if it's true," she said firmly and paused, awaiting his response.

"Listen up," Rome said. "What happened here last night was unfortunate and definitely not what I would have asked for. But at the same time it was a blessing because it opened my eyes and gave me some clarity about where things were going with me and Courtney." He exchanged looks with them all, and then set his focus on his mother. "As much as I hate to admit this because usually Mother is off the mark when it comes to affairs of the heart, but this one time she was right. She told me that Courtney was not the right girl for me; and it turns out she was absolutely correct." He smiled at his mother. "Just because you were right this time, doesn't mean I'll me taking relationship advice from you in the future," he said and held out both arms. "So, there you have it, I agreed with Mother and told Courtney she wasn't the one for me."

"I take it, you gave Miss Ross her walking papers," Catherine laughed. "Good for you. That young lady crossed the line when she did what she did."

Rome held up one finger. "Aunt Catherine, please don't get into what took place. That's behind me and I have moved on."

Veronica glanced toward the Christmas tree and did a double take when she noticed the gifts for Courtney was gone from under the tree. "Did you give that young lady all those expensive gifts you had purchased for her?"

"Yes, Mother, I gave her the gifts. I had the choice of keeping them after her little stunt, but my conscience wouldn't allow me to do so. I purchased the presents for her and told her to keep them."

"Did she ask to give them back to you?" Catherine asked.

"Yes, she called and asked me did I want them back so I could get a refund, but I told her to keep them."

"Sweetheart, you should have let her returned the gifts to you. My goodness, that would have been punishment for her unspeakable behavior," Veronica said.

"Mother, I have no desire to punish Courtney. She's out of my life and that's what counts."

"Yes, she's out of your life along with a lot of your cash. Those gifts were too expensive to give to someone you never plan to see again," Veronica explained.

"Mother, I agree, but I would have felt worse to not give them to her, since she already knew about them."

"Okay, I'm just glad she's out of your life and won't be able to lead you on with anymore of her lies," Veronica said firmly.

"I have to agree with your mother," Catherine told him. "I always thought you and Courtney made a cute couple, but I'm glad she's out of your life too. I'm not behind any female that's going to cause any of you big headaches. Now you can move on and find yourself a nice young lady who you won't have to worry about running off to your brothers' room when you turn your back," Catherine stated seriously.

"Thank you, Aunt Catherine, for your concern about my love life, but I have already moved on," Rome announced and winked at Britain.

Britain, Paris and Sydney all said at the same time. "Who is she?"

After a moment of waiting for Rome to speak, Britain turned his glass up and finished his eggnog. "I think I know who she is. Sabrina mentioned something about her cousin." He narrowed his eyes at Rome.

"You mean, Amber, who works for us, right?" Sydney asked.

Britain nodded and they all looked toward Rome waiting for his confirmation.

Veronica smiled. "If that's true, its obvious Amber really likes you; and with that old policy off the books, there's nothing standing in your way," Veronica said with subdued excitement, not to give away her extreme enthusiasm and approval.

Rome smiled at his mother. "Mother, you mean you would approve of me dating one of my employees?" he said in a joking manner. "I thought policy or no policy; you were totally against the idea of us dating who works for us?"

Veronica didn't know what to say because she was against the policy, but in regards to Amber she felt differently. "Well, you did remove the policy from the books and I have to accept that."

"Mother, do you accept the policy or do you just accept Amber?" He smiled.

Veronica smiled. "Okay, you got me. I didn't want you to remove that policy, but I do accept Amber. That young lady is quite unique and in a class by herself."

"I think so as well." Rome smiled. "That's why I asked her to marry me."

For a moment silence fell over the room and all that could be hear was the vague tick tock of the tall grandfather clock in the corner of the room. Veronica coughed and took a minute to clear her throat. "Did you just say marriage?"

"Yes, Mother, I asked Amber to marry me."

"I'm stunned, Sweetheart. I had no idea you felt that strongly about Amber. Besides, you just broke off with Courtney. I think Amber is a wonderful young lady, but asking her to marry you right after just breaking off with the other girl doesn't sound too proper. Are you sure you asked her for the right reasons?"

Rome nodded. "Amber wanted to know the same thing and after I convinced her that I knew what I was doing and how much I loved her and wanted her to be apart of my life, she accepted my proposal."

"Did you go over with the intent of asking her to be your wife?" Veronica asked.

"No, Mother, I did not. I had no idea I even wanted to get married." He paused. "It's hard to explain. It was something about being with her that pulled it out of me, and the next thing I realized I was asking her to marry me. I wasn't ready or prepared; therefore, I had no ring and now I have to get one and make the engagement official."

"Wow, you didn't let any grass grow under your feet," Catherine said, smiling. "You sent Courtney packing this morning, and by evening you had a prettier and much richer girl to take her place. I'm proud of you for moving on at lightning speed," Catherine grinned.

"Thanks, Aunt Catherine, but there's a saying that if you do good, it will come back to you, two folds. Therefore, I would like to think that the good I sow has a little to do with the good that comes back my way," Rome said sincerely.

"That is true and it's one of the golden rules that your father use to live by. He would be so proud of all of you, because you are all the finest, most decent bunch of young men I have ever known," Catherine said lovingly.

"Thank you, Aunt Catherine." Britain smiled at her.

"Yes, thank you, Aunt Catherine," Sydney nodded toward her. "We think you are a pretty cool Aunt too."

"That's right, Aunt Catherine, you are the coolest; and just like a second mother to us," Paris said warmly. "Growing up, we missed our father but having you around made it feel like less of a void."

"If you guys keep this up, I just might cry," Catherine said, smiling.

"So, Mother, what do you think about my engagement to Amber?"

"There's no question about it, you have my approval of course. My only hesitation had to do with the timing, considering this all did happen rather suddenly."

"I realize the timing isn't ideal, but I love her, Mother." He turned up his glass to his lips and swallowed the last of his drink. "I'm blown away by this sudden realization, but I love her and want her as my wife." He placed his empty glass on the coffee table and Catherine pointed toward the eggnog on the serving tray.

He nodded and she fetched his glass and walked across the room to pour more eggnog in it. She filled his glass and handed it to him. "You better watch it, this stuff is fattening, you know. You don't want to end up with my figure, now do you?" she said, jokingly as she sat back on the sofa beside him.

He shook his head. "No, Aunt Catherine, I think I'll keep my own," he joked and took a sip of the eggnog.

"Since the engagement isn't official, I can assume the two of you didn't set a date about any arrangements?" Veronica asked.

"That's correct, Mother. We were both so thrown by the fact that I had asked her until we couldn't concentrate on anything else except our joy of finding each other. But one thing I can say, after we are married, I figured we could move into the east wing that's been closed off since father died."

Veronica shifted in her seat and did not comment as he continued.

"I know you and father lived in the east wing for a few years when you were first married. Then after father folks passed away, you two took over the entire house. But after father's death you closed off the east wing."

Catherine exchanged looks with Veronica, because she was aware of the reason that section of the house was closed off. She was waiting and hoping that Veronica would share that information with her sons. She wanted Veronica to tell them that it wasn't closed off due to sad memories of their father, but closed off because it had become too expensive to maintain the heating and lighting for that section of the house.

Catherine blood boiled because she wanted her nephews to know what was going on at Franklin House. She wanted to tell them but she knew better than to upset Veronica or boldly interfere with the rearing of her sons. But this time she couldn't hold her peace. "Are you going to tell them about the east wing?"

Veronica smiled at Catherine so she wouldn't give away the fury inside of her that she wanted to let go on Catherine for her indiscretion of bringing up the east wing in front of her sons. "They don't need to hear about that." Veronica waved her hand.

"We don't need to hear about what?" Paris asked. "Maybe we want to hear about it; although, I'm assuming it's closed off to keep sad memories of Father hidden behind those doors?"

"Yes, Mother, what's up with the east wing?" Britain looked toward his mother and narrowed his eyes curiously.

"Is it haunted or something?" Sydney joked.

"It's nothing like that and you wouldn't be wasting your efforts inquiring if Catherine wasn't making a mountain out of a mole hill. She's just referring to how stuffy and dusty that section of the house is. It has nothing to do with ghosts and sad memories of Ryan," Veronica explained.

"I'm glad to hear that because Amber and I will most likely live in that section of the house when we are married," Rome said eagerly. "So, Mother, what do you think of that, having your son and his new bride under one roof with the rest of the family? Does that meet your approval?"

"I'm sure you don't have to ask. I can't think of anything that would please me more; although, I do think we are jumping the gun here and getting a little bit ahead of ourselves. You just asked Amber to marry you. And as much as I adore Amber and would love to see the two of you together as husband and wife, I think the two of you need to have a talk and discuss where you would like to live. She may not want to live at Franklin House," Veronica warmly pointed out.

"Mother, I know there's a slim chance that she may not want to live here, but by my instincts I'm sure she will. Therefore, I would like to open the east wing right away." He looked toward Catherine. "Aunt Catherine, can you have the staff open all the windows and air that section of the house out. And have them do whatever needs to be done like vacuuming and dusting."

Catherine nodded. "Consider it done. I'll have them get right on it."

"And, Mother, maybe we can donate the old furniture that's in there and have all new furniture delivered. How many rooms are in that section?" Rome asked.

Veronica wasn't sure and looked toward Catherine who was born and raised at Franklin House. "Do you know off hand how many rooms are in the east wing, Catherine?" Veronica asked.

"Like the back of my hand," Catherine grinned. "I used to run and play in all of those rooms when I was about seven years old. I would sometime hide from friends when we would play hide and go seek in that part of the house. Plus, that's where Ma and Pa used to have all their parties," Catherine said, not readily answering the question of how many rooms were in that section.

"Thanks for sharing your childhood, but could you please answer the question now and let us all know how many rooms are in the east wing?" Veronica demanded.

"Twelve rooms are in that section, just like the west wing, but not all twelve rooms are bedrooms. That's where my folks had all their parties, in the large living room, which was used as a ballroom. Then there are eleven other rooms, not including the five bathrooms: a large sitting room, a library, a study, a home office, a sewing room and six bedrooms," Catherine relayed.

"What's a sewing room?" Sydney asked.

"Just that, sweetheart," Catherine smiled toward Sydney. "Your grandmother Ellen used to live in that room from day in to day out."

"That's right," Veronica recalled. "Ryan told me that his mother was a professional drapery maker years ago when he was a young boy."

Catherine nodded. "That's true. Almost from the time Ma and Pa married, she worked tirelessly in that sewing room making mostly draperies, but other bedding items as well. Her sewing helped built their fortune," Catherine shared. "I'm sure you all have read in some of the old newspapers that my father amassed his fortune from the stock market and solid investments, but the foundation of the cash flow came from Franklin Gas and my mother's homemade draperies. Plus, it didn't hurt that my father's parents had left him an undisclosed inheritance along with the main section of Franklin House. My parents had the east wing added to the house after my grandparents passed away a couple years before I was born."

"That's sensation, I never knew draperies were apart of our heritage," Rome said, smiling. "I don't think any of us knew that about Grandma Ellen. Therefore, when we refurnish the east wing, I think we should leave the sewing room as is and not change it into a den or anything like that," he suggested. "Although, none of us sew around here, I just think it's a good way to preserve the memory of Grandma Ellen's passion for sewing."

"I think that's an excellent idea, sweetheart," Veronica agreed.

"So do I, and when we start donating items from that section of the house, I'll make sure Ma's old Elias Howe sewing machine, which is in mint condition, stays right where it is. That thing is probably worth a fortune now."

"So, Aunt Catherine, did Grandma Ellen ever sew anything other than draperies and bed items? What about clothing?" Britain asked. "Could she make clothes?"

Catherine shook her head. "If she could make clothes, she never made any for us. I just recall the draperies and bed items. And I'll have you know at that time in the early 1960's, especially 1963, when I was seven and my mother was only thirty-three, she was quite popular for a woman in her times. She made the local paper a few times in articles about how she couldn't make her draperies and linens fast enough. As soon as she finished a stack of elegant draperies in an assortment of colors all from the finest materials, she would have several orders waiting. She was a whiz on the sewing machine and made all her draperies singlehandedly," Catherine shared eagerly.

"Ryan mentioned that his mother's draperies sold for mega bucks at that time," Veronica recalled.

Propped against the fireplace mantle, Paris picked up a picture from the mantle of his Grandma Ellen and looked at the photograph for a moment and then placed the old black and white picture back on the mantle.

"Maybe we need to get back into the drapery business," Paris said, smiling and turned his glass up to his mouth and took a swallow of eggnog.

Everyone looked toward Paris and he shook his head. "I'm just kidding, but I'm quite impressed with my Grandma Ellen's drive to achieve such an accomplishment, especially during that time when there wasn't as many women in the workforce."

Sydney nodded. "I agree. For that time period in the mid-1950's and early 1960's women rights were much worse than they are now. They still are not perfect but much better." He took a swallow of his drink. "I'm glad to hear that our grandmother rose above the norm and shook up the system with her moneymaking sewing skills."

"I read some of Father's old notes," Britain added. "He mentioned how Grandpa Samuel explicitly had the builders design a sewing room for Grandma Ellen, and he encouraged her from the start to pursue her idea of making and selling draperies," Britain said with admiration. "I barely remember Father, but I know he was all about women's rights, civil rights and all rights that didn't step on the dignity of others." He nodded toward Catherine. "Now I realize how those values were passed on from his parents. During that period, without Grandpa Samuel's encouragement, Grandma Ellen most likely would not have achieved her goal of making and selling draperies."

Rome touched Catherine on the shoulder. "Thanks Aunt Catherine for sharing with us about Grandma Ellen's accomplishments. But now that we have shared enough intriguing, enlightening talk about Grandma Ellen's sewing room, and her money making draperies being key in helping to amass the Franklin fortune, let's move on to the current business at hand," Rome suggested and then looked toward his mother. "Mother, do I have your approval to donate the old furniture that's in the east wing and replace it with all new pieces and maybe have a decorator come in and brighten up that section of the house to coordinate with the main section of the house?" Rome asked.

"Of course, you have my approval. Whatever you want or decide about the east wing is fine with me. I'll call and schedule a pick up for the old furniture to be removed. And after the staff air out and clean those rooms, I'll place an order for all new furnishing to coordinate with the decorator's recommendations."

Rome smiled and touched his mother on the shoulder warmly. "That's great, Mother. We are on a roll here. Once we get the east wing situated the way we want it, I would like to show Amber her new future living quarters." He looked at Catherine. "So, Aunt Catherine, please have the staff open up and start cleaning that section as soon as their schedules will allow. Is it possible that they could start tomorrow?"

Before Catherine could answer, Veronica interrupted anxiously.

"Sweetheart, what's the rush?"

Rome stared at his mother. "What's the hold up?"

Veronica coughed and fumbled with her reply, not expecting his question. "Sweetheart, there's no hold up," she quickly replied and paused. "Oh, yes, I remember, there is a slight hold up."

"Okay, what is it, Mother?" Rome curiously inquired.

All eyes were on Veronica waiting to hear what she had to say. She waved her hand as if it was nothing. "It's nothing really, it's just that there's no heat or lights in that section of the house right now. It's too cold for the staff to do any work in those rooms. But hold your horses, I'll just call tomorrow and have the heat and lights turned back on, and after that the staff can open up that section of the house and do whatever needs to be done."

Rome and his brother exchanged looks. "Mother, why would you turn off the lights and heat in that section of the house?" He curiously inquired, and then answered his own question before she could speak. "To save on utilities for space that's not being used. That makes sense."

"Yes, dear, that's it. I figured why throw money out of the window."

Catherine slightly shook her head. She was thinking to herself how Veronica had dodged a bullet by not sharing the real reasons for having the heating and lighting turned off in that section of the house.

Paris stepped over and extended his hand to Rome. "Congratulations, Amber is a beauty. She's going to make you an incredible wife." Paris smiled and nodded at him.

Everyone congratulated Rome and by ten o'clock the Franklin guys had all cleared out of the living room.

Catherine and Veronica were still seated on the sofa finishing up the eggnog in the crystal pitcher, which was now sitting on the coffee table instead of the serving tray.

"You are on a roll," Catherine said as she turned her glass up to her mouth.

"What do you mean by that," Veronica snapped, not holding back her emotions now that her sons were out of the room.

"Let's see, Courtney is out of Rome's life and your golden girl who is heir to billions is in. How is that for hitting the jackpot?"

"Yes, I'm quite please, but I didn't have to lift a finger to make it happen. Courtney Ross was bound to break his heart, because when all was said and done she had used my son to get close to the other one."

Catherine nodded. "Yes, I'll give you that. You had her number from the start. But what do you think of this engagement to Amber Taylor all of a sudden? It's a little bit too soon for comfort if you ask me."

"But I'm not asking you, so just drop it. Rome is happy and that's all that matters," Veronica Snapped.

Catherine lifted the pitcher and poured more eggnog into her glass. "I'm sure that's all that matters, now that he's with your choice. When he was with the other girl and was happy, it wasn't all that mattered," Catherine pointed out.

"Catherine, what is your beef here? Rome is happy with Amber, what's not to like? Besides, you were so sure that he was off somewhere nursing a broken heart and that he would come home miserable. Just be happy for him that he isn't sad."

"I'm happy for him; I'm just stumped by the suddenness and I thought you would be as well." Catherine took a swallow of her drink.

"I agree with you there; I am stumped by the abruptness of the engagement and wish the timing was better. But if I know anything, I know my son is one of the most levelheaded individuals I know. Therefore, his explanation fits just fine with me, and I couldn't be happier that he and Amber has found each other," Veronica said seriously.

"Who would have thought among us that he was having a good Christmas? We all thought he was off somewhere trying to forget old memories, but he was off somewhere making new memories," Catherine yawned. "He's a remarkable young man and too compassionate for his own good, because I agree with you that he never should have given Courtney all those nice expensive presents after what happened here last night. But that's who he is; and you got to love him for his kindness."

"This is the best Christmas gift I could have asked for." Veronica smiled. "You'll have to get the staff right on cleaning up and airing out the east wing; and I'll call and have the lights and heat turned on tomorrow."

Catherine looked at Veronica and asked. "Why did you do it?"

"Why did I do what?" Veronica asked.

"Why did you leave your sons in the dark about why the lights and heating was turned off in the east wing? Why didn't you tell them you have spent most of their father's fortune and we are going broke? He left you a billionaire, but you have almost drained the account."

"Catherine, you need to zip it up. You don't know everything. Let you tell it, we are all headed to the soup line. I don't need your gloom and doom. I'm so fed up with your pessimistic attitude," Veronica argued. "You know as well as I do, that by all accounts we are still quite wealthy."

"Well, quite wealthy isn't the same as quite rich. When my brother and parents were alive and living here at Franklin House we were quite rich with a combined wealth of 2.2 billion. Twenty years later and your management of the funds and I guess a few zeros have disappeared. Of course, you won't share with me the bottomline in the account. But you bark when I excessively use my credit card and you bark about salary increases for the staff and you bark about the household bills, but the only thing you don't bark about is what your sons spend. I'm starting to think you're barking to make me think we're broke, so I won't give large raises to the staff or spend much on myself. The more I think about it, the more I think I'm right," Catherine said suspiciously.

Veronica waved her hand. "Catherine you always think you're right."

"You're wrong, I don't always think I'm right, but I think I'm right now."

"What do you think you're right about?"

"I think I'm right about the fact that nobody is going broke in this house except for me and the staff."

"What are you talking about? The staff gets a raise every year and you're not hurting for anything."

"That's where you are wrong. I'm hurting for a new car. My car is five years old; and you haven't approved more than a three percent raise for the staff in the past five years. Whenever I mention more of a salary increase you always bring up the fact that we are going broke. Hell, you have said it so often until you had me convinced. Whenever I mentioned buying a new Mercedes, you would give me a song and dance about we are going broke. The account is always fading when I want to make a big purchase and you make me feel too guilty to make the purchase." Catherine lifted her glass and finished the drink. "So are you pulling my leg about the fading account?" Catherine stared at Veronica. "You know I'm the one who have to tell the staff things are tight and that's why they can't have more of an increase. That's why Natalie and Fred were working here today on Christmas. I'm sure they would have preferred to have the day off, but they wanted to make extra money since they can barely live off their pay."

"Just drop it, Catherine," Veronica suggested. "And no, I'm not going to answer your question or statement or whatever it was."

"You don't have to answer. I'm sure I hit the nail on the head and have you dead for rights."

"Catherine, I dare you make it sound as if I'm taking advantage of the staff. What would my sons think if they heard you mention something like that? I never want to hear you say that again. Do I make myself clear?"

"Crystal," Catherine nodded. "But while we are on the subject of being clear, do I make myself clear? Raises are due in a couple weeks, is it okay to give the staff a five percent increase this time?" Catherine asked.

Veronica nodded without hesitation. "Sure, give them a five percent increase. I think that's okay for this year. But always run it by me for my approval."

"I always run it by you, and you know that; but thanks. I'm pleased to have some good news for the staff. They'll be quite pleased."

"I'm sure they will. But explain how we had a good year and that the five percent is not a permanent percentage to expect."

Catherine sat there on the sofa and shook her head and smiled while looking at Veronica. "You never cease to shock me. Just like that you are approving a five percent raise for the staff. That's incredible, considering you haven't bulged in the past five years. What changed your mind? You usually say the account is fading."

"It is fading, but we can spare a five percent increase for the staff this year?"

Catherine narrowed her eyes toward Veronica. "Can we also spare the purchase of my new car?"

"Catherine, why are you asking me? You have your own credit card to use how you see fit. If you want a new car, go out and buy it."

"What about the fading bank account? You are not going to tell me that we are going broke and need to hold on to every extra dime?"

Veronica stared at Catherine with irritated eyes. "What do you want from me? If I complaint about the purchase, you question it, and if I don't complaint you question it." She waved her hand.

"I guess I'm just skeptical since that's what you usually say when I mention anything about buying a new car," Catherine reminded her. "And you say that to me, inspite of the fact that you buy a new car every two years, and all your sons are driving the most expensive cars out there. But for the past five years you have made me feel that the fading bank account needed to be spared of what a new car would cost me."

"Okay, but now I'm not saying that. Just be grateful and go out and buy your car," Veronica said firmly.

"You don't have to tell me twice," Catherine said, smiling. "Purchasing a new car is on my agenda for tomorrow."

"I'm sure it is, Catherine," Veronica mumbled with a smirk on her face.

Catherine stared toward the east wing in silence for a moment. "You know, talking about the reopening of the east wing brought back a lot of old memories including, as a little girl I remember that large living room in the east wing was used as a ballroom. It would be packed with guest every other Saturday night. It reminded me of something out of an old movie. My parents knew how to throw a party. There hasn't been a party in this house since Ryan died," Catherine pointed out.

"You're right, but now we have something to celebrate. When Rome makes his engagement to Amber official, the sky will be the limit. We'll have an all out celebration for my son and his beautiful future bride."

"Don and Angela Taylor may have something to say about that," Catherine said.

"What do you mean by that?"

"Amber is their daughter and their only child, most likely they will want to throw the engagement party," Catherine reminded her.

"I didn't think of that. But I plan to have some input about the party to celebrate my son's engagement. Don and Angela will just have to get used to me butting in because I will not leave my son's celebration to chance."

"What do you mean leave it to chance? Amber parents are filthy rich; do you think they would give their only child anything but the best engagement party ever?

"That slipped my mind as well."

"Well, I hope the fact that I'll be driving home in a new Mercedes tomorrow doesn't slip your mind," Catherine teased.

Veronica stood up from the sofa and headed toward the staircase. Catherine walked along side her, but stopped at the bottom of the stairs as Veronica headed up the staircase. After walking up three steps, Veronica faced Catherine and leaned her back against the railing. "I forgot something."

"What's that?" Catherine asked.

"I forgot to unplug the tree. Could you unplug it before you head up?"

"Sure, I'll take care of it, but when you said you forgot something I thought you were going to confirm my suspicions?" Catherine smiled.

"Confirm your suspicions about what?"

"That your going broke talk has just been a song and dance?"

Veronica stared annoyingly at Catherine for a moment. "Catherine, this conversation is over. Goodnight," Veronica said and headed up the staircase.

Chapter Twenty-Eight

Courtney and Trina left home and drove to the Christmas Party that was taking place at the local nightclub down the street. They stood in the club near the front entrance and just sort of looked around the place. Trina was in good spirits but Courtney was weighed down with despair due to her drunken, disrespectful behavior displayed at Franklin House that caused Rome to break up with her. She stood beside Trina not saying a word as Trina's body movement indicated she wanted to get on the dance floor. She pulled Courtney by the arm.

"I love this song. Let's dance," Trina suggested.

Courtney pulled her arm away from Trina and braced her stand, not moving toward the dance floor. "No, I don't want to dance," Courtney told her.

"C'mon, it's Christmas. Everyone is dancing and enjoying themselves." She pulled Courtney by the arm again.

Courtney jerked her arm away and snapped. "I said no. The floor is crowded. Just get out there and dance. Nobody will notice that you're dancing alone."

"I will notice. What's with you? You have been in a rotten mood all day," Trina said as she scanned the club and held up her arm for a waiter.

A tall, thin waiter approached them. "What can I get you two?"

"I'll take a glass of white wine and also one for her." Trina pointed to Courtney.

Courtney stood there staring out into space, looking at the crowded dance floor but not really focusing on the dancers. Her mind was preoccupied with the storm that was still brewing inside of her over the fallout of her actions. Then moments later she found herself standing near the nightclub Christmas tree but Trina was nowhere in sight. She focused on the here and now and spotted Trina headed across the floor walking toward her from the bar area. She was carrying two glasses of white wine.

"Here's your drink." Trina passed her the glass.

"Thank you," Courtney said. "I thought the waiter would have brought our drinks to us. Did you have to go get them?"

"No, I didn't have to go get them. I went to the ladies room and bumped into our waiter on my way back." Trina took a sip of her wine and looked at Courtney's sad face. "I can see you are still in knots about something. Just tell me what's going on with you?"

"What makes you think something is going on with me?" Courtney asked calmly, trying to conceal her emotions.

"I have eyes and also a brain!" Trina stated irritated and pointed to her head. "It's obvious you are upset and miserable about something. Even Kenny noticed before we left the house. He asked me were you feeling okay."

"Why didn't he ask me if he wanted to know?" Courtney snapped.

"He probably didn't ask you because he didn't want you to snap his head off as you are doing me right now. So what's eating you? And don't tell me it's nothing." Trina gave her a solid look. "It's clear something is bothering you. You haven't smiled since you walked in the door with all those expensive gifts from Rome. Two bags of fine gifts from Neiman Marcus seems to me you would be on top of the world. So what gives with your sour attitude?"

Courtney turned her glass up to her lips and took a long sip of wine before swallowing and lowering her glass. She looked at Trina and shook her head. "Okay, you're right. Something is eating at me and I feel just awful about it."

"Okay, what is it?" Trina asked curiously.

"I'll tell you, but not in here. It's too crowded and the music is too loud. I'll tell you when we get to the house."

"That's fine because we are leaving now," Trina announced and placed her empty wine glass on the empty table next to them.

"Sure, that's fine if you're ready," Courtney mumbled and placed her half finished glass of wine on the table next to Trina's glass.

When Courtney and Trina arrived home, Kenney and Vickie waved at them from across the room. They were seated on the floor under the Christmas tree working on a five thousand piece puzzle. It was ten forty-five and Christmas evening was coming to a close at the Ross's home. The tall silver Christmas tree in the far corner of the room lit up the living room with red, green and blue lights as Courtney placed her purse on the coffee table and then removed her coat and threw it across the arm of the sofa. She dropped down on the far right end of the sofa as her whole insides were saturated with agony.

Trina removed her coat and threw it on a nearby chair as she walked into the kitchen to locate the leftover red wine that was served with Christmas dinner. She spotted the bottle on the kitchen counter, grabbed the bottle and two glasses and hurried back into the living room. She placed the two glasses and the half drank wine bottle on the end table and then proceeded to pour the two glasses full. She stepped to the opposite end of the sofa and handed Courtney a glass.

"Thank you, I can use this," Courtney said and quickly took a sip.

"I'm sure you can use it after that disaster you shared with me during our drive home from the club," Trina said, taking a seat on the sofa at the opposite end.

"Keep your voice down, please. I don't want Kenny and Vickie to hear us," Courtney said in a low voice. "What happened at Franklin House is not something that I want anyone else to know."

"Don't worry, they can't hear us. They are too wrapped up in that puzzle. But you need to get ready for the gossip. You know everybody is going to find out. I know you don't think this is something that can remain a secret, do you?" Trina asked.

"I know people will find out that Rome broke up with me but I just don't want everybody to know why."

"That you got wasted and ended up in his brother's bedroom?"

"Yes that, and also how I ended up telling Britain I loved him right in front of Rome." Courtney grabbed her face. "I can't believe I was so..."

"Is stupid the word you're looking for?" Trina sipped her wine.

"Maybe it is, because I completely messed up big time," Courtney said sadly.

They spoke in low voices as Kenny and Vickie voices were also low as they were preoccupied in their task. But louder voices and laughter floated up from the basement as their parents and other family members were engaged in Christmas board games.

"How could you have been so reckless to allow a filthy rich man like Rome Franklin to slip between your fingers? Not to mention he's one of the best looking men in this town." Trina asked confused, as she sat with her legs propped beneath her. "But at least the folks won't hold you up as an example I need to follow, saying I need to find a fellow like Rome Franklin with class and money."

"They'll just call us both old maids," Courtney mumbled.

"They will not; besides, old maids are single females over thirty. We still have several years before we reach old maid hood," Trina joked.

"Speak for yourself. You may have several years, seven to be exact before you hit thirty, but I only have six before I'm over the hill." Courtney waved her hand. "Besides, that's the least of my worries. I don't care about that."

"Well, what do you care about? I thought you cared about Rome Franklin. I thought the guy was it for you. I know he would have been it for me or anybody else in their right mind. So what gives with your little mess up?" Trina asked seriously.

"I just messed up that's what gives."

"I know you messed up. But you're smarter than that."

"Nobody is smart when they're wasted," Courtney snapped.

"Maybe you were full of booze, but hearing about your actions at Franklin House has really thrown me for a loop. I just can't get over what you have told me." Trina shook her head. "I thought you were crazy about Rome and not his brother."

Courtney stared at Trina. "What do you want me to say? I thought I was crazy about Rome and not his brother also, but it turns out I never got over Britain. You try sharing your lunch with the guy every day for two months and see how well you fair?"

"That's the difference between us, Courtney. I would never be lucky enough to get that chance to louse up."

"What is that supposed to mean?"

"It means I may be the younger sibling, but you are the attractive sibling. In a nutshell, I didn't end up with your good looks."

"Don't be silly. You look just fine."

"Sure, I may look just fine to you if you think overweightness looks good. But even you would have to agree that I need to lose a few pounds. But even if I was skinny I wouldn't be their type. Those guys are not looking for some female who look just fine. They may be gentlemen but they definitely have an eye for beauty; and why shouldn't they when they are all pretty boys."

"Thanks, Trina. That makes me feel even worse to know I had a rare chance but blew it. But my biggest mistake was not being able to get over Britain. I do love him," Courtney mumbled sadly, wiping tears from her eyes with the back of her hand.

"What about Rome? What do you feel for him? He's the guy that you couldn't stop talking about when you first got that job."

"I know and I have thought about it, and I guess I love them both."

"You guess you love them both? That's a good answer when you don't have either one of them. And on top of that you lost your job!" Trina lifted the wine bottle from the end table and poured more wine into her glass.

"I don't care about the job. I was leaving away, you know that."

"All I know is that you messed up big time. For a smart girl, you have done a really dumb thing. But knowing how compassionate the Franklins are. I don't think all is lost," Trina winked at her.

Courtney stared hard at her sister. "What do you mean by that? I think all is lost. I have lost Rome and my job. Not to mention that Britain probably hates me too! So tell me, how did you come up with the idea that not all is lost?"

"I'm just saying, I think if you talk to Rome he'll probably give you your job back," Trina encouraged her. "He's upset right now, of course, but you know how compassionate those Franklin guys are. I bet you anything he'll give you your job back," Trina assured her.

"I'm not as convinced as you are. I saw how disappointed he was with me. You didn't hear how firm he sounded when he had that talk with me. Besides, he knew I was leaving at the first of the year, which is only a week from now."

"Yes, you were leaving the company but only after you had landed another job. So I think it would be wise to try to get your job back in the meantime."

"Trina, I'm not sure I should bother. I don't want to feel like I'm begging them for anything. Besides, I'm not looking to do that kind of work forever. I didn't get my degree to be a counter assistant; I got my degree to teach school and that's what I want to get into," she said with both legs propped on the coffee table.

"Who said anything about forever? I'm talking about for now," Trina stressed strongly. "I know you want a teaching job and I'm sure you'll get one, but in the meantime who's going to pay you a better salary than Franklin Gas. They pay top dollars to their workers. They were paying you more as a counter assistant than you'll probably earn as a teacher."

"I doubt that. I'm sure a teacher's salary is a lot more than a counter assistant at a gas station, but I do agree that they do pay their employees very well."

"So, does that mean you're going to ask for your job back?"

"I can ask of course, but it doesn't mean Rome will rehire me."

"I think you should talk to Sydney and plead your case. Explain that you are sorry and didn't mean to hurt anyone. Just let him know how much you need your job back. I'm sure he'll understand and give you another chance."

"So, you think Sydney will go behind Rome's back and rehire me after Rome let me go? They don't operate that way. They stick together like glue and have each other's back all the way."

"I know that. I'm just saying, I think you should talk to Sydney and of course, Sydney will most likely talk to Rome and suggest that they give you another chance. It's worth a shot. Besides, you always received glowing reviews for your work. You were reliable and all the customers loved you; and they know that."

"Okay, I'll give Sydney a call and see what he says, but I doubt they will rehire me. That scene at their house was something I'm sure none of them will forget anytime soon. That was the mistake of my life. I had the love and respect of a nearly perfect man and I threw it all away at the mercy of too much booze and pinning away for someone I couldn't have."

"Stop feeling sorry for yourself. You need to focus on thinking clearly and putting your best self forward to win over the Franklin guys again."

Courtney grabbed her face and cried uncontrollably for a few seconds, and then she wiped her eyes with the back of her hands, grabbed her purse from the coffee table and pulled a bottle of vodka from it.

Trina shook her head at the sight of the liquor bottle. "Do you think it's a good idea to start drinking again? That's what landed you in the predicament you're in," Trina reminded her.

"Give me one good reason why I shouldn't take a drink? It's Christmas a time to be happy and thankful, but I feel worse than I ever have." She touched her stomach. "I just feel so sick and hopeless inside. I really need a drink right now with all this stress I'm dealing with."

"Yeah, I'm sure you feel pretty rotten, but that bottle is only going to make it worse." Trina pointed toward the bottle.

"Who cares about that right now? Besides, it's Christmas and everyone drinks a little wine or champagne on Christmas," Courtney fussed. "We are both drinking wine; plus you drank some vodka earlier, so why shouldn't I have some of this vodka?"

"The difference is that I can handle my liquor and you can't." Trina waved her hand and glanced over at Kenny and Vickie in the far corner of the room. "You see he's not drinking, and I'm sure he would love to. But he knows he can't."

"Blah, blah, blah, Kenny isn't dealing with what I'm dealing with right now," Courtney snapped.

"Maybe he isn't dealing with what you are; but the point is, you are just like Dad and Kenny. Therefore, you shouldn't be drinking since you can't handle your booze. That's why you gave up drinking after college."

Courtney ignored Trina and twisted the top off the bottle and then turned it up to her mouth and took a quick swallow. She exchanged looks with Trina, frowning and shaking her head from the burning sting in her throat.

"Wow, look at you," Trina shouted. "You're drinking straight vodka from the bottle now? I guess you really are in a bad way. You would think all those nice gifts from Rome would have you in a better mood."

"Nothing is going to put me in a better mood except to wake up and find this nightmare was a sick dream." She held out both arms. "But we both know it's not a dream. Therefore, I'm depending on this bottle to fade my reality," Courtney cried. "I know the gifts are nice, but they mean nothing, because there's no meaning behind them. Rome only gave them to me because he had already bought them and he's too much of a gentleman to have not given them to me. I'm sure he couldn't stomach the fact that he spent all that money on someone he kicked to the curb."

"Just be careful with that bottle. You could end up really sick if you drink too much of that vodka on top of all the wine you had this evening. Remember how sick wine and vodka made you back in college when you had to miss a week of classes?"

"I'll watch it, but it's all that Sabrina Taylor's fault that Britain didn't ask me out. I'm sure he wanted to. He was so sweet and kind to me for those two months before she moved to town."

"That may be true, but he's with her now and you know how devoted those guys are when they are with someone. I think you need to forget Britain and concentrate on Rome. You probably have a better chance of getting him back than ever having a relationship with Britain."

Courtney took another swallow of the vodka and passed the bottle to her left to Trina. "Have a sip. Get in the Christmas spirit and be merry."

Trina took the bottle. "You are telling me to get in the Christmas spirit and be merry. I think you need to take your own advice. I am merry," Trina said, turned the bottle up to her mouth and took a sip. "Thanks, I needed that sip of booze. I can stomach it a lot better than this cheap red wine we're drinking that was left over from Christmas dinner." Trina passed the bottle back to Courtney.

"Well, it's plenty more where this bottle came from. I have a couple more bottles in my room. Those bottles have been in my closet for over a year now. Like you said, I gave up drinking when I finished college. But I fell off the wagon soon after starting at my job at Franklin Gas."

"You hid your drinking well," Trina said. "We started working for the Franklins at the same time right after I finished college. You had worked at the college for a year just so I could see a familiar face. And if I never thanked you, I really appreciated your gesture. But I have to tell you, after we started at Franklin Gas I didn't see any signs that you were problem drinking again."

"That's because I hid it so well and were mostly drinking alone in my room before bed. It would numb the pain of wanting Rome and then it started numbing the pain of wanting Britain; and right now it's the only thing that can numb me and get me through this agony I'm going through."

"Are you in agony over losing Rome or is Britain who you're pinning away for? I know you said you love them both. But that's not an answer. I'm sure you love one of them more than the other, so which one you love the most?"

"It's obvious?" Courtney snapped. "Think about what landed me in this mess. It's Britain, okay! I love Britain Franklin the most!"

"Wrong answer, being in love with Britain Franklin is useless. He's a man that is completely off the radar to you?"

"He wouldn't be off the radar if Sabrina Taylor was out of the picture."

"That may be true, but she's not out of the picture. It's obvious he's totally into her. She's his type!"

"What type is that?"

"She is skinny as a noodle with super long hair and filthy rich to boot," Trina stared toward Courtney. "Can you match up to that?"

"I guess not, since I'm not skinny as a noodle and I don't have super long hair; and I don't want super long hair and I'm definitely not rich." She paused. "But Britain doesn't care about how rich she is. You know they don't care about that."

"Maybe not, but being filthy rich is definite a plus," Trina laughed.

Courtney glanced at Trina and shook her head. "Why are you laughing? I don't find anything the least bit funny about our conversation. I just wish Sabrina Taylor would leave town and then Britain and I would have some fragment of a chance."

"Hello, wake up!" Trina said loudly, but quickly lowered her voice. "That's your liquor talking. You have a zero chance with Britain. You have a better chance of taking a trip to the moon than you do with that guy. You need to face facts and move on."

"I believe Sabrina Taylor is blocking my chances with Britain."

"If that is true what can you do about it?"

"I don't know what I can do about it, but it's tearing me up inside. I detest her for messing up my life the way she has. My misery is all on her head."

"I don't think you can blame Sabrina for your misery. You need to take a look in the mirror."

Courtney exchanged looks with Trina. "Who side are you on?

"I'm on your side, of course. But I just don't think it's fair and it's not like you to blame someone else for your mistakes the way you are doing."

"You are right. It's not like me, because the old me was destroyed when Britain rejected me. I'm tired of being the nice girl who ends up with nothing to show for it. Sabrina Taylor has destroyed my life and now I want to destroy hers."

"How do you plan to do that? I hope it's nothing stupid."

"I'm not sure yet. I just know I hate that female and her penalty for messing up my life needs to be more than a couple curse words thrown her way."

"Courtney, I really don't like where your head is right now. You are sounding dumber as this conversation continues. You need to accept the facts and leave that girl alone. If you think you have a problem now, you will have a much bigger problem if you do something stupid like pick a fight with Sabrina Taylor. I say drop the attitude and forget that girl," Trina suggested strongly. "Right now it's the booze talking, but you still need to shake yourself out of your funk!"

"I'm not in a funk, I'm just upset!"

"Same difference; the best advice I can give you is, please apology to the Franklin family and ask for their forgiveness for that scene you caused at their house and see if they will give you your job back."

After a long silent pause, Courtney dried her tears with the back of her hands and looked over at Trina. "You are right, of course. You may be my younger sister, but you give good advice," she said, and then looked at the bottle of vodka that sat on the coffee table. "Drinking this hard liquor isn't really helping me feel any better." She lifted the bottle, turned toward Trina and passed it to her.

Trina took the bottle and took a sip. When she tried to hand the bottle back to Courtney, Courtney shook her head. "Keep it. I need to clear my mind and get back on track. I need to wake up as you have suggested and open my eyes to the fact that there's no chance for me with Britain." She grabbed her cheeks with both hands for a moment and stared into space, and then looked toward Trina. "If I'm totally honest, there's no chance with Rome either. I burnt my bridges with them both. The most I can hope for is a second chance to work at their company. I can ask for my job back and be thankful if they rehire me."

"Now that's good thinking, but there is something else you should think about as well," Trina suggested.

"And what's that?"

"Wally Simpson, the one guy who has always been crazy about you."

"I'm not really into Wally Simpson anymore; my heart is in pieces for Britain and Rome Franklin. Besides, I haven't heard from him since my birthday, which was over three months ago. What makes you think he's still pinning away for me?"

"It doesn't matter how long its been since you heard from him. You know Wally wants to get back together with you."

"Just drop it; I'm not looking to get back together with Wally." Courtney waved her hand. "I just said I'm no longer into the man."

Trina shook her head. "Listen, Courtney, you need to get over it and suck it up! The most important thing here is that Wally is into you, and that's more than you can say for Rome and Britain Franklin since they are not. You better think about giving Wally another chance. At least he actually gives a damn," Trina said with conviction. "Rome and Britain is never going to look your way again. Besides, Wally may not be a Franklin, but he's a decent guy and the new principal over at Barrington High. He's in a position to offer you a job at the school if you apply there."

Chapter Twenty-Nine

On Friday morning, shortly after ten o'clock, two days after Christmas, it was snowing steadily as Courtney parked her six year old green Ford Focus down the street from Franklin Gas. She was wearing a pair of neatly pressed blue jeans and a cranberry pull over sweater beneath coat. She sat there in her car anxious with nerves as she wondered if she should go inside or not. Rome had dismissed her and had asked her to stay away from the building, but she was determined to talk to Britain. Therefore, after five minutes of trying to decide whether she should go inside or not, she turned off the engine and stepped out of the car. The moment she stepped out of her warm car, the cold wind hit her face and made her frown, but she was warmly wrapped in her long black wool coat as she walked quickly up the street toward the building.

She managed to sneak in the building and took the elevator up to the fourth floor without any of the workers noticing her. She went straight to Britain's office. When she arrived at his door, it was ajar. She peeked in and saw Britain sitting at his desk talking on the phone with his back to her. She stepped into his office and closed the door as he continued his call with no awareness of her presence. When he swirled around at his desk and noticed her standing with her back against his office door, he immediately ended his call as surprise showed on his face.

"Good morning, Courtney. What are you doing here?" he asked politely.

"I didn't mean to startle you but I had to come so I could apologize to you for my awful behavior at your house," she said humbly.

"You didn't have to come here for that. I understand you had had too much to drink." He nodded. "It happens."

"Yes it happens, but it shouldn't have happened. I made a fool of myself in front of your entire family."

"I'm sure you wish you could take it back, but you can't un-spill milk. Don't worry about. Just forget the whole thing," he suggested.

"How can I forget? I made Rome hate me and so do you." She grabbed her face with both hands and began to cry.

"Courtney, it's not as bad as that. Nobody hates you."

"But Rome fired me and you probably don't want to have anything else to do with me either. But I do love you, Britain." She wiped her tears with her fingers.

Britain shifted in his seat. He was a bit uncomfortable hearing Courtney confession of love. "I'm flattered, Courtney, of course. What guy wouldn't be?" He stood up from his seat and walked in front of his desk and leaned against it with his arms folded. "But I don't think we need to have this conversation."

"We do need to have this conversation because I think you and I deserve a chance to try," she mumbled.

"I'm not following, a chance to try what?"

"A chance for us to try at a relationship," she paused looking in his eyes. "I'm no longer with your brother."

"But I'm with someone, remember Sabrina?"

"Sure, I remember her, but I'm sure I can make you a lot happier than that poor little rich girl," she said slipping out of her coat.

"You should probably keep your coat on. I don't want to be rude but I need to get back to work and you need to leave before Rome catches you in my office."

"Who cares if he catches me in your office?"

"I care, Courtney. Seeing you in here would just remind him of Christmas Eve when you stood in front of him and confessed your feelings for me."

"I'm sorry it happened that way but I'm not sorry that I told you, because it's true. I love you and I think you care for me as well." She placed her coat in the chair near the door. Beneath the coat revealed her sexy outfit.

Britain threw a quick glance at her outfit and then turned his back to her and occupied himself with some files on his desk. He picked up a stack of files and stepped over to the file cabinet near his desk and placed them on top of the cabinet. "I really must get back to work," he said with his back to her.

Courtney had stepped across the room, standing right behind him when he turned around. She stood about twenty inches from him. "Your outfit is really nice," she said. "But all your outfits are nice." He was wearing a brown three piece suit with a white shirt and a narrow brown tie.

"You are the best dressed guy in this building besides your brothers, of course." She smiled. "You all dress like movie stars, and you will be pretty soon when you start performing in your first movie," she said excitedly. "Rome told me all about it and mentioned they are shooting the film here in town because it's sort of about your life."

Britain nodded. "That's correct." He felt uncomfortable small talking with her.

"Do you have your scripts and who gets top billing?" she asked.

"We received the scripts yesterday and Sydney has the leading role," he said, and then swallowed hard. "Courtney, with all due respect, if you don't mind I would rather not discuss our movie project with you. Besides, I'm sure Rome has already filled you in on a lot of details."

She nodded. "Yes, he told me a lot, but he didn't mention the exact date of the filming and what section of town is being blocked off. Do you know?"

"They start shooting the film in about three weeks. That's all I can tell you; and I'm not trying to be rude, but it feels awkward having you here in my office exchanging talk as if all is well when it really isn't. Rome ended your relationship and dismissed you from the company and I'm sure he wouldn't take to well to your visit here this morning. Besides, you and I don't have that kind of small talk connection any more."

She changed the subject and reached out and touched his tie. "Your tie is really chic," she said, smiling.

He kept his composure. "Thank you, but I think it would be best if you would just leave now, Courtney. You have said what you came to say and now you need to leave. I heard you out, I know how you feel, but I can't return your feelings."

"I know you feel that way now," she mumbled.

"My feelings are not going to change," Britain stressed. "I know you feel there's a chance for us somewhere down the road, but I want to make it crystal clear that we could never be more than acquaintances."

"Acquaintance, not even friends?" she asked. "We used to be good friends."

He nodded. "Yes, we used to be good friends, but there's no way we could pick up and be friends again. Too much has happened; and with your current feelings for me it won't work. I hope you can understand that."

"All I understand is that I have fallen in love with you and you can't understand that," she said, looking sadly in his eyes.

"Courtney, I have empathy for you. But I'm in a relationship and even if I wasn't I would never consider asking you out," he said firmly.

"Britain, why do you say never? Maybe a few months down the road things will fall apart for you and Sabrina and you'll be single again."

"Courtney, that's not a nice prediction to make." He shook his head. "And you're not listening to me. I just said even if I wasn't already in a relationship I would never ask you out."

"You really know how to make a girl feel lousy," Courtney mumbled.

"I'm not trying to make you feel lousy. I'm just being on the level with you."

"Okay, but why do you feel you can never ask me out?"

"Because you were my brother's girl, I would never cross that line."

"But I'm in love with you," she threw her arms around him and he stiffened his stand. He felt uneasy but kept his composure and didn't push her away. He felt empathy for her and knew she was having a hard time being rejected, but he couldn't be anything but honest with her.

"Courtney, I'm sorry but you need to try to accept things the way they are."

"I don't want to accept things the way they are. I believe we can find away. I know you are in a relationship and I'm not asking you to leave Sabrina to be with me." She held him tightly as he stood there with both arms at his side.

"Okay, what are you saying?" he asked, awaiting release of her arms from him.

"I'm saying I want to be with you anyway I can. Nobody needs to know. I want you to make love to me," she blurted out.

He swallowed hard, stunned by her words. "Courtney, I could never use you in that way."

"But I want you to use me if that's the only way I can be with you, I'll take it."

Britain reflected back to what his mother had told him on Christmas Eve that Courtney came to his room because she wanted him to have his way with her. Now he had to face the reality that his mother instincts were true. He didn't like the picture in his head as he gently pushed Courtney away.

He shook his head. "Courtney, you are not thinking clearly. I'm sure you don't want what you are asking."

"I do want what I'm asking," she mumbled in a low voice and then looked toward the floor. "I haven't been drinking this early in the morning. I know exactly what I'm asking." She looked in his eyes. "I know I love you and want to be with you in that way right now. It can be our secret and if you never want to see me again afterward, I'll deal with that."

Britain was suddenly heated from their awkward conversation. He removed his suit jacket and stepped across his office to place it on the coat stand in the corner. Then he stepped across the room and locked the door. He looked at Courtney with a serious expression. "I'm a gentleman and I have asked you to leave, but you are trying my patience and that's not cool."

"But I see you locked the door, so are you considering what I said?"

"Courtney, no way am I considering what you said. The only thing on my mind is Rome walking in here and seeing you. That's why I locked the door." He pointed to the door. "My brother doesn't need to be reminded of what took place on Christmas Eve. Seeing you here would do that."

"Britain, why do you keep slamming the door in my face?"

"I have told you why. You are a beautiful woman and it's nothing personal. But if you know me at all, you already know that I could never use you or any female in the manner you are asking. I need to be able to look myself in the mirror everyday. It would be easy to throw my values out of the window for a beautiful woman that's willing, but I'm not that guy to do it."

"I guess not. You're too damn moral," Courtney snapped.

"Courtney, you have morals as well. Therefore, you need to forget me and move on. Pursuing me is a waste of your time. I can not and will not push my principles aside in the face of any amount of desire."

"So, you do have desire for me?" she asked.

"No, Courtney, I do not. I do not have those kinds of feelings for you. It was just a figure of speech. So I'm asking you to please put your coat back on and leave this office before Rome runs in to you here."

Courtney grabbed her coat and tore out of his office without looking back. She rushed down the hall two doors down to Sydney's office. She knocked.

"Please come in," he said.

She walked in and he nodded. "Hi Courtney, what can I do for you this morning?" he was seated at his desk with both arms folded on his desk in front of him.

"I came here to discuss something with you. Do you have a minute?" she asked, standing in front of his desk holding her coat in her arms.

He was dressed in a navy blue two piece pinstripe suit, white shirt and solid navy tie. He was wearing a pair of shiny navy Louis Vuitton shoes; and his diamond blue face Rolex offset his attire. He nodded and then pointed to either chair sitting on either side of his desk. She took a seat and he pointed to the coffee stand in the corner of his office. "Would you care for some coffee I'm about to have a cup." He got out of his seat and headed toward the coffee stand.

"Sure, coffee sounds great."

"How do you take it?"

"Cream and sugar, please," she said nervously.

She couldn't read Sydney, because the Franklin guys were all gentlemen and always kept their composure. But he didn't seem as shocked to see her face as Britain had appeared when she walked into his office. Sydney seemed less awkward around her and she knew it was probably due to the fact that he hadn't been directly affected by her behavior at Franklin House.

"Here you are." Sydney passed her a shiny black mug with a white S on it.

"Thank you, this is a nice mug." She sipped the coffee.

He nodded. "They are pretty cool. My father purchased a dozen for us all before he died," he said as he took a seat at his desk. "We were just little boys. But on one of his trips abroad he purchased and shipped home these wonderful mugs with our initials on them: Black for me, Gray for Rome, White for Britain and Blue for Paris." He took a sip from the mug, holding it with both hands. "That's pretty much how we all ended up with our color schemes."

"I see. Its incredible how your father had such a huge effect on your lives in amazing ways that he didn't even know he would." She took another sip of coffee.

"I agree with that," Sydney smiled. "Father isn't with us, but he has always been with us in one way or another." He stacked some files on his desk. "But I'm sure you didn't stop by my office to find out the history of my coffee mugs. You said you wanted to discuss something with me, so what can I do for you this morning?"

"I would like my job back," she said.

"But you were planning on leaving at the first of the year, which is just a few days from now."

"But what you don't know is that I wasn't going to leave until I had another job lined up and since I don't, I was wondering if maybe I could work on here until I do."

Sydney shifted in his seat and loosened his tie a bit. "Courtney, this puts me in an awkward position. Although, I'm in charge of hiring and dismissing employees, Paris originally hired you and Rome dismissed you. But you are coming to me and asking for your job back." He lifted his mug and took a long sip of coffee as if he was in deep thought. "I don't see how I could rehire you without Rome's approval. I could get him in here and see what he has to say. I know he let you go because of what happened at the house a couple nights ago, but he might feel differently now. I could buzz his office and ask him to step in here, if you like." He nodded.

"Please, don't. I'm sure Rome doesn't want me working here."

"But you feel comfortable working here inspite of that?" he asked.

"Not really, but I need the job. My salary helps out the household. My parents fell behind and my pay check helps with the mortgage. If I don't get my job back we could end up losing our house," Courtney explained.

"No kidding, I didn't know. We would never want that to happen, but you being here on the premises isn't a good fit for you and Rome or Britain for that matter." He shook his head. "So giving you your old job back is out of the question."

"Where is your compassionate? I thought you guys were so caring toward others like your father used to be," she snapped. "I just told you how we could end up losing our home and you still won't rehire me," Courtney said angrily.

"Courtney, I won't rehire you for a position that my brother dismissed you from. But I didn't say I wouldn't help you. I'm willing to rehire you in a different capacity if you are in agreement with it."

"What kind of different capacity?"

"The position would not be here in this building."

"Where would it be?"

"I'm willing to give you the same salary to work for us out of your home."

"I don't understand," she said with confusion in her eyes. "What could I do for the company out of my home?"

"There's a lot of work that you can do for us offsite, but are you in favor of it?"

"Sure, I'm in favor to be rehired with the same salary, especially since I don't have to leave home. But what would I be doing?"

"Basically, you would be answering all calls that come in for myself, Rome, Britain and Paris. You would screen our calls and take messages and you would notify us of important calls that need our immediate attention. You would work from home from nine to five, the same schedule you had here with an hour for lunch."

"It sounds great. When can I start?"

"We'll have it all set up for Monday, how is that?" he smiled.

"I think Monday will be perfect. Thank you so much, Sydney. You are so compassionate and a Godsend," she said excitedly. "You are doing me a huge favor giving me this opportunity to help my folks keep our home." She grabbed her face. "But what about your brothers, especially Rome when you tell them you rehired me?"

"Well, I'm not technically rehiring you. I'm giving you a new job and its offsite. I think you working here in the building was Rome's main objection. He felt it would be too awkward to keep you on after what happened. But giving you a position to earn a living to help yourself and your parents, I'm sure they will all be for it." He stood from his seat and walked around to shake her hand. "Welcome back onboard. The calls will start being forward to your phone Monday morning. We will give you a company's credit card for all your business supplies." Sydney pulled open his desk drawer and pulled out a credit card and passed it to her.

Courtney stood from her seat and took the card and just as she took her seat back in the chair, there was a slight knock on Sydney's door. A lump reached in her throat and she was hoping the knocker wasn't Rome. But before Sydney knew who was at his door he said, "Please come in." He and Courtney looked toward the door as Paris opened the door and stepped inside, closing the door behind him. He looked the picture of chic elegance dressed in a two piece black suit, hunter green shirt with a black tie with hunter green stripes on it. He was wearing a pair of exclusive shoes that reflected glowingly from the overhead office light.

"Hi Courtney," Paris said and exchanged looks with Sydney. "I'm sorry to barge in like this. I hope I'm not interrupting anything. I can come back later. I just wanted to pick up that file we discussed." He stepped across the room to stand in front of Sydney's desk.

"Sure, it's right here." Sydney pulled open his desk drawer and pulled out the file and handed it to Paris.

"Thanks, I'll take this file and be on my way," Paris nodded at him.

"No, hold up for a moment," Sydney said. "You might as well hear it now," Sydney said and paused, looking at his brother.

"Okay, I'm listening. What is it?" Paris asked.

"I just gave Courtney that phone answering position we wanted to fill."

"You did, okay," Paris nodded. He wasn't sure if Sydney had done the proper thing or not due to the circumstances.

"I'm sure you are wondering about the timing and considering what happened at home you're wondering if Courtney is the right choice; but she'll be working offsite."

Paris just stood there with a solemn face not commenting.

"Her parents are having some difficulties meeting their monthly mortgage and without our salary from here, they could lose their home," Sydney explained.

Concern immediately ripped across Paris face as he looked at Courtney. "I'm sorry about your family difficulties, but I'm glad we were able to find something for you. The circumstances are a bit sticky, but working offsite will help you and your family and not cause an awkward situation at the workplace."

"Thank you, Paris, and I would like to apologize to you and Sydney for my drunken behavior at your house on Christmas Eve," she said humbly.

"Apology accepted," Paris said. "We all make mistakes. The reward comes from forgiveness." Paris looked toward Sydney.

Sydney nodded. "And when we forgive others, it's easier to forgive ourselves. My mother told us how Father used to live by that rule."

Paris nodded. "And he also lived by the rule that it's better to give than to receive." Paris stepped over to the coffee stand and poured himself a cup of coffee.

"So I take it, you don't have a coffee machine in your office," Courtney asked.

"I do, but it's not working at the moment," Paris explained and took a seat in the chair across from Courtney in front of Sydney's desk. But just minutes after he took his seat his phone rang. It was an important business call. "Excuse me," he held up one finger to Sydney. "I need to take this call." He stepped out of the office and closed the door behind him.

Courtney smiled. "One down and two to go," she said jokingly.

Sydney stood from his seat. "There's no need to concern yourself with that. All will be well. Regardless of the situation between you, Rome and Britain, they would not want you and your family to lose your home. They'll both be onboard with this decision because it's the right one to make." Sydney nodded. "I think we are all set."

Courtney stood from the chair as he walked around his desk and reached out his hand to shake hers; and as they shook hands he said, "One last thing, you will continue receiving your pay through direct deposit into your checking account."

She walked over to his office door and pulled it open. "Thank you, Sydney, so much. This means a lot to me and my family," she said and then closed the door and headed down the hallway toward the elevators.

The phone rang on Sydney's desk just minutes after Courtney left. He answered the call that kept him engaged until nearly noon. Immediately after the call, he sent all his brothers a text and asked them to join him in the cafeteria for lunch. And at straight up noon, they were all gathered at one of the reserved tables in the lunch room; and after they finished their lunches and were finishing up their iced-tea, Rome picked up a peanut from the dish in the middle of the table and threw one at Sydney. "Hey, I thought you wanted us to meet for lunch for a business reason," Rome smiled. "It was cool breaking bread together, but I thought you had some business in mind."

Sydney picked up a peanut out of the dish and threw one across the table at Rome. "Two can play this game," he joked. "I do have some business but I wanted everyone to finish their meals before I mentioned it." He exchanged looks with Paris. "Except Paris already knows the business I'm going to bring up."

"Okay, I'm curious to hear what it is," Britain lifted his bottle of iced-tea and turned it up to his mouth in a quick swallow. When he lowered the bottle and sat it on the table, he noticed Paris and Sydney exchanging serious looks with each other.

"Okay, I'm really curious now. What's this business you have to share?"

"I hired Courtney this morning," Sydney announced and reached in the little crystal bowl and grabbed two peanuts and placed in his mouth.

Britain and Rome exchanged surprise looks and then looked at Sydney. Rome kept his composure. "Did she come here asking for her job back?" Rome asked.

Sydney nodded. "Yes, she did, and I informed her that working here wouldn't be a good fit for you or Britain because of what happened at the house."

"But you felt compelled to give her the job back anyway?" Rome asked. "I thought we had a policy of not interfering or rehiring workers that one of us let go."

"That is correct, but in this case it wasn't quite that way," Sydney explained.

Britain held up one finger and looked at Sydney. "I'm not questioning your authority to hire whomever you please, but this is a sticky situation. I'm sure you realize that, therefore, I must admit I'm thrown that you would rehire Courtney." He took a sip of iced-tea. "With all due respect to Courtney's job skills, working here is going to be quite awkward to say the least."

"It's not going to be awkward," Paris added as he took a swallow from his iced-tea bottle; and then continued. "She won't be around."

"What do you mean she won't be around?" Britain asked.

Paris pointed to Sydney. "He'll explain."

"Okay, I guess we are waiting for you to explain," Britain looked at Sydney. He didn't want another awkward visit from her that had taken place in his office earlier.

"I didn't rehire Courtney as a counter assistance. I would never rehire a worker for an old position that one of you let that person go from. It would be your call to rehire the person for the position you dismissed them from. I gave her that new position we discussed," Sydney explained.

"The job we discussed about someone answering phones offsite," Rome asked.

"Yes, that's the job I hired her for."

Rome nodded. "That should work. At least she won't be here in the building. That was my concern. I felt it would have been too awkward for me and Britain."

"She'll be working from home the way we set up the position?" Britain asked.

"That's correct, and there will be no need for her to come here. Whenever any contact is needed, I'll meet with her," Sydney assured them. "This will be a smooth transition with no intrusion to the workplace. Besides, we know she's a good worker."

"Her work ethics are not the issue," Britain stated. "Her personal emotions are. We need to be levelheaded about this situation." He looked toward Rome. "Are you comfortable with Courtney being back on the payroll. I know she'll be working out of her home, but are you comfortable with that?" Britain asked.

Rome didn't readily answer Britain's question as he sat there in thought, reflecting on the situation.

Sydney looked at Rome. "Are you comfortable with this set up? I thought her working out of her home would be workable for us, but I don't want my giving her this job to be stressful. If you're not okay with it, I'll have to think of something else."

"Look, Courtney is a good worker. I see no real issue with her working offsite," Rome said. "I'm no longer emotionally attached to her, but would like to spare the workplace unnecessary rumors and gossip if possible."

Sydney nodded. "You don't see a problem with Courtney working offsite, that's good. I think it will work out." He looked at Britain. "Do you see a problem with her on payroll? I know she put you in an awkward spot with what she said to you."

Britain looked Sydney in the eyes. "I know you have hired her, but it probably would have been for the best if you had not. She was in my office this morning before she went to yours and her visit was quite awkward." Britain looked toward Rome. "I'm sorry, but she just showed up and I handled the meeting with as much respect as I could, making it crystal clear that there could never be anything between her and me."

Rome nodded at Britain. "You don't have to feel weird to tell me about her visit. You have done nothing wrong. It's not your fault if she's into you. Besides, I have no emotions for Courtney. She wasn't the one for me, but Amber is and I'm quite happy."

Sydney looked at Britain. "I think having Courtney on payroll is going to affect you more because of the awkward position she put you in by her announcement in your room. Just say the word and I'll let her go," Sydney assured him.

"It would be less stressful knowing she's not on payroll because even offsite, she's going to be taking calls and messages for all of us. It's quite uncomfortable communicating with her in person," Britain explained to Sydney.

"So, are you saying I should call her up and tell her the job offer is not going to work out? I wouldn't want to do it, but would figure out some other way to help her if her keeping the job would be too stressful for you," Sydney explained.

Before Britain could answer, Paris looked at Sydney. "What about their home?"

"That will work out, I'll take care of it," Sydney said.

"What about whose home?" Britain asked.

"Yeah, what's that about?" Rome asked.

"The reason I offered Courtney the offsite job is because without the income from Franklin Gas right now, they could lose their home," Sydney explained. "Her income is helping her parents keep their home right now."

"But she was quitting at the first of the year, days from now," Rome pointed out.

"Her intentions are to seek a teacher's position but had no intentions of leaving the company until she had landed another position. They could lose their home without her income from here," Sydney explained.

Britain held out both arms. "Say no more, keeping their home is a lot more important than the awkwardness I'll feel with her being on payroll," he said. "I had no idea they were in financial trouble." He looked at Rome.

"She never mentioned it to me," Rome said. "This is most disturbing that she and her family have been suffering financially and she didn't mention it while we were together. I could have helped them out."

"We can still help them out," Paris suggested. "This is still the Christmas season. We could issue an anonymous payment toward their mortgage. It's the sort of thing Father did all the time when he was alive."

Britain nodded. "That's a great idea, because I don't think Courtney would straight out accept a donation from us due to her pride."

Rome nodded. "I agree. She wouldn't accept a donation from us. But if we make the payment anonymous they wouldn't know it was from us."

Sydney shook his head. "It's a great idea and I wish we could do this for Courtney and her family, but she would figure out it came from us. She knows she shared the information with me."

"So, what if she knows, by the time she figures it out the house payment will be paid. It will be our good deed for the year," Paris said. "We would have helped a family that's struggling. I know there's tension between you and Courtney," he said to Rome. "And Britain is uncomfortable to be around her, but we need to take a stand and help out this woman and her family. We clearly know they are in need and could lose their home. Keeping the job is going to help, but who is to say they still won't end up losing their home. I had a talk with her brother, Kenny, and he believes in a lot of the things Father believed in. He's a decent guy but he's struggling with alcoholism just as his father and if I may be so bold, I think Courtney has the same disease. But they are all trying to cope and keep it under control. Kenny Ross did something priceless for me a couple months ago and I would very much like to do this for his family," Paris said with conviction. "Without his confession and insight the love of my life could have been lost to me. I told him on that day if he ever needed a job to come to me. I'm sure he has too much pride to come to me, but I want to help them because it's the right thing to do and it's what Father would do."

Britain nodded. "It is what Father would do. He died at 38 but he had helped hundredth of people keep their homes. We do what we can but Paris is right, we haven't begun to make an impact in helping others as our father. I agree with Paris, this can be our Secret Santa project. We can talk to Trina and let her know what we are planning for her family. I'm sure she would be onboard and keep the information to herself after we explain we want to stay anonymous." He took a sip from his iced-tea bottle. "And I realize that staying anonymous would be best if we didn't mention it to Trina, but we have to share our plans with her since she is needed to get the mortgage account number and billing information for the payment," Britain explained.

"We also have to keep this information from Mother for a little while," Sydney reminded them. "She'll have a fit, of course, but this is something we want to do for someone who is struggling financially."

"Who's going to talk to Trina? The sooner we get the mortgage information the sooner we can make the payment. They won't have the thought of losing their home hanging over their heads after that," Paris said.

Rome held up one finger. "I'll talk with Trina and let her know what our Secret Santa plan is and that we would like to stay anonymous until Courtney finds another job and is no longer working for us. But I will also let her know that she can feel free to inform her parents after we have made the payment. I think they should be told."

Paris nodded. "I agree; this way they won't have to worry about that debt."

"Do we have a ceiling of how much we'll pay on their home?" Sydney asked.

"I figured six months of payments, which will probably run us about eighteen thousand. I figured anything up to, but over twenty thousand," Paris said.

"It's definitely less than twenty thousand," Rome said. "I have seen their home and my best guess puts their mortgage at a couple thousand a month." Rome paused. "I know why you're looking at me as if I'm off target with that amount, but their home is quite modest. But, if I guessed on the low side we still know it won't be over twenty thousand. Any amount over that will get to Mother's attention quicker."

"That's true." Paris nodded. "That's why I suggested up to, but not over. Mother gets phones and emails alerts for any transactions over that amount."

"She does get those alerts," Britain agreed. "But it really doesn't matter if it does get to her attention. She knows we spend about hundred thousand yearly on charities, helping the needy. So far this year, and the year is almost over, we have only donated half of that amount. Besides, Mother has never questioned who we donated too."

Sydney smiled. "With all due respect, we all know Mother. She would never object to someone in need, but this situation is different. She knows Courtney and isn't that fond of her. She didn't think she was the right person for you." Sydney looked toward Rome. "And after that incident on Christmas Eve her feelings are probably less warm toward Courtney. My point is, once she finds out, she will have plenty to say."

"Maybe, but we have to keep our emotions separate from our humanitarian side," Paris added. "We can all agree that Courtney behaved shockingly on Christmas Eve; and we can also agree that her dishonesty to Rome was appalling."

Britain added. "We can also agree we're more at ease with her working offsite."

Paris nodded. "That's true, but my point is, we can also agree that paying their mortgage for six months so they won't be in jeopardy of losing their home is the charitable thing to do. We'll be making a real difference with someone that we know personally is having difficulties. I'm especially pleased to have this opportunity to help out her family, in light of the very generous thing that her brother did for me. It took a bighearted person to do what he did."

"I agree with you Paris, of course," Rome nodded. "Mother will not be pleased since Courtney is involved, but after we make the payment, we'll talk to Mother and explain why we felt compelled to give Courtney a job offsite and to help her family."

That Friday evening at Franklin House while they were all gathered at the dinner table, Veronica was excited about the movie scripts that they had received in the mail yesterday and she wanted to discuss the dialogue, especially Sydney's part, the leading role; but she noticed he wasn't at the dinner table. She glanced toward his empty seat and then exchanged looks with her other sons.

"Have any of you heard from Sydney?" she asked.

Everyone shook their heads as they busied themselves with their meals.

"It's not like your brother to be late for dinner without letting someone know. I checked with all the staff and even Dillion outside and nobody has seen or heard from him since he left work this afternoon," Veronica stressed. "Did he mention anything about an appointment after work?"

They all shook their heads and Britain smiled. "Maybe he's out to dinner with Starlet. He's a big boy if he wants to miss Friday evening meatloaf," Britain joked.

"This is no joking matter," Veronica said firmly. "You boys never miss dinner; and if any of you would ever miss calling, it wouldn't be Sydney."

"Mother, you worry too much," Rome reminded her. "He left work at 4:30 and it's only 6:00, I'm sure he got tied up and couldn't make it home on time for dinner."

They got through dinner and Veronica waited up all night. She waited on the living room sofa and ended up falling to sleep there with no sign or call from Sydney throughout the night. They knew he wasn't with Starlet because she had called the main house a couple times during the night asking to speak to him.

Chapter Thirty

On Saturday morning after a heavy heart breakfast, Veronica and Catherine paced the living room floor, looking out of the windows and grabbing the house phone at every ring. Rome, Britain and Paris sit restless scattered throughout the living room on their cell phones calling every one of their friends that they could think of. They were calling to check if any of them had seen or knew the whereabouts of Sydney. But after calling everyone they could think of to no avail, their concern level reached its peak. After a small discussion they decided that they had waited a reasonable enough time for Sydney to call home or show up. When he hadn't shown up by noon and still wasn't answering his cell, Veronica noticed the local police department.

It wasn't like Sydney to make his family worry. They were a close knit group and this was extremely uncustomary for Sydney. By twelve-thirty the department called her back and asked for information; and by 2:30 two officers, Hal Ford and Pete Fields arrived at Franklin House. Veronica rushed to answer the door and when the two officers walked in, they all gathered around the officers. The tall officer reached out his hand to Veronica. "Are you Mrs. Franklin?"

She nodded. "Yes, I'm Veronica Franklin; these are my sons, Rome, Britain and Paris." She pointed to them, and this is my sister-in-law, Catherine." She pointed to Catherine. "We called because it's unusual for my youngest son, Sydney, to stay away like this without contacting any of us; plus he's not answering his cell."

"You did the right thing to call us." The officer shook her hand. "I'm Officer Hal Ford and this is my partner, Officer Pete Fields. We will do all we can to locate your son. We already have some news," the officer said with sad eyes.

"You already have some news? Have you located my son? Is he okay; was he in an accident or something?" Veronica anxiously inquired.

Officer Ford looked at Veronica with compassion in his eyes. "I'm sorry to deliver this news but your son, Sydney."

Standing sandwiched between Rome and Britain, it was something about the distress look in the officer's eyes that caused Veronica to faint before the officer could finish his statement. Rome and Britain stopped her fall and placed her on one of the sofas. Catherine quickly hurried to the nearest bathroom and soaked a towel in cold water. Then she rushed to Veronica and placed the cold towel against her face. Seconds later, Veronica was revived. She sat up and held the cold wet towel against her face.

The tall officer took a seat on the sofa beside her and patted her back.

"I'm sorry, Mrs. Franklin that I scared you," Officer Ford apologized. "I could have used a bit more tact," he said and paused, looking her in the eyes. "But we have received information that your son is being held against his will."

They were all stunned and exchanged looks with each other. Catherine interrupted Officer Ford. "You mean kidnapped?"

Officer Ford nodded. "Yes, we are apparently dealing with a kidnapping."

"We received a tip after Mrs. Franklin notified us that her youngest son, Sydney, was missing," Officer Fields shared.

"That's outrageous. I can't believe it." Catherine eyes filled with tears as she grabbed her stomach and dropped down on the sofa in disbelief of the situation.

Veronica grabbed her forehead as she sat there on the sofa in tears. "I can't lose my son, not my baby. I can't go through this again. Why is this happening? My sons are fine, decent young men. They work hard and don't bother a soul."

Officer Ford read the notes on his note pad. "It appears that your son is being held by a one Jack Coleman."

They all exchanged looks; and then Rome glanced at his mother and then turned to the officer. "We know him. Jack Coleman is our new agent."

"He was also our father's agent before our father passed away," Paris shared.

Veronica found the strength and stood to her feet. "This can't be true, Officer. Do you have the right man?" She dried her eyes with her fingers. "Jack Coleman has always been a friend of the family. It doesn't make any sense that he would be holding my son against his will?" Veronica tears poured again as she ached inside from agony. She felt as if someone was stabbing her with knife right in the stomach with every breath she took. "Please double check. What tip are you referring to? There has to be some kind of mistake, Jack would never do something like this."

"There is no mistake, Mrs. Franklin, according to our information Jack Coleman notified headquarters to relay that he was holding your son," Officer Ford announced.

"Something doesn't add up, here, Officer Ford," Rome stated. "If our agent kidnapped our brother, why would he contact the police to inform them of his crime?"

Office Ford exchanged looks with Officer Fields. "We'll get to that."

Rome looked at Paris and Britain and the three of them shook their heads feeling helpless and confused.

"Officers, no harm intended but someone has botched up your information. I'm not convinced that Jack Coleman kidnapped my son. Frankly, because if he was out of his mind to do such a thing; as my son pointed out, I don't think he would voluntarily alert the authorities, it is a federal offense afterall," Veronica stated tearfully.

"There has been no mistake made with our information. It was all verified before it was handed over to us," Officer Ford assured her.

"But it makes no sense that an old family friend would kidnap my son?" Veronica grabbed her cheeks with both hands as the agony of feeling helpless overwhelmed her. "It just doesn't make any sense.

Jack is their agent and he was their father's best friend. I have known Jack Coleman all my life. We went to school together. And as my son mentioned, Jack was also my husband's agent," she stressed.

"Mrs. Franklin, we sympathize that Mr. Coleman was a friend of your family, but the facts are the facts. He committed this crime and he has admitted to it. We realize that this is a tough pill to swallow, but try to find comfort in the facts that the department is in hot pursuit of this man. We know he's holding your son somewhere in the Barrington area. We haven't figured out where because he's communicating with a non-traceable phone. However, we will find this man," Officer Fields assured her.

Just as the short officer was relaying that message, Officer Ford received a phone call where his only words were. "Yes, we are still at the Franklins, 605 Academy Place. Please, send it over."

The room was quiet and all eyes were on the tall officer when he put his phone in his left jacket pocket. He showed no reaction as he pulled his tablet from his right jacket pocket. Then he shifted his standing position when he noticed a message on the tablet. He looked toward Veronica. "The department is still in communication with Mr. Coleman and we just received a note from him that he would like for us to read to you."

"If this is about money, I'll give him whatever he wants. How much is he asking for?" Veronica cried out.

"Mrs. Franklin, I'm not sure how to tell you this ma'am," Officer Ford exchanged looks with Officer Fields.

"Just tell me, I'm not concerned with the amount and rest assured that there's no amount that he could request that I couldn't supply your department with," Veronica said and exchanged looks with Catherine.

Catherine nodded toward her and she nodded back at Catherine. Catherine knew that was her answer to her question that the Franklin fortune was still solid and all the talk from Veronica about going broke had just been a song and dance.

"You have my word; Jack Coleman can have whatever amount of cash he's asking for! I just want him to release my son! My son means more to me than anything I have or own. They all do! Everything I do,

I do for them!" She raised both arms. "Therefore, whatever he wants he will get, he just need to release Sydney and let him come home," she said between tears.

"Mrs. Franklin, that's just it. He isn't asking for anything except your son," Officer Ford replied.

"I beg you pardon? What do you mean he isn't asking for anything? He has to want something for the release of my son!"

"Mrs. Franklin, please listen and we'll read Mr. Coleman's note that he asked us to read to you. After I read his note it might shed a little light on the situation," Officer Ford suggested.

Veronica was panicky and couldn't hold her words. "It won't shed light on anything. I only want this man to release my son. That's the only thing I want," she shouted angrily. "I can see the sadness and devastation in the eyes of my other sons." She exchanged looks with Rome, Britain and Paris and she could see their silent pain, and that ripped at her even more. "I would rather tear out my own heart than for my sons to have ever faced the uncertainty and pain of something like this. How could I have put my sons in the hands of a lunatic?" she cried.

Rome, Britain, Paris and Catherine embraced Veronica to calm her down.

"Veronica, you can't blame yourself. You had no idea Jack Coleman had lost his marbles. Because that's certainly what has happened to him, pulling a stunt like this," Catherine said sadly as tears rolled down her face. She was deeply saddened by the incident, but quickly dried her tears, trying to be strong for the rest of them.

Veronica collected herself and mumbled toward the tall officer. "Please proceed and read the note, I'm listening."

Officer Ford held up one finger. "Please bear in mind, Mrs. Franklin that this note is not from a sane person. Mr. Coleman has apparently had a breakdown of some sort because his words are not in accord with reality. Therefore, no matter what he has written in this note to you, we want you to know that we will find this man and deliver your son back to you."

Dear Veronica Franklin, December 28, 2013

This is going to be a sad time for you. Sadness catches up with all of us at some point in life. It grabbed me at an early age from the day you walked down the isle with Ryan. It jumped on my back and I couldn't wrestle it off until now. I'm pleased to announce that my sad days are over, thanks to you! It's a hard blow to you, but this is how it has to be: your despair ends my sadness. It's a pity, of course, to shatter your life. You are such a beauty, almost as gorgeous as Ryan. But it would take extreme radiance to outshine Ryan Franklin, and you had four.

Therefore, however cruel my actions may appear to you, this had to be done in part to reprimand you for stealing my boyfriend all those years ago. He was mine before he was yours. But only in my heart, since I never had the nerves to tell him. Besides, he was a world class actor and I was just his agent who had helped him get his career off the ground. He was strictly into women and never knew I was in love with him. I was obsessed with Ryan Franklin because no other man could measure up to his kindness, his compassion, his incredible smile and good looks. Then after years of coping by the skin of my teeth without him, you lit up my world when you brought your sons, Rome, Britain, Paris and Sydney into my office on that lonely hot day back in August. I kept my cool, but my heart was racing with admiration for the four of them. Then unsuspecting you, handed them over to the lion's den when you asked me to be their agent and manage their career. You could not see the man-eating look in my eyes; you could only see the fame and prestige that would come their way after starring in a successful movie.

On that day, you would have sold a piece of yourself to get your sons in the movies; and that's exactly what you did. You sold your boys down the river without looking back. Those were two things that I always admired about you, your relentless confidence and smooth powers of persuasion. You are a master at manipulation. But this time you were preaching to the chorus, because I was waiting for those young men to walk into my office. One look at them and Ryan was alive again in all of their eyes; those same mesmerizing clear brown eyes that I thought I would never see again. Ryan had the eyes of divinity, but that's not where their similarities end. Their flawless tan skin, polite manners and stunning features are a carbon copy of their father's.

That single visit changed my life and set my mission in place. I would not lose out again. And just in case you are wondering why I grabbed Sydney; it wasn't personal. I would have been happy with anyone of your sons, but I snatched Sydney because he seemed more enthusiastic about the upcoming movie than the others. Plus, he was in and out of my office more and when he dropped by Friday evening after work, it was a perfect opportunity to finally have the carbon copy of the person I have wanted all my life.

Sydney isn't pleased to be held here, but he seems quite calm for a man in distress. But I will keep him tied up until he accepts his new home with me. If you are worried about his well-being, you don't have to fret. I would never harm him. A man this precious need to be cherished and not harmed. I'll do anything for Sydney. I asked him what he wanted but he said my question didn't dignify an answer. But I'm sure he wants his mother. A twenty-three-year-old man shouldn't be tied to his mother's apron strings. I think it's high time that he stands on his own with me. Being with me will toughen him up and let him see how the real world works with every man for himself without his mother to cushion his fall.

I want to marry Sydney, but he doesn't want to hear that right now. Therefore, I don't want to force him into a marriage that he isn't ready for. I'll give him all the time he needs because all we have is time. He's with me and that's where he will remain. Just the short time he has been in my custody, he has brought me endless happiness. But my happiness is somewhat subdued having to hide out in this little shack in the middle of nowhere with no central heating.

I know Sydney is used to the good life since you have given him everything on a silver platter. We won't be in this dump much longer. I have the funds and the means to disappear with your son to a remote location off the radar and law enforcement will not be able to track us down. Right now we are lying low to avoid a credit card or paper trail. Sydney is mute, but doesn't appear to be uncomfortable, tied in that chair with a blanket over his shoulders. I'm keeping this hut warm with a roaring fire. We also have plenty of food until we can blow this joint.

Your Sydney has a compassionate side that is the equivalent of his father's. He said in memory of his father and the fact that I was his father's best friend that if I turned him loose he wouldn't press charges. He had one condition but I couldn't accept it. I turned him down flat. He wanted me to seek counseling. He thinks I'm off my rocker. I told him I'm not out of my mind; I'm just in love with Ryan's baby!

Veronica, open your eyes and accept the fact that Sydney has slipped through your fingers while you watched. Just as Ryan slipped through my fingers when I thought it was going to be just the two of us forever, in the business of making movies and celebrating together. Then you came along and wrecked my life. No points awarded for making your sons a sitting duck when you brought them into my office. Now I have come to wreck your life. Sydney is lost to you, and your charm and gifts of persuasion can't help you get your son back. The two of us will travel the world and make movies. You'll never see Sydney again, but the latter should make you happy. You always wanted him to make movies. Does it surprise you that the tables are turned this time? You came out the winner when Ryan took you as his bride all those years ago. I was left to long for the man until his death. We can't all win every time! This time, Veronica Franklin, you lose!"

Signed: Jack Coleman

Would you like to see your manuscript become a book?

If you are interested in becoming a PublishAmerica author, please submit your manuscript for possible publication to us at:

mybook@publishamerica.com

You may also mail in your manuscript to:

**PublishAmerica
PO Box 151
Frederick, MD 21705**

www.publishamerica.com

CPSIA information can be obtained at www.ICGtesting.com
Printed in the USA
BVOW07s1002060115

382139BV00001B/88/P

9 781630 842062